SPIDER-MAN
SPIDER-VERSE
SPIDER-WOMEN

SPIDER-MAN
SPIDER-VERSE
SPIDER-WOMEN

SPIDER-WOMAN #1

WRITER: **MARV WOLFMAN**
PENCILER: **CARMINE INFANTINO**
INKER: **TONY DeZUNIGA**
COLORIST: **GLYNIS WEIN**
LETTERER: **JOE ROSEN**
EDITOR: **MARV WOLFMAN**
CONSULTING EDITOR: **ARCHIE GOODWIN**

SPIDER-WOMAN #20

WRITER: **MARK GRUENWALD**
PENCILER: **FRANK SPINGER**
INKER: **MIKE ESPOSITO**
COLORIST: **NEL YOMTOV**
LETTERER: **JOHN COSTANZA**
EDITOR: **JIM SHOOTER**

WHAT IF? #105

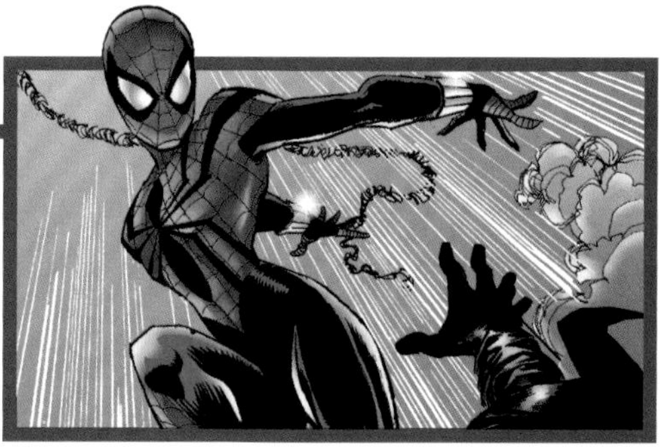

CO-PLOTTER/WRITER: **TOM DeFALCO**
CO-PLOTTER/PENCILER: **RON FRENZ**
INKER: **BILL SIENKIEWICZ**
COLORIST: **MATT WEBB**
LETTERER: **CHRIS ELIOPOULOS & VIRTUAL CALLIGRAPHY**
EDITOR: **KELLY CORVESE**

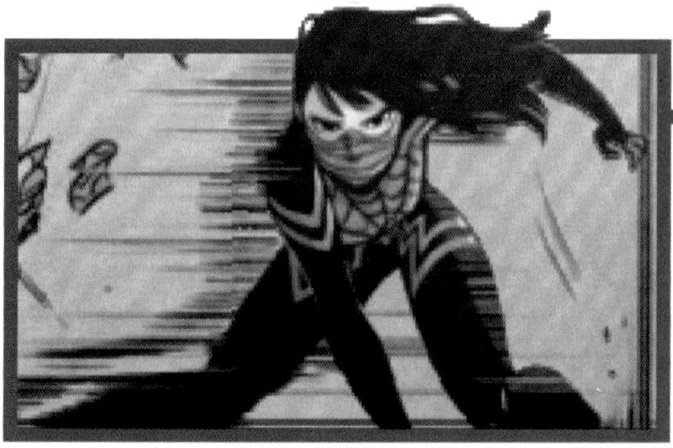

SILK #2

WRITER: **ROBBIE THOMPSON**
ARTIST: **STACEY LEE**
COLOR ARTIST: **IAN HERRING**
LETTERER: **VC's TRAVIS LANHAM**
COVER ART: **DAVE JOHNSON**
ASSISTANT EDITOR: **DEVIN LEWIS**
EDITORS: **ELLIE PYLE & NICK LOWE**

AMAZING SPIDER-MAN: RENEW YOUR VOWS #13

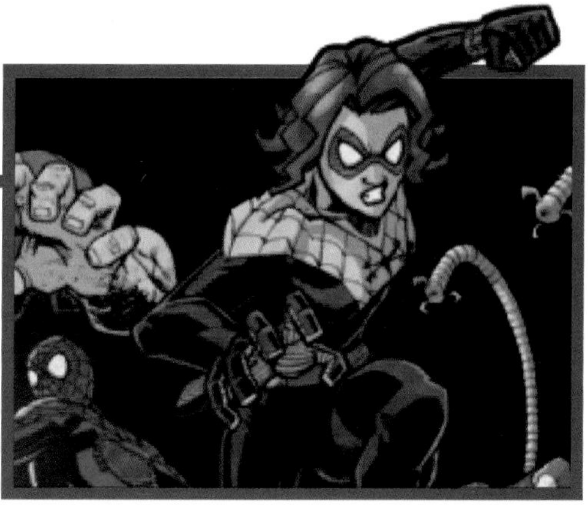

WRITER: **JODY HOUSER**
ARTIST: **NICK ROCHE**
COLORIST: **RUTH REDMOND**
LETTERER: **VC's JOE CARAMAGNA**
COVER ART: **RYAN STEGMAN & JESUS ABURTOV**
EDITOR: **HEATHER ANTOS**
SUPERVISING EDITOR: **JORDAN D. WHITE**

THESE COMICS ARE PRESENTED AS ORIGINALLY CREATED. THEY MAY CONTAIN OUTDATED DEPICTIONS.

SPIDER-MAN CREATED BY STAN LEE & STEVE DITKO

SPECIAL THANKS TO **JACQUE PORTE**

COLLECTION EDITOR: **JENNIFER GRÜNWALD** ASSISTANT MANAGING EDITOR: **MAIA LOY**
ASSISTANT MANAGING EDITOR: **LISA MONTALBANO** EDITOR, SPECIAL PROJECTS: **MARK D. BEAZLEY**
VP PRODUCTION & SPECIAL PROJECTS: **JEFF YOUNGQUIST** RESEARCH: **JESS HARROLD & JEPH YORK**
PRODUCTION: **COLORTEK, DIGIKORE, JOE FRONTIRRE & DAN KIRCHHOFFER**
BOOK DESIGNER: **JAY BOWEN** SVP PRINT, SALES & MARKETING: **DAVID GABRIEL** EDITOR IN CHIEF: **C.B. CEBULSKI**

SPIDER-MAN: SPIDER-VERSE — SPIDER-WOMEN. Contains material originally published in magazine form as SPIDER-WOMAN (1978) #1 and #20, WHAT IF? (1989) #105, SILK (2015A) #2, and AMAZING SPIDER-MAN: RENEW YOUR VOWS (2016) #13. First printing 2020. ISBN 978-1-302-92522-2. Published by MARVEL WORLDWIDE, INC., a subsidiary of MARVEL ENTERTAINMENT, LLC. OFFICE OF PUBLICATION: 1290 Avenue of the Americas, New York, NY 10104. **Printed in Canada.** KEVIN FEIGE, Chief Creative Officer; DAN BUCKLEY, President, Marvel Entertainment; JOHN NEE, Publisher; JOE QUESADA, EVP & Creative Director; TOM BREVOORT, SVP of Publishing; DAVID BOGART, Associate Publisher & SVP of Talent Affairs; Publishing & Partnership; DAVID GABRIEL, VP of Print & Digital Publishing; JEFF YOUNGQUIST, VP of Production & Special Projects; DAN CARR, Executive Director of Publishing Technology; ALEX MORALES, Director of Publishing Operations; DAN EDINGTON, Managing Editor; SUSAN CRESPI, Production Manager; STAN LEE, Chairman Emeritus. For information regarding advertising in Marvel Comics or on Marvel.com, please contact Vit DeBellis, Custom Solutions & Integrated Advertising Manager, at vdebellis@marvel.com. For Marvel subscription inquiries, please call 888-511-5480. **Manufactured between 7/24/2020 and 8/31/2020 by SOLISCO PRINTERS, SCOTT, QC, CANADA.**

10 9 8 7 6 5 4 3 2 1

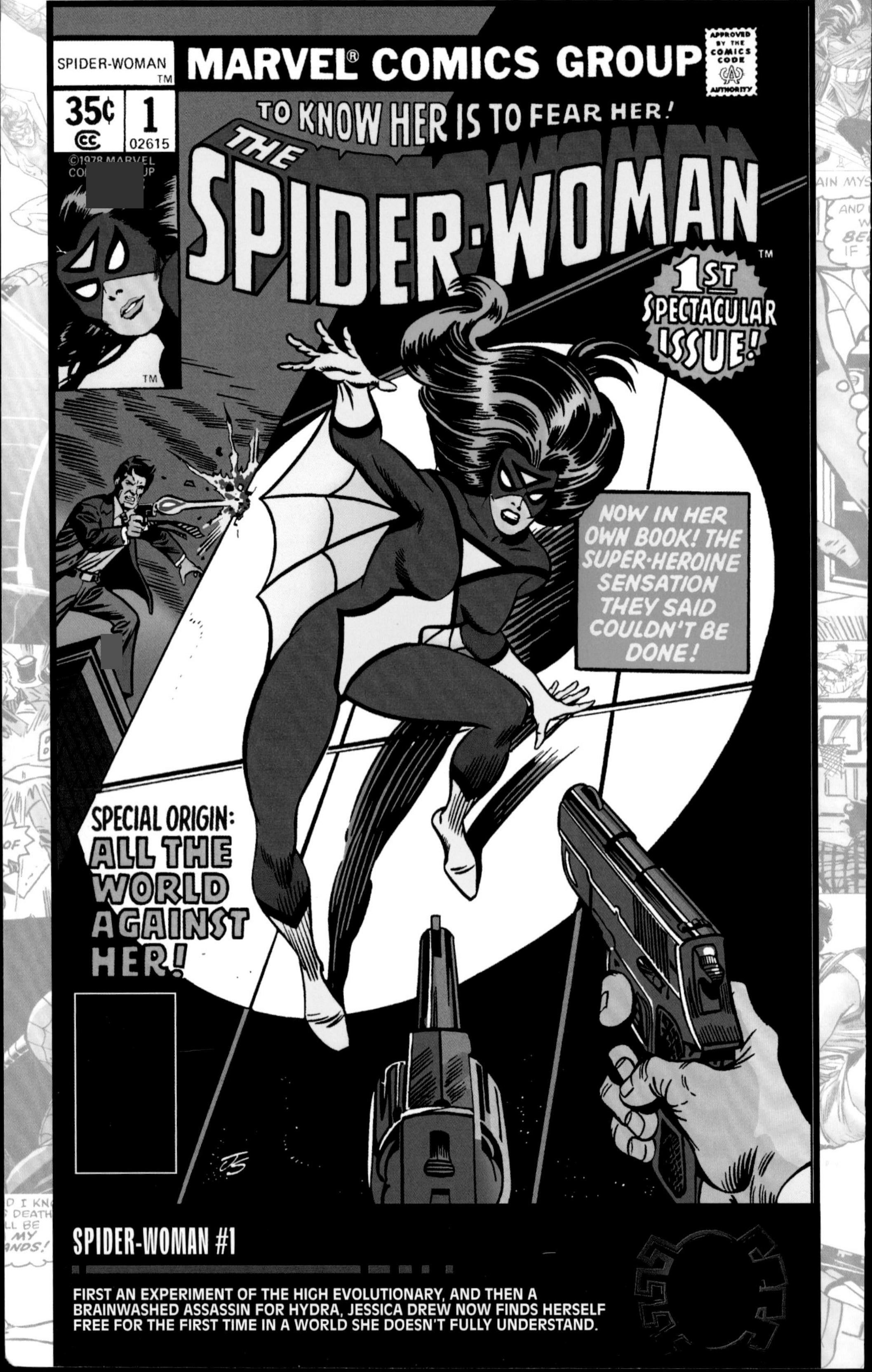
SPIDER-WOMAN TM
MARVEL® COMICS GROUP
APPROVED BY THE COMICS CODE AUTHORITY
35¢ 1
02615
©1978 MARVEL
TO KNOW HER IS TO FEAR HER!
THE SPIDER-WOMAN TM
1ST SPECTACULAR ISSUE!
NOW IN HER OWN BOOK! THE SUPER-HEROINE SENSATION THEY SAID COULDN'T BE DONE!
SPECIAL ORIGIN:
ALL THE WORLD AGAINST HER!

SPIDER-WOMAN #1

FIRST AN EXPERIMENT OF THE HIGH EVOLUTIONARY, AND THEN A BRAINWASHED ASSASSIN FOR HYDRA, JESSICA DREW NOW FINDS HERSELF FREE FOR THE FIRST TIME IN A WORLD SHE DOESN'T FULLY UNDERSTAND.

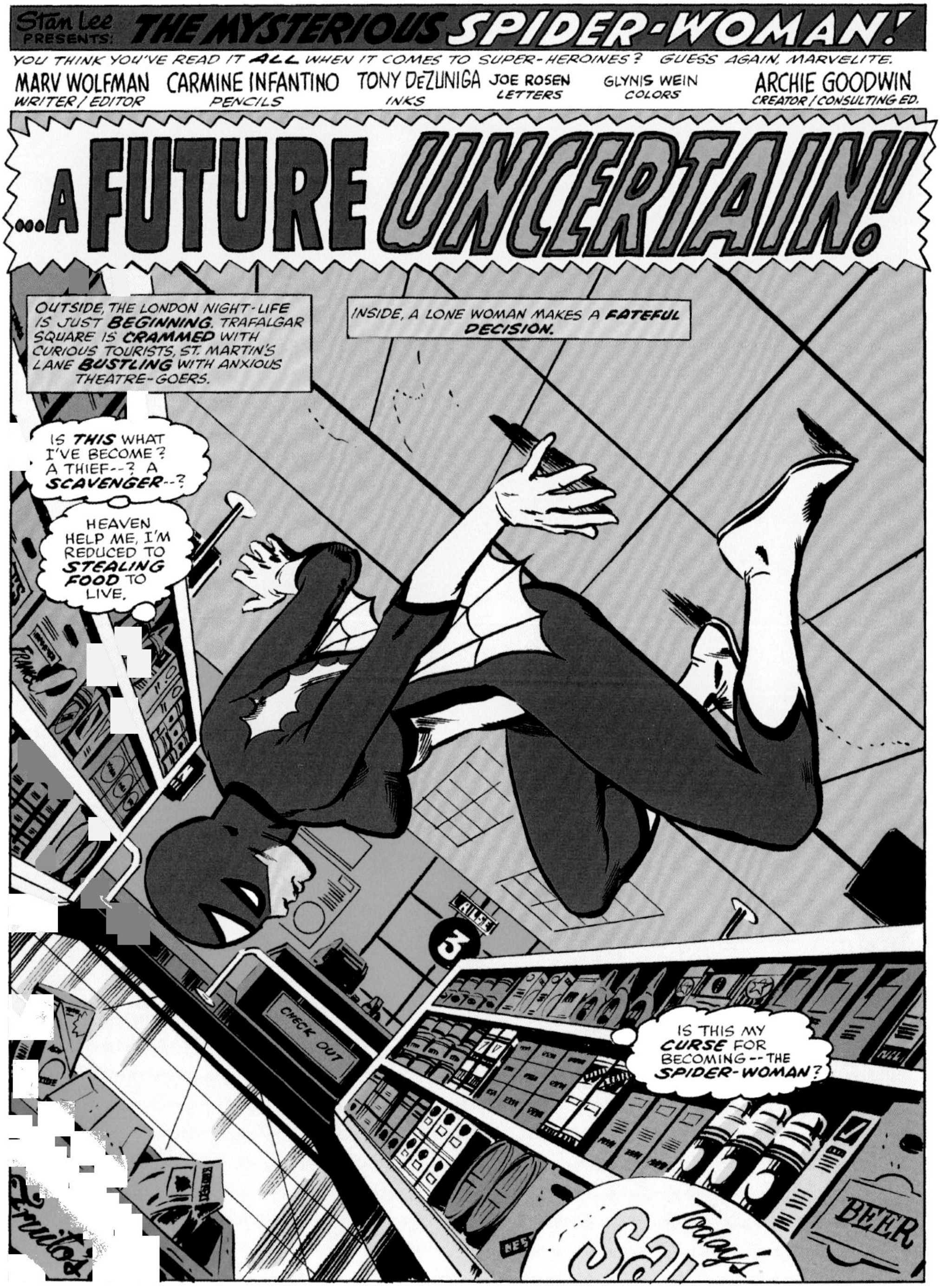

Stan Lee PRESENTS: THE MYSTERIOUS SPIDER-WOMAN!
YOU THINK YOU'VE READ IT ALL WHEN IT COMES TO SUPER-HEROINES? GUESS AGAIN, MARVELITE.
MARV WOLFMAN WRITER / EDITOR
CARMINE INFANTINO PENCILS
TONY DeZUNIGA INKS
JOE ROSEN LETTERS
GLYNIS WEIN COLORS
ARCHIE GOODWIN CREATOR / CONSULTING ED.
...A FUTURE UNCERTAIN!
OUTSIDE, THE LONDON NIGHT-LIFE IS JUST BEGINNING. TRAFALGAR SQUARE IS CRAMMED WITH CURIOUS TOURISTS, ST. MARTIN'S LANE BUSTLING WITH ANXIOUS THEATRE-GOERS.
INSIDE, A LONE WOMAN MAKES A FATEFUL DECISION.
IS THIS WHAT I'VE BECOME? A THIEF--? A SCAVENGER--?
HEAVEN HELP ME, I'M REDUCED TO STEALING FOOD TO LIVE.
IS THIS MY CURSE FOR BECOMING--THE SPIDER-WOMAN?
CHECK OUT
3
BEER
Today's

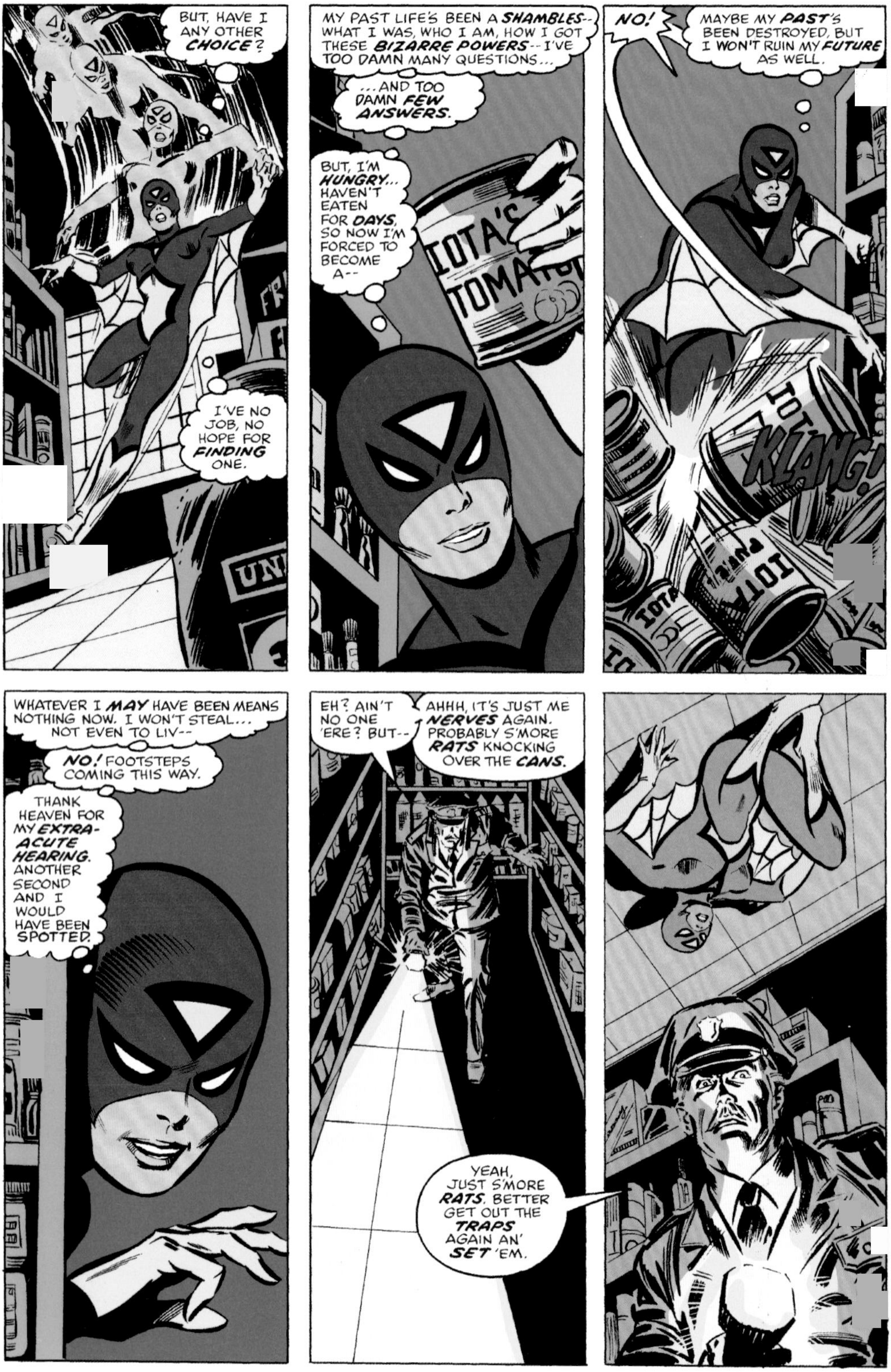
BUT, HAVE I ANY OTHER CHOICE?
I'VE NO JOB, NO HOPE FOR FINDING ONE.
MY PAST LIFE'S BEEN A SHAMBLES-- WHAT I WAS, WHO I AM, HOW I GOT THESE BIZARRE POWERS--I'VE TOO DAMN MANY QUESTIONS...
...AND TOO DAMN FEW ANSWERS.
BUT, I'M HUNGRY... HAVEN'T EATEN FOR DAYS, SO NOW I'M FORCED TO BECOME A--
IOTA'S TOMATO
NO!
MAYBE MY PAST'S BEEN DESTROYED, BUT I WON'T RUIN MY FUTURE AS WELL.
KLANG!
WHATEVER I MAY HAVE BEEN MEANS NOTHING NOW. I WON'T STEAL... NOT EVEN TO LIV--
NO! FOOTSTEPS COMING THIS WAY.
THANK HEAVEN FOR MY EXTRA-ACUTE HEARING. ANOTHER SECOND AND I WOULD HAVE BEEN SPOTTED.
EH? AIN'T NO ONE 'ERE? BUT--
AHHH, IT'S JUST ME NERVES AGAIN. PROBABLY S'MORE RATS KNOCKING OVER THE CANS.
YEAH, JUST S'MORE RATS. BETTER GET OUT THE TRAPS AGAIN AN' SET 'EM.

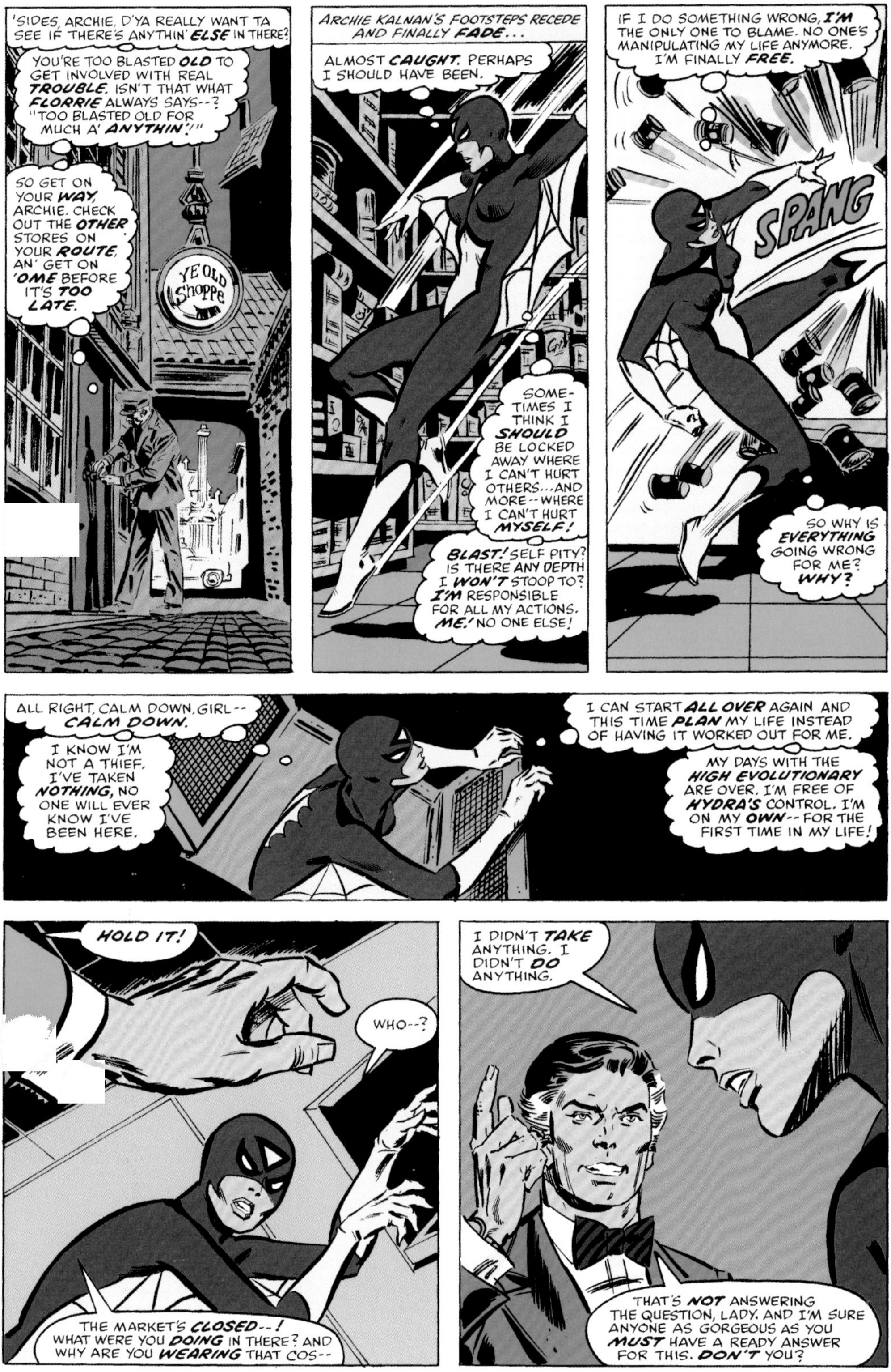

'SIDES, ARCHIE, D'YA REALLY WANT TA SEE IF THERE'S ANYTHIN' ELSE IN THERE?
YOU'RE TOO BLASTED OLD TO GET INVOLVED WITH REAL TROUBLE. ISN'T THAT WHAT FLORRIE ALWAYS SAYS--? "TOO BLASTED OLD FOR MUCH A' ANYTHIN'!"
SO GET ON YOUR WAY, ARCHIE. CHECK OUT THE OTHER STORES ON YOUR ROUTE, AN' GET ON 'OME BEFORE IT'S TOO LATE.
YE OLD Shoppe
ARCHIE KALNAN'S FOOTSTEPS RECEDE AND FINALLY FADE...
ALMOST CAUGHT. PERHAPS I SHOULD HAVE BEEN.
SOMETIMES I THINK I SHOULD BE LOCKED AWAY WHERE I CAN'T HURT OTHERS...AND MORE--WHERE I CAN'T HURT MYSELF!
BLAST! SELF PITY? IS THERE ANY DEPTH I WON'T STOOP TO? I'M RESPONSIBLE FOR ALL MY ACTIONS. ME! NO ONE ELSE!
IF I DO SOMETHING WRONG, I'M THE ONLY ONE TO BLAME. NO ONE'S MANIPULATING MY LIFE ANYMORE. I'M FINALLY FREE.
SPANG
SO WHY IS EVERYTHING GOING WRONG FOR ME? WHY?
ALL RIGHT, CALM DOWN, GIRL-- CALM DOWN.
I KNOW I'M NOT A THIEF. I'VE TAKEN NOTHING. NO ONE WILL EVER KNOW I'VE BEEN HERE.
I CAN START ALL OVER AGAIN AND THIS TIME PLAN MY LIFE INSTEAD OF HAVING IT WORKED OUT FOR ME.
MY DAYS WITH THE HIGH EVOLUTIONARY ARE OVER. I'M FREE OF HYDRA'S CONTROL. I'M ON MY OWN--FOR THE FIRST TIME IN MY LIFE!
HOLD IT!
WHO--?
THE MARKET'S CLOSED--! WHAT WERE YOU DOING IN THERE? AND WHY ARE YOU WEARING THAT COS--
I DIDN'T TAKE ANYTHING. I DIDN'T DO ANYTHING.
THAT'S NOT ANSWERING THE QUESTION, LADY. AND I'M SURE ANYONE AS GORGEOUS AS YOU MUST HAVE A READY ANSWER FOR THIS. DON'T YOU?

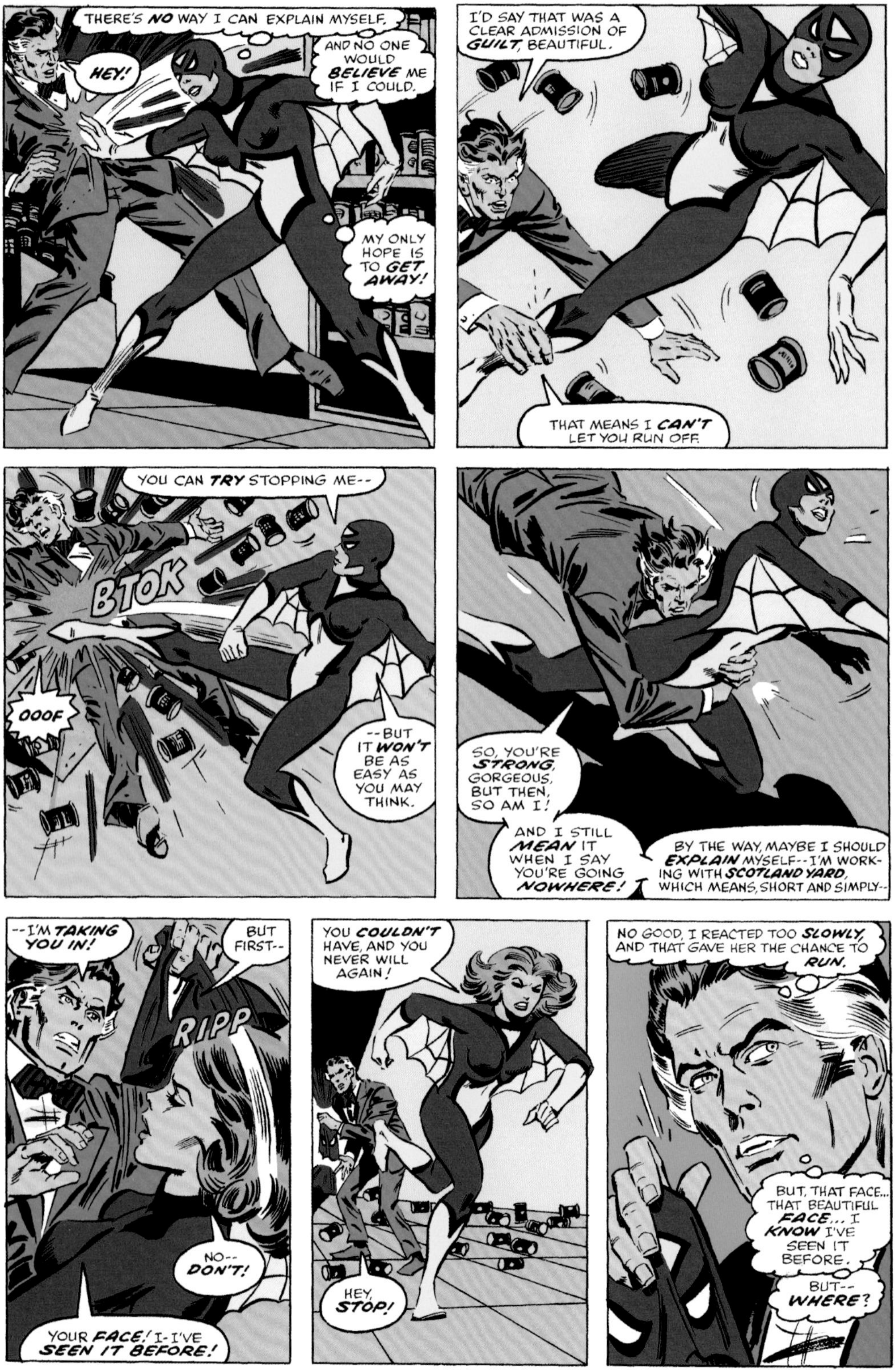
THERE'S NO WAY I CAN EXPLAIN MYSELF.
HEY!
AND NO ONE WOULD BELIEVE ME IF I COULD.
MY ONLY HOPE IS TO GET AWAY!
I'D SAY THAT WAS A CLEAR ADMISSION OF GUILT, BEAUTIFUL.
THAT MEANS I CAN'T LET YOU RUN OFF.
YOU CAN TRY STOPPING ME--
BTOK
OOOF
--BUT IT WON'T BE AS EASY AS YOU MAY THINK.
SO, YOU'RE STRONG, GORGEOUS, BUT THEN, SO AM I!
AND I STILL MEAN IT WHEN I SAY YOU'RE GOING NOWHERE!
BY THE WAY, MAYBE I SHOULD EXPLAIN MYSELF--I'M WORKING WITH SCOTLAND YARD, WHICH MEANS, SHORT AND SIMPLY--
--I'M TAKING YOU IN!
BUT FIRST--
RIPP
NO-- DON'T!
YOUR FACE! I-I'VE SEEN IT BEFORE!
YOU COULDN'T HAVE, AND YOU NEVER WILL AGAIN!
HEY, STOP!
NO GOOD, I REACTED TOO SLOWLY, AND THAT GAVE HER THE CHANCE TO RUN.
BUT, THAT FACE... THAT BEAUTIFUL FACE... I KNOW I'VE SEEN IT BEFORE.
BUT-- WHERE?

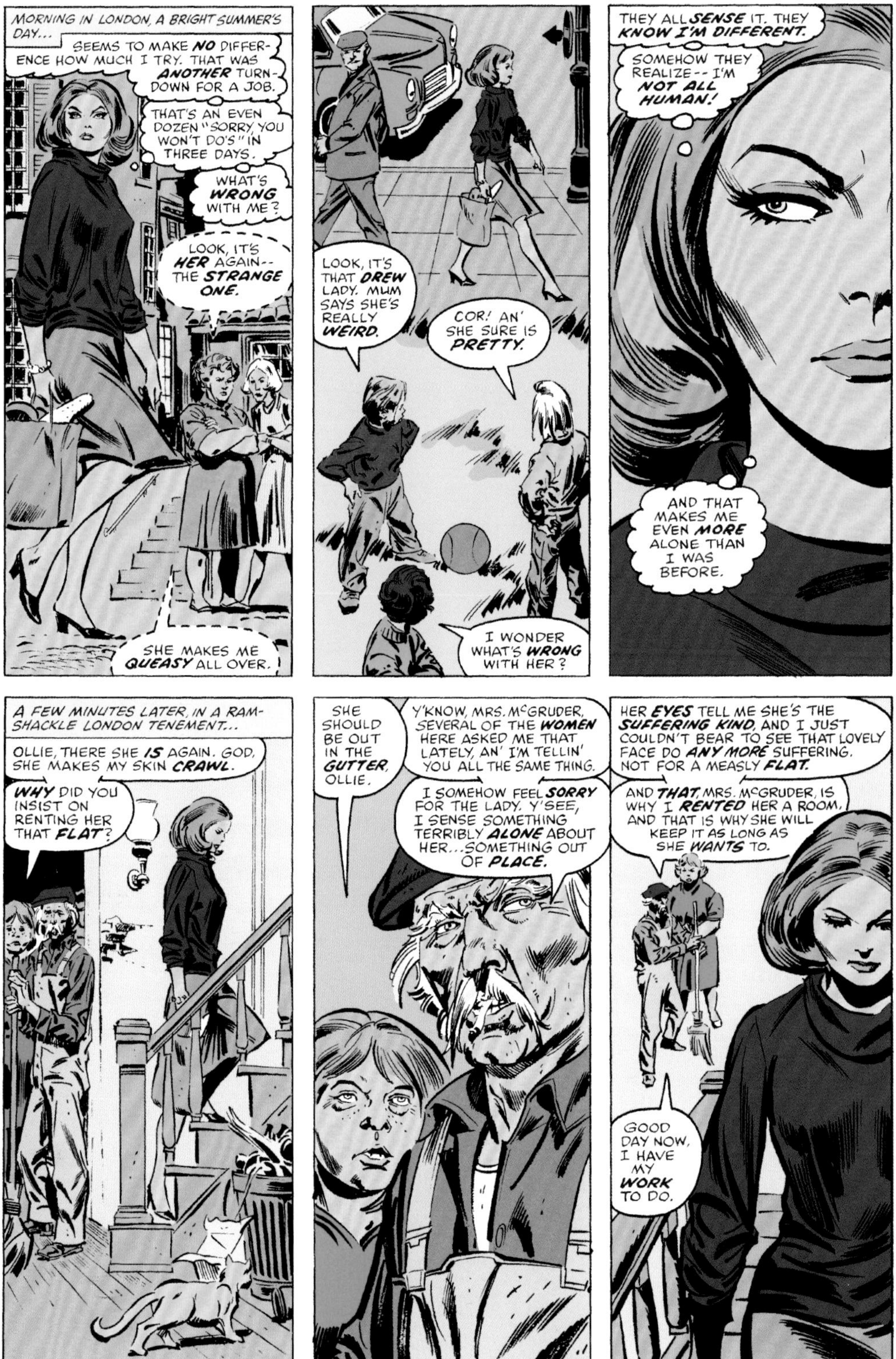
MORNING IN LONDON, A BRIGHT SUMMER'S DAY...
SEEMS TO MAKE NO DIFFERENCE HOW MUCH I TRY. THAT WAS ANOTHER TURN-DOWN FOR A JOB.
THAT'S AN EVEN DOZEN "SORRY, YOU WON'T DO'S" IN THREE DAYS.
WHAT'S WRONG WITH ME?
LOOK, IT'S HER AGAIN-- THE STRANGE ONE.
SHE MAKES ME QUEASY ALL OVER.
LOOK, IT'S THAT DREW LADY. MUM SAYS SHE'S REALLY WEIRD.
COR! AN' SHE SURE IS PRETTY.
I WONDER WHAT'S WRONG WITH HER?
THEY ALL SENSE IT. THEY KNOW I'M DIFFERENT.
SOMEHOW THEY REALIZE-- I'M NOT ALL HUMAN!
AND THAT MAKES ME EVEN MORE ALONE THAN I WAS BEFORE.
A FEW MINUTES LATER, IN A RAMSHACKLE LONDON TENEMENT...
OLLIE, THERE SHE IS AGAIN. GOD, SHE MAKES MY SKIN CRAWL.
WHY DID YOU INSIST ON RENTING HER THAT FLAT?
SHE SHOULD BE OUT IN THE GUTTER, OLLIE.
Y'KNOW, MRS. McGRUDER, SEVERAL OF THE WOMEN HERE ASKED ME THAT LATELY, AN' I'M TELLIN' YOU ALL THE SAME THING.
I SOMEHOW FEEL SORRY FOR THE LADY. Y'SEE, I SENSE SOMETHING TERRIBLY ALONE ABOUT HER... SOMETHING OUT OF PLACE.
HER EYES TELL ME SHE'S THE SUFFERING KIND, AND I JUST COULDN'T BEAR TO SEE THAT LOVELY FACE DO ANY MORE SUFFERING. NOT FOR A MEASLY FLAT.
AND THAT, MRS. McGRUDER, IS WHY I RENTED HER A ROOM, AND THAT IS WHY SHE WILL KEEP IT AS LONG AS SHE WANTS TO.
GOOD DAY NOW, I HAVE MY WORK TO DO.

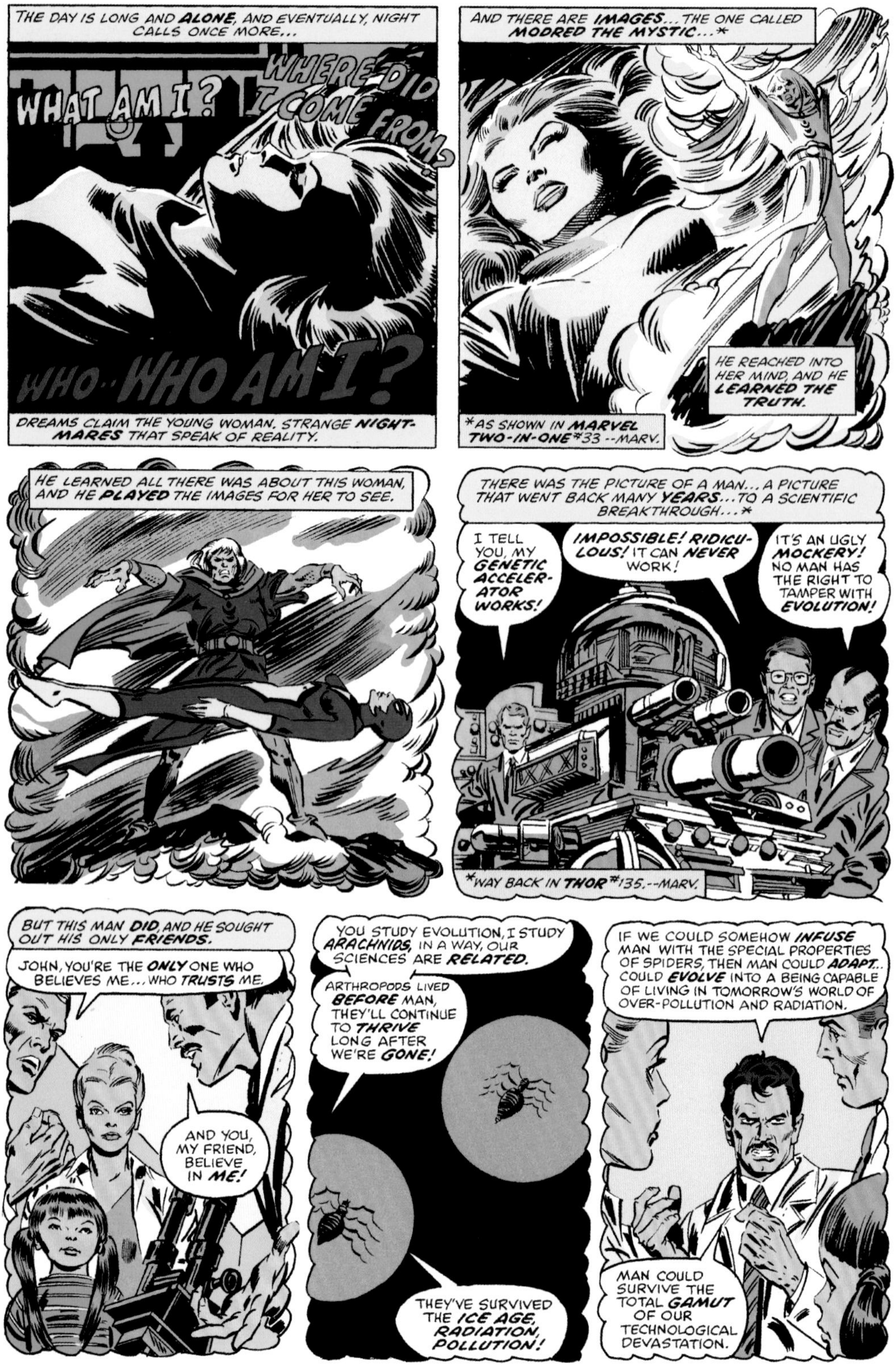
THE DAY IS LONG AND ALONE, AND EVENTUALLY, NIGHT CALLS ONCE MORE...
WHAT AM I? WHERE DID I COME FROM?
WHO.. WHO AM I?
DREAMS CLAIM THE YOUNG WOMAN. STRANGE NIGHTMARES THAT SPEAK OF REALITY.
AND THERE ARE IMAGES... THE ONE CALLED MODRED THE MYSTIC...*
HE REACHED INTO HER MIND, AND HE LEARNED THE TRUTH.
*AS SHOWN IN MARVEL TWO-IN-ONE #33 --MARV.
HE LEARNED ALL THERE WAS ABOUT THIS WOMAN, AND HE PLAYED THE IMAGES FOR HER TO SEE.
THERE WAS THE PICTURE OF A MAN... A PICTURE THAT WENT BACK MANY YEARS... TO A SCIENTIFIC BREAKTHROUGH...*
I TELL YOU, MY GENETIC ACCELERATOR WORKS!
IMPOSSIBLE! RIDICULOUS! IT CAN NEVER WORK!
IT'S AN UGLY MOCKERY! NO MAN HAS THE RIGHT TO TAMPER WITH EVOLUTION!
*WAY BACK IN THOR #135.--MARV.
BUT THIS MAN DID, AND HE SOUGHT OUT HIS ONLY FRIENDS.
JOHN, YOU'RE THE ONLY ONE WHO BELIEVES ME... WHO TRUSTS ME.
AND YOU, MY FRIEND, BELIEVE IN ME!
YOU STUDY EVOLUTION, I STUDY ARACHNIDS. IN A WAY, OUR SCIENCES ARE RELATED.
ARTHROPODS LIVED BEFORE MAN, THEY'LL CONTINUE TO THRIVE LONG AFTER WE'RE GONE!
THEY'VE SURVIVED THE ICE AGE, RADIATION, POLLUTION!
IF WE COULD SOMEHOW INFUSE MAN WITH THE SPECIAL PROPERTIES OF SPIDERS, THEN MAN COULD ADAPT... COULD EVOLVE INTO A BEING CAPABLE OF LIVING IN TOMORROW'S WORLD OF OVER-POLLUTION AND RADIATION.
MAN COULD SURVIVE THE TOTAL GAMUT OF OUR TECHNOLOGICAL DEVASTATION.

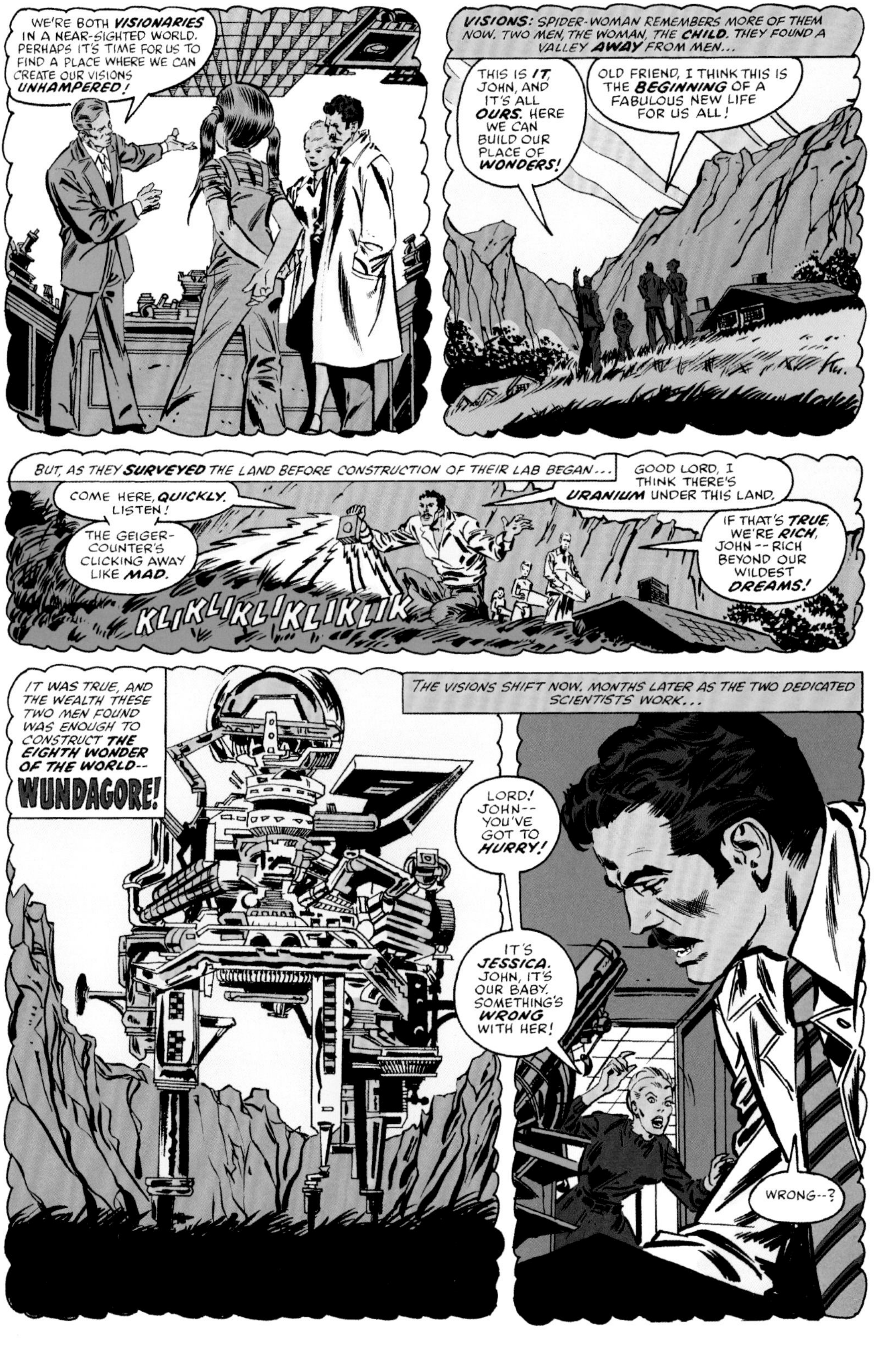
WE'RE BOTH VISIONARIES IN A NEAR-SIGHTED WORLD. PERHAPS IT'S TIME FOR US TO FIND A PLACE WHERE WE CAN CREATE OUR VISIONS UNHAMPERED!
VISIONS: SPIDER-WOMAN REMEMBERS MORE OF THEM NOW. TWO MEN, THE WOMAN, THE CHILD. THEY FOUND A VALLEY AWAY FROM MEN...
THIS IS IT, JOHN, AND IT'S ALL OURS. HERE WE CAN BUILD OUR PLACE OF WONDERS!
OLD FRIEND, I THINK THIS IS THE BEGINNING OF A FABULOUS NEW LIFE FOR US ALL!
BUT, AS THEY SURVEYED THE LAND BEFORE CONSTRUCTION OF THEIR LAB BEGAN...
COME HERE, QUICKLY. LISTEN!
THE GEIGER-COUNTER'S CLICKING AWAY LIKE MAD.
KLIKLIKLIKLIKLIK
GOOD LORD, I THINK THERE'S URANIUM UNDER THIS LAND.
IF THAT'S TRUE, WE'RE RICH, JOHN -- RICH BEYOND OUR WILDEST DREAMS!
IT WAS TRUE, AND THE WEALTH THESE TWO MEN FOUND WAS ENOUGH TO CONSTRUCT THE EIGHTH WONDER OF THE WORLD--
WUNDAGORE!
THE VISIONS SHIFT NOW. MONTHS LATER AS THE TWO DEDICATED SCIENTISTS WORK...
LORD! JOHN-- YOU'VE GOT TO HURRY!
IT'S JESSICA. JOHN, IT'S OUR BABY. SOMETHING'S WRONG WITH HER!
WRONG--?

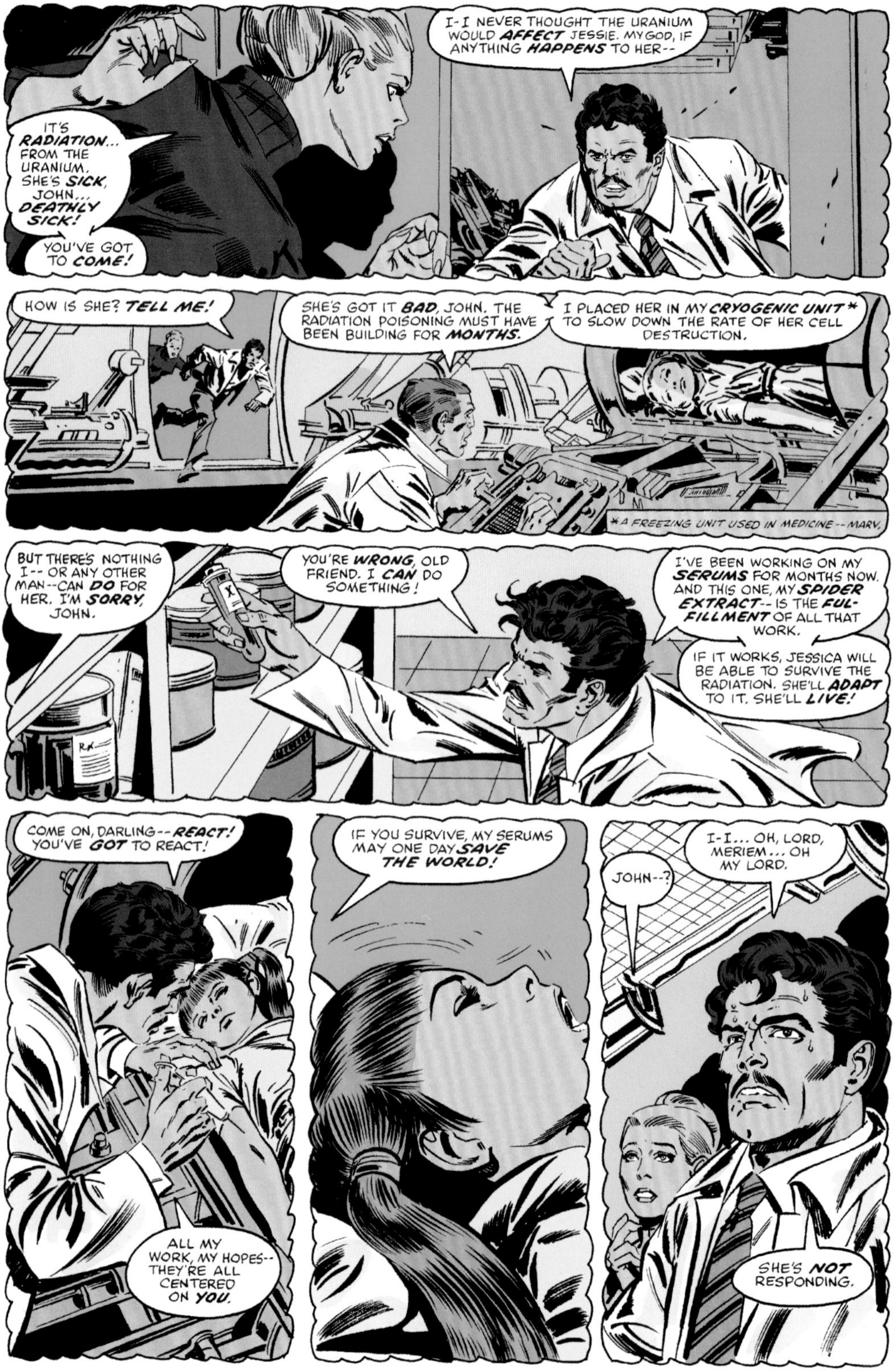
IT'S RADIATION... FROM THE URANIUM. SHE'S SICK, JOHN... DEATHLY SICK!
YOU'VE GOT TO COME!
I-I NEVER THOUGHT THE URANIUM WOULD AFFECT JESSIE. MY GOD, IF ANYTHING HAPPENS TO HER--
HOW IS SHE? TELL ME!
SHE'S GOT IT BAD, JOHN. THE RADIATION POISONING MUST HAVE BEEN BUILDING FOR MONTHS.
I PLACED HER IN MY CRYOGENIC UNIT* TO SLOW DOWN THE RATE OF HER CELL DESTRUCTION.
*A FREEZING UNIT USED IN MEDICINE--MARV.
BUT THERE'S NOTHING I-- OR ANY OTHER MAN--CAN DO FOR HER. I'M SORRY, JOHN.
YOU'RE WRONG, OLD FRIEND. I CAN DO SOMETHING!
I'VE BEEN WORKING ON MY SERUMS FOR MONTHS NOW. AND THIS ONE, MY SPIDER EXTRACT-- IS THE FULFILLMENT OF ALL THAT WORK.
IF IT WORKS, JESSICA WILL BE ABLE TO SURVIVE THE RADIATION. SHE'LL ADAPT TO IT. SHE'LL LIVE!
COME ON, DARLING--REACT! YOU'VE GOT TO REACT!
ALL MY WORK, MY HOPES-- THEY'RE ALL CENTERED ON YOU.
IF YOU SURVIVE, MY SERUMS MAY ONE DAY SAVE THE WORLD!
JOHN--?
I-I... OH, LORD, MERIEM... OH MY LORD.
SHE'S NOT RESPONDING.

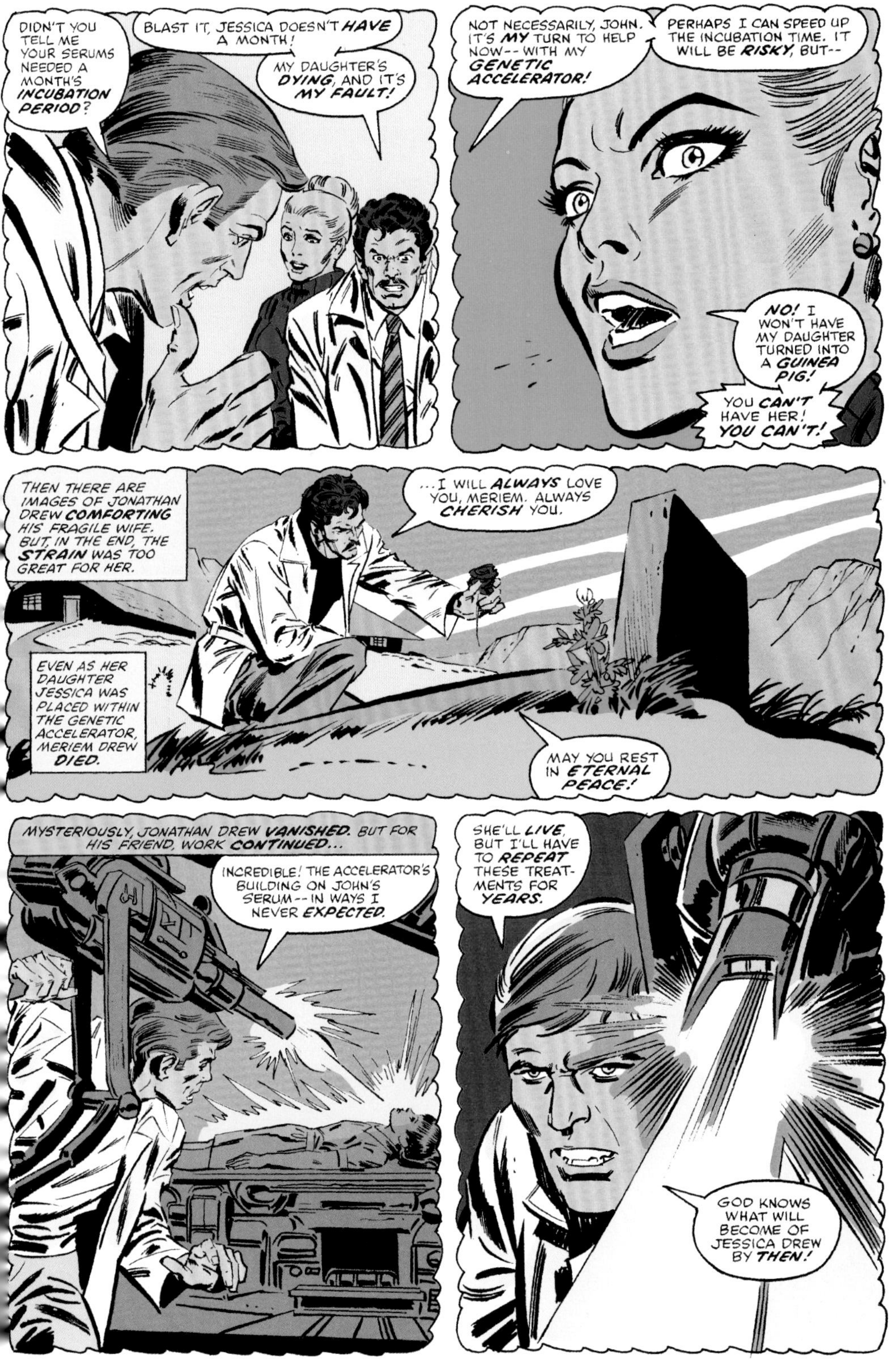
DIDN'T YOU TELL ME YOUR SERUMS NEEDED A MONTH'S INCUBATION PERIOD?
BLAST IT, JESSICA DOESN'T HAVE A MONTH!
MY DAUGHTER'S DYING, AND IT'S MY FAULT!
NOT NECESSARILY, JOHN. IT'S MY TURN TO HELP NOW-- WITH MY GENETIC ACCELERATOR!
PERHAPS I CAN SPEED UP THE INCUBATION TIME. IT WILL BE RISKY, BUT--
NO! I WON'T HAVE MY DAUGHTER TURNED INTO A GUINEA PIG!
YOU CAN'T HAVE HER! YOU CAN'T!
THEN THERE ARE IMAGES OF JONATHAN DREW COMFORTING HIS FRAGILE WIFE. BUT, IN THE END, THE STRAIN WAS TOO GREAT FOR HER.
...I WILL ALWAYS LOVE YOU, MERIEM. ALWAYS CHERISH YOU.
EVEN AS HER DAUGHTER JESSICA WAS PLACED WITHIN THE GENETIC ACCELERATOR, MERIEM DREW DIED.
MAY YOU REST IN ETERNAL PEACE!
MYSTERIOUSLY, JONATHAN DREW VANISHED. BUT FOR HIS FRIEND, WORK CONTINUED...
INCREDIBLE! THE ACCELERATOR'S BUILDING ON JOHN'S SERUM-- IN WAYS I NEVER EXPECTED.
SHE'LL LIVE, BUT I'LL HAVE TO REPEAT THESE TREATMENTS FOR YEARS.
GOD KNOWS WHAT WILL BECOME OF JESSICA DREW BY THEN!

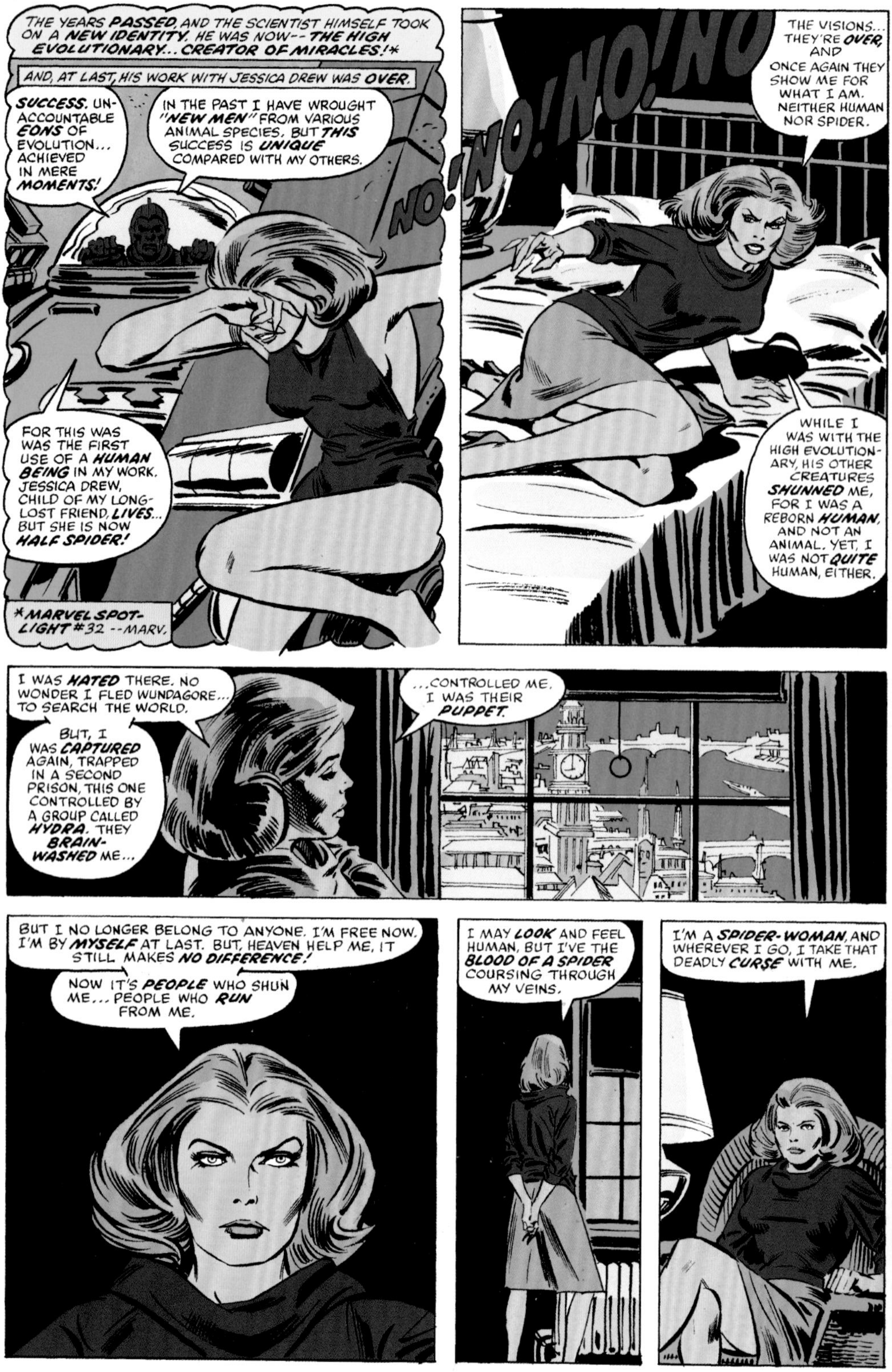

THE YEARS PASSED, AND THE SCIENTIST HIMSELF TOOK ON A NEW IDENTITY. HE WAS NOW-- THE HIGH EVOLUTIONARY... CREATOR OF MIRACLES!*
AND, AT LAST, HIS WORK WITH JESSICA DREW WAS OVER.
SUCCESS. UNACCOUNTABLE EONS OF EVOLUTION... ACHIEVED IN MERE MOMENTS!
IN THE PAST I HAVE WROUGHT "NEW MEN" FROM VARIOUS ANIMAL SPECIES. BUT THIS SUCCESS IS UNIQUE COMPARED WITH MY OTHERS.
FOR THIS WAS THE FIRST USE OF A HUMAN BEING IN MY WORK. JESSICA DREW, CHILD OF MY LONG-LOST FRIEND, LIVES... BUT SHE IS NOW HALF SPIDER!
*MARVEL SPOTLIGHT #32 --MARV.
NO! NO! NO! NO
THE VISIONS... THEY'RE OVER, AND ONCE AGAIN THEY SHOW ME FOR WHAT I AM. NEITHER HUMAN NOR SPIDER.
WHILE I WAS WITH THE HIGH EVOLUTIONARY, HIS OTHER CREATURES SHUNNED ME, FOR I WAS A REBORN HUMAN, AND NOT AN ANIMAL. YET, I WAS NOT QUITE HUMAN, EITHER.
I WAS HATED THERE. NO WONDER I FLED WUNDAGORE... TO SEARCH THE WORLD.
BUT, I WAS CAPTURED AGAIN, TRAPPED IN A SECOND PRISON, THIS ONE CONTROLLED BY A GROUP CALLED HYDRA. THEY BRAIN-WASHED ME...
...CONTROLLED ME. I WAS THEIR PUPPET.
BUT I NO LONGER BELONG TO ANYONE. I'M FREE NOW. I'M BY MYSELF AT LAST. BUT, HEAVEN HELP ME, IT STILL MAKES NO DIFFERENCE!
NOW IT'S PEOPLE WHO SHUN ME... PEOPLE WHO RUN FROM ME.
I MAY LOOK AND FEEL HUMAN, BUT I'VE THE BLOOD OF A SPIDER COURSING THROUGH MY VEINS.
I'M A SPIDER-WOMAN, AND WHEREVER I GO, I TAKE THAT DEADLY CURSE WITH ME.

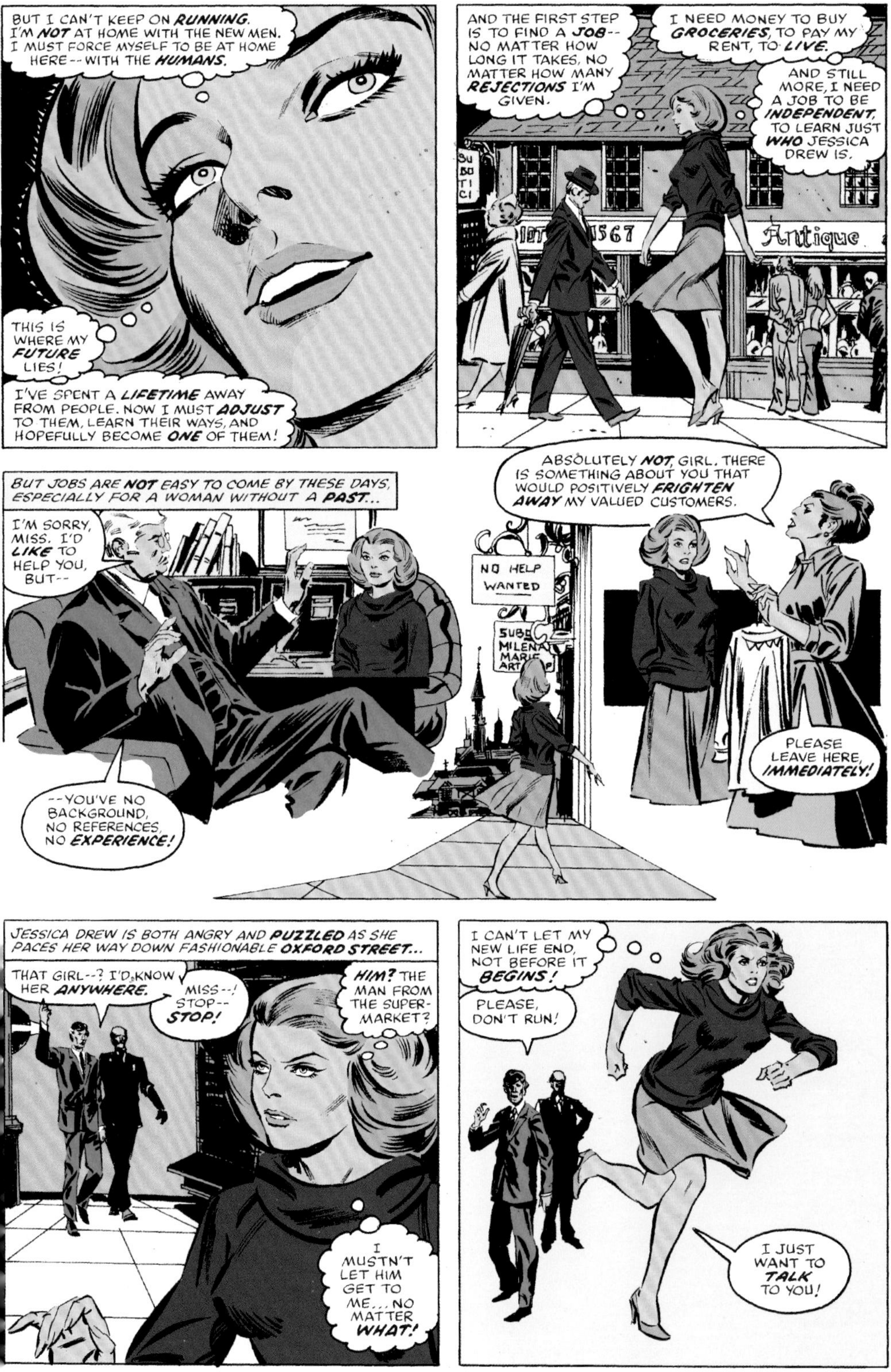
BUT I CAN'T KEEP ON RUNNING. I'M NOT AT HOME WITH THE NEW MEN. I MUST FORCE MYSELF TO BE AT HOME HERE--WITH THE HUMANS.
THIS IS WHERE MY FUTURE LIES!
I'VE SPENT A LIFETIME AWAY FROM PEOPLE. NOW I MUST ADJUST TO THEM, LEARN THEIR WAYS, AND HOPEFULLY BECOME ONE OF THEM!
AND THE FIRST STEP IS TO FIND A JOB--NO MATTER HOW LONG IT TAKES, NO MATTER HOW MANY REJECTIONS I'M GIVEN.
I NEED MONEY TO BUY GROCERIES, TO PAY MY RENT, TO LIVE.
AND STILL MORE, I NEED A JOB TO BE INDEPENDENT, TO LEARN JUST WHO JESSICA DREW IS.
Antique
BUT JOBS ARE NOT EASY TO COME BY THESE DAYS, ESPECIALLY FOR A WOMAN WITHOUT A PAST...
I'M SORRY, MISS. I'D LIKE TO HELP YOU, BUT--
--YOU'VE NO BACKGROUND, NO REFERENCES, NO EXPERIENCE!
NO HELP WANTED
ABSOLUTELY NOT, GIRL. THERE IS SOMETHING ABOUT YOU THAT WOULD POSITIVELY FRIGHTEN AWAY MY VALUED CUSTOMERS.
PLEASE LEAVE HERE, IMMEDIATELY!
JESSICA DREW IS BOTH ANGRY AND PUZZLED AS SHE PACES HER WAY DOWN FASHIONABLE OXFORD STREET...
THAT GIRL--? I'D KNOW HER ANYWHERE.
MISS--! STOP--STOP!
HIM? THE MAN FROM THE SUPER-MARKET?
I MUSTN'T LET HIM GET TO ME... NO MATTER WHAT!
I CAN'T LET MY NEW LIFE END, NOT BEFORE IT BEGINS!
PLEASE, DON'T RUN!
I JUST WANT TO TALK TO YOU!

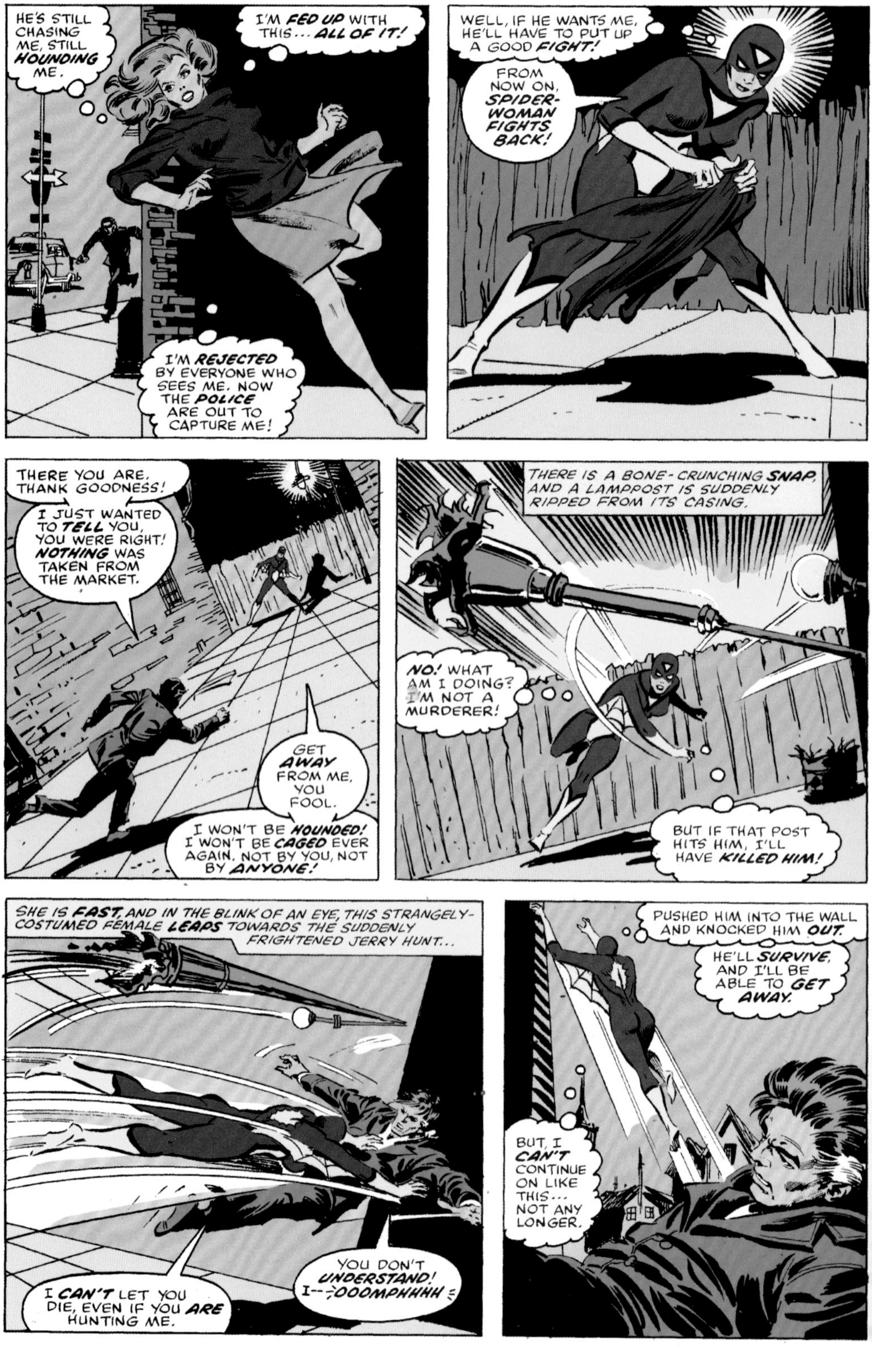

HE'S STILL CHASING ME, STILL HOUNDING ME.
I'M FED UP WITH THIS... ALL OF IT!
I'M REJECTED BY EVERYONE WHO SEES ME. NOW THE POLICE ARE OUT TO CAPTURE ME!
WELL, IF HE WANTS ME, HE'LL HAVE TO PUT UP A GOOD FIGHT!
FROM NOW ON, SPIDER-WOMAN FIGHTS BACK!
THERE YOU ARE. THANK GOODNESS!
I JUST WANTED TO TELL YOU, YOU WERE RIGHT! NOTHING WAS TAKEN FROM THE MARKET.
GET AWAY FROM ME, YOU FOOL.
I WON'T BE HOUNDED! I WON'T BE CAGED EVER AGAIN. NOT BY YOU, NOT BY ANYONE!
THERE IS A BONE-CRUNCHING SNAP, AND A LAMPPOST IS SUDDENLY RIPPED FROM ITS CASING.
NO! WHAT AM I DOING? I'M NOT A MURDERER!
BUT IF THAT POST HITS HIM, I'LL HAVE KILLED HIM!
SHE IS FAST, AND IN THE BLINK OF AN EYE, THIS STRANGELY-COSTUMED FEMALE LEAPS TOWARDS THE SUDDENLY FRIGHTENED JERRY HUNT...
I CAN'T LET YOU DIE, EVEN IF YOU ARE HUNTING ME.
YOU DON'T UNDERSTAND! I-- OOOMPHHHH
PUSHED HIM INTO THE WALL AND KNOCKED HIM OUT.
HE'LL SURVIVE, AND I'LL BE ABLE TO GET AWAY.
BUT, I CAN'T CONTINUE ON LIKE THIS... NOT ANY LONGER.

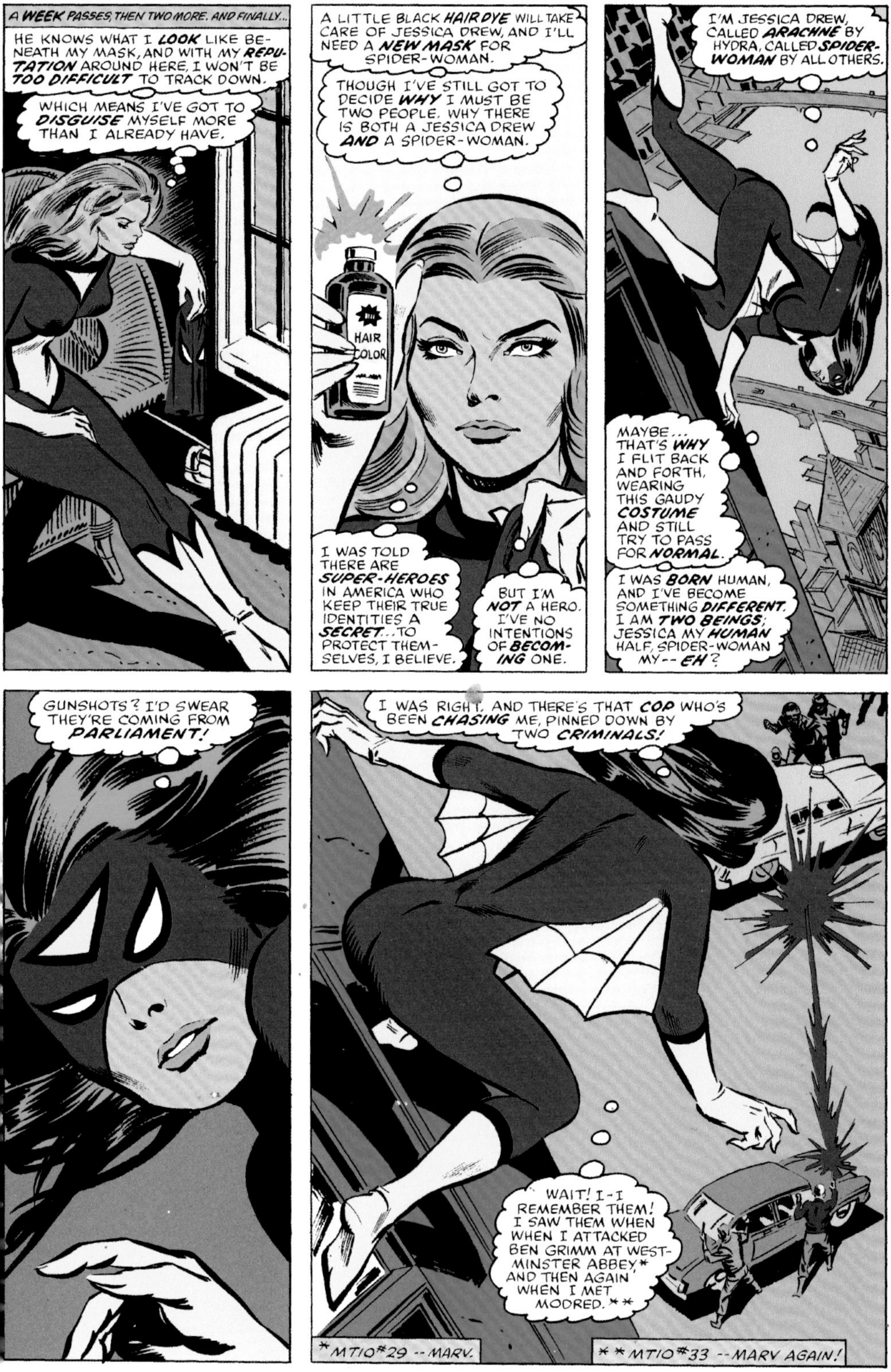
A WEEK PASSES, THEN TWO MORE. AND FINALLY...
HE KNOWS WHAT I LOOK LIKE BENEATH MY MASK, AND WITH MY REPUTATION AROUND HERE, I WON'T BE TOO DIFFICULT TO TRACK DOWN.
WHICH MEANS I'VE GOT TO DISGUISE MYSELF MORE THAN I ALREADY HAVE.
A LITTLE BLACK HAIR DYE WILL TAKE CARE OF JESSICA DREW, AND I'LL NEED A NEW MASK FOR SPIDER-WOMAN.
THOUGH I'VE STILL GOT TO DECIDE WHY I MUST BE TWO PEOPLE. WHY THERE IS BOTH A JESSICA DREW AND A SPIDER-WOMAN.
HAIR COLOR
I WAS TOLD THERE ARE SUPER-HEROES IN AMERICA WHO KEEP THEIR TRUE IDENTITIES A SECRET... TO PROTECT THEMSELVES, I BELIEVE.
BUT I'M NOT A HERO. I'VE NO INTENTIONS OF BECOMING ONE.
I'M JESSICA DREW, CALLED ARACHNE BY HYDRA, CALLED SPIDER-WOMAN BY ALL OTHERS.
MAYBE... THAT'S WHY I FLIT BACK AND FORTH, WEARING THIS GAUDY COSTUME AND STILL TRY TO PASS FOR NORMAL.
I WAS BORN HUMAN, AND I'VE BECOME SOMETHING DIFFERENT. I AM TWO BEINGS; JESSICA MY HUMAN HALF, SPIDER-WOMAN MY-- EH?
GUNSHOTS? I'D SWEAR THEY'RE COMING FROM PARLIAMENT!
I WAS RIGHT. AND THERE'S THAT COP WHO'S BEEN CHASING ME, PINNED DOWN BY TWO CRIMINALS!
WAIT! I-I REMEMBER THEM! I SAW THEM WHEN WHEN I ATTACKED BEN GRIMM AT WESTMINSTER ABBEY,* AND THEN AGAIN WHEN I MET MODRED.**
*MTIO #29 -- MARV.
**MTIO #33 -- MARV AGAIN!

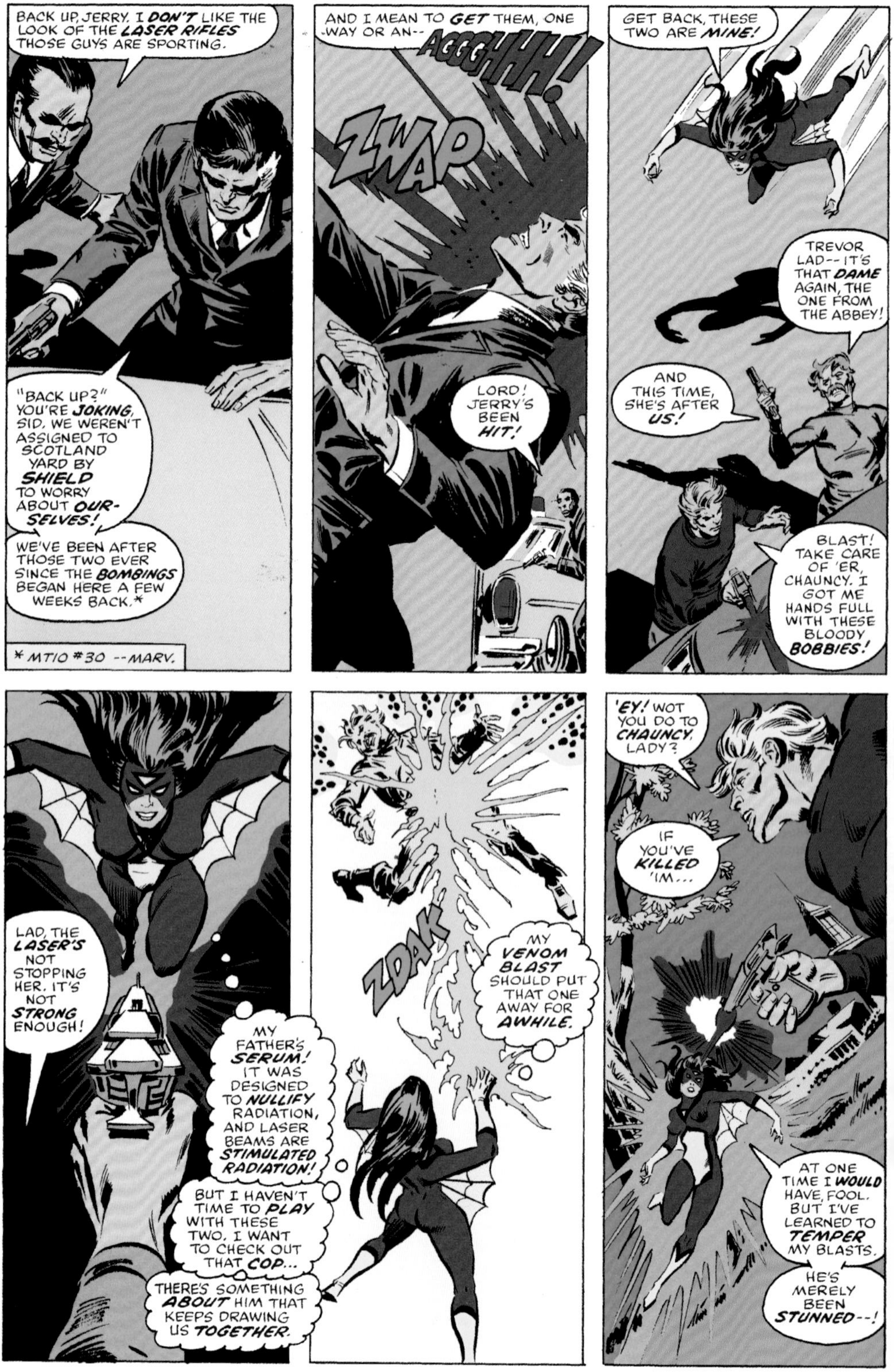
BACK UP, JERRY. I DON'T LIKE THE LOOK OF THE LASER RIFLES THOSE GUYS ARE SPORTING.
"BACK UP?" YOU'RE JOKING, SID. WE WEREN'T ASSIGNED TO SCOTLAND YARD BY SHIELD TO WORRY ABOUT OUR-SELVES!
WE'VE BEEN AFTER THOSE TWO EVER SINCE THE BOMBINGS BEGAN HERE A FEW WEEKS BACK.*
* MTIO #30 --MARV.
AND I MEAN TO GET THEM, ONE WAY OR AN--
AGGGHHH!
ZWAP
LORD! JERRY'S BEEN HIT!
GET BACK, THESE TWO ARE MINE!
TREVOR LAD-- IT'S THAT DAME AGAIN, THE ONE FROM THE ABBEY!
AND THIS TIME, SHE'S AFTER US!
BLAST! TAKE CARE OF 'ER, CHAUNCY. I GOT ME HANDS FULL WITH THESE BLOODY BOBBIES!
LAD, THE LASER'S NOT STOPPING HER. IT'S NOT STRONG ENOUGH!
MY FATHER'S SERUM! IT WAS DESIGNED TO NULLIFY RADIATION, AND LASER BEAMS ARE STIMULATED RADIATION!
BUT I HAVEN'T TIME TO PLAY WITH THESE TWO. I WANT TO CHECK OUT THAT COP...
THERE'S SOMETHING ABOUT HIM THAT KEEPS DRAWING US TOGETHER.
ZDAK
MY VENOM BLAST SHOULD PUT THAT ONE AWAY FOR AWHILE.
'EY! WOT YOU DO TO CHAUNCY, LADY?
IF YOU'VE KILLED 'IM...
AT ONE TIME I WOULD HAVE, FOOL. BUT I'VE LEARNED TO TEMPER MY BLASTS.
HE'S MERELY BEEN STUNNED--!

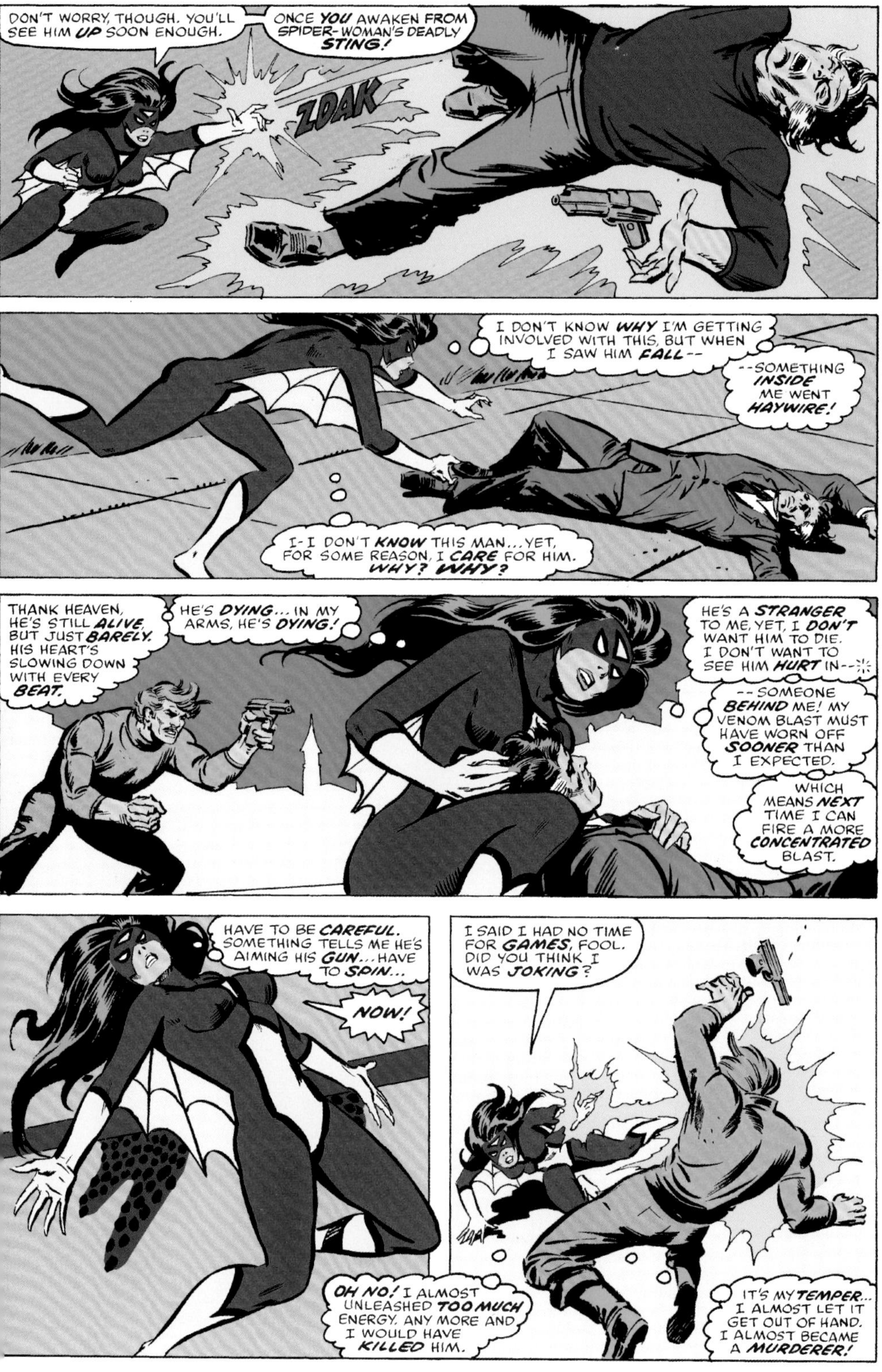
DON'T WORRY, THOUGH. YOU'LL SEE HIM UP SOON ENOUGH.
ONCE YOU AWAKEN FROM SPIDER-WOMAN'S DEADLY STING!
ZDAK
I DON'T KNOW WHY I'M GETTING INVOLVED WITH THIS, BUT WHEN I SAW HIM FALL--
--SOMETHING INSIDE ME WENT HAYWIRE!
I-I DON'T KNOW THIS MAN... YET, FOR SOME REASON, I CARE FOR HIM. WHY? WHY?
THANK HEAVEN, HE'S STILL ALIVE, BUT JUST BARELY. HIS HEART'S SLOWING DOWN WITH EVERY BEAT.
HE'S DYING... IN MY ARMS, HE'S DYING!
HE'S A STRANGER TO ME, YET, I DON'T WANT HIM TO DIE. I DON'T WANT TO SEE HIM HURT IN--
--SOMEONE BEHIND ME! MY VENOM BLAST MUST HAVE WORN OFF SOONER THAN I EXPECTED.
WHICH MEANS NEXT TIME I CAN FIRE A MORE CONCENTRATED BLAST.
HAVE TO BE CAREFUL. SOMETHING TELLS ME HE'S AIMING HIS GUN... HAVE TO SPIN...
NOW!
I SAID I HAD NO TIME FOR GAMES, FOOL. DID YOU THINK I WAS JOKING?
OH NO! I ALMOST UNLEASHED TOO MUCH ENERGY. ANY MORE AND I WOULD HAVE KILLED HIM.
IT'S MY TEMPER... I ALMOST LET IT GET OUT OF HAND. I ALMOST BECAME A MURDERER!

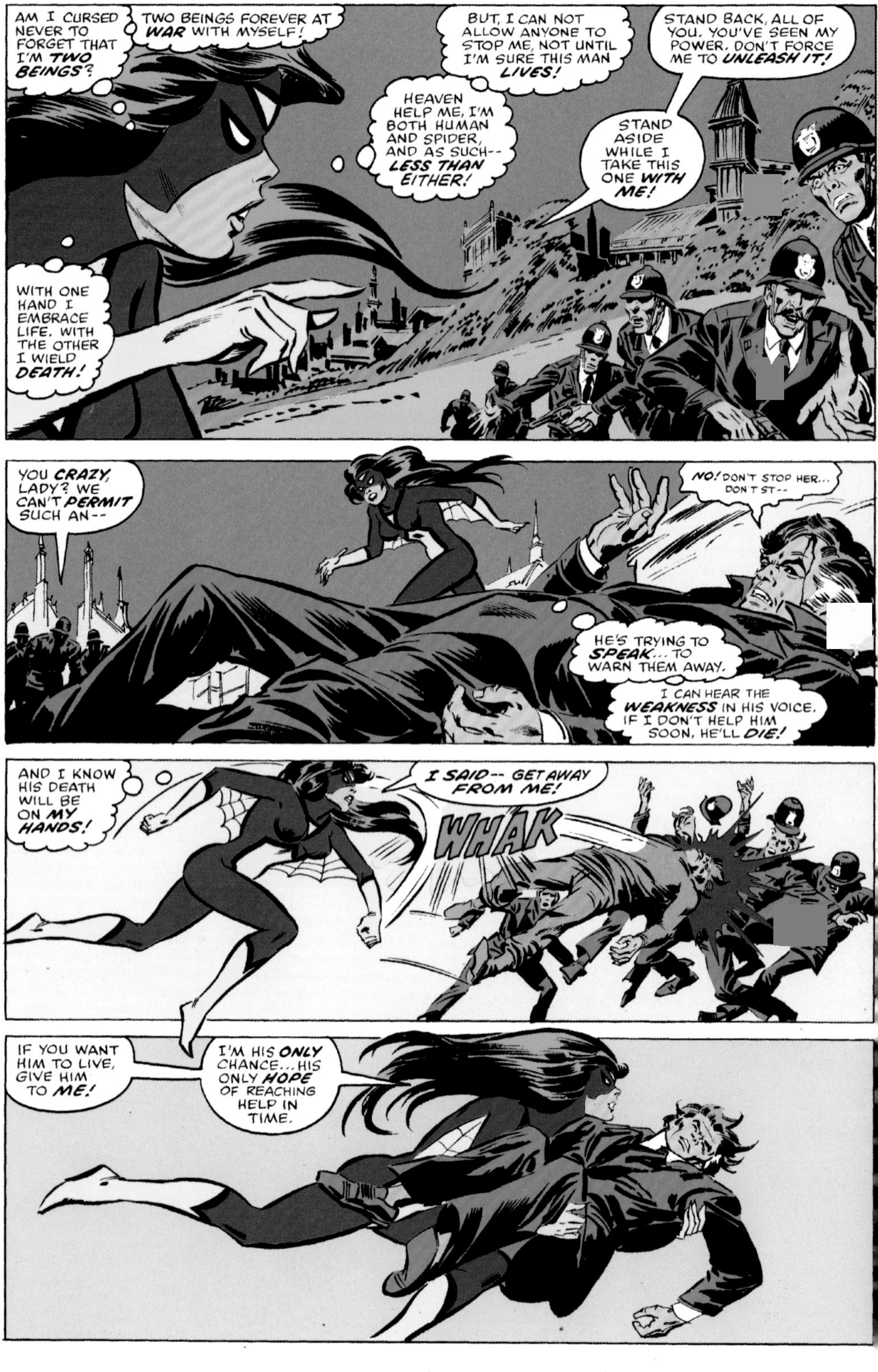
AM I CURSED NEVER TO FORGET THAT I'M TWO BEINGS?
TWO BEINGS FOREVER AT WAR WITH MYSELF!
BUT, I CAN NOT ALLOW ANYONE TO STOP ME, NOT UNTIL I'M SURE THIS MAN LIVES!
STAND BACK, ALL OF YOU. YOU'VE SEEN MY POWER. DON'T FORCE ME TO UNLEASH IT!
HEAVEN HELP ME, I'M BOTH HUMAN AND SPIDER, AND AS SUCH-- LESS THAN EITHER!
STAND ASIDE WHILE I TAKE THIS ONE WITH ME!
WITH ONE HAND I EMBRACE LIFE. WITH THE OTHER I WIELD DEATH!
YOU CRAZY, LADY? WE CAN'T PERMIT SUCH AN--
NO! DON'T STOP HER... DON'T ST--
HE'S TRYING TO SPEAK... TO WARN THEM AWAY.
I CAN HEAR THE WEAKNESS IN HIS VOICE. IF I DON'T HELP HIM SOON, HE'LL DIE!
AND I KNOW HIS DEATH WILL BE ON MY HANDS!
I SAID-- GET AWAY FROM ME!
WHAK
IF YOU WANT HIM TO LIVE, GIVE HIM TO ME!
I'M HIS ONLY CHANCE... HIS ONLY HOPE OF REACHING HELP IN TIME.

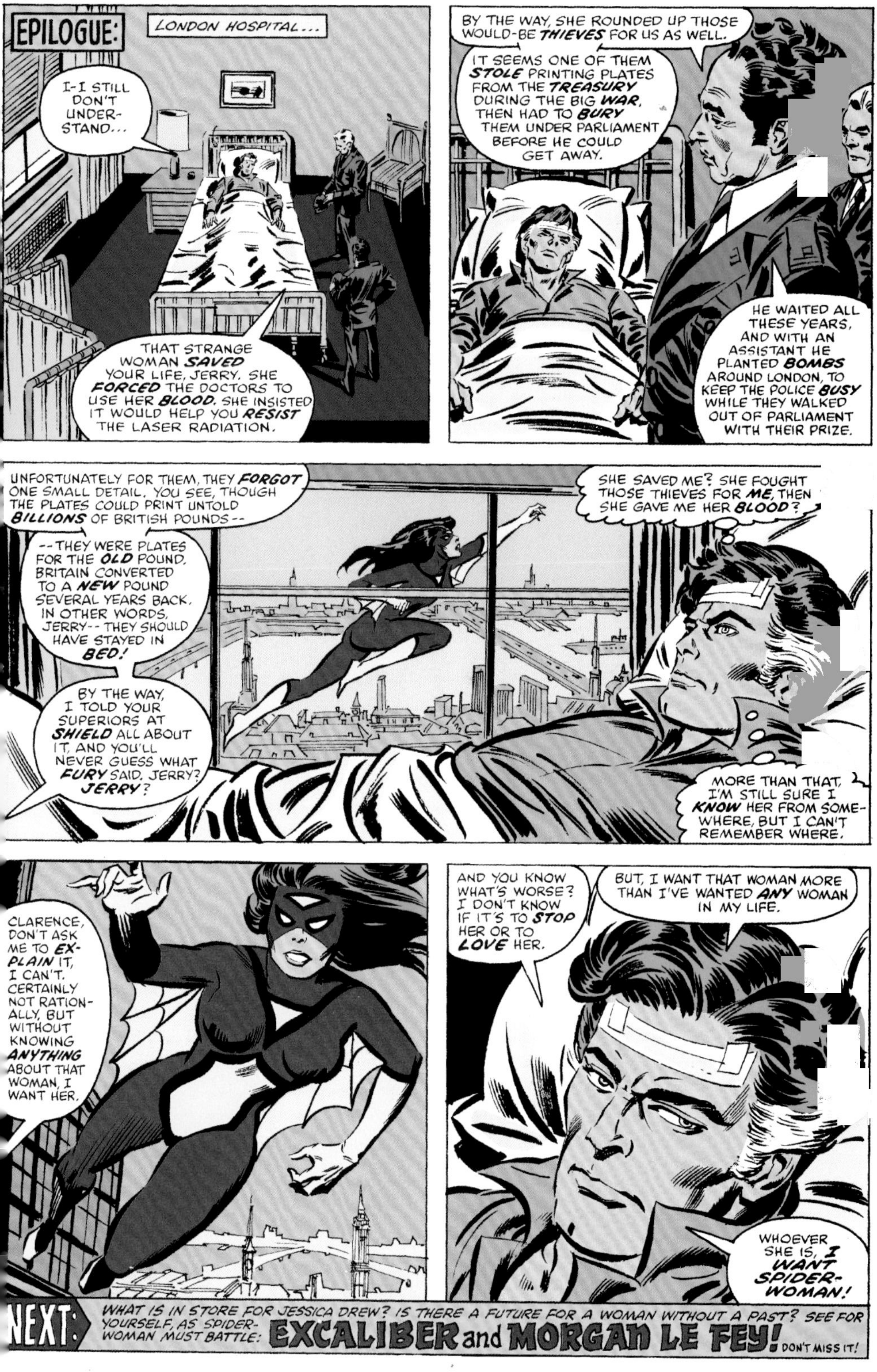
EPILOGUE:
LONDON HOSPITAL...
I-I STILL DON'T UNDER-STAND...
THAT STRANGE WOMAN SAVED YOUR LIFE, JERRY. SHE FORCED THE DOCTORS TO USE HER BLOOD. SHE INSISTED IT WOULD HELP YOU RESIST THE LASER RADIATION.
BY THE WAY, SHE ROUNDED UP THOSE WOULD-BE THIEVES FOR US AS WELL.
IT SEEMS ONE OF THEM STOLE PRINTING PLATES FROM THE TREASURY DURING THE BIG WAR, THEN HAD TO BURY THEM UNDER PARLIAMENT BEFORE HE COULD GET AWAY.
HE WAITED ALL THESE YEARS, AND WITH AN ASSISTANT HE PLANTED BOMBS AROUND LONDON, TO KEEP THE POLICE BUSY WHILE THEY WALKED OUT OF PARLIAMENT WITH THEIR PRIZE.
UNFORTUNATELY FOR THEM, THEY FORGOT ONE SMALL DETAIL. YOU SEE, THOUGH THE PLATES COULD PRINT UNTOLD BILLIONS OF BRITISH POUNDS--
--THEY WERE PLATES FOR THE OLD POUND. BRITAIN CONVERTED TO A NEW POUND SEVERAL YEARS BACK. IN OTHER WORDS, JERRY-- THEY SHOULD HAVE STAYED IN BED!
BY THE WAY, I TOLD YOUR SUPERIORS AT SHIELD ALL ABOUT IT, AND YOU'LL NEVER GUESS WHAT FURY SAID. JERRY? JERRY?
SHE SAVED ME? SHE FOUGHT THOSE THIEVES FOR ME, THEN SHE GAVE ME HER BLOOD?
MORE THAN THAT, I'M STILL SURE I KNOW HER FROM SOME-WHERE, BUT I CAN'T REMEMBER WHERE.
CLARENCE, DON'T ASK ME TO EX-PLAIN IT, I CAN'T. CERTAINLY NOT RATION-ALLY, BUT WITHOUT KNOWING ANYTHING ABOUT THAT WOMAN, I WANT HER.
AND YOU KNOW WHAT'S WORSE? I DON'T KNOW IF IT'S TO STOP HER OR TO LOVE HER.
BUT, I WANT THAT WOMAN MORE THAN I'VE WANTED ANY WOMAN IN MY LIFE.
WHOEVER SHE IS, I WANT SPIDER-WOMAN!
NEXT: WHAT IS IN STORE FOR JESSICA DREW? IS THERE A FUTURE FOR A WOMAN WITHOUT A PAST? SEE FOR YOURSELF, AS SPIDER-WOMAN MUST BATTLE: EXCALIBER and MORGAN LE FEY! DON'T MISS IT!

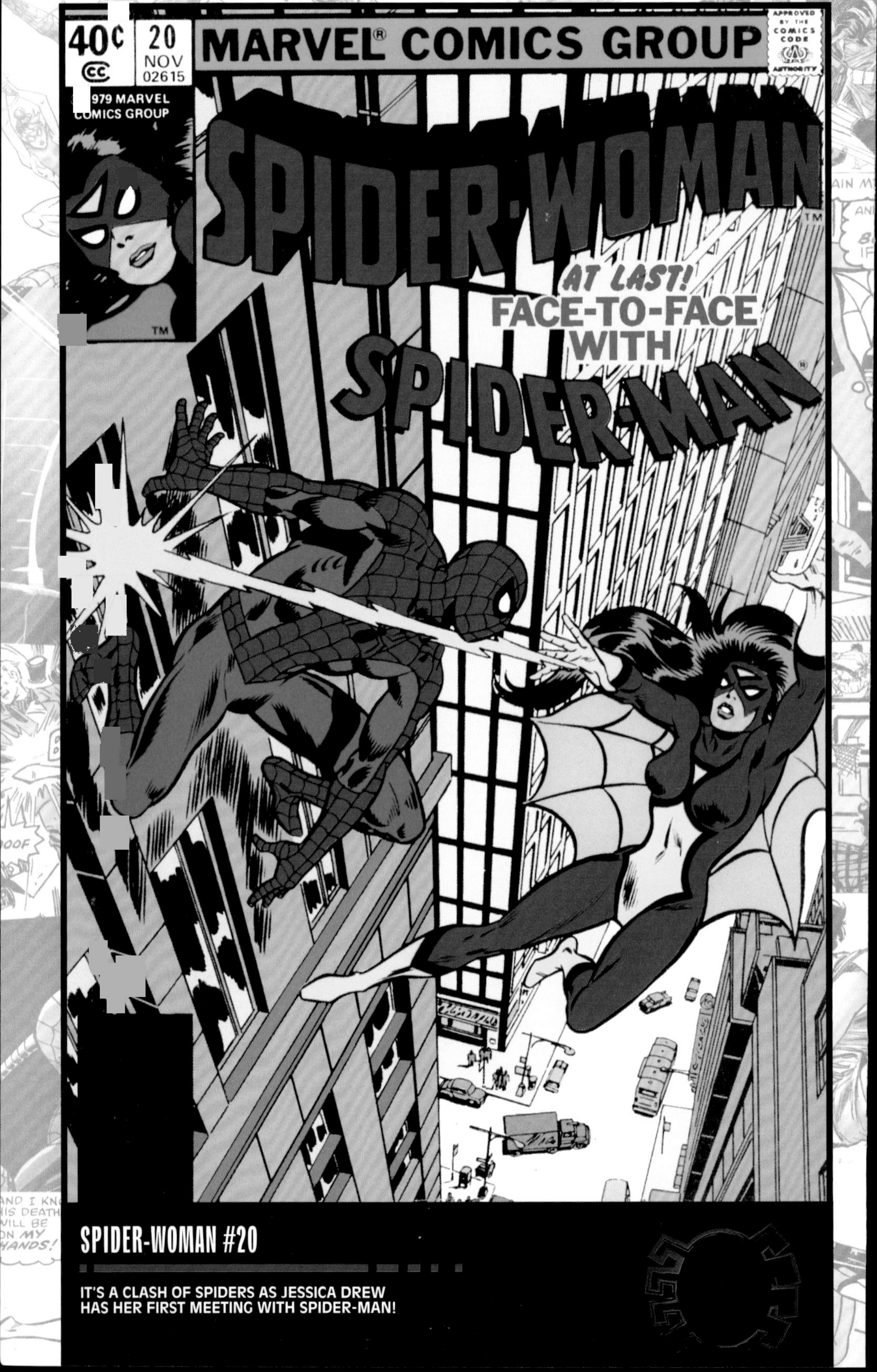
40¢
20
NOV
02615
MARVEL COMICS GROUP
APPROVED BY THE COMICS CODE AUTHORITY
979 MARVEL COMICS GROUP
SPIDER-WOMAN
AT LAST!
FACE-TO-FACE WITH
SPIDER-MAN

SPIDER-WOMAN #20

IT'S A CLASH OF SPIDERS AS JESSICA DREW HAS HER FIRST MEETING WITH SPIDER-MAN!

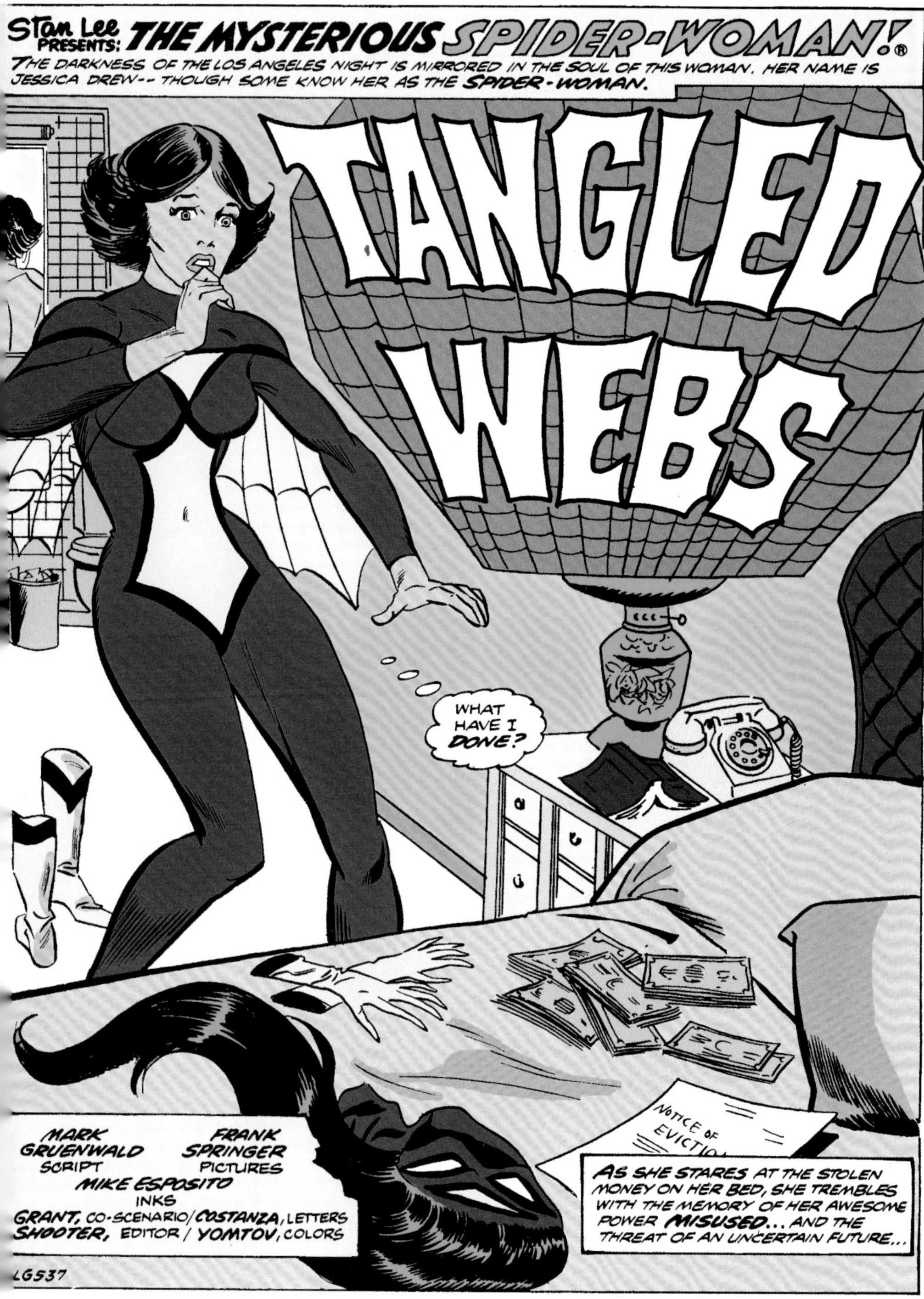

STAN LEE PRESENTS: THE MYSTERIOUS SPIDER-WOMAN!®
THE DARKNESS OF THE LOS ANGELES NIGHT IS MIRRORED IN THE SOUL OF THIS WOMAN. HER NAME IS JESSICA DREW-- THOUGH SOME KNOW HER AS THE SPIDER-WOMAN.
TANGLED WEBS
WHAT HAVE I DONE?
NOTICE OF EVICTION
MARK GRUENWALD SCRIPT
FRANK SPRINGER PICTURES
MIKE ESPOSITO INKS
GRANT, CO-SCENARIO/COSTANZA, LETTERS
SHOOTER, EDITOR / YOMTOV, COLORS
AS SHE STARES AT THE STOLEN MONEY ON HER BED, SHE TREMBLES WITH THE MEMORY OF HER AWESOME POWER MISUSED... AND THE THREAT OF AN UNCERTAIN FUTURE...
LG537

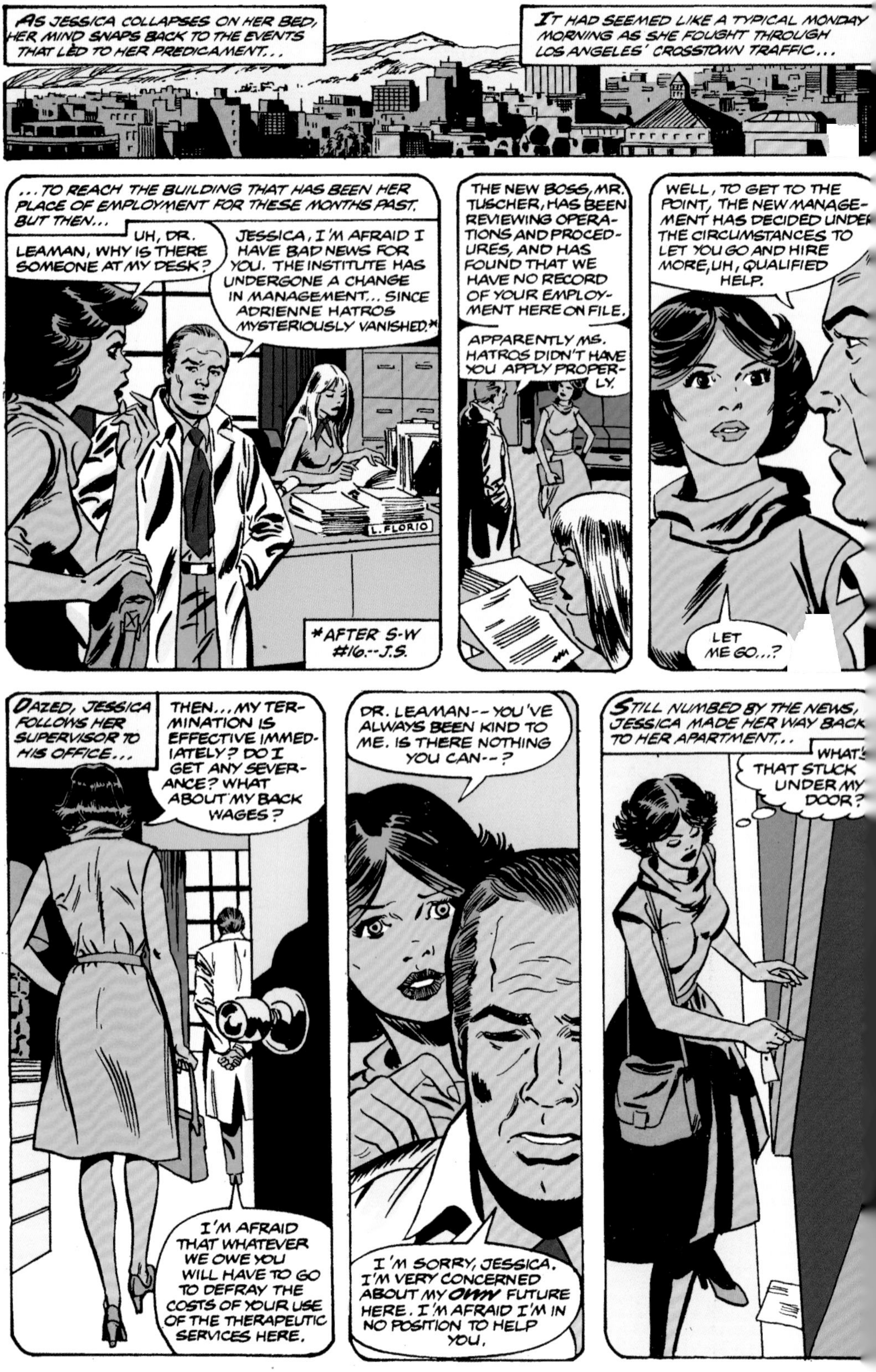
AS JESSICA COLLAPSES ON HER BED, HER MIND SNAPS BACK TO THE EVENTS THAT LED TO HER PREDICAMENT...
IT HAD SEEMED LIKE A TYPICAL MONDAY MORNING AS SHE FOUGHT THROUGH LOS ANGELES' CROSSTOWN TRAFFIC...
...TO REACH THE BUILDING THAT HAS BEEN HER PLACE OF EMPLOYMENT FOR THESE MONTHS PAST. BUT THEN...
UH, DR. LEAMAN, WHY IS THERE SOMEONE AT MY DESK?
JESSICA, I'M AFRAID I HAVE BAD NEWS FOR YOU. THE INSTITUTE HAS UNDERGONE A CHANGE IN MANAGEMENT... SINCE ADRIENNE HATROS MYSTERIOUSLY VANISHED.*
L. FLORIO
*AFTER S-W #16.--J.S.
THE NEW BOSS, MR. TUSCHER, HAS BEEN REVIEWING OPERATIONS AND PROCEDURES, AND HAS FOUND THAT WE HAVE NO RECORD OF YOUR EMPLOYMENT HERE ON FILE.
APPARENTLY MS. HATROS DIDN'T HAVE YOU APPLY PROPERLY.
WELL, TO GET TO THE POINT, THE NEW MANAGEMENT HAS DECIDED UNDER THE CIRCUMSTANCES TO LET YOU GO AND HIRE MORE, UH, QUALIFIED HELP.
LET ME GO...?
DAZED, JESSICA FOLLOWS HER SUPERVISOR TO HIS OFFICE...
THEN... MY TERMINATION IS EFFECTIVE IMMEDIATELY? DO I GET ANY SEVERANCE? WHAT ABOUT MY BACK WAGES?
I'M AFRAID THAT WHATEVER WE OWE YOU WILL HAVE TO GO TO DEFRAY THE COSTS OF YOUR USE OF THE THERAPEUTIC SERVICES HERE.
DR. LEAMAN-- YOU'VE ALWAYS BEEN KIND TO ME. IS THERE NOTHING YOU CAN--?
I'M SORRY, JESSICA. I'M VERY CONCERNED ABOUT MY OWN FUTURE HERE. I'M AFRAID I'M IN NO POSITION TO HELP YOU.
STILL NUMBED BY THE NEWS, JESSICA MADE HER WAY BACK TO HER APARTMENT...
WHAT'S THAT STUCK UNDER MY DOOR?

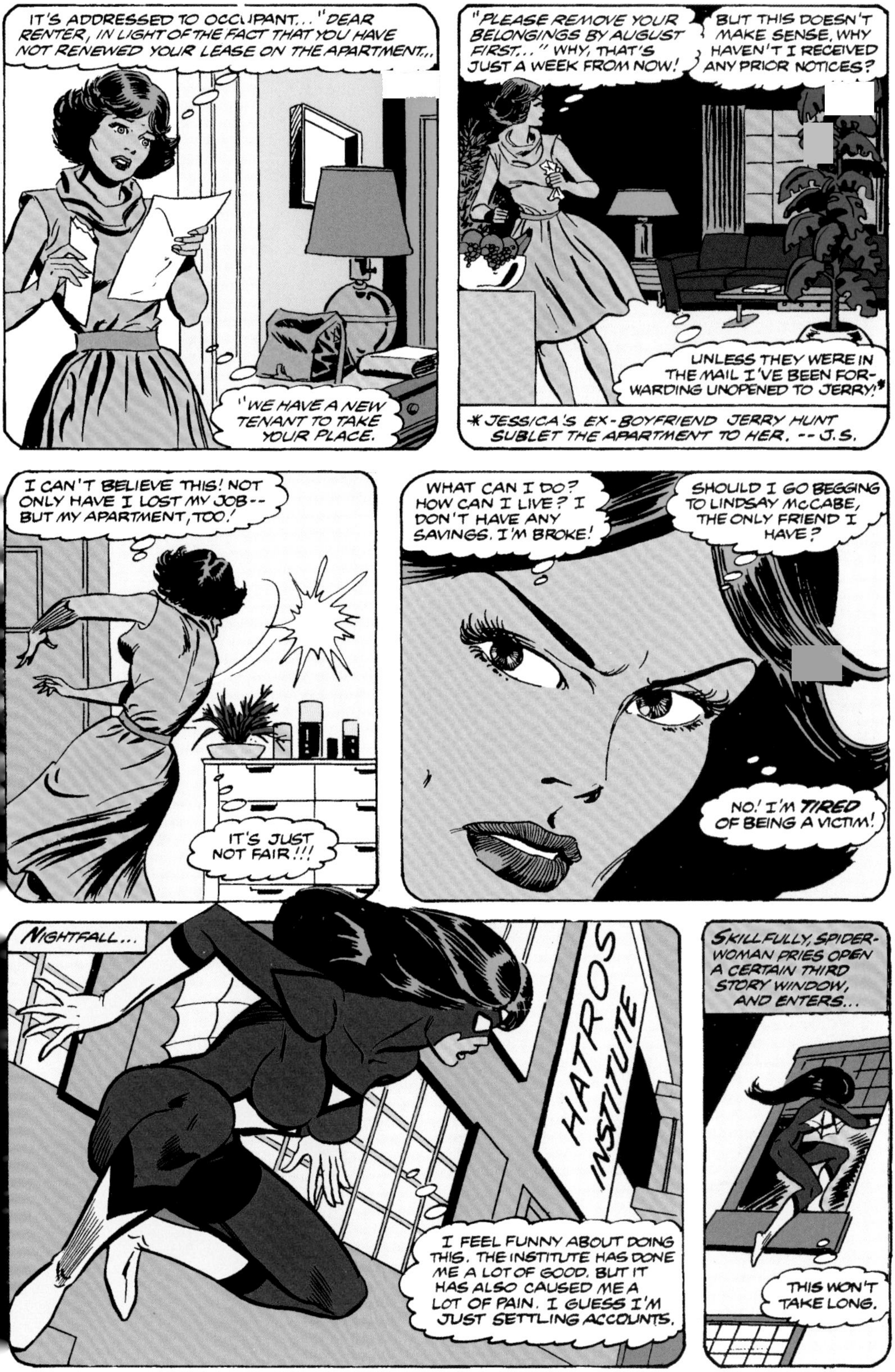
IT'S ADDRESSED TO OCCUPANT..."DEAR RENTER, IN LIGHT OF THE FACT THAT YOU HAVE NOT RENEWED YOUR LEASE ON THE APARTMENT...
"WE HAVE A NEW TENANT TO TAKE YOUR PLACE.
"PLEASE REMOVE YOUR BELONGINGS BY AUGUST FIRST..." WHY, THAT'S JUST A WEEK FROM NOW!
BUT THIS DOESN'T MAKE SENSE, WHY HAVEN'T I RECEIVED ANY PRIOR NOTICES?
UNLESS THEY WERE IN THE MAIL I'VE BEEN FORWARDING UNOPENED TO JERRY!*
* JESSICA'S EX-BOYFRIEND JERRY HUNT SUBLET THE APARTMENT TO HER. -- J.S.
I CAN'T BELIEVE THIS! NOT ONLY HAVE I LOST MY JOB-- BUT MY APARTMENT, TOO!
IT'S JUST NOT FAIR!!!
WHAT CAN I DO? HOW CAN I LIVE? I DON'T HAVE ANY SAVINGS. I'M BROKE!
SHOULD I GO BEGGING TO LINDSAY McCABE, THE ONLY FRIEND I HAVE?
NO! I'M TIRED OF BEING A VICTIM!
NIGHTFALL...
HATROS INSTITUTE
I FEEL FUNNY ABOUT DOING THIS. THE INSTITUTE HAS DONE ME A LOT OF GOOD. BUT IT HAS ALSO CAUSED ME A LOT OF PAIN. I GUESS I'M JUST SETTLING ACCOUNTS.
SKILLFULLY, SPIDER-WOMAN PRIES OPEN A CERTAIN THIRD STORY WINDOW, AND ENTERS...
THIS WON'T TAKE LONG.

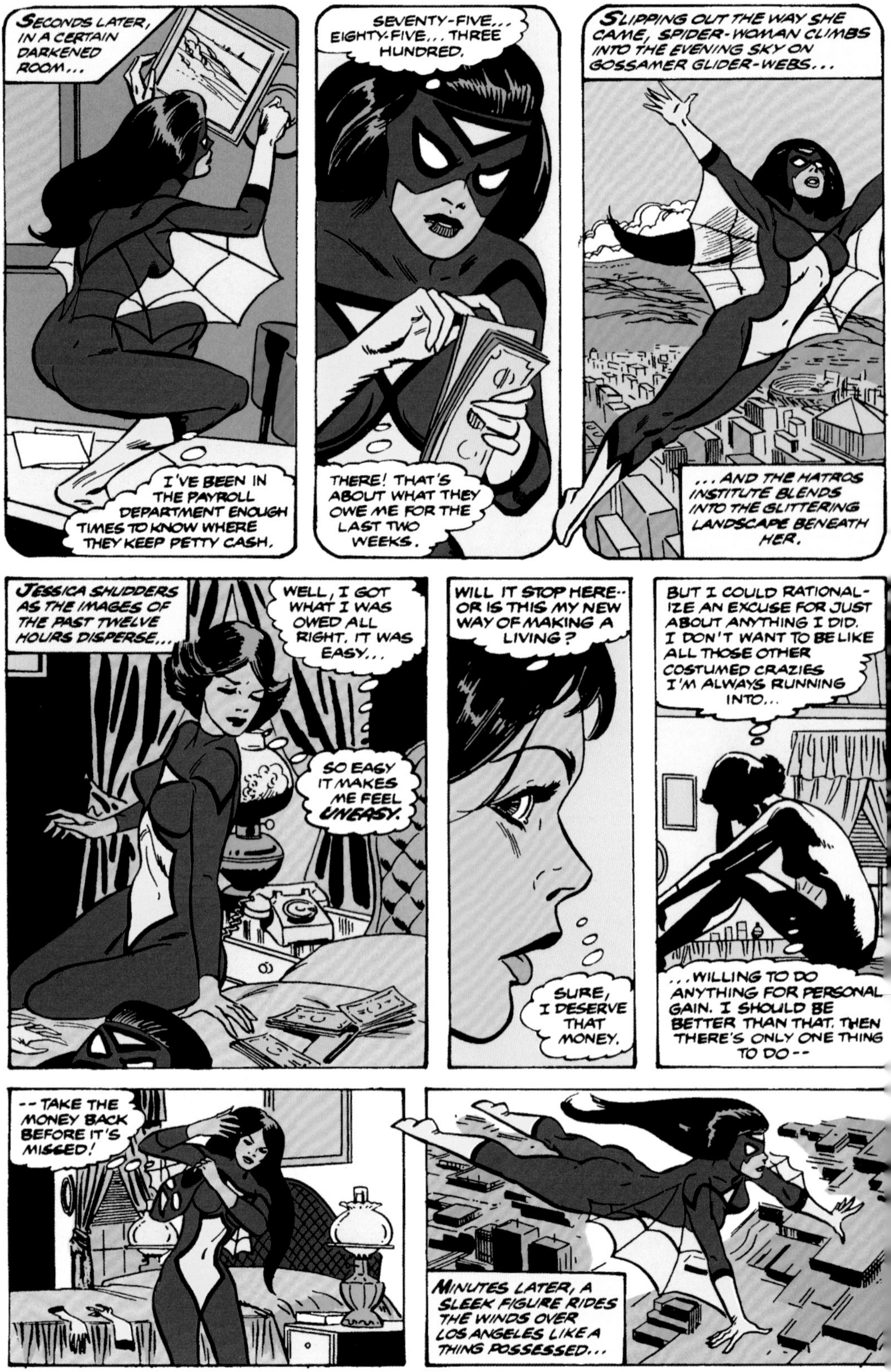
SECONDS LATER, IN A CERTAIN DARKENED ROOM...
I'VE BEEN IN THE PAYROLL DEPARTMENT ENOUGH TIMES TO KNOW WHERE THEY KEEP PETTY CASH.
SEVENTY-FIVE... EIGHTY-FIVE... THREE HUNDRED.
THERE! THAT'S ABOUT WHAT THEY OWE ME FOR THE LAST TWO WEEKS.
SLIPPING OUT THE WAY SHE CAME, SPIDER-WOMAN CLIMBS INTO THE EVENING SKY ON GOSSAMER GLIDER-WEBS...
...AND THE HATROS INSTITUTE BLENDS INTO THE GLITTERING LANDSCAPE BENEATH HER.
JESSICA SHUDDERS AS THE IMAGES OF THE PAST TWELVE HOURS DISPERSE...
WELL, I GOT WHAT I WAS OWED ALL RIGHT. IT WAS EASY...
SO EASY IT MAKES ME FEEL UNEASY.
WILL IT STOP HERE-- OR IS THIS MY NEW WAY OF MAKING A LIVING?
SURE, I DESERVE THAT MONEY.
BUT I COULD RATIONAL-IZE AN EXCUSE FOR JUST ABOUT ANYTHING I DID. I DON'T WANT TO BE LIKE ALL THOSE OTHER COSTUMED CRAZIES I'M ALWAYS RUNNING INTO...
...WILLING TO DO ANYTHING FOR PERSONAL GAIN. I SHOULD BE BETTER THAN THAT. THEN THERE'S ONLY ONE THING TO DO--
--TAKE THE MONEY BACK BEFORE IT'S MISSED!
MINUTES LATER, A SLEEK FIGURE RIDES THE WINDS OVER LOS ANGELES LIKE A THING POSSESSED...

UNKNOWN TO HER, THERE ARE THREE OTHERS WHO HAVE AFTER-HOURS BUSINESS AT THE HATROS INSTITUTE...

THIS ASSIGNMENT ISN'T HALF AS INTERESTING AS I HOPED IT WOULD BE.

HATROS INSTITUTE

BUT IF THE DAILY GLOBE WANTS TO SPRING FOR A WEEKEND TRIP TO L.A.--

--JUST SO I CAN SNAP A FEW ROLLS OF SOME POP PSYCH CLINICS... WHO IS PETER PARKER, BOY SHUTTERBUG, TO TELL 'EM NO THANKS? BESIDES, I COULD USE A BREAK FROM THE OL' SPIDER-MAN GRIND.

I THINK YOU'RE GOING TO BE QUITE IMPRESSED WITH OUR FACILITIES HERE, MR. MULLANEY. THE HATROS INSTITUTE IS NOT AT ALL LIKE MOST OF THE GROUP ENCOUNTER CLINICS THAT HAVE BECOME POPULAR IN RECENT YEARS...

HOW SO?

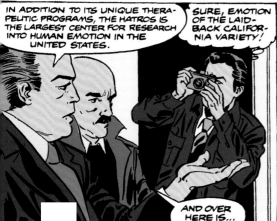

IN ADDITION TO ITS UNIQUE THERA-PEUTIC PROGRAMS, THE HATROS IS THE LARGEST CENTER FOR RESEARCH INTO HUMAN EMOTION IN THE UNITED STATES.

SURE, EMOTION OF THE LAID-BACK CALIFOR-NIA VARIETY!

AND OVER HERE IS...

SOME TIME LATER... SHEESH, I DON'T KNOW WHO'S THE BIGGER WINDBAG-- THIS DR. LEAMAN OR MY PARTNER MIKE. AFTER A DAY OF TRAIPSING FROM ONE BLAND CLINIC TO THE NEXT I'M READY TO PACK IT IN. DON'T CALIFORNIANS HAVE ANYTHING BETTER TO DO THAN--

HEY, WHAT'S THIS? MY SPIDER-SENSE IS TINGLING LIKE A GEIGER COUNTER IN A NUCLEAR REACTOR!

SOMETHING WEIRD IS GOING ON AROUND HERE...

...AND I'VE GOT AN ITCH TO SEE WHAT IT IS!

DR. LEAMAN-- IS IT OKAY IF I USE THE MEN'S ROOM?

CERTAINLY.

DON'T GET LOST, KID.

I SHOULD PROBABLY CHANGE TO MY SPIDER-MAN TOGS, BUT I WANT TO AVOID LETTING ANY-ONE KNOW BOTH PARKER AND SPIDEY ARE OUT ON THE COAST AT THE SAME TIME.

MMM. THE TINGLING'S STRONGER. I MUST BE GETTING CLOSE.

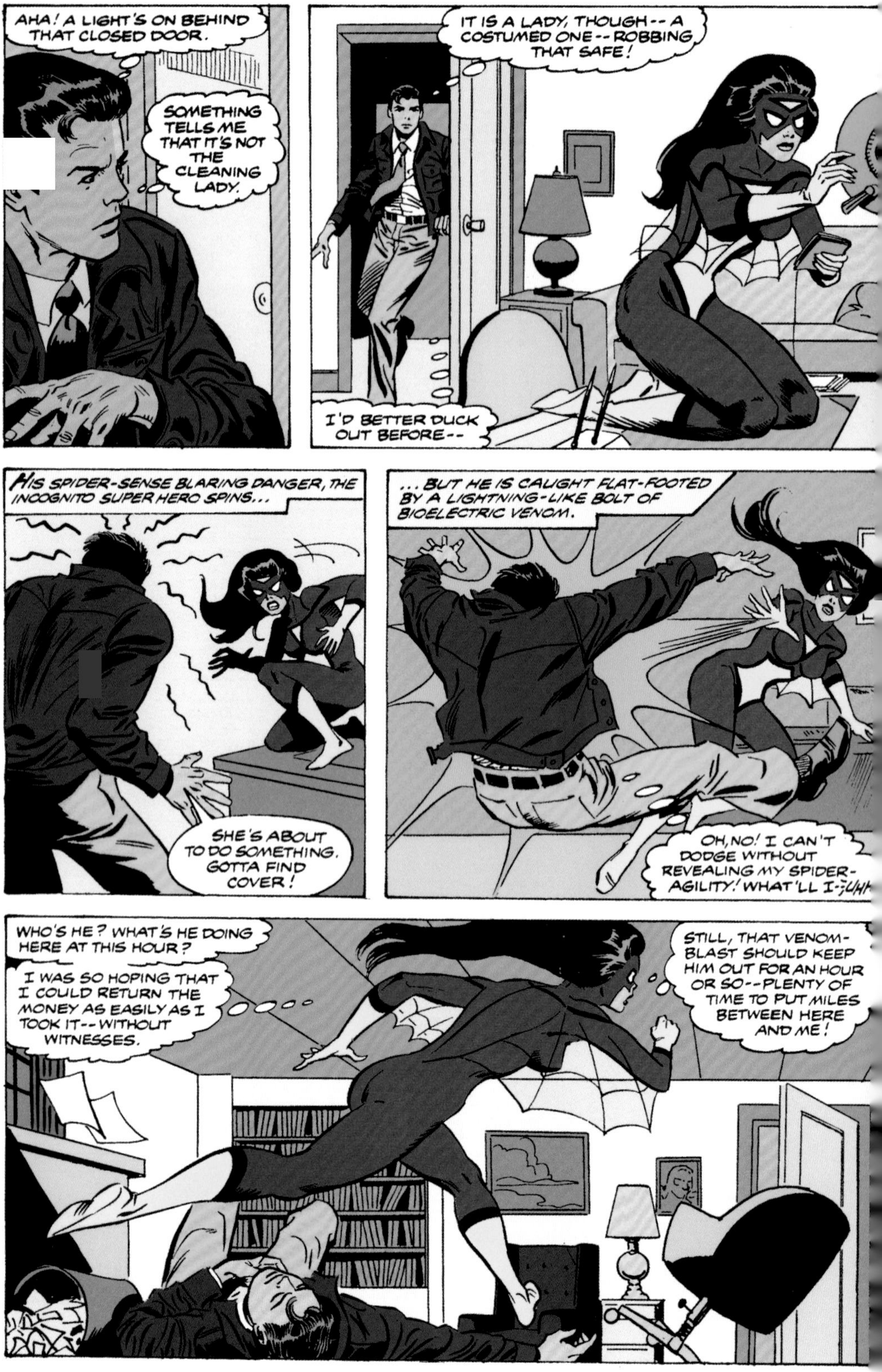
AHA! A LIGHT'S ON BEHIND THAT CLOSED DOOR.
SOMETHING TELLS ME THAT IT'S NOT THE CLEANING LADY.
IT IS A LADY, THOUGH-- A COSTUMED ONE-- ROBBING THAT SAFE!
I'D BETTER DUCK OUT BEFORE--
HIS SPIDER-SENSE BLARING DANGER, THE INCOGNITO SUPER HERO SPINS...
SHE'S ABOUT TO DO SOMETHING. GOTTA FIND COVER!
... BUT HE IS CAUGHT FLAT-FOOTED BY A LIGHTNING-LIKE BOLT OF BIOELECTRIC VENOM.
OH, NO! I CAN'T DODGE WITHOUT REVEALING MY SPIDER-AGILITY! WHAT'LL I--UHH
WHO'S HE? WHAT'S HE DOING HERE AT THIS HOUR?
I WAS SO HOPING THAT I COULD RETURN THE MONEY AS EASILY AS I TOOK IT-- WITHOUT WITNESSES.
STILL, THAT VENOM-BLAST SHOULD KEEP HIM OUT FOR AN HOUR OR SO-- PLENTY OF TIME TO PUT MILES BETWEEN HERE AND ME!

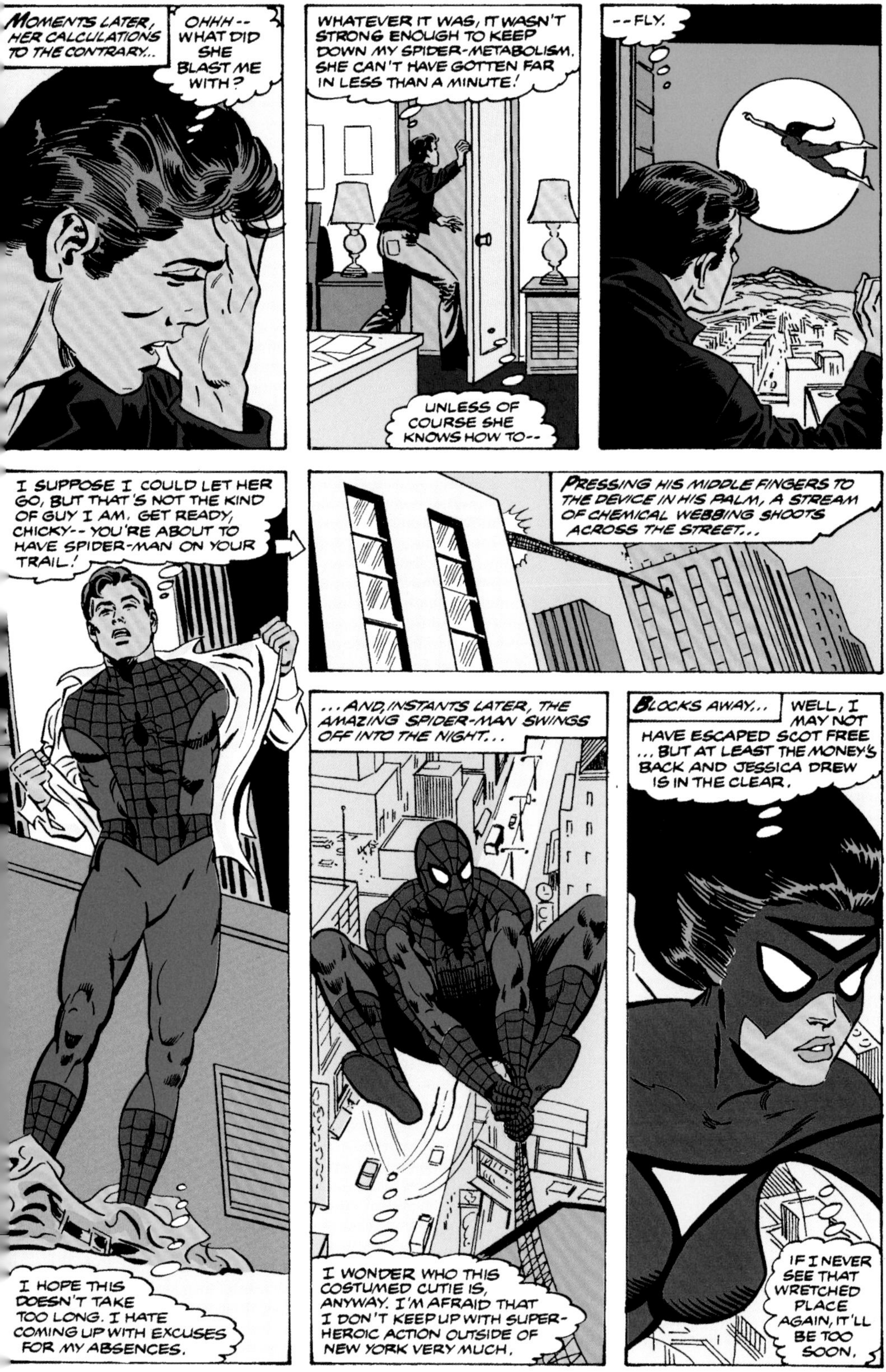
MOMENTS LATER, HER CALCULATIONS TO THE CONTRARY...
OHHH-- WHAT DID SHE BLAST ME WITH?
WHATEVER IT WAS, IT WASN'T STRONG ENOUGH TO KEEP DOWN MY SPIDER-METABOLISM. SHE CAN'T HAVE GOTTEN FAR IN LESS THAN A MINUTE!
UNLESS OF COURSE SHE KNOWS HOW TO--
--FLY.
I SUPPOSE I COULD LET HER GO, BUT THAT'S NOT THE KIND OF GUY I AM. GET READY, CHICKY-- YOU'RE ABOUT TO HAVE SPIDER-MAN ON YOUR TRAIL!
I HOPE THIS DOESN'T TAKE TOO LONG. I HATE COMING UP WITH EXCUSES FOR MY ABSENCES.
PRESSING HIS MIDDLE FINGERS TO THE DEVICE IN HIS PALM, A STREAM OF CHEMICAL WEBBING SHOOTS ACROSS THE STREET...
...AND, INSTANTS LATER, THE AMAZING SPIDER-MAN SWINGS OFF INTO THE NIGHT...
I WONDER WHO THIS COSTUMED CUTIE IS, ANYWAY. I'M AFRAID THAT I DON'T KEEP UP WITH SUPER-HEROIC ACTION OUTSIDE OF NEW YORK VERY MUCH.
BLOCKS AWAY...
WELL, I MAY NOT HAVE ESCAPED SCOT FREE ...BUT AT LEAST THE MONEY'S BACK AND JESSICA DREW IS IN THE CLEAR.
IF I NEVER SEE THAT WRETCHED PLACE AGAIN, IT'LL BE TOO SOON.

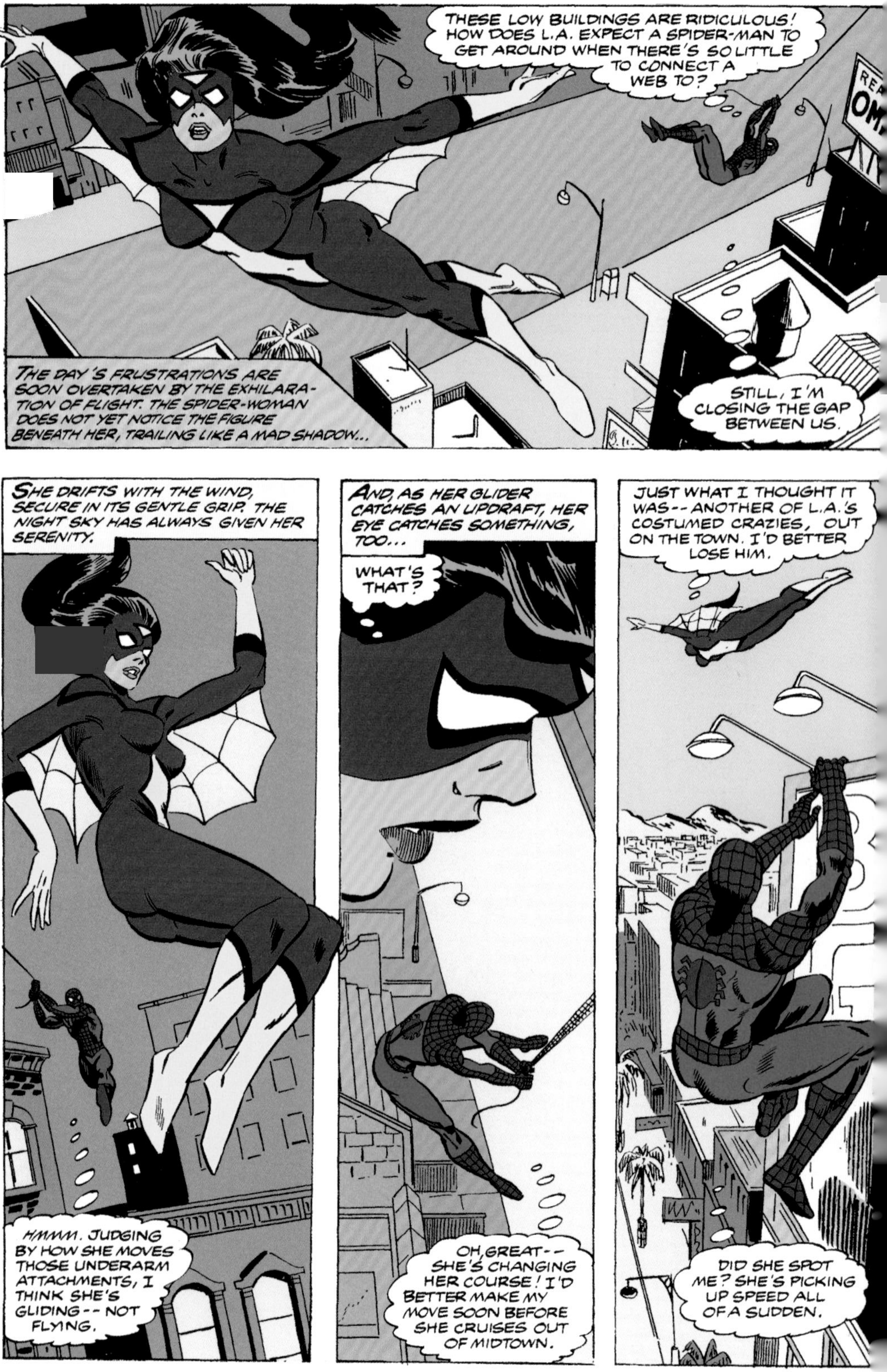
THESE LOW BUILDINGS ARE RIDICULOUS! HOW DOES L.A. EXPECT A SPIDER-MAN TO GET AROUND WHEN THERE'S SO LITTLE TO CONNECT A WEB TO?
THE DAY'S FRUSTRATIONS ARE SOON OVERTAKEN BY THE EXHILARATION OF FLIGHT. THE SPIDER-WOMAN DOES NOT YET NOTICE THE FIGURE BENEATH HER, TRAILING LIKE A MAD SHADOW...
STILL, I'M CLOSING THE GAP BETWEEN US.
SHE DRIFTS WITH THE WIND, SECURE IN ITS GENTLE GRIP. THE NIGHT SKY HAS ALWAYS GIVEN HER SERENITY.
HMMM. JUDGING BY HOW SHE MOVES THOSE UNDERARM ATTACHMENTS, I THINK SHE'S GLIDING-- NOT FLYING.
AND, AS HER GLIDER CATCHES AN UPDRAFT, HER EYE CATCHES SOMETHING, TOO...
WHAT'S THAT?
OH, GREAT-- SHE'S CHANGING HER COURSE! I'D BETTER MAKE MY MOVE SOON BEFORE SHE CRUISES OUT OF MIDTOWN.
JUST WHAT I THOUGHT IT WAS-- ANOTHER OF L.A.'S COSTUMED CRAZIES, OUT ON THE TOWN. I'D BETTER LOSE HIM.
DID SHE SPOT ME? SHE'S PICKING UP SPEED ALL OF A SUDDEN.

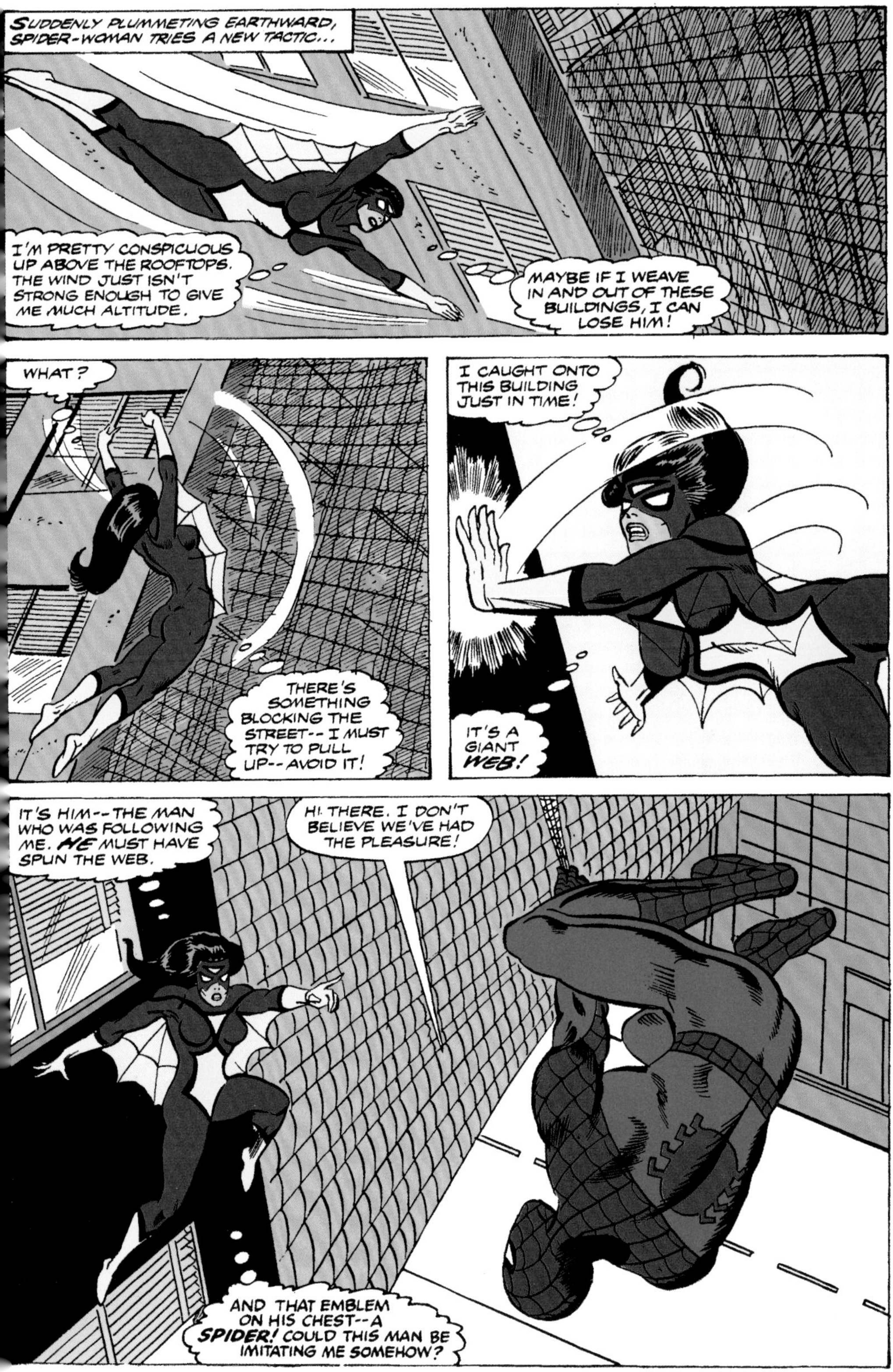
SUDDENLY PLUMMETING EARTHWARD, SPIDER-WOMAN TRIES A NEW TACTIC...
I'M PRETTY CONSPICUOUS UP ABOVE THE ROOFTOPS. THE WIND JUST ISN'T STRONG ENOUGH TO GIVE ME MUCH ALTITUDE.
MAYBE IF I WEAVE IN AND OUT OF THESE BUILDINGS, I CAN LOSE HIM!
WHAT?
THERE'S SOMETHING BLOCKING THE STREET-- I MUST TRY TO PULL UP-- AVOID IT!
I CAUGHT ONTO THIS BUILDING JUST IN TIME!
IT'S A GIANT WEB!
IT'S HIM--THE MAN WHO WAS FOLLOWING ME. HE MUST HAVE SPUN THE WEB.
HI. THERE. I DON'T BELIEVE WE'VE HAD THE PLEASURE!
AND THAT EMBLEM ON HIS CHEST--A SPIDER! COULD THIS MAN BE IMITATING ME SOMEHOW?

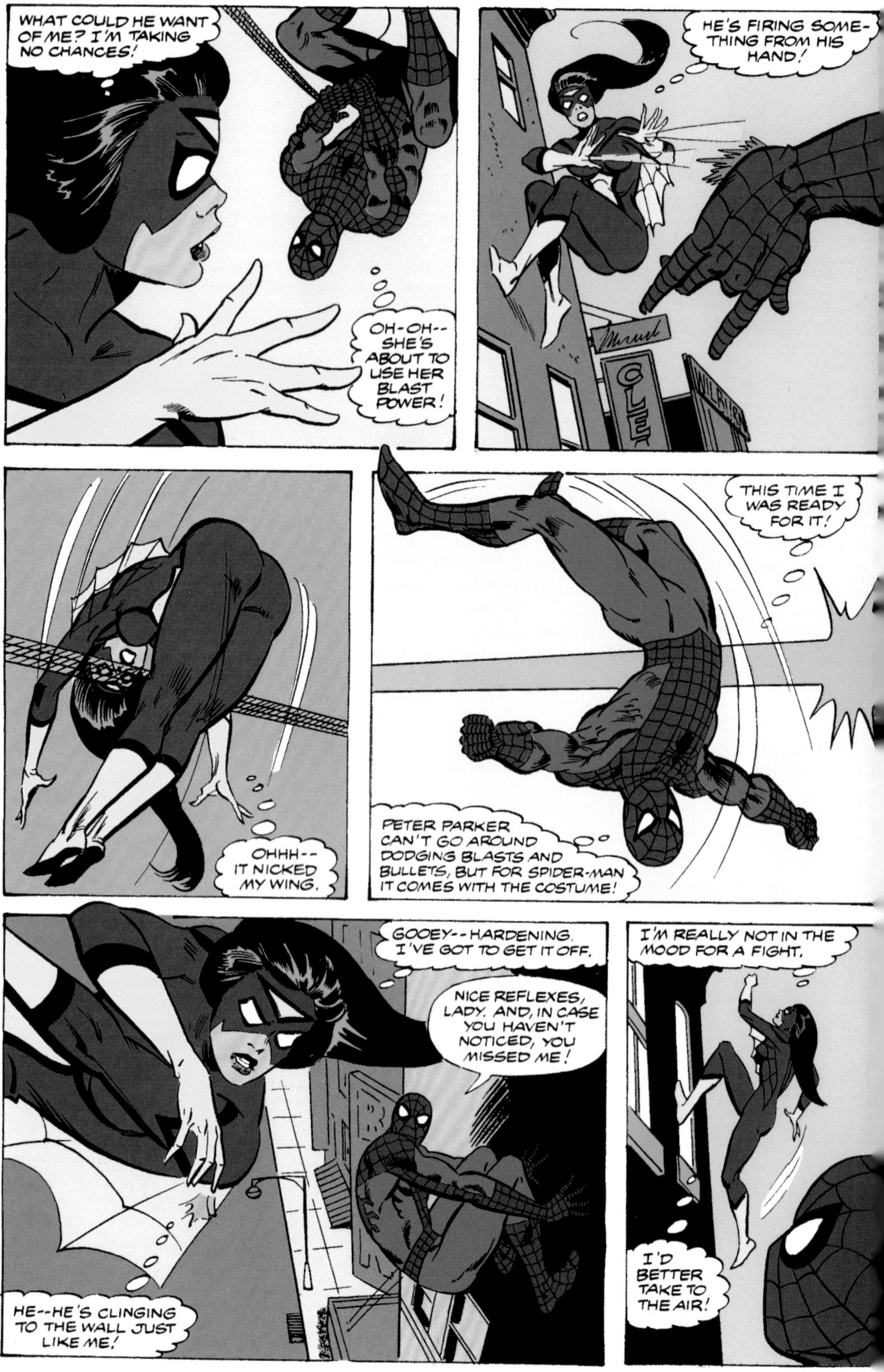
WHAT COULD HE WANT OF ME? I'M TAKING NO CHANCES!
OH-OH-- SHE'S ABOUT TO USE HER BLAST POWER!
HE'S FIRING SOME-THING FROM HIS HAND!
OHHH-- IT NICKED MY WING.
THIS TIME I WAS READY FOR IT!
PETER PARKER CAN'T GO AROUND DODGING BLASTS AND BULLETS, BUT FOR SPIDER-MAN IT COMES WITH THE COSTUME!
GOOEY--HARDENING. I'VE GOT TO GET IT OFF.
NICE REFLEXES, LADY. AND, IN CASE YOU HAVEN'T NOTICED, YOU MISSED ME!
HE--HE'S CLINGING TO THE WALL JUST LIKE ME!
I'M REALLY NOT IN THE MOOD FOR A FIGHT.
I'D BETTER TAKE TO THE AIR!

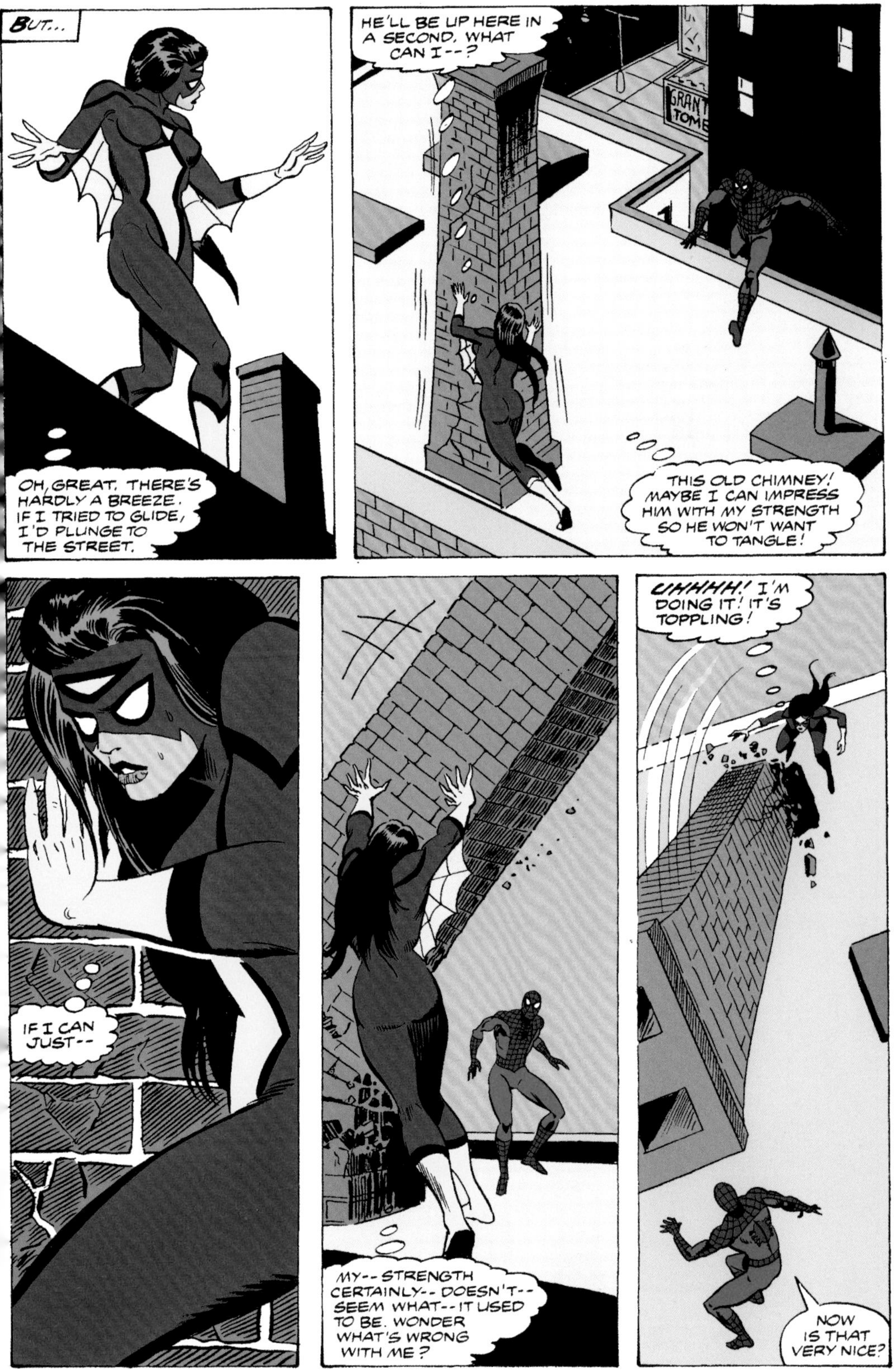
BUT...
OH, GREAT. THERE'S HARDLY A BREEZE. IF I TRIED TO GLIDE, I'D PLUNGE TO THE STREET.
HE'LL BE UP HERE IN A SECOND. WHAT CAN I--?
GRANT TOMB
THIS OLD CHIMNEY! MAYBE I CAN IMPRESS HIM WITH MY STRENGTH SO HE WON'T WANT TO TANGLE!
IF I CAN JUST--
MY-- STRENGTH CERTAINLY-- DOESN'T-- SEEM WHAT--IT USED TO BE. WONDER WHAT'S WRONG WITH ME?
UHHHH! I'M DOING IT! IT'S TOPPLING!
NOW IS THAT VERY NICE?

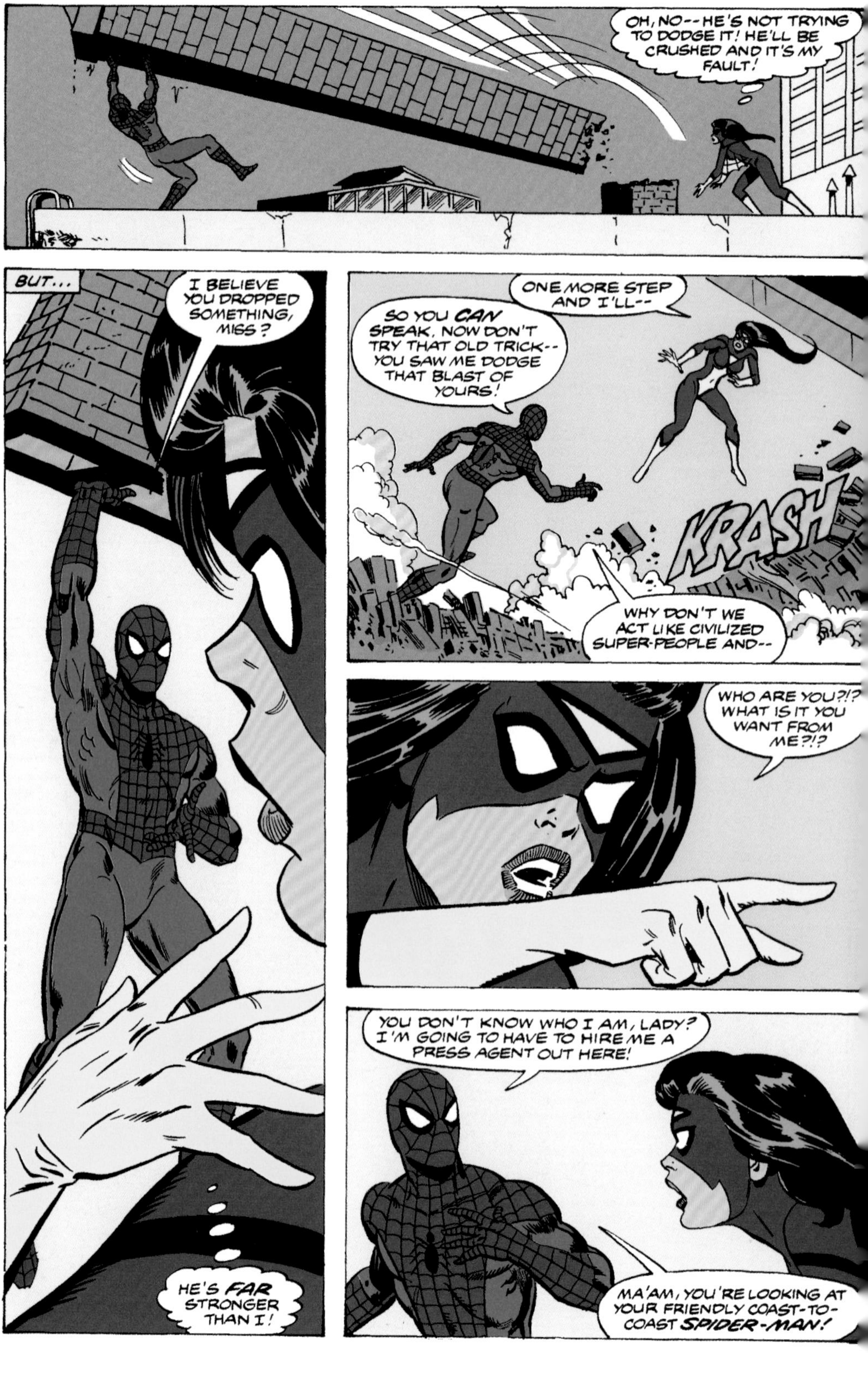

OH, NO--HE'S NOT TRYING TO DODGE IT! HE'LL BE CRUSHED AND IT'S MY FAULT!
BUT...
I BELIEVE YOU DROPPED SOMETHING, MISS?
HE'S FAR STRONGER THAN I!
ONE MORE STEP AND I'LL--
SO YOU CAN SPEAK. NOW DON'T TRY THAT OLD TRICK--YOU SAW ME DODGE THAT BLAST OF YOURS!
KRASH
WHY DON'T WE ACT LIKE CIVILIZED SUPER-PEOPLE AND--
WHO ARE YOU?!? WHAT IS IT YOU WANT FROM ME?!?
YOU DON'T KNOW WHO I AM, LADY? I'M GOING TO HAVE TO HIRE ME A PRESS AGENT OUT HERE!
MA'AM, YOU'RE LOOKING AT YOUR FRIENDLY COAST-TO-COAST SPIDER-MAN!

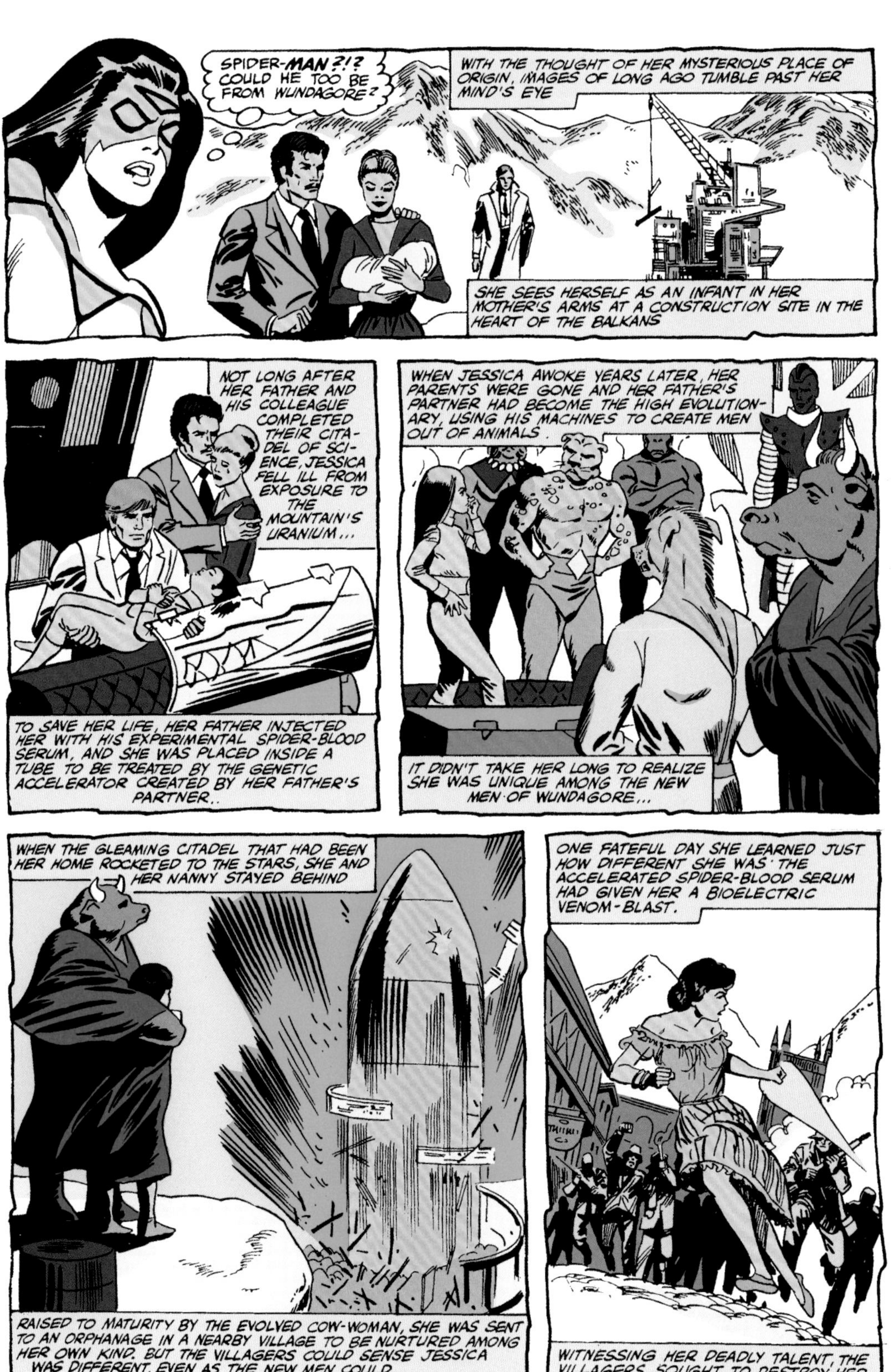

SPIDER-MAN?!? COULD HE TOO BE FROM WUNDAGORE?
WITH THE THOUGHT OF HER MYSTERIOUS PLACE OF ORIGIN, IMAGES OF LONG AGO TUMBLE PAST HER MIND'S EYE
SHE SEES HERSELF AS AN INFANT IN HER MOTHER'S ARMS AT A CONSTRUCTION SITE IN THE HEART OF THE BALKANS
NOT LONG AFTER HER FATHER AND HIS COLLEAGUE COMPLETED THEIR CITADEL OF SCIENCE, JESSICA FELL ILL FROM EXPOSURE TO THE MOUNTAIN'S URANIUM...
TO SAVE HER LIFE, HER FATHER INJECTED HER WITH HIS EXPERIMENTAL SPIDER-BLOOD SERUM, AND SHE WAS PLACED INSIDE A TUBE TO BE TREATED BY THE GENETIC ACCELERATOR CREATED BY HER FATHER'S PARTNER..
WHEN JESSICA AWOKE YEARS LATER, HER PARENTS WERE GONE AND HER FATHER'S PARTNER HAD BECOME THE HIGH EVOLUTIONARY, USING HIS MACHINES TO CREATE MEN OUT OF ANIMALS.
IT DIDN'T TAKE HER LONG TO REALIZE SHE WAS UNIQUE AMONG THE NEW MEN OF WUNDAGORE...
WHEN THE GLEAMING CITADEL THAT HAD BEEN HER HOME ROCKETED TO THE STARS, SHE AND HER NANNY STAYED BEHIND
RAISED TO MATURITY BY THE EVOLVED COW-WOMAN, SHE WAS SENT TO AN ORPHANAGE IN A NEARBY VILLAGE TO BE NURTURED AMONG HER OWN KIND. BUT THE VILLAGERS COULD SENSE JESSICA WAS DIFFERENT, EVEN AS THE NEW MEN COULD.
ONE FATEFUL DAY SHE LEARNED JUST HOW DIFFERENT SHE WAS: THE ACCELERATED SPIDER-BLOOD SERUM HAD GIVEN HER A BIOELECTRIC VENOM-BLAST.
WITNESSING HER DEADLY TALENT, THE VILLAGERS SOUGHT TO DESTROY HER...

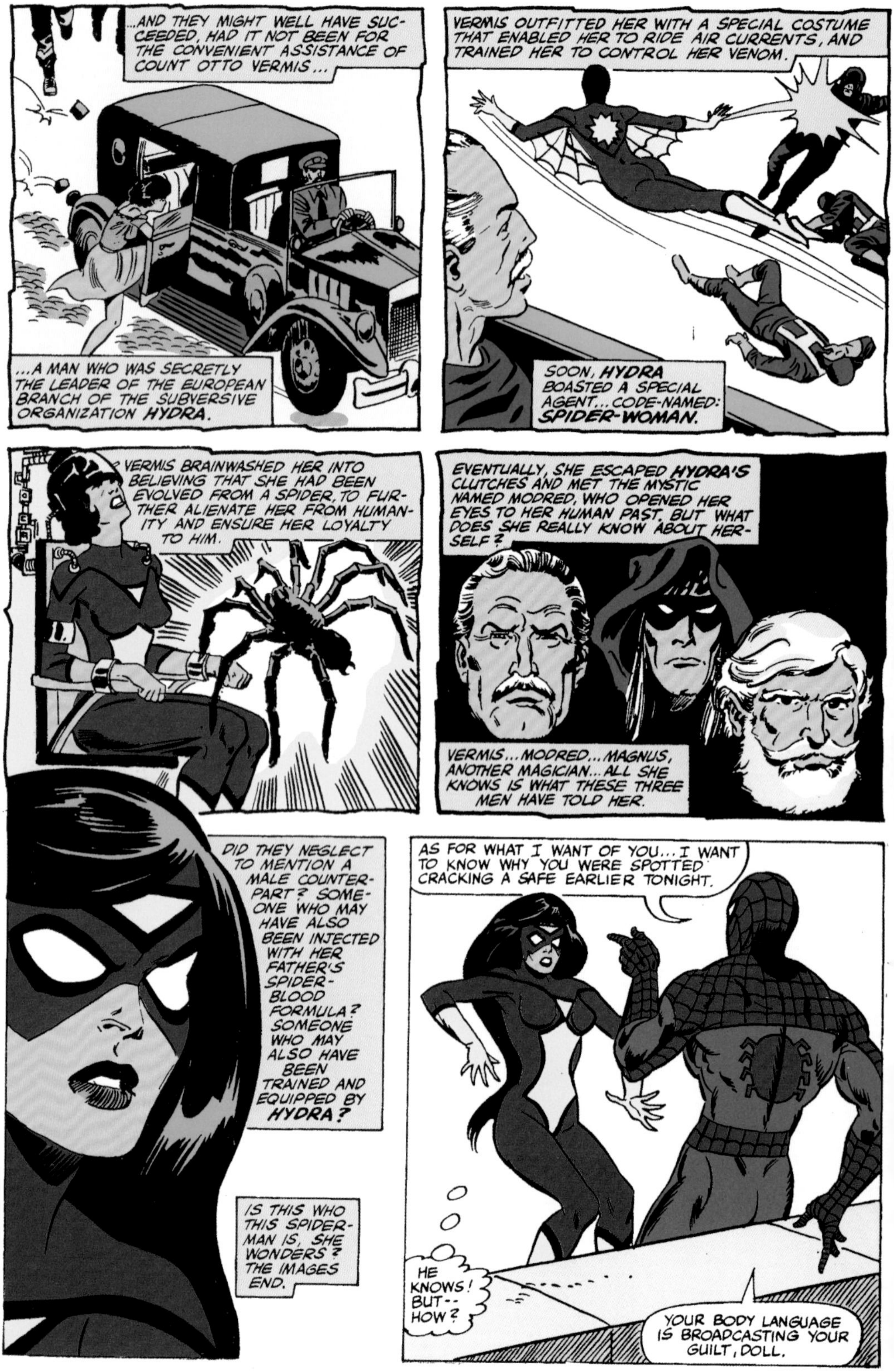
...AND THEY MIGHT WELL HAVE SUCCEEDED, HAD IT NOT BEEN FOR THE CONVENIENT ASSISTANCE OF COUNT OTTO VERMIS...
...A MAN WHO WAS SECRETLY THE LEADER OF THE EUROPEAN BRANCH OF THE SUBVERSIVE ORGANIZATION HYDRA.
VERMIS OUTFITTED HER WITH A SPECIAL COSTUME THAT ENABLED HER TO RIDE AIR CURRENTS, AND TRAINED HER TO CONTROL HER VENOM.
SOON, HYDRA BOASTED A SPECIAL AGENT... CODE-NAMED: SPIDER-WOMAN.
VERMIS BRAINWASHED HER INTO BELIEVING THAT SHE HAD BEEN EVOLVED FROM A SPIDER, TO FURTHER ALIENATE HER FROM HUMANITY AND ENSURE HER LOYALTY TO HIM.
EVENTUALLY, SHE ESCAPED HYDRA'S CLUTCHES AND MET THE MYSTIC NAMED MODRED, WHO OPENED HER EYES TO HER HUMAN PAST, BUT WHAT DOES SHE REALLY KNOW ABOUT HERSELF?
VERMIS... MODRED... MAGNUS, ANOTHER MAGICIAN... ALL SHE KNOWS IS WHAT THESE THREE MEN HAVE TOLD HER.
DID THEY NEGLECT TO MENTION A MALE COUNTERPART? SOMEONE WHO MAY HAVE ALSO BEEN INJECTED WITH HER FATHER'S SPIDER-BLOOD FORMULA? SOMEONE WHO MAY ALSO HAVE BEEN TRAINED AND EQUIPPED BY HYDRA?
IS THIS WHO THIS SPIDER-MAN IS, SHE WONDERS? THE IMAGES END.
AS FOR WHAT I WANT OF YOU... I WANT TO KNOW WHY YOU WERE SPOTTED CRACKING A SAFE EARLIER TONIGHT.
HE KNOWS! BUT-- HOW?
YOUR BODY LANGUAGE IS BROADCASTING YOUR GUILT, DOLL.

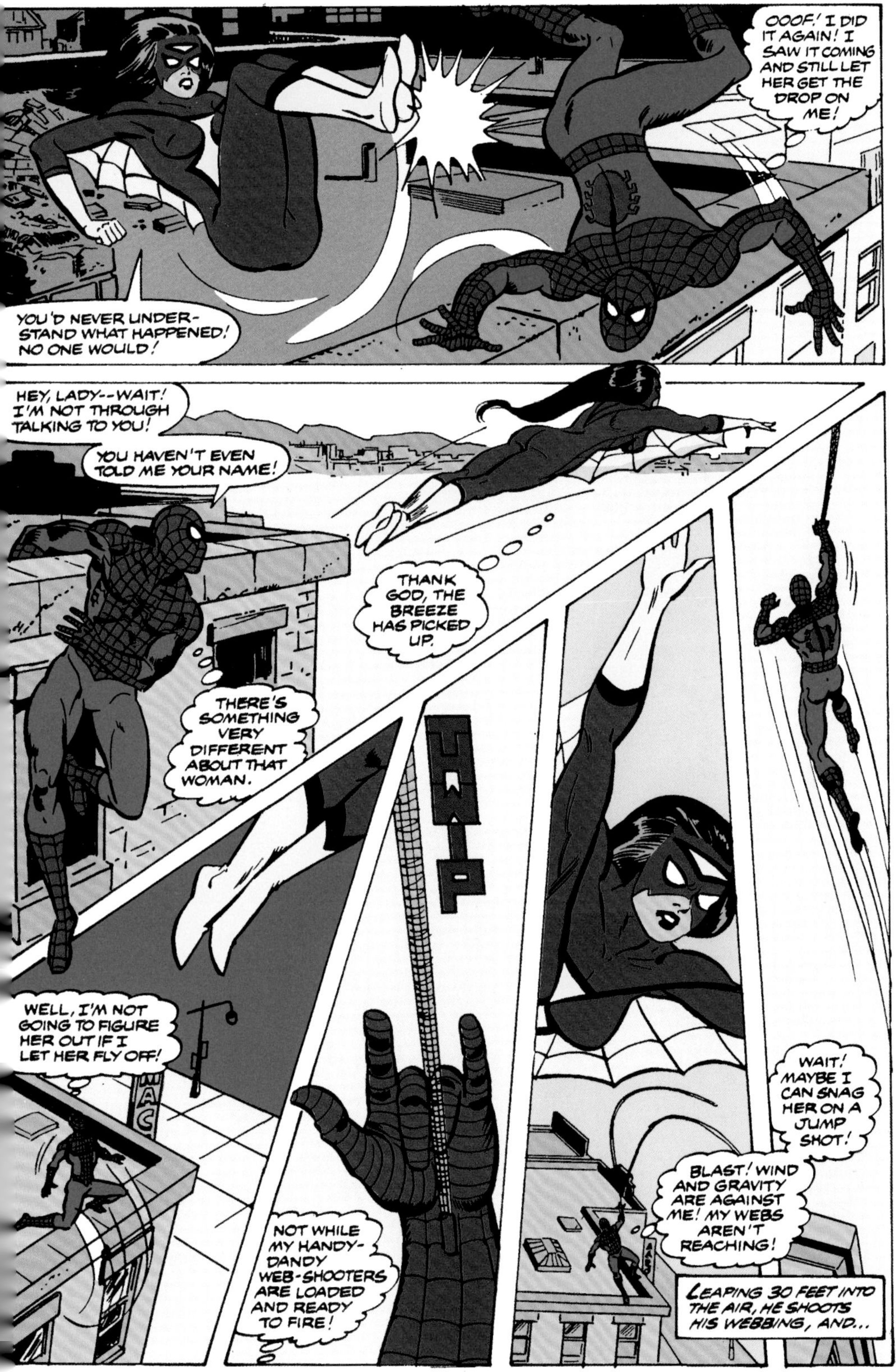
OOOF! I DID IT AGAIN! I SAW IT COMING AND STILL LET HER GET THE DROP ON ME!
YOU'D NEVER UNDERSTAND WHAT HAPPENED! NO ONE WOULD!
HEY, LADY--WAIT! I'M NOT THROUGH TALKING TO YOU!
YOU HAVEN'T EVEN TOLD ME YOUR NAME!
THANK GOD, THE BREEZE HAS PICKED UP.
THERE'S SOMETHING VERY DIFFERENT ABOUT THAT WOMAN.
THWIP
WELL, I'M NOT GOING TO FIGURE HER OUT IF I LET HER FLY OFF!
NOT WHILE MY HANDY-DANDY WEB-SHOOTERS ARE LOADED AND READY TO FIRE!
WAIT! MAYBE I CAN SNAG HER ON A JUMP SHOT!
BLAST! WIND AND GRAVITY ARE AGAINST ME! MY WEBS AREN'T REACHING!
LEAPING 30 FEET INTO THE AIR, HE SHOOTS HIS WEBBING, AND...

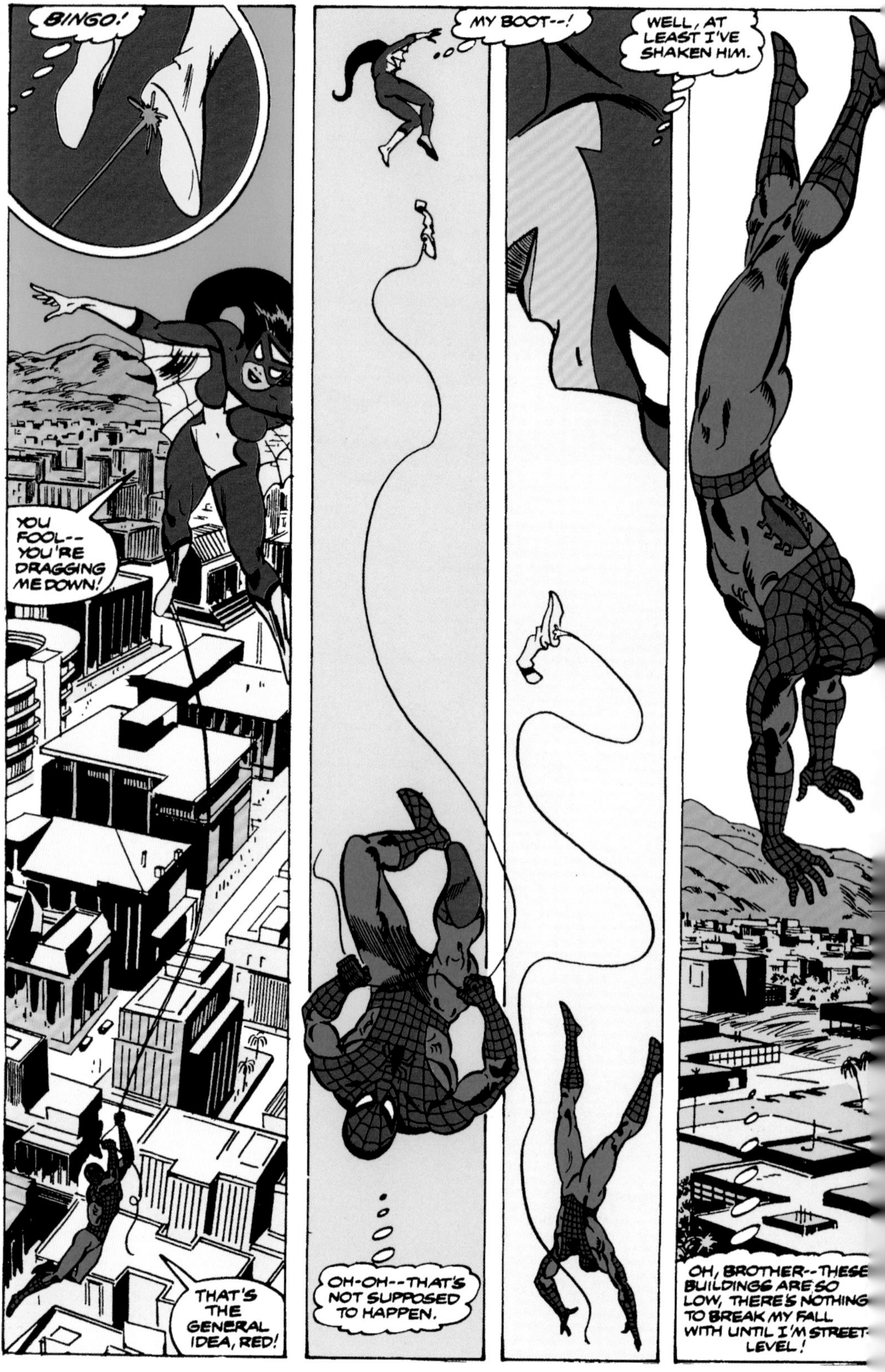
BINGO!
YOU FOOL-- YOU'RE DRAGGING ME DOWN!
THAT'S THE GENERAL IDEA, RED!
MY BOOT--!
OH-OH--THAT'S NOT SUPPOSED TO HAPPEN.
WELL, AT LEAST I'VE SHAKEN HIM.
OH, BROTHER--THESE BUILDINGS ARE SO LOW, THERE'S NOTHING TO BREAK MY FALL WITH UNTIL I'M STREET-LEVEL!

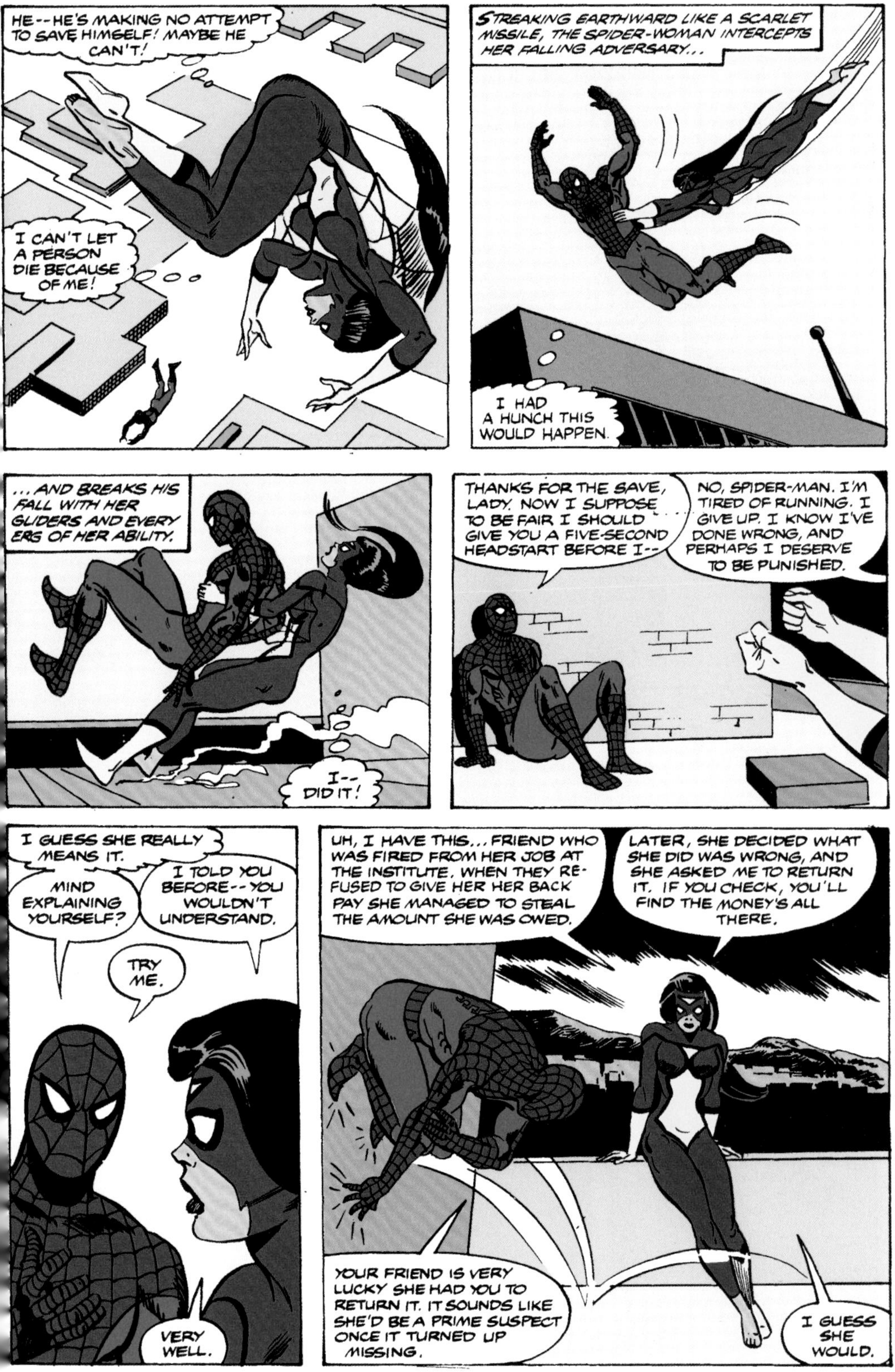
HE--HE'S MAKING NO ATTEMPT TO SAVE HIMSELF! MAYBE HE CAN'T!
I CAN'T LET A PERSON DIE BECAUSE OF ME!
STREAKING EARTHWARD LIKE A SCARLET MISSILE, THE SPIDER-WOMAN INTERCEPTS HER FALLING ADVERSARY...
I HAD A HUNCH THIS WOULD HAPPEN.
...AND BREAKS HIS FALL WITH HER GLIDERS AND EVERY ERG OF HER ABILITY.
I-- DID IT!
THANKS FOR THE SAVE, LADY. NOW I SUPPOSE TO BE FAIR I SHOULD GIVE YOU A FIVE-SECOND HEADSTART BEFORE I--
NO, SPIDER-MAN. I'M TIRED OF RUNNING. I GIVE UP. I KNOW I'VE DONE WRONG, AND PERHAPS I DESERVE TO BE PUNISHED.
I GUESS SHE REALLY MEANS IT.
MIND EXPLAINING YOURSELF?
I TOLD YOU BEFORE--YOU WOULDN'T UNDERSTAND.
TRY ME.
VERY WELL.
UH, I HAVE THIS... FRIEND WHO WAS FIRED FROM HER JOB AT THE INSTITUTE. WHEN THEY REFUSED TO GIVE HER HER BACK PAY SHE MANAGED TO STEAL THE AMOUNT SHE WAS OWED.
LATER, SHE DECIDED WHAT SHE DID WAS WRONG, AND SHE ASKED ME TO RETURN IT. IF YOU CHECK, YOU'LL FIND THE MONEY'S ALL THERE.
YOUR FRIEND IS VERY LUCKY SHE HAD YOU TO RETURN IT. IT SOUNDS LIKE SHE'D BE A PRIME SUSPECT ONCE IT TURNED UP MISSING.
I GUESS SHE WOULD.

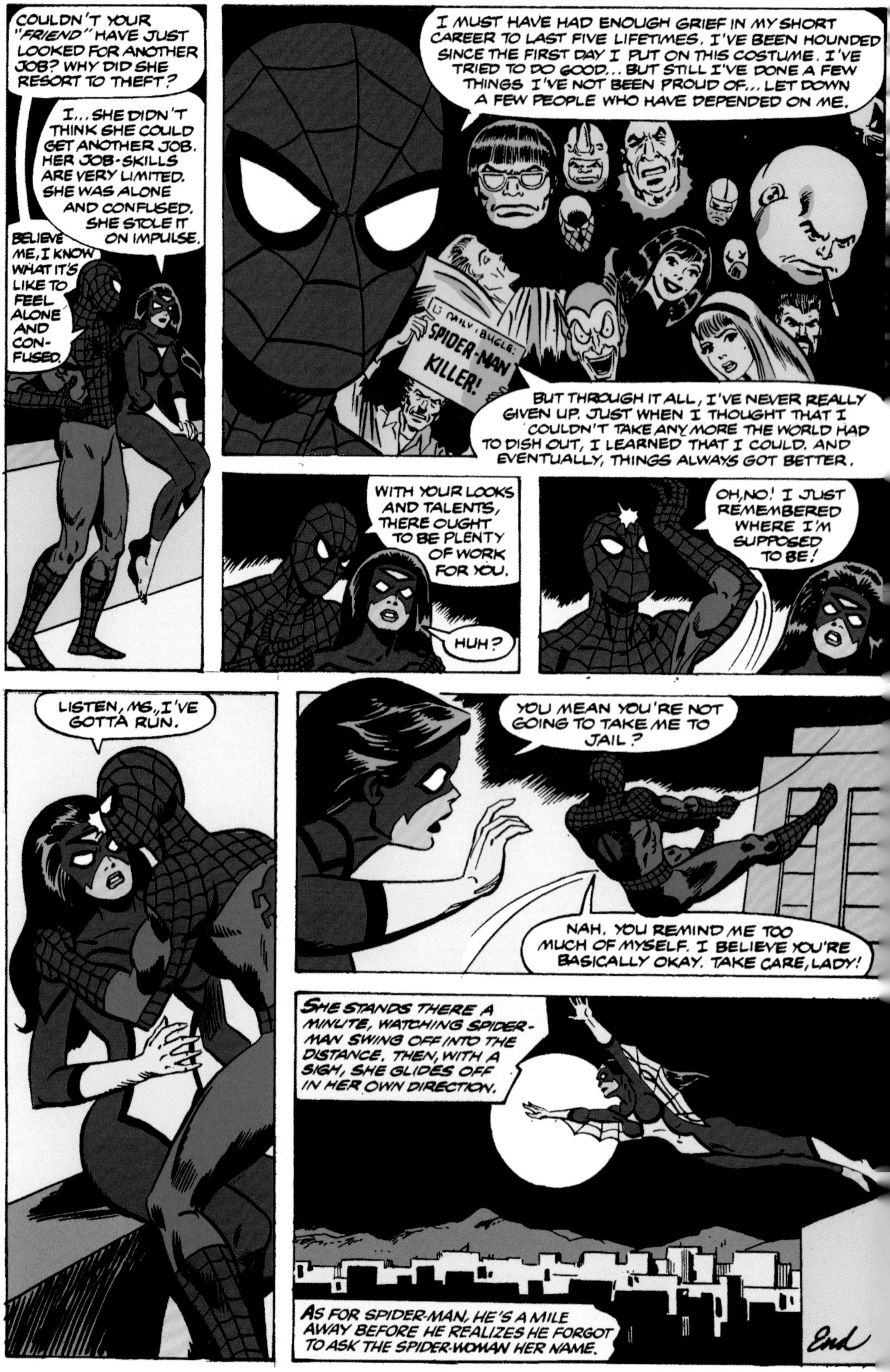

COULDN'T YOUR "FRIEND" HAVE JUST LOOKED FOR ANOTHER JOB? WHY DID SHE RESORT TO THEFT?
I... SHE DIDN'T THINK SHE COULD GET ANOTHER JOB. HER JOB-SKILLS ARE VERY LIMITED. SHE WAS ALONE AND CONFUSED. SHE STOLE IT ON IMPULSE.
BELIEVE ME, I KNOW WHAT IT'S LIKE TO FEEL ALONE AND CON-FUSED.
I MUST HAVE HAD ENOUGH GRIEF IN MY SHORT CAREER TO LAST FIVE LIFETIMES. I'VE BEEN HOUNDED SINCE THE FIRST DAY I PUT ON THIS COSTUME. I'VE TRIED TO DO GOOD... BUT STILL I'VE DONE A FEW THINGS I'VE NOT BEEN PROUD OF... LET DOWN A FEW PEOPLE WHO HAVE DEPENDED ON ME.
DAILY BUGLE: SPIDER-MAN KILLER!
BUT THROUGH IT ALL, I'VE NEVER REALLY GIVEN UP. JUST WHEN I THOUGHT THAT I COULDN'T TAKE ANY MORE THE WORLD HAD TO DISH OUT, I LEARNED THAT I COULD. AND EVENTUALLY, THINGS ALWAYS GOT BETTER.
WITH YOUR LOOKS AND TALENTS, THERE OUGHT TO BE PLENTY OF WORK FOR YOU.
HUH?
OH, NO! I JUST REMEMBERED WHERE I'M SUPPOSED TO BE!
LISTEN, MS., I'VE GOTTA RUN.
YOU MEAN YOU'RE NOT GOING TO TAKE ME TO JAIL?
NAH. YOU REMIND ME TOO MUCH OF MYSELF. I BELIEVE YOU'RE BASICALLY OKAY. TAKE CARE, LADY!
SHE STANDS THERE A MINUTE, WATCHING SPIDER-MAN SWING OFF INTO THE DISTANCE. THEN, WITH A SIGH, SHE GLIDES OFF IN HER OWN DIRECTION.
AS FOR SPIDER-MAN, HE'S A MILE AWAY BEFORE HE REALIZES HE FORGOT TO ASK THE SPIDER-WOMAN HER NAME.
End

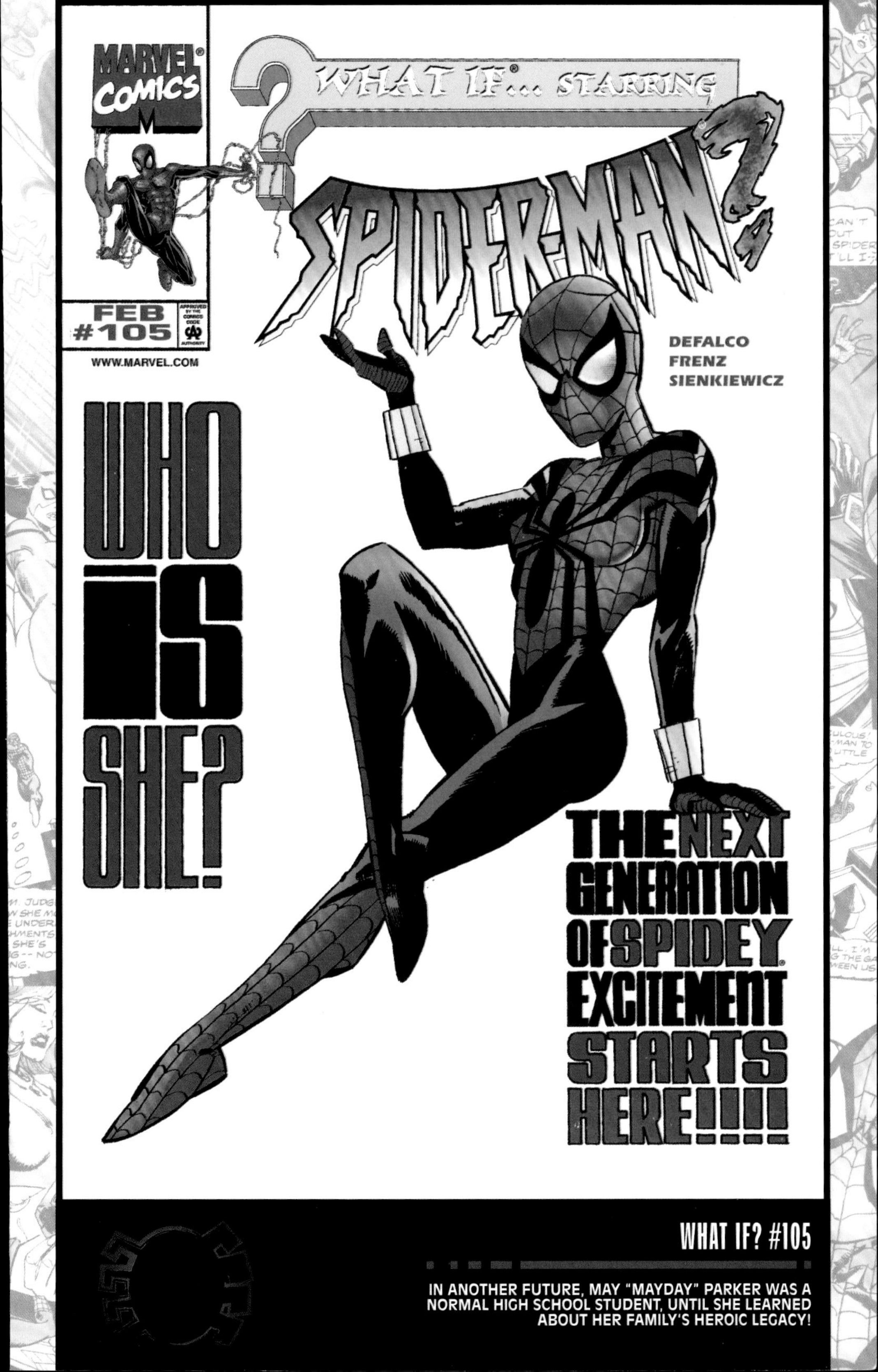
MARVEL COMICS
WHAT IF... STARRING
SPIDER-MAN
FEB #105
WWW.MARVEL.COM
DEFALCO
FRENZ
SIENKIEWICZ
WHO IS SHE?
THE NEXT GENERATION OF SPIDEY EXCITEMENT STARTS HERE!!!!

WHAT IF? #105

IN ANOTHER FUTURE, MAY "MAYDAY" PARKER WAS A NORMAL HIGH SCHOOL STUDENT, UNTIL SHE LEARNED ABOUT HER FAMILY'S HEROIC LEGACY!

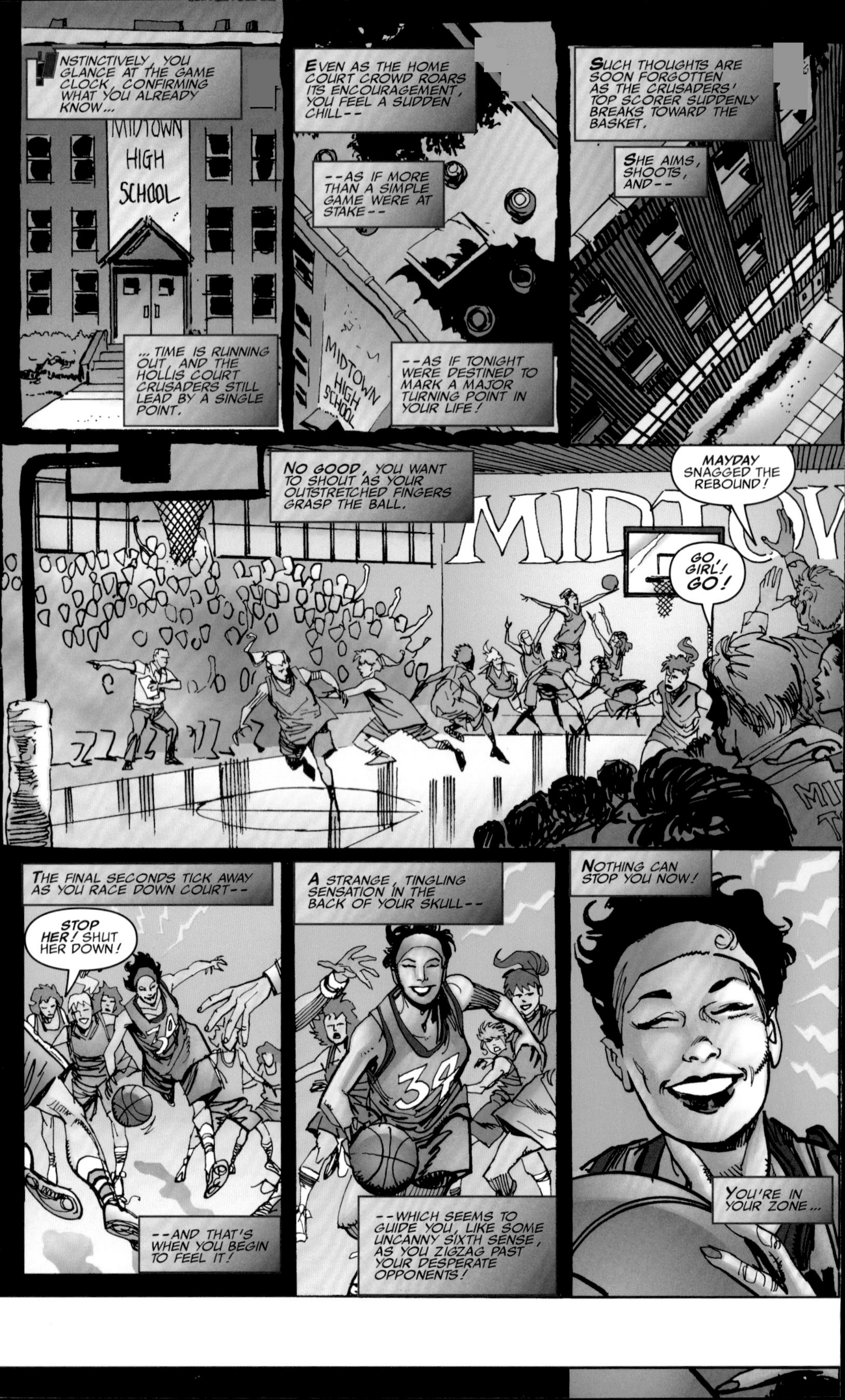
INSTINCTIVELY, YOU GLANCE AT THE GAME CLOCK, CONFIRMING WHAT YOU ALREADY KNOW...
MIDTOWN HIGH SCHOOL
...TIME IS RUNNING OUT, AND THE HOLLIS COURT CRUSADERS STILL LEAD BY A SINGLE POINT.
EVEN AS THE HOME COURT CROWD ROARS ITS ENCOURAGEMENT, YOU FEEL A SUDDEN CHILL--
--AS IF MORE THAN A SIMPLE GAME WERE AT STAKE--
MIDTOWN HIGH SCHOOL
--AS IF TONIGHT WERE DESTINED TO MARK A MAJOR TURNING POINT IN YOUR LIFE!
SUCH THOUGHTS ARE SOON FORGOTTEN AS THE CRUSADERS' TOP SCORER SUDDENLY BREAKS TOWARD THE BASKET.
SHE AIMS, SHOOTS, AND--
NO GOOD, YOU WANT TO SHOUT AS YOUR OUTSTRETCHED FINGERS GRASP THE BALL.
MAYDAY SNAGGED THE REBOUND!
GO, GIRL! GO!
THE FINAL SECONDS TICK AWAY AS YOU RACE DOWN COURT--
STOP HER! SHUT HER DOWN!
--AND THAT'S WHEN YOU BEGIN TO FEEL IT!
A STRANGE, TINGLING SENSATION IN THE BACK OF YOUR SKULL--
--WHICH SEEMS TO GUIDE YOU, LIKE SOME UNCANNY SIXTH SENSE, AS YOU ZIGZAG PAST YOUR DESPERATE OPPONENTS!
NOTHING CAN STOP YOU NOW!
YOU'RE IN YOUR ZONE...

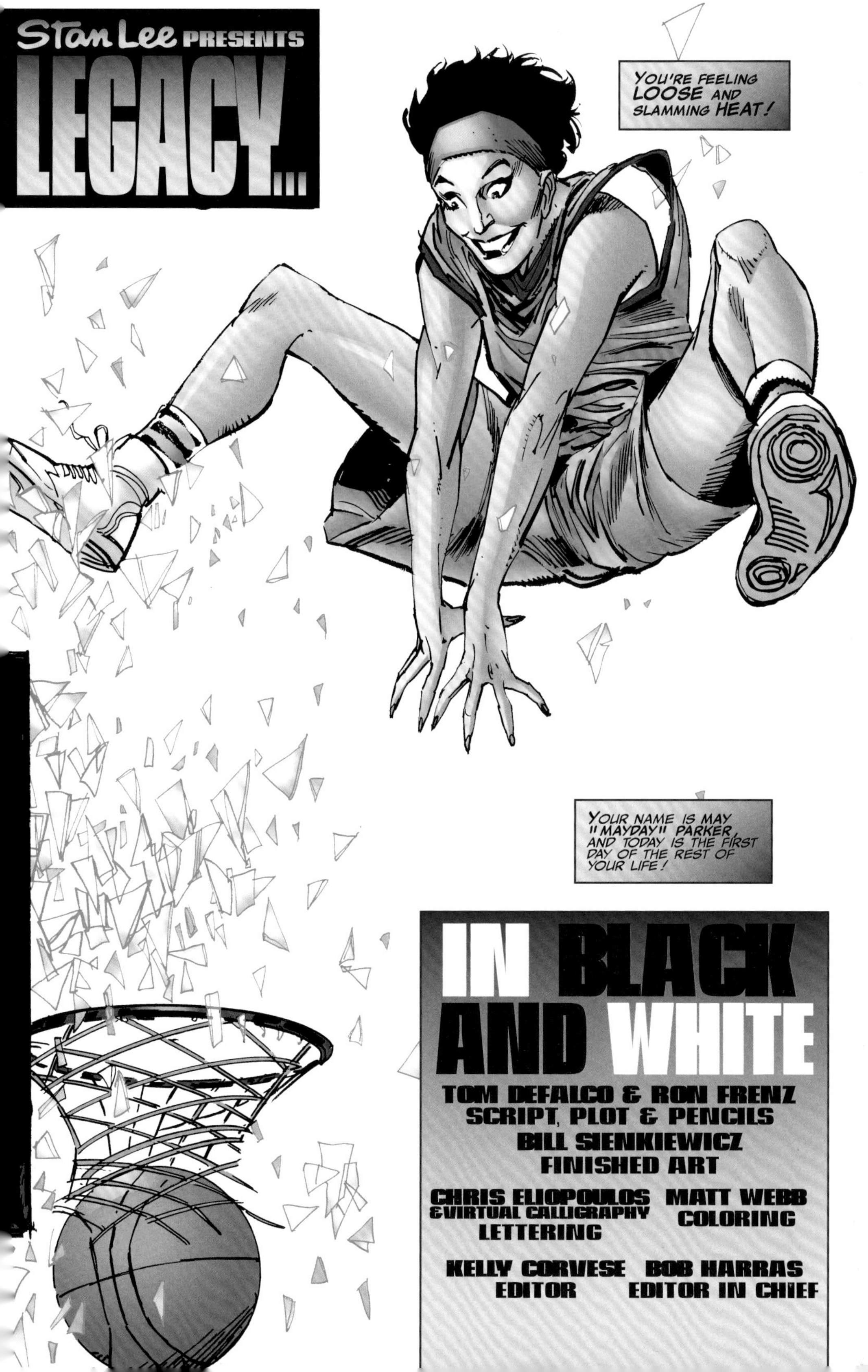
Stan Lee PRESENTS
LEGACY...
YOU'RE FEELING LOOSE AND SLAMMING HEAT!
YOUR NAME IS MAY "MAYDAY" PARKER, AND TODAY IS THE FIRST DAY OF THE REST OF YOUR LIFE!
IN BLACK AND WHITE
TOM DEFALCO & RON FRENZ
SCRIPT, PLOT & PENCILS
BILL SIENKIEWICZ
FINISHED ART
CHRIS ELIOPOULOS & VIRTUAL CALLIGRAPHY
LETTERING
MATT WEBB
COLORING
KELLY CORVESE
EDITOR
BOB HARRAS
EDITOR IN CHIEF

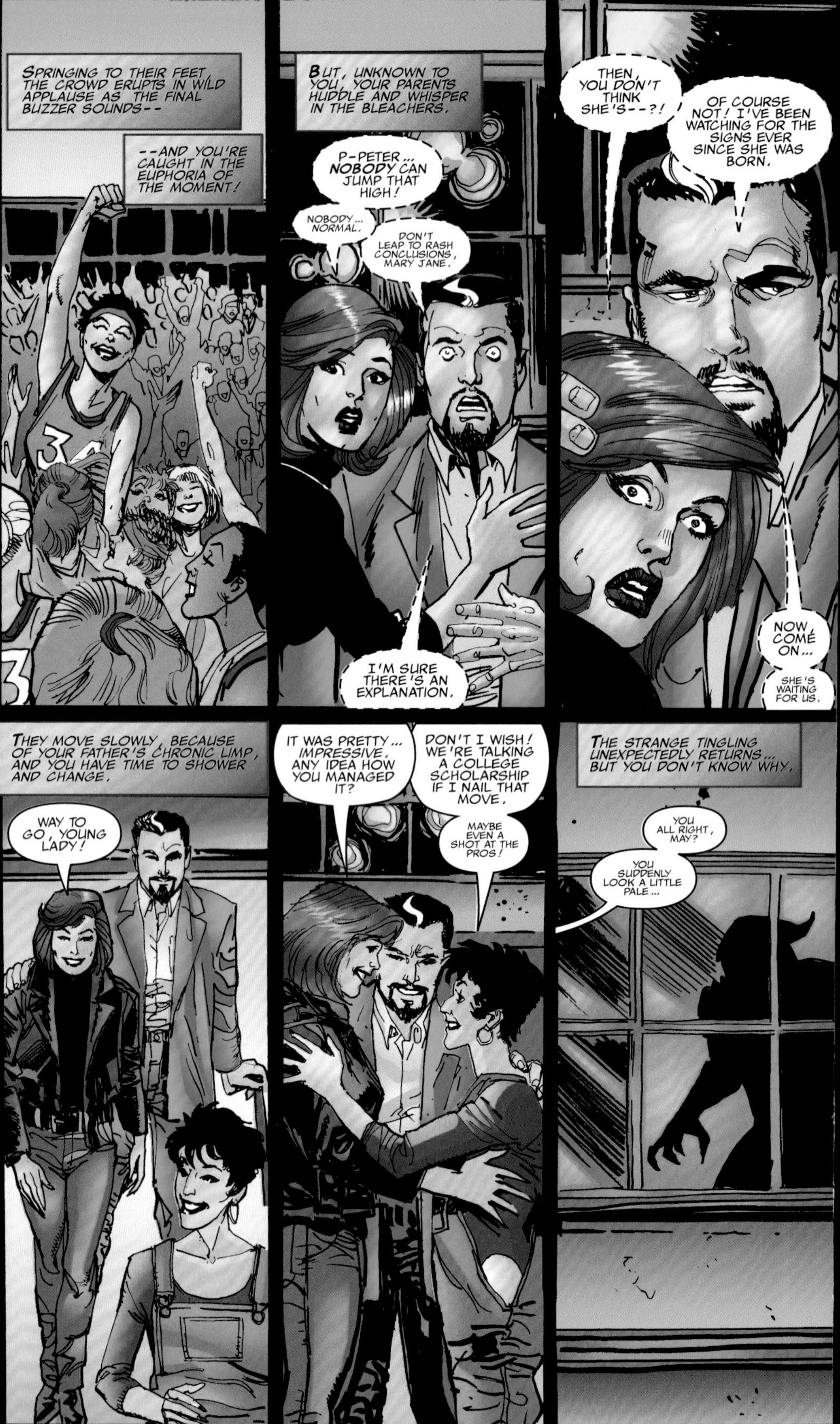
SPRINGING TO THEIR FEET THE CROWD ERUPTS IN WILD APPLAUSE AS THE FINAL BUZZER SOUNDS--
--AND YOU'RE CAUGHT IN THE EUPHORIA OF THE MOMENT!
BUT, UNKNOWN TO YOU, YOUR PARENTS HUDDLE AND WHISPER IN THE BLEACHERS.
P-PETER... NOBODY CAN JUMP THAT HIGH!
NOBODY... NORMAL.
DON'T LEAP TO RASH CONCLUSIONS, MARY JANE.
I'M SURE THERE'S AN EXPLANATION.
THEN, YOU DON'T THINK SHE'S--?!
OF COURSE NOT! I'VE BEEN WATCHING FOR THE SIGNS EVER SINCE SHE WAS BORN.
NOW, COME ON...
SHE'S WAITING FOR US.
THEY MOVE SLOWLY, BECAUSE OF YOUR FATHER'S CHRONIC LIMP, AND YOU HAVE TIME TO SHOWER AND CHANGE.
WAY TO GO, YOUNG LADY!
IT WAS PRETTY... IMPRESSIVE. ANY IDEA HOW YOU MANAGED IT?
DON'T I WISH! WE'RE TALKING A COLLEGE SCHOLARSHIP IF I NAIL THAT MOVE.
MAYBE EVEN A SHOT AT THE PROS!
THE STRANGE TINGLING UNEXPECTEDLY RETURNS... BUT YOU DON'T KNOW WHY.
YOU ALL RIGHT, MAY?
YOU SUDDENLY LOOK A LITTLE PALE...

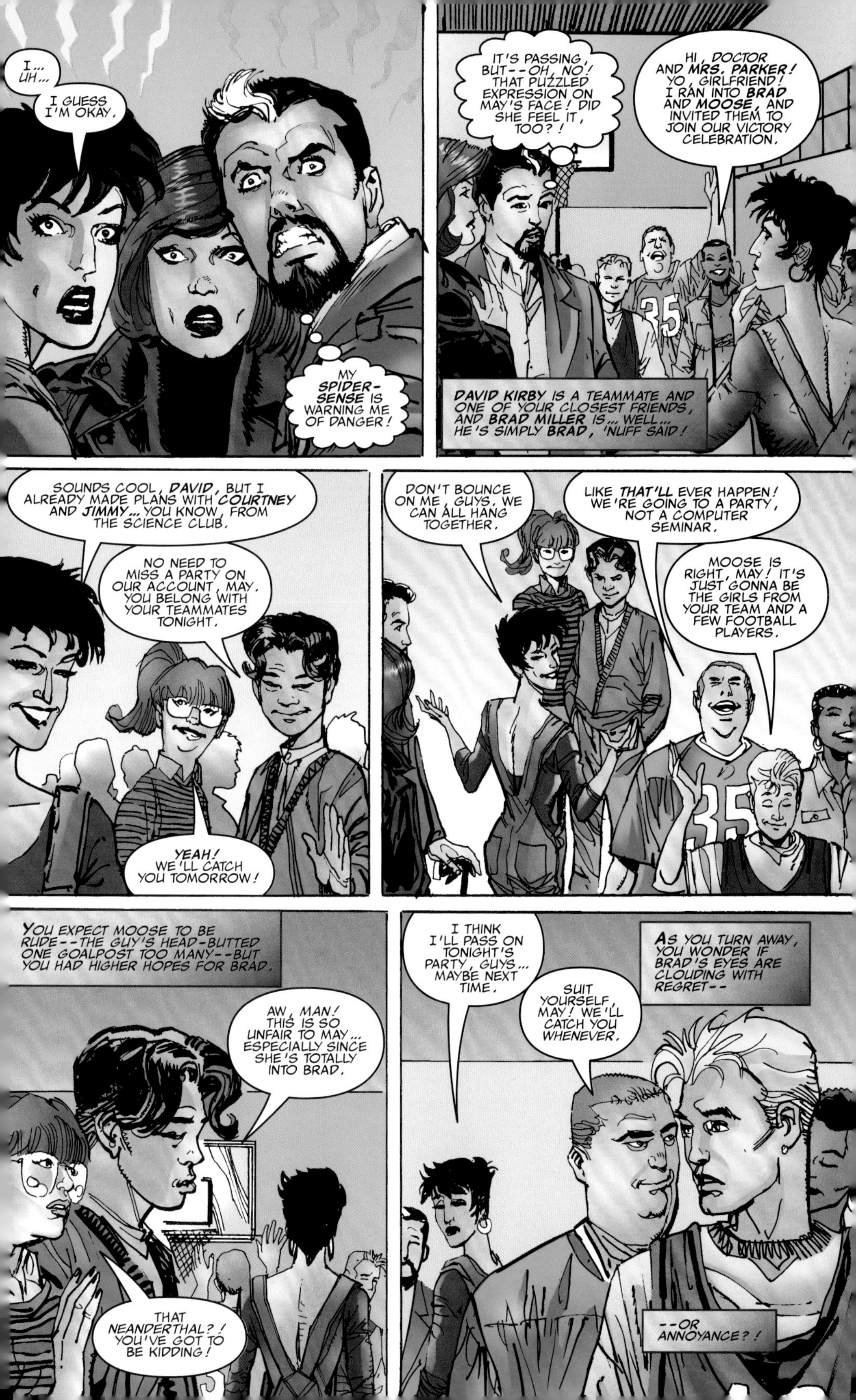
I... UH...
I GUESS I'M OKAY.
MY SPIDER-SENSE IS WARNING ME OF DANGER!
IT'S PASSING, BUT--OH, NO! THAT PUZZLED EXPRESSION ON MAY'S FACE! DID SHE FEEL IT, TOO?!
HI, DOCTOR AND MRS. PARKER! YO, GIRLFRIEND! I RAN INTO BRAD AND MOOSE, AND INVITED THEM TO JOIN OUR VICTORY CELEBRATION.
DAVID KIRBY IS A TEAMMATE AND ONE OF YOUR CLOSEST FRIENDS, AND BRAD MILLER IS... WELL... HE'S SIMPLY BRAD, 'NUFF SAID!
SOUNDS COOL, DAVID, BUT I ALREADY MADE PLANS WITH COURTNEY AND JIMMY... YOU KNOW, FROM THE SCIENCE CLUB.
NO NEED TO MISS A PARTY ON OUR ACCOUNT, MAY. YOU BELONG WITH YOUR TEAMMATES TONIGHT.
YEAH! WE'LL CATCH YOU TOMORROW!
DON'T BOUNCE ON ME, GUYS. WE CAN ALL HANG TOGETHER.
LIKE THAT'LL EVER HAPPEN! WE'RE GOING TO A PARTY, NOT A COMPUTER SEMINAR.
MOOSE IS RIGHT, MAY! IT'S JUST GONNA BE THE GIRLS FROM YOUR TEAM AND A FEW FOOTBALL PLAYERS.
YOU EXPECT MOOSE TO BE RUDE--THE GUY'S HEAD-BUTTED ONE GOALPOST TOO MANY--BUT YOU HAD HIGHER HOPES FOR BRAD.
AW, MAN! THIS IS SO UNFAIR TO MAY... ESPECIALLY SINCE SHE'S TOTALLY INTO BRAD.
THAT NEANDERTHAL?! YOU'VE GOT TO BE KIDDING!
I THINK I'LL PASS ON TONIGHT'S PARTY, GUYS... MAYBE NEXT TIME.
AS YOU TURN AWAY, YOU WONDER IF BRAD'S EYES ARE CLOUDING WITH REGRET--
SUIT YOURSELF, MAY! WE'LL CATCH YOU WHENEVER.
--OR ANNOYANCE?!

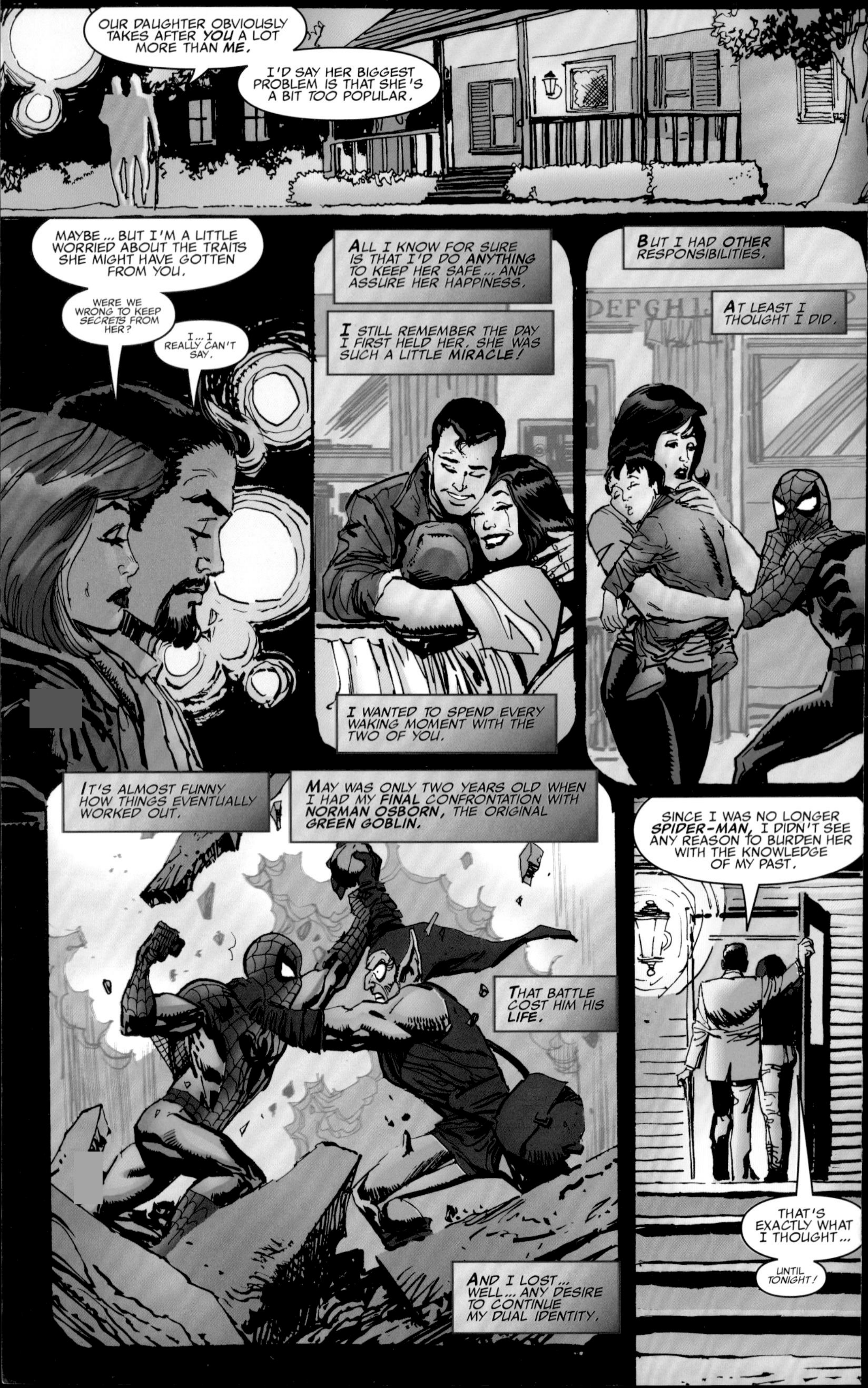
OUR DAUGHTER OBVIOUSLY TAKES AFTER YOU A LOT MORE THAN ME.
I'D SAY HER BIGGEST PROBLEM IS THAT SHE'S A BIT TOO POPULAR.
MAYBE ... BUT I'M A LITTLE WORRIED ABOUT THE TRAITS SHE MIGHT HAVE GOTTEN FROM YOU.
WERE WE WRONG TO KEEP SECRETS FROM HER?
I ... I REALLY CAN'T SAY.
ALL I KNOW FOR SURE IS THAT I'D DO ANYTHING TO KEEP HER SAFE ... AND ASSURE HER HAPPINESS.
I STILL REMEMBER THE DAY I FIRST HELD HER. SHE WAS SUCH A LITTLE MIRACLE!
I WANTED TO SPEND EVERY WAKING MOMENT WITH THE TWO OF YOU.
BUT I HAD OTHER RESPONSIBILITIES.
AT LEAST I THOUGHT I DID.
IT'S ALMOST FUNNY HOW THINGS EVENTUALLY WORKED OUT.
MAY WAS ONLY TWO YEARS OLD WHEN I HAD MY FINAL CONFRONTATION WITH NORMAN OSBORN, THE ORIGINAL GREEN GOBLIN.
THAT BATTLE COST HIM HIS LIFE.
AND I LOST ... WELL ... ANY DESIRE TO CONTINUE MY DUAL IDENTITY.
SINCE I WAS NO LONGER SPIDER-MAN, I DIDN'T SEE ANY REASON TO BURDEN HER WITH THE KNOWLEDGE OF MY PAST.
THAT'S EXACTLY WHAT I THOUGHT ...
UNTIL TONIGHT!

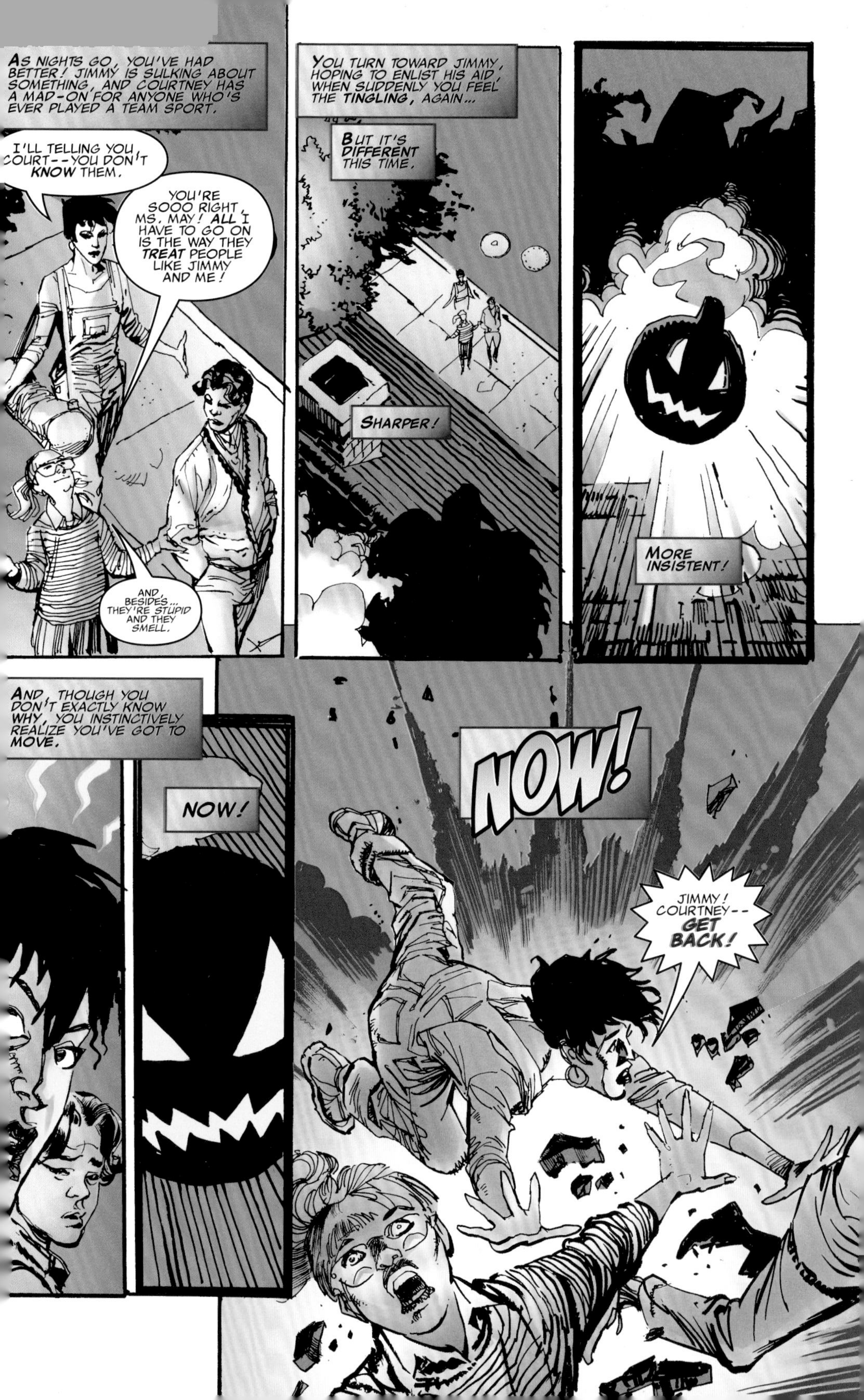
AS NIGHTS GO, YOU'VE HAD BETTER! JIMMY IS SULKING ABOUT SOMETHING, AND COURTNEY HAS A MAD-ON FOR ANYONE WHO'S EVER PLAYED A TEAM SPORT.
I'LL TELLING YOU, COURT--YOU DON'T KNOW THEM.
YOU'RE SOOO RIGHT, MS. MAY! ALL I HAVE TO GO ON IS THE WAY THEY TREAT PEOPLE LIKE JIMMY AND ME!
AND, BESIDES... THEY'RE STUPID AND THEY SMELL.
YOU TURN TOWARD JIMMY, HOPING TO ENLIST HIS AID, WHEN SUDDENLY YOU FEEL THE TINGLING, AGAIN...
BUT IT'S DIFFERENT THIS TIME.
SHARPER!
MORE INSISTENT!
AND, THOUGH YOU DON'T EXACTLY KNOW WHY, YOU INSTINCTIVELY REALIZE YOU'VE GOT TO MOVE.
NOW!
NOW!
JIMMY! COURTNEY--GET BACK!

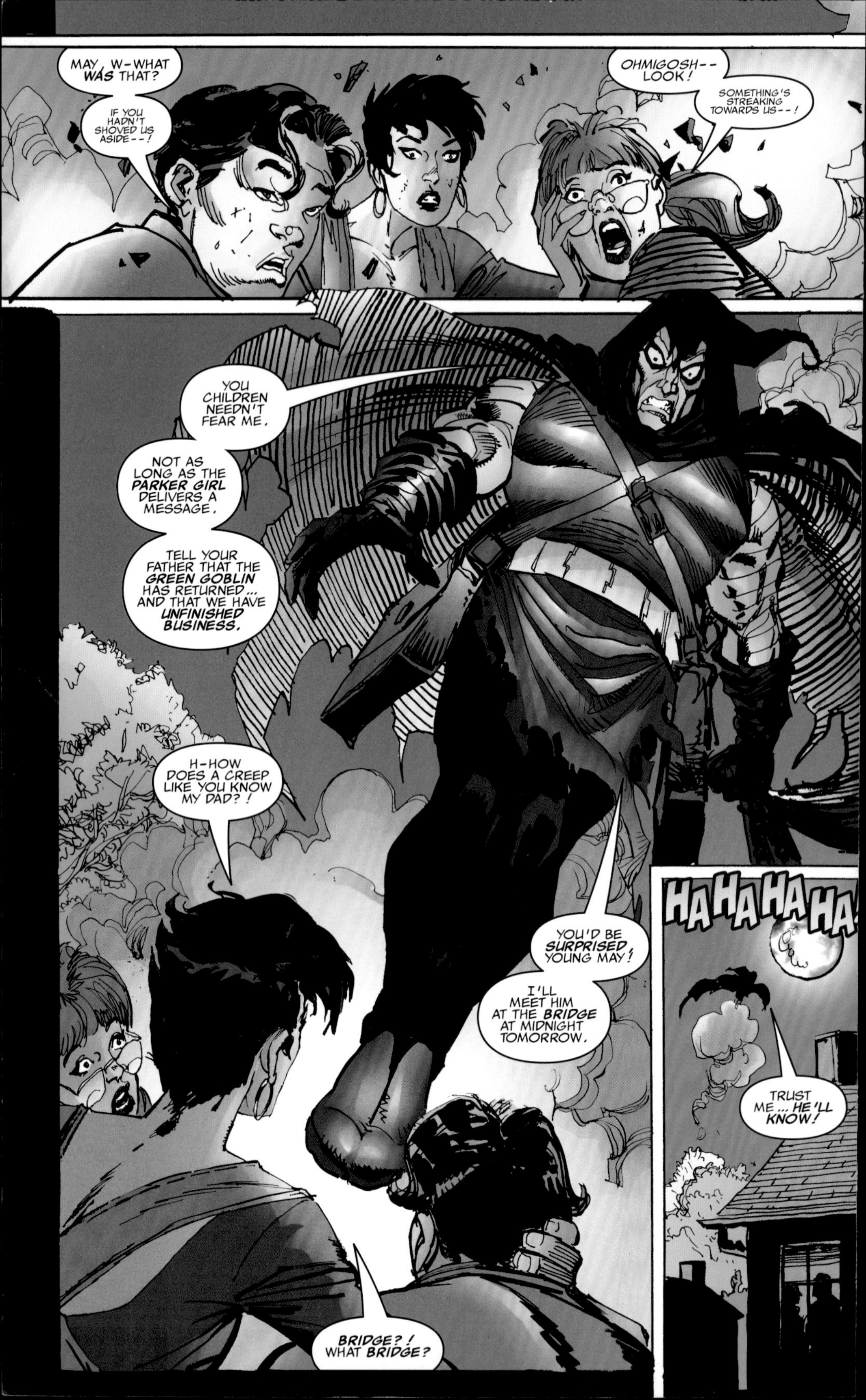

MAY, W-WHAT WAS THAT?
IF YOU HADN'T SHOVED US ASIDE--!
OHMIGOSH--LOOK!
SOMETHING'S STREAKING TOWARDS US--!
YOU CHILDREN NEEDN'T FEAR ME.
NOT AS LONG AS THE PARKER GIRL DELIVERS A MESSAGE.
TELL YOUR FATHER THAT THE GREEN GOBLIN HAS RETURNED... AND THAT WE HAVE UNFINISHED BUSINESS.
H-HOW DOES A CREEP LIKE YOU KNOW MY DAD?!
YOU'D BE SURPRISED, YOUNG MAY!
I'LL MEET HIM AT THE BRIDGE AT MIDNIGHT TOMORROW.
BRIDGE?! WHAT BRIDGE?
HA HA HA HA!
TRUST ME... HE'LL KNOW!

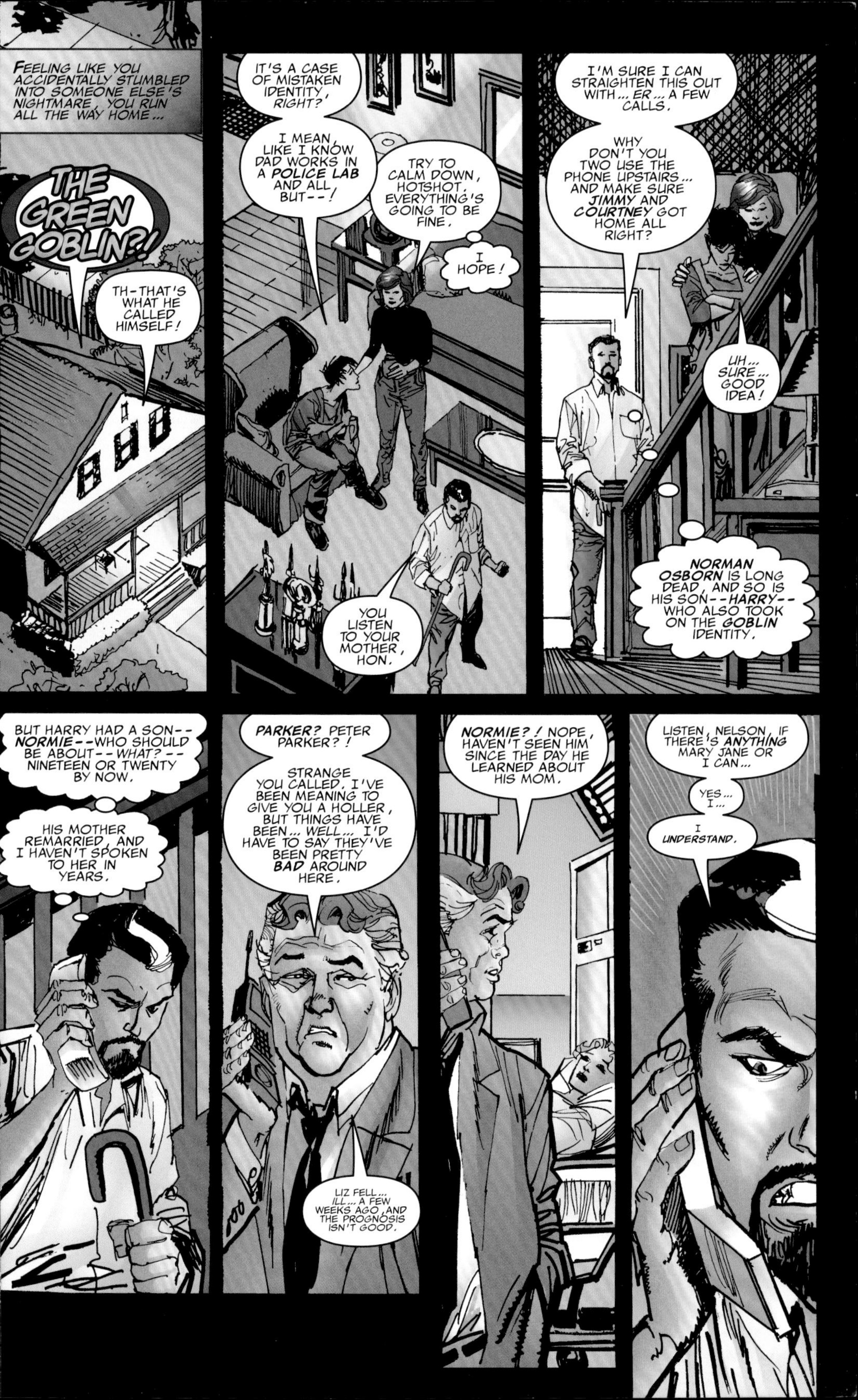
FEELING LIKE YOU ACCIDENTALLY STUMBLED INTO SOMEONE ELSE'S NIGHTMARE, YOU RUN ALL THE WAY HOME...
THE GREEN GOBLIN?!
TH-THAT'S WHAT HE CALLED HIMSELF!
IT'S A CASE OF MISTAKEN IDENTITY, RIGHT?
I MEAN, LIKE I KNOW DAD WORKS IN A POLICE LAB AND ALL, BUT--!
TRY TO CALM DOWN, HOTSHOT. EVERYTHING'S GOING TO BE FINE.
I HOPE!
YOU LISTEN TO YOUR MOTHER, HON.
I'M SURE I CAN STRAIGHTEN THIS OUT WITH... ER... A FEW CALLS.
WHY DON'T YOU TWO USE THE PHONE UPSTAIRS... AND MAKE SURE JIMMY AND COURTNEY GOT HOME ALL RIGHT?
UH... SURE... GOOD IDEA!
NORMAN OSBORN IS LONG DEAD, AND SO IS HIS SON--HARRY--WHO ALSO TOOK ON THE GOBLIN IDENTITY.
BUT HARRY HAD A SON--NORMIE--WHO SHOULD BE ABOUT--WHAT?--NINETEEN OR TWENTY BY NOW.
HIS MOTHER REMARRIED, AND I HAVEN'T SPOKEN TO HER IN YEARS.
PARKER? PETER PARKER?!
STRANGE YOU CALLED. I'VE BEEN MEANING TO GIVE YOU A HOLLER, BUT THINGS HAVE BEEN... WELL... I'D HAVE TO SAY THEY'VE BEEN PRETTY BAD AROUND HERE.
LIZ FELL... ILL... A FEW WEEKS AGO, AND THE PROGNOSIS ISN'T GOOD.
NORMIE?! NOPE, HAVEN'T SEEN HIM SINCE THE DAY HE LEARNED ABOUT HIS MOM.
LISTEN, NELSON, IF THERE'S ANYTHING MARY JANE OR I CAN...
YES... I...
I UNDERSTAND.

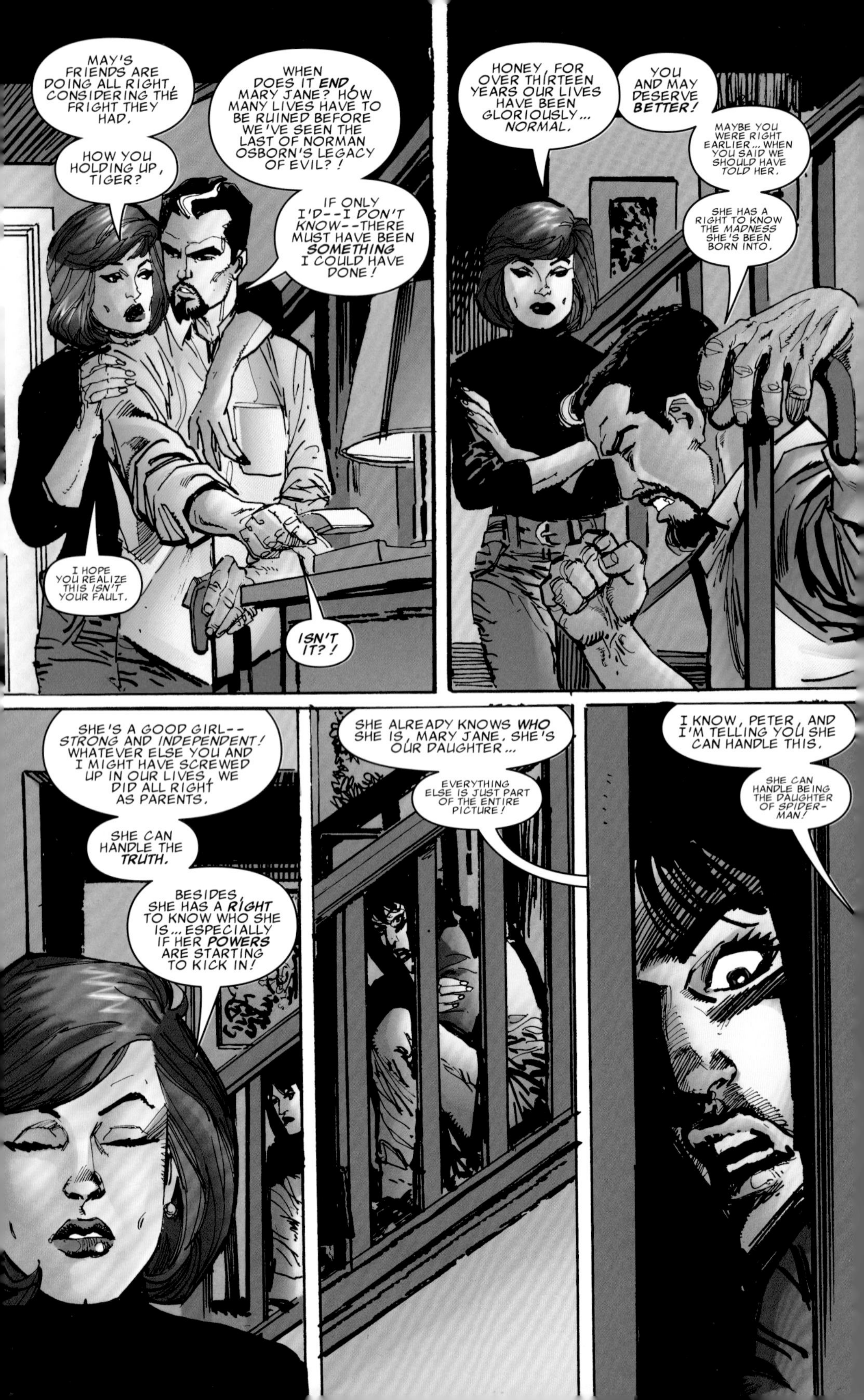
MAY'S FRIENDS ARE DOING ALL RIGHT, CONSIDERING THE FRIGHT THEY HAD.
HOW YOU HOLDING UP, TIGER?
WHEN DOES IT END, MARY JANE? HOW MANY LIVES HAVE TO BE RUINED BEFORE WE'VE SEEN THE LAST OF NORMAN OSBORN'S LEGACY OF EVIL?!
IF ONLY I'D--I DON'T KNOW--THERE MUST HAVE BEEN SOMETHING I COULD HAVE DONE!
I HOPE YOU REALIZE THIS ISN'T YOUR FAULT.
ISN'T IT?!
HONEY, FOR OVER THIRTEEN YEARS OUR LIVES HAVE BEEN GLORIOUSLY... NORMAL.
YOU AND MAY DESERVE BETTER!
MAYBE YOU WERE RIGHT EARLIER... WHEN YOU SAID WE SHOULD HAVE TOLD HER.
SHE HAS A RIGHT TO KNOW THE MADNESS SHE'S BEEN BORN INTO.
SHE'S A GOOD GIRL--STRONG AND INDEPENDENT! WHATEVER ELSE YOU AND I MIGHT HAVE SCREWED UP IN OUR LIVES, WE DID ALL RIGHT AS PARENTS.
SHE CAN HANDLE THE TRUTH.
BESIDES, SHE HAS A RIGHT TO KNOW WHO SHE IS... ESPECIALLY IF HER POWERS ARE STARTING TO KICK IN!
SHE ALREADY KNOWS WHO SHE IS, MARY JANE. SHE'S OUR DAUGHTER...
EVERYTHING ELSE IS JUST PART OF THE ENTIRE PICTURE!
I KNOW, PETER, AND I'M TELLING YOU SHE CAN HANDLE THIS.
SHE CAN HANDLE BEING THE DAUGHTER OF SPIDER-MAN!

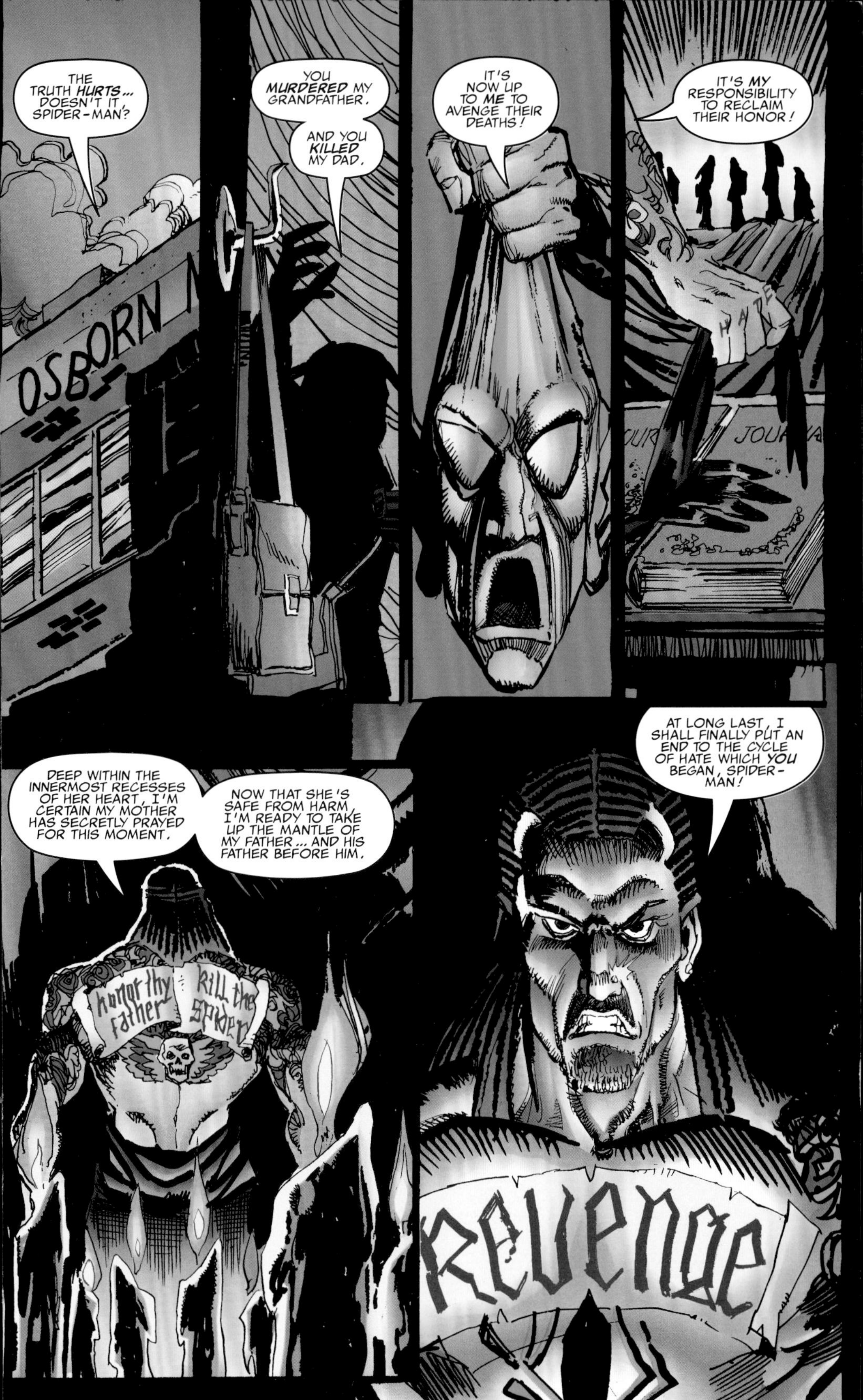
THE TRUTH HURTS... DOESN'T IT, SPIDER-MAN?
YOU MURDERED MY GRANDFATHER.
AND YOU KILLED MY DAD.
OSBORN
IT'S NOW UP TO ME TO AVENGE THEIR DEATHS!
IT'S MY RESPONSIBILITY TO RECLAIM THEIR HONOR!
HATE
JOUR
DEEP WITHIN THE INNERMOST RECESSES OF HER HEART, I'M CERTAIN MY MOTHER HAS SECRETLY PRAYED FOR THIS MOMENT.
NOW THAT SHE'S SAFE FROM HARM, I'M READY TO TAKE UP THE MANTLE OF MY FATHER... AND HIS FATHER BEFORE HIM.
honor thy father
kill the spider
AT LONG LAST, I SHALL FINALLY PUT AN END TO THE CYCLE OF HATE WHICH YOU BEGAN, SPIDER-MAN!
Revenge

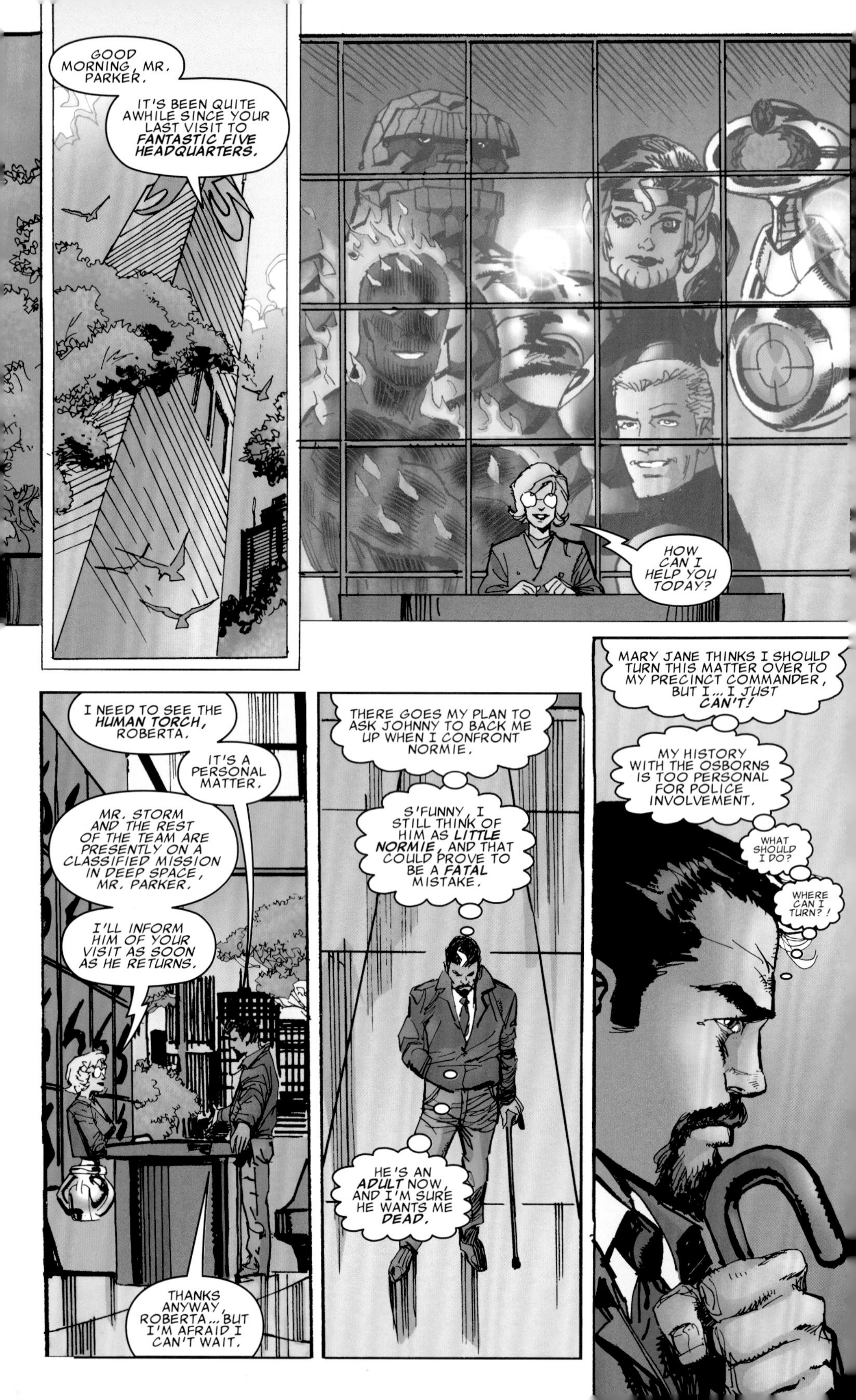
GOOD MORNING, MR. PARKER.
IT'S BEEN QUITE AWHILE SINCE YOUR LAST VISIT TO FANTASTIC FIVE HEADQUARTERS.
HOW CAN I HELP YOU TODAY?
I NEED TO SEE THE HUMAN TORCH, ROBERTA.
IT'S A PERSONAL MATTER.
MR. STORM AND THE REST OF THE TEAM ARE PRESENTLY ON A CLASSIFIED MISSION IN DEEP SPACE, MR. PARKER.
I'LL INFORM HIM OF YOUR VISIT AS SOON AS HE RETURNS.
THANKS ANYWAY, ROBERTA... BUT I'M AFRAID I CAN'T WAIT.
THERE GOES MY PLAN TO ASK JOHNNY TO BACK ME UP WHEN I CONFRONT NORMIE.
S'FUNNY, I STILL THINK OF HIM AS LITTLE NORMIE, AND THAT COULD PROVE TO BE A FATAL MISTAKE.
HE'S AN ADULT NOW, AND I'M SURE HE WANTS ME DEAD.
MARY JANE THINKS I SHOULD TURN THIS MATTER OVER TO MY PRECINCT COMMANDER, BUT I... I JUST CAN'T!
MY HISTORY WITH THE OSBORNS IS TOO PERSONAL FOR POLICE INVOLVEMENT.
WHAT SHOULD I DO?
WHERE CAN I TURN?!

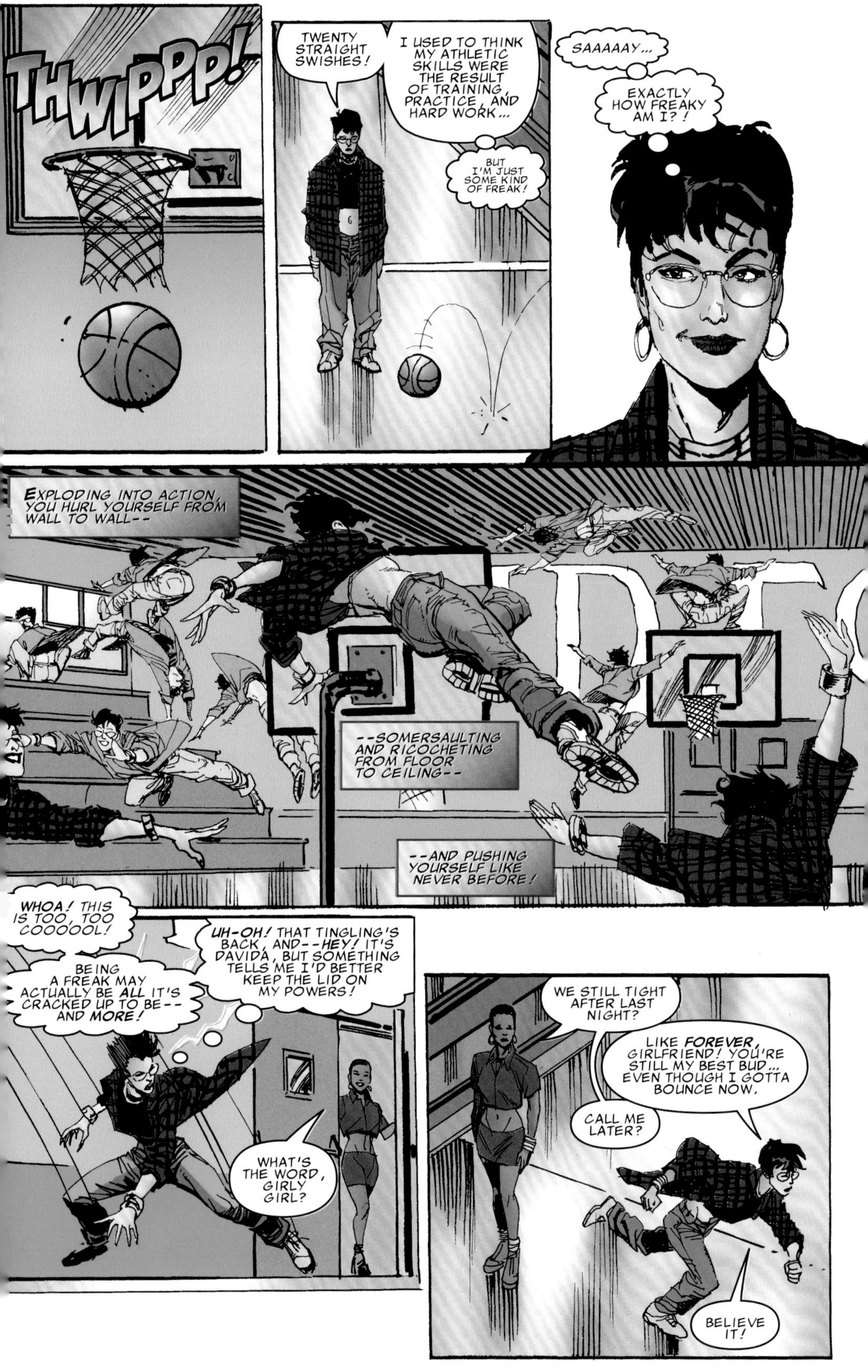
THWIPPP!
TWENTY STRAIGHT SWISHES!
I USED TO THINK MY ATHLETIC SKILLS WERE THE RESULT OF TRAINING, PRACTICE, AND HARD WORK...
BUT I'M JUST SOME KIND OF FREAK!
SAAAAAY...
EXACTLY HOW FREAKY AM I?!
EXPLODING INTO ACTION, YOU HURL YOURSELF FROM WALL TO WALL--
--SOMERSAULTING AND RICOCHETING FROM FLOOR TO CEILING--
--AND PUSHING YOURSELF LIKE NEVER BEFORE!
WHOA! THIS IS TOO, TOO COOOOOL!
BEING A FREAK MAY ACTUALLY BE ALL IT'S CRACKED UP TO BE--AND MORE!
UH-OH! THAT TINGLING'S BACK, AND--HEY! IT'S DAVIDA, BUT SOMETHING TELLS ME I'D BETTER KEEP THE LID ON MY POWERS!
WHAT'S THE WORD, GIRLY GIRL?
WE STILL TIGHT AFTER LAST NIGHT?
LIKE FOREVER, GIRLFRIEND! YOU'RE STILL MY BEST BUD... EVEN THOUGH I GOTTA BOUNCE NOW.
CALL ME LATER?
BELIEVE IT!

WELCOME TO *AVENGERS MANSION*, MR. PARKER.

I UNDERSTAND YOU'RE A CIVILIAN SCIENTIST EMPLOYED BY THE MANHATTAN POLICE DEPARTMENT.

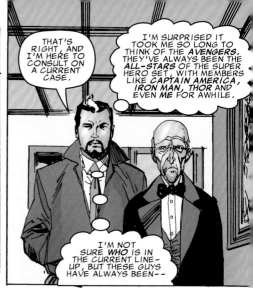

THAT'S RIGHT, AND I'M HERE TO CONSULT ON A CURRENT CASE.

I'M SURPRISED IT TOOK ME SO LONG TO THINK OF THE *AVENGERS*. THEY'VE ALWAYS BEEN THE *ALL-STARS* OF THE SUPER HERO SET, WITH MEMBERS LIKE *CAPTAIN AMERICA, IRON MAN, THOR* AND EVEN *ME* FOR AWHILE.

I'M NOT SURE *WHO* IS IN THE CURRENT LINE-UP, BUT THESE GUYS HAVE ALWAYS BEEN--

--EARTH'S *MIGHTIEST HEROES?!*

AFTERNOON, SIR.

WHAT'S THE *PROB*, POPS?

WHAT WAS I *THINKING?!*

THEY ALL SEEM SO ...SO *YOUNG!*

I KNOW I'M BEING UNFAIR! HECK, I WAS EVEN *YOUNGER* WHEN I FIRST DONNED MY WEBS, BUT IT WAS A DIFFERENT WORLD ...A DIFFERENT TIME.

⸴WHEW⸴ I BARELY MANAGED TO MAKE AN EXIT WITH MY DIGNITY STILL INTACT, BUT I... I JUST COULDN'T ASK THOSE ...THOSE *KIDS*... TO PUT THEMSELVES AT RISK!

NORMIE IS MY PROBLEM!

MY RESPONSIBILITY!

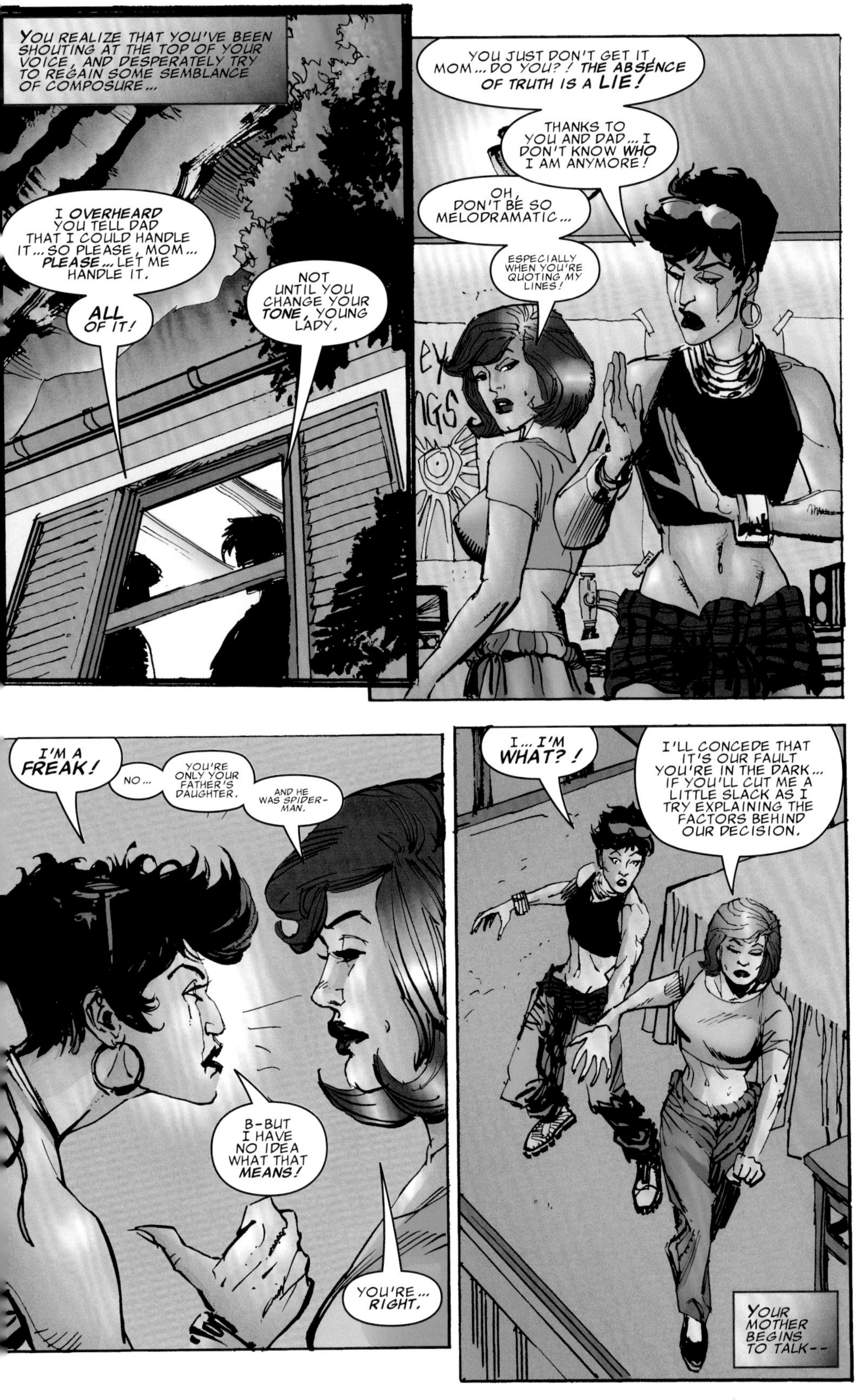

YOU REALIZE THAT YOU'VE BEEN SHOUTING AT THE TOP OF YOUR VOICE, AND DESPERATELY TRY TO REGAIN SOME SEMBLANCE OF COMPOSURE...
I OVERHEARD YOU TELL DAD THAT I COULD HANDLE IT... SO PLEASE, MOM... PLEASE... LET ME HANDLE IT.
ALL OF IT!
NOT UNTIL YOU CHANGE YOUR TONE, YOUNG LADY.
YOU JUST DON'T GET IT, MOM... DO YOU?! THE ABSENCE OF TRUTH IS A LIE!
THANKS TO YOU AND DAD... I DON'T KNOW WHO I AM ANYMORE!
OH, DON'T BE SO MELODRAMATIC...
ESPECIALLY WHEN YOU'RE QUOTING MY LINES!
I'M A FREAK!
NO...
YOU'RE ONLY YOUR FATHER'S DAUGHTER.
AND HE WAS SPIDER-MAN.
B-BUT I HAVE NO IDEA WHAT THAT MEANS!
YOU'RE... RIGHT.
I... I'M WHAT?!
I'LL CONCEDE THAT IT'S OUR FAULT YOU'RE IN THE DARK... IF YOU'LL CUT ME A LITTLE SLACK AS I TRY EXPLAINING THE FACTORS BEHIND OUR DECISION.
YOUR MOTHER BEGINS TO TALK--

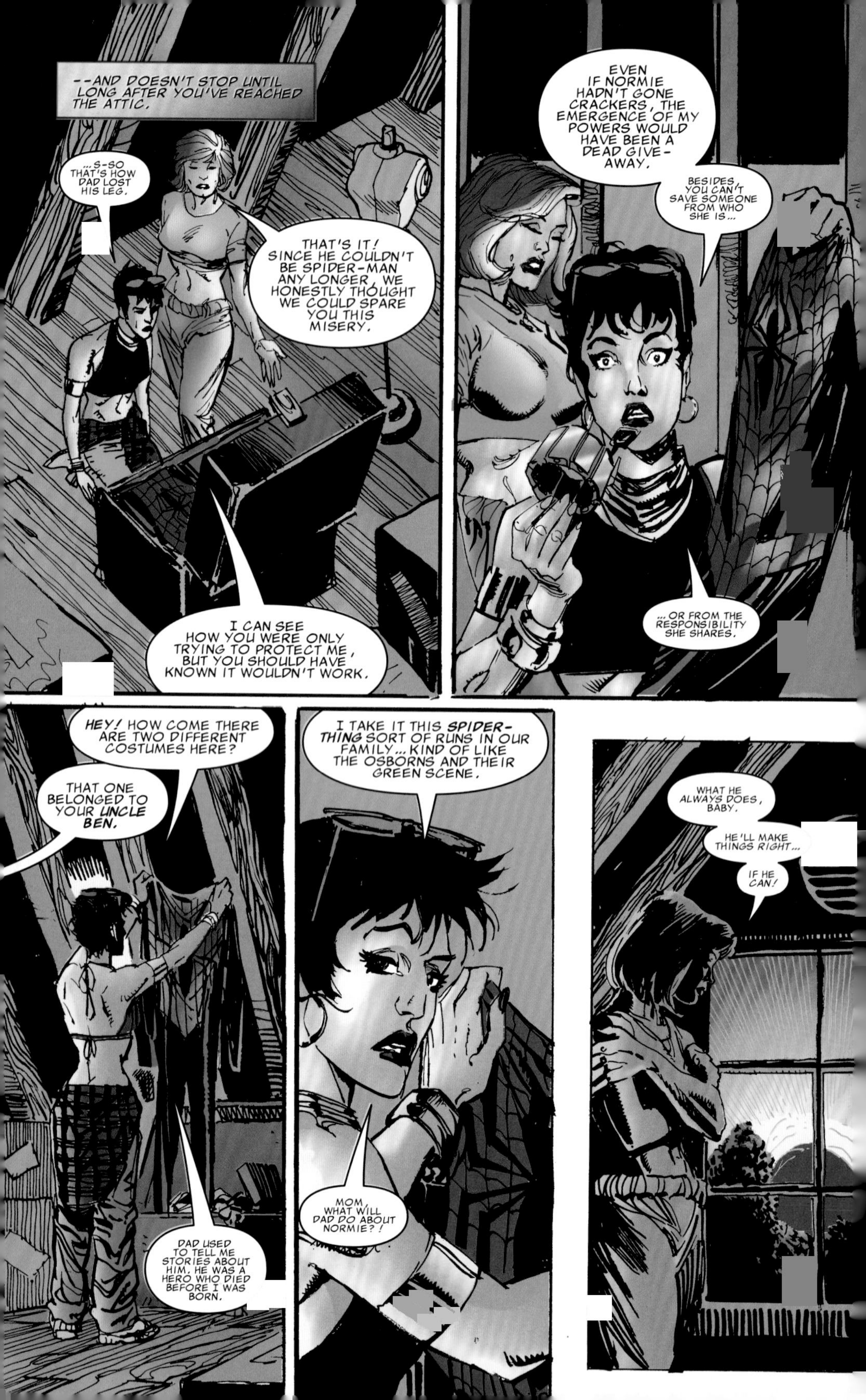
--AND DOESN'T STOP UNTIL LONG AFTER YOU'VE REACHED THE ATTIC.
...S-SO THAT'S HOW DAD LOST HIS LEG.
THAT'S IT! SINCE HE COULDN'T BE SPIDER-MAN ANY LONGER, WE HONESTLY THOUGHT WE COULD SPARE YOU THIS MISERY.
I CAN SEE HOW YOU WERE ONLY TRYING TO PROTECT ME, BUT YOU SHOULD HAVE KNOWN IT WOULDN'T WORK.
EVEN IF NORMIE HADN'T GONE CRACKERS, THE EMERGENCE OF MY POWERS WOULD HAVE BEEN A DEAD GIVE-AWAY.
BESIDES, YOU CAN'T SAVE SOMEONE FROM WHO SHE IS...
...OR FROM THE RESPONSIBILITY SHE SHARES.
HEY! HOW COME THERE ARE TWO DIFFERENT COSTUMES HERE?
THAT ONE BELONGED TO YOUR UNCLE BEN.
DAD USED TO TELL ME STORIES ABOUT HIM. HE WAS A HERO WHO DIED BEFORE I WAS BORN.
I TAKE IT THIS SPIDER-THING SORT OF RUNS IN OUR FAMILY... KIND OF LIKE THE OSBORNS AND THEIR GREEN SCENE.
MOM, WHAT WILL DAD DO ABOUT NORMIE?!
WHAT HE ALWAYS DOES, BABY.
HE'LL MAKE THINGS RIGHT...
IF HE CAN!

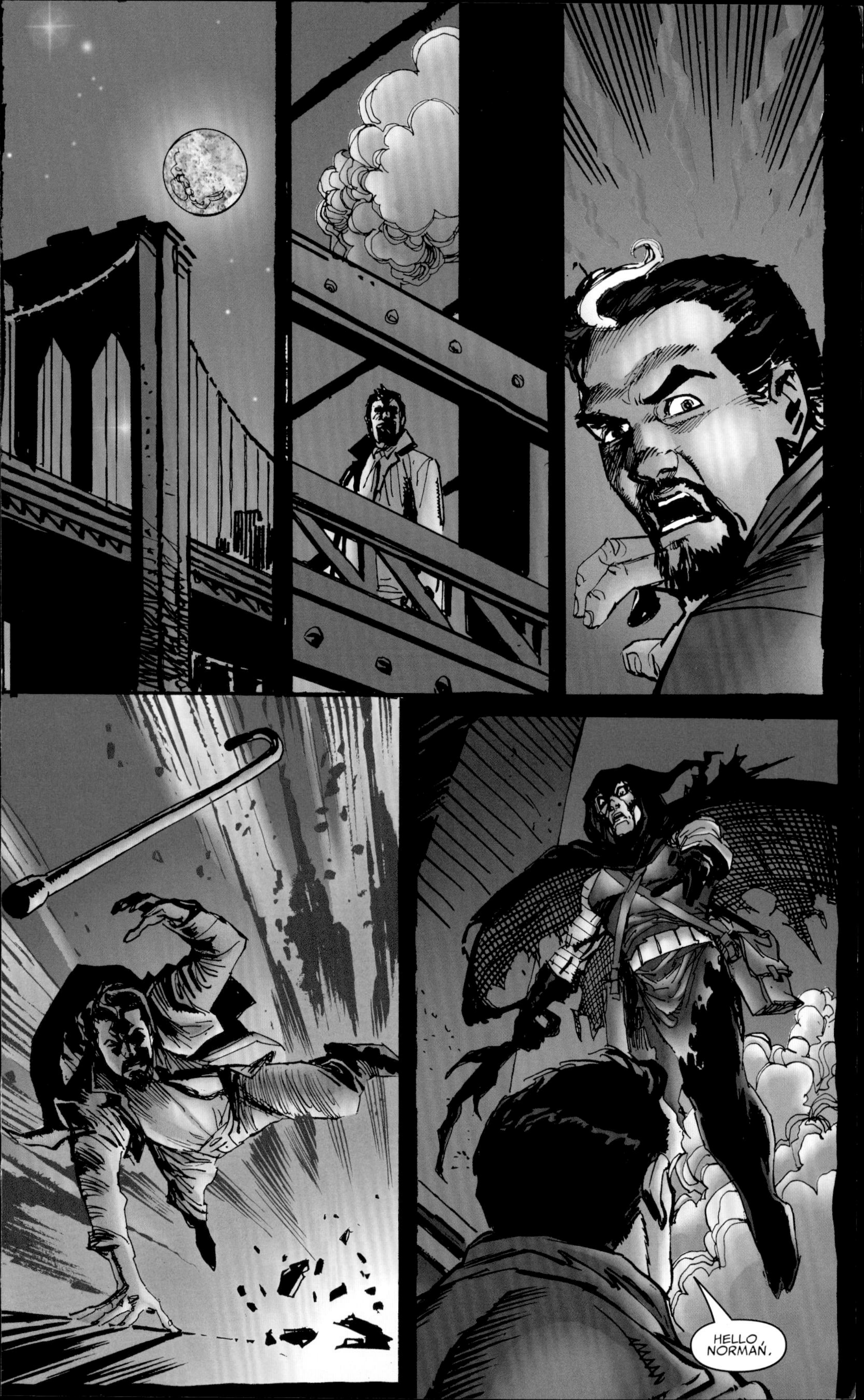
HELLO, NORMAN.

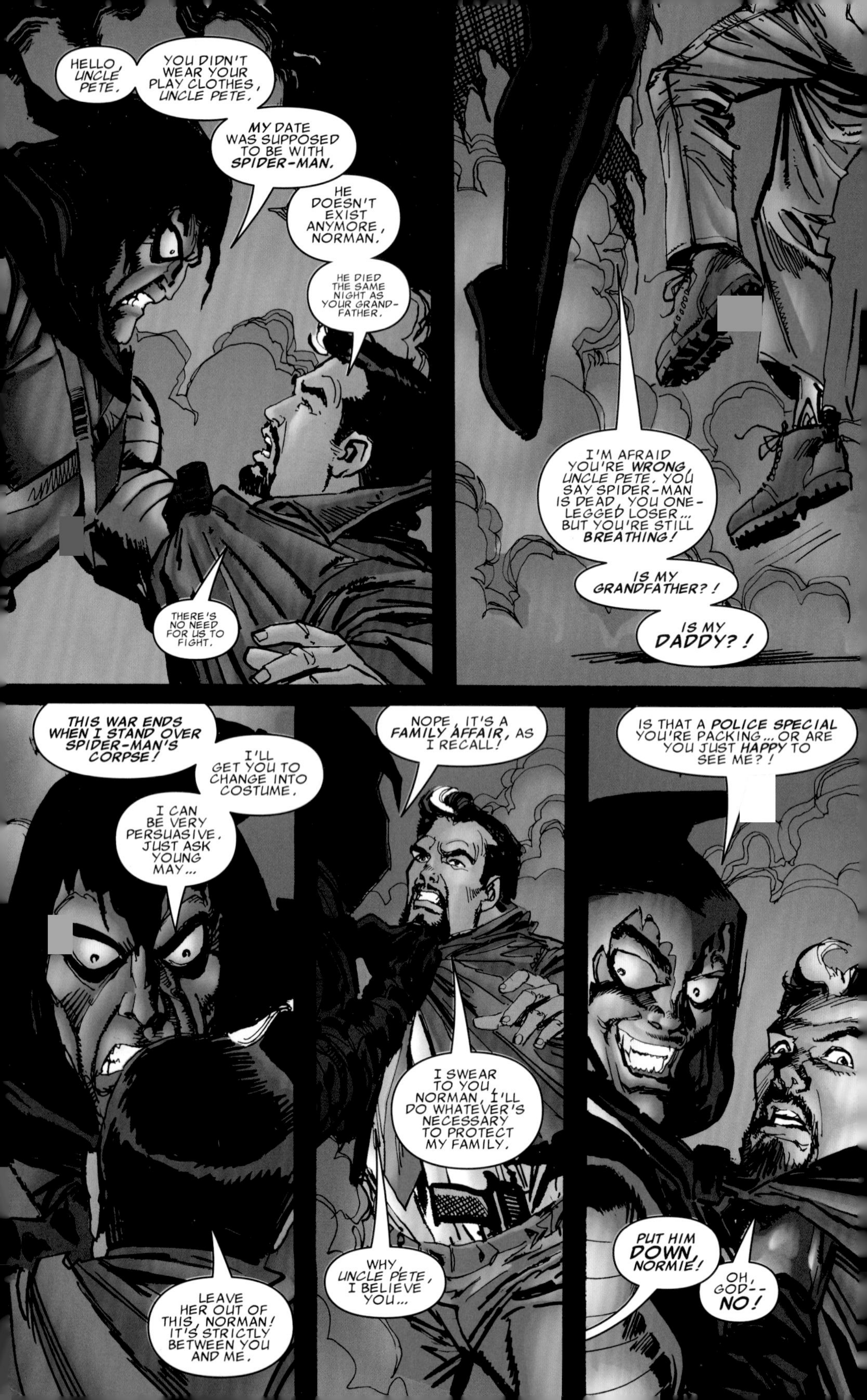
HELLO, UNCLE PETE.
YOU DIDN'T WEAR YOUR PLAY CLOTHES, UNCLE PETE.
MY DATE WAS SUPPOSED TO BE WITH SPIDER-MAN.
HE DOESN'T EXIST ANYMORE, NORMAN.
HE DIED THE SAME NIGHT AS YOUR GRAND-FATHER.
THERE'S NO NEED FOR US TO FIGHT.
I'M AFRAID YOU'RE WRONG, UNCLE PETE. YOU SAY SPIDER-MAN IS DEAD, YOU ONE-LEGGED LOSER... BUT YOU'RE STILL BREATHING!
IS MY GRANDFATHER?!
IS MY DADDY?!
THIS WAR ENDS WHEN I STAND OVER SPIDER-MAN'S CORPSE!
I'LL GET YOU TO CHANGE INTO COSTUME.
I CAN BE VERY PERSUASIVE. JUST ASK YOUNG MAY...
LEAVE HER OUT OF THIS, NORMAN! IT'S STRICTLY BETWEEN YOU AND ME.
NOPE, IT'S A FAMILY AFFAIR, AS I RECALL!
I SWEAR TO YOU, NORMAN, I'LL DO WHATEVER'S NECESSARY TO PROTECT MY FAMILY.
WHY, UNCLE PETE, I BELIEVE YOU...
IS THAT A POLICE SPECIAL YOU'RE PACKING... OR ARE YOU JUST HAPPY TO SEE ME?!
PUT HIM DOWN, NORMIE!
OH, GOD--NO!

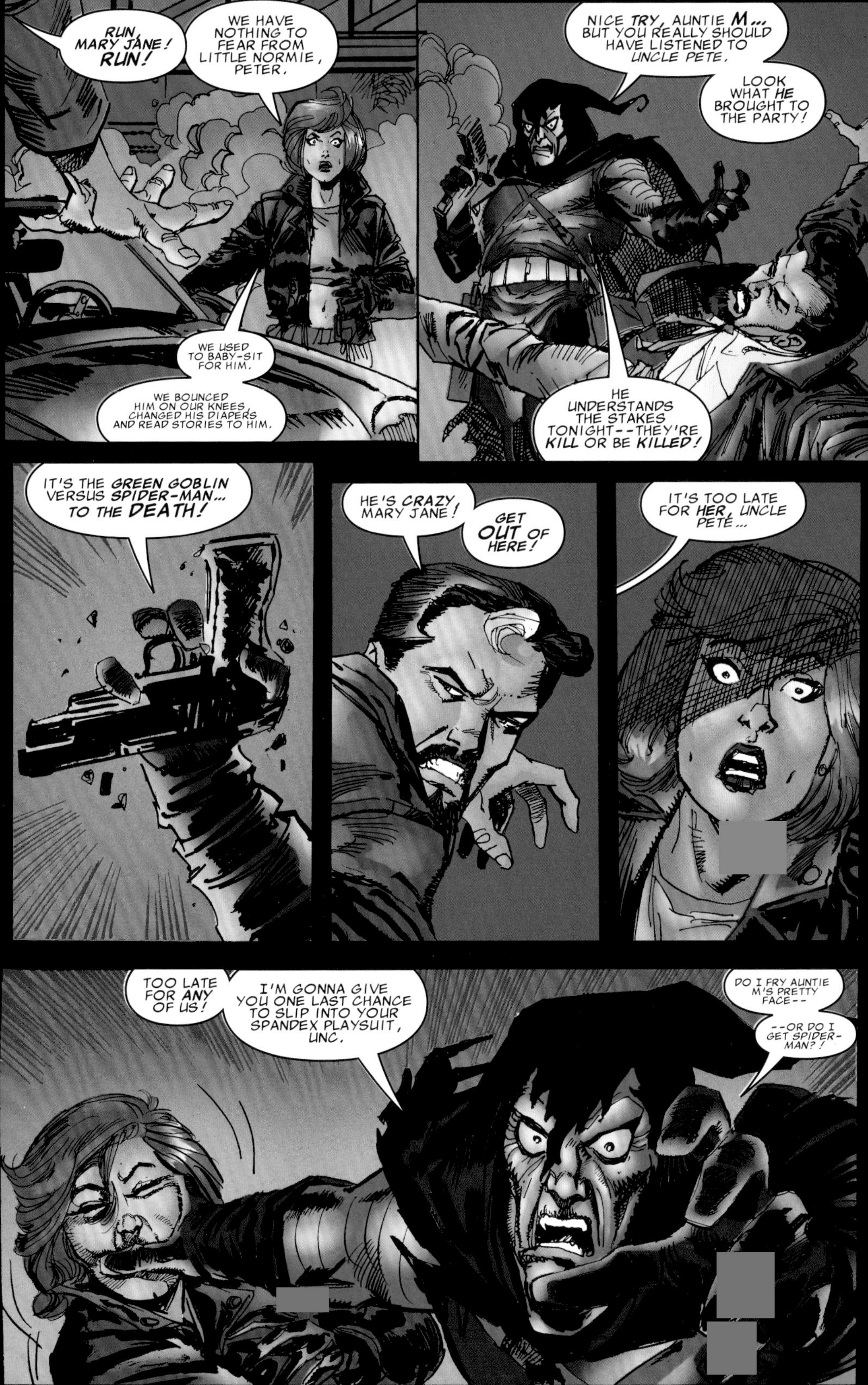
RUN, MARY JANE! RUN!
WE HAVE NOTHING TO FEAR FROM LITTLE NORMIE, PETER.
WE USED TO BABY-SIT FOR HIM.
WE BOUNCED HIM ON OUR KNEES, CHANGED HIS DIAPERS AND READ STORIES TO HIM.
NICE TRY, AUNTIE M... BUT YOU REALLY SHOULD HAVE LISTENED TO UNCLE PETE.
LOOK WHAT HE BROUGHT TO THE PARTY!
HE UNDERSTANDS THE STAKES TONIGHT--THEY'RE KILL OR BE KILLED!
IT'S THE GREEN GOBLIN VERSUS SPIDER-MAN... TO THE DEATH!
HE'S CRAZY, MARY JANE!
GET OUT OF HERE!
IT'S TOO LATE FOR HER, UNCLE PETE...
TOO LATE FOR ANY OF US!
I'M GONNA GIVE YOU ONE LAST CHANCE TO SLIP INTO YOUR SPANDEX PLAYSUIT, UNC.
DO I FRY AUNTIE M'S PRETTY FACE--
--OR DO I GET SPIDER-MAN?!

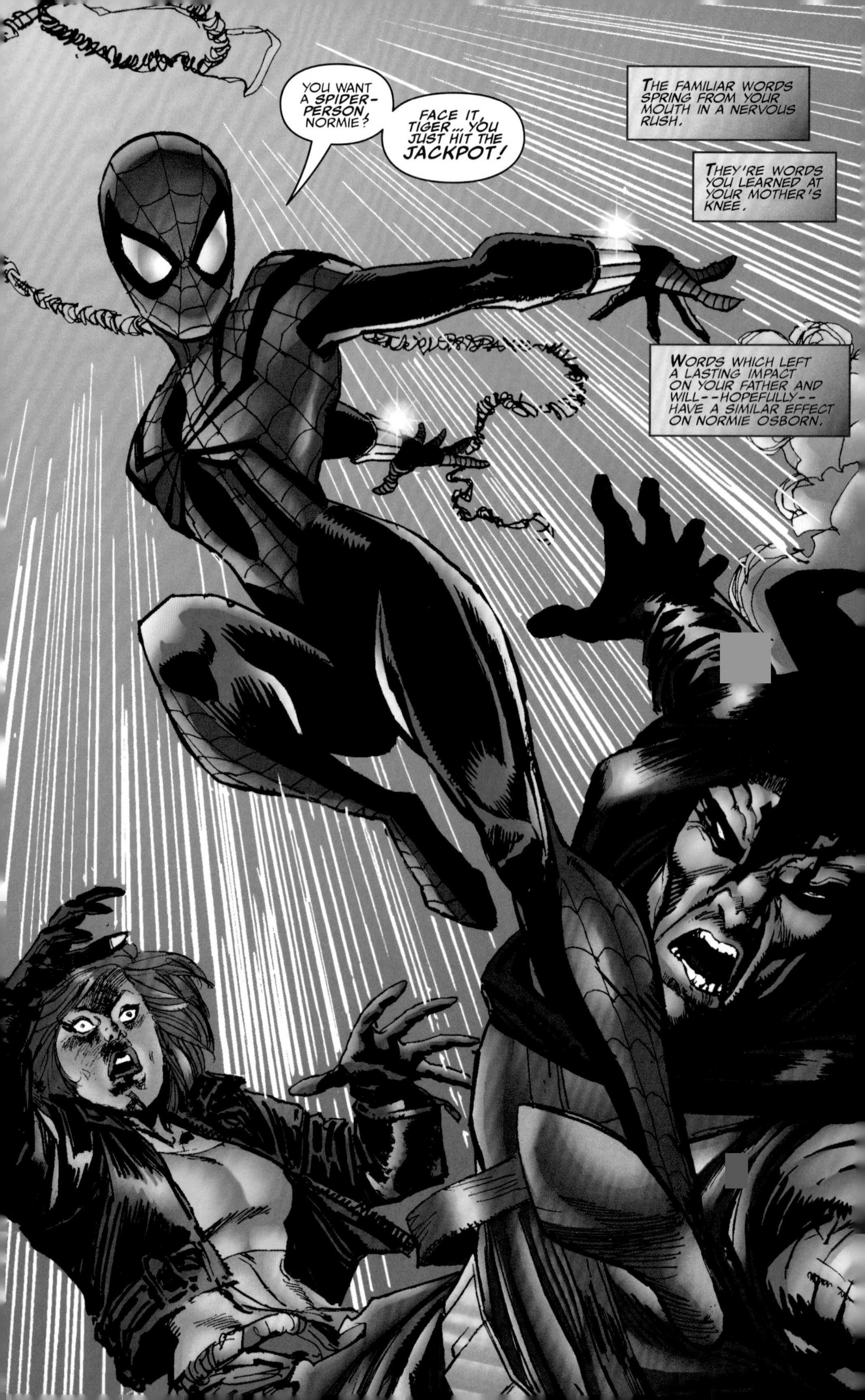

YOU WANT A SPIDER-PERSON, NORMIE?
FACE IT, TIGER... YOU JUST HIT THE JACKPOT!
THE FAMILIAR WORDS SPRING FROM YOUR MOUTH IN A NERVOUS RUSH.
THEY'RE WORDS YOU LEARNED AT YOUR MOTHER'S KNEE.
WORDS WHICH LEFT A LASTING IMPACT ON YOUR FATHER AND WILL--HOPEFULLY--HAVE A SIMILAR EFFECT ON NORMIE OSBORN.

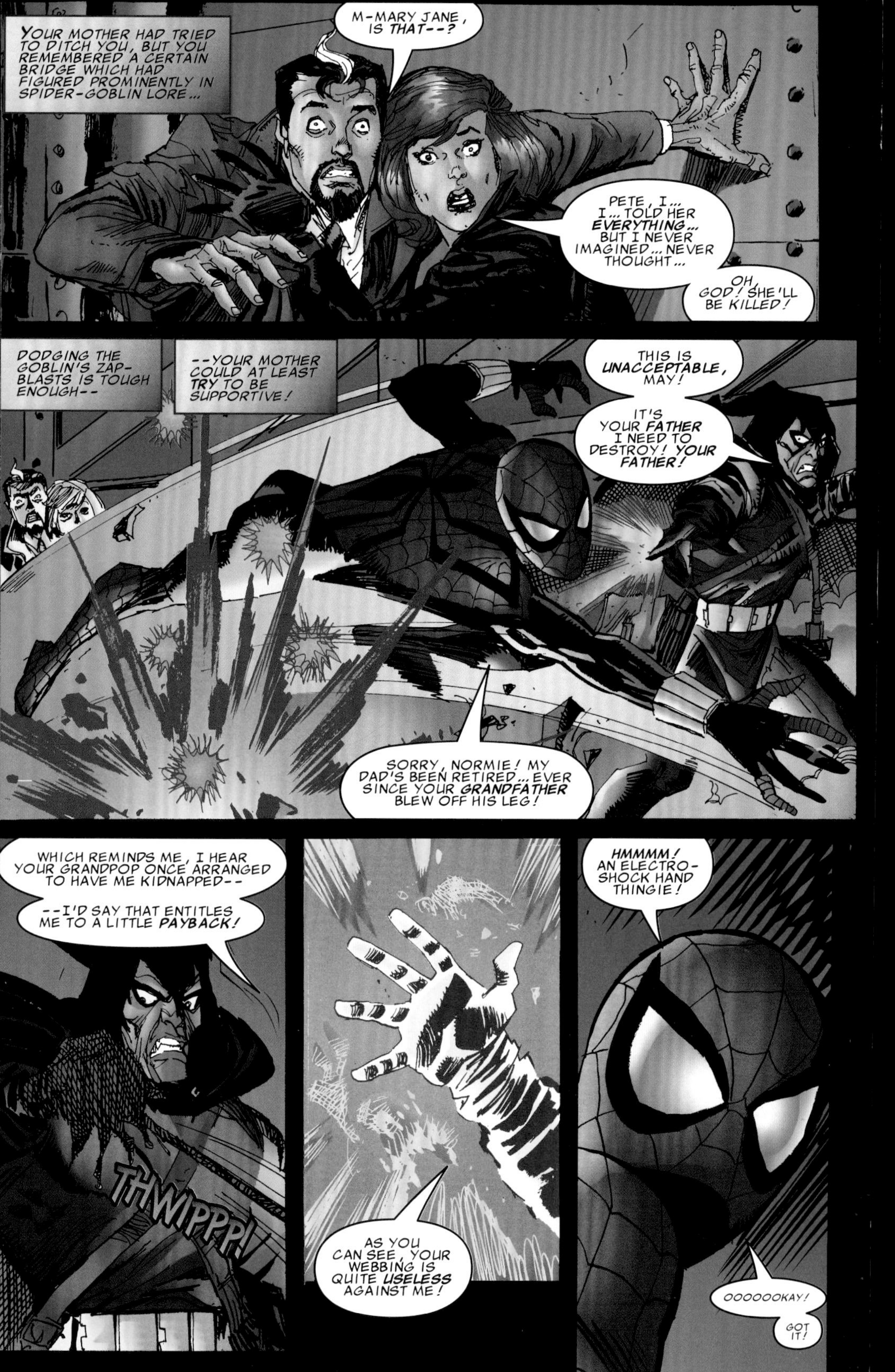
YOUR MOTHER HAD TRIED TO DITCH YOU, BUT YOU REMEMBERED A CERTAIN BRIDGE WHICH HAD FIGURED PROMINENTLY IN SPIDER-GOBLIN LORE...
M-MARY JANE, IS THAT--?
PETE, I... I... TOLD HER EVERYTHING... BUT I NEVER IMAGINED... NEVER THOUGHT...
OH, GOD! SHE'LL BE KILLED!
DODGING THE GOBLIN'S ZAP-BLASTS IS TOUGH ENOUGH--
--YOUR MOTHER COULD AT LEAST TRY TO BE SUPPORTIVE!
THIS IS UNACCEPTABLE, MAY!
IT'S YOUR FATHER I NEED TO DESTROY! YOUR FATHER!
SORRY, NORMIE! MY DAD'S BEEN RETIRED... EVER SINCE YOUR GRANDFATHER BLEW OFF HIS LEG!
WHICH REMINDS ME, I HEAR YOUR GRANDPOP ONCE ARRANGED TO HAVE ME KIDNAPPED--
--I'D SAY THAT ENTITLES ME TO A LITTLE PAYBACK!
THWIPPP!
AS YOU CAN SEE, YOUR WEBBING IS QUITE USELESS AGAINST ME!
HMMMM! AN ELECTRO-SHOCK HAND THINGIE!
OOOOOOKAY!
GOT IT!

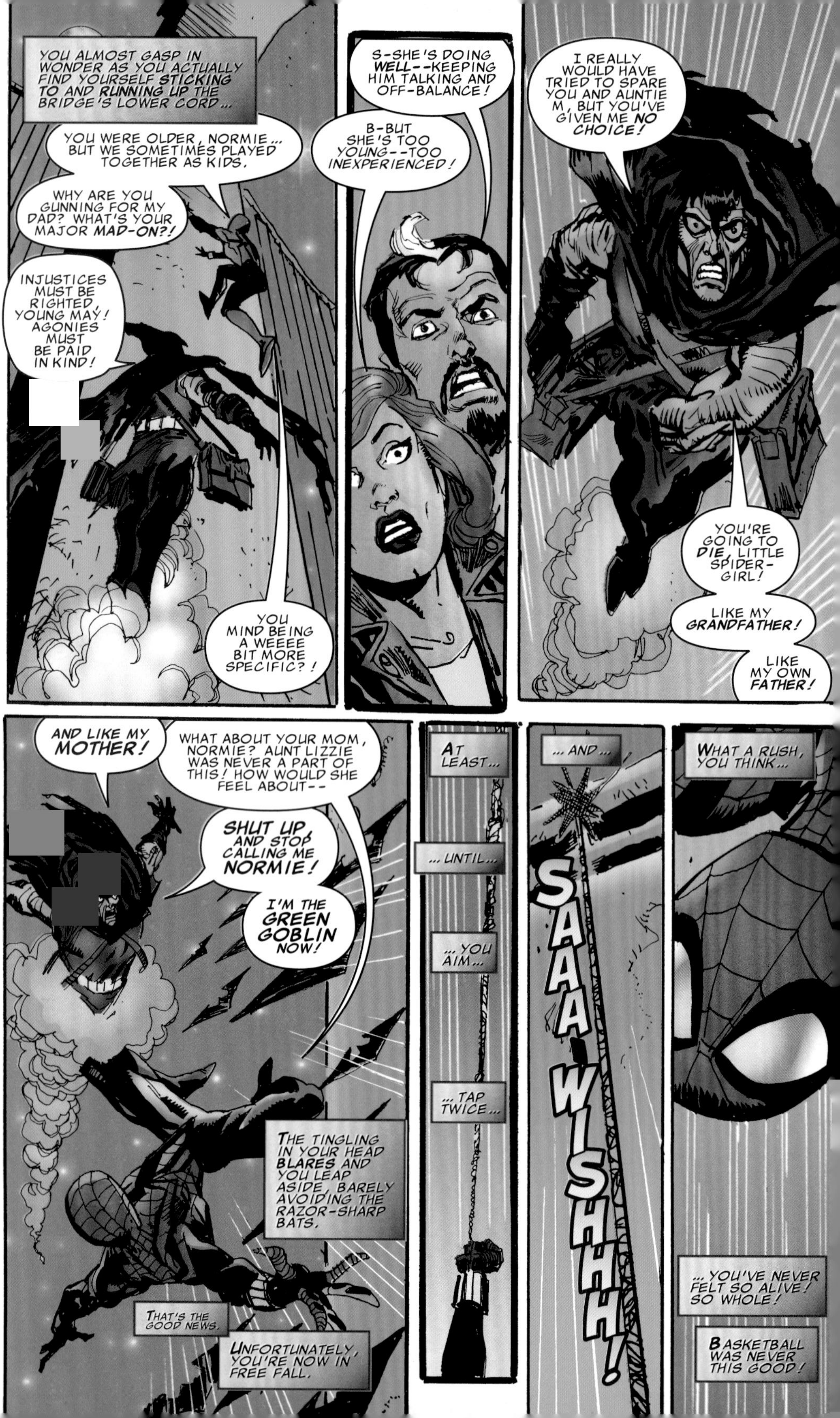
YOU ALMOST GASP IN WONDER AS YOU ACTUALLY FIND YOURSELF STICKING TO AND RUNNING UP THE BRIDGE'S LOWER CORD...
YOU WERE OLDER, NORMIE... BUT WE SOMETIMES PLAYED TOGETHER AS KIDS.
WHY ARE YOU GUNNING FOR MY DAD? WHAT'S YOUR MAJOR MAD-ON?!
INJUSTICES MUST BE RIGHTED, YOUNG MAY! AGONIES MUST BE PAID IN KIND!
YOU MIND BEING A WEEEE BIT MORE SPECIFIC?!
S-SHE'S DOING WELL--KEEPING HIM TALKING AND OFF-BALANCE!
B-BUT SHE'S TOO YOUNG--TOO INEXPERIENCED!
I REALLY WOULD HAVE TRIED TO SPARE YOU AND AUNTIE M, BUT YOU'VE GIVEN ME NO CHOICE!
YOU'RE GOING TO DIE, LITTLE SPIDER-GIRL!
LIKE MY GRANDFATHER!
LIKE MY OWN FATHER!
AND LIKE MY MOTHER!
WHAT ABOUT YOUR MOM, NORMIE? AUNT LIZZIE WAS NEVER A PART OF THIS! HOW WOULD SHE FEEL ABOUT--
SHUT UP, AND STOP CALLING ME NORMIE!
I'M THE GREEN GOBLIN NOW!
THE TINGLING IN YOUR HEAD BLARES AND YOU LEAP ASIDE, BARELY AVOIDING THE RAZOR-SHARP BATS.
THAT'S THE GOOD NEWS.
UNFORTUNATELY, YOU'RE NOW IN FREE FALL.
AT LEAST...
...UNTIL...
...YOU AIM...
...TAP TWICE...
...AND...
SAAA-WISHHH!
WHAT A RUSH, YOU THINK...
...YOU'VE NEVER FELT SO ALIVE! SO WHOLE!
BASKETBALL WAS NEVER THIS GOOD!

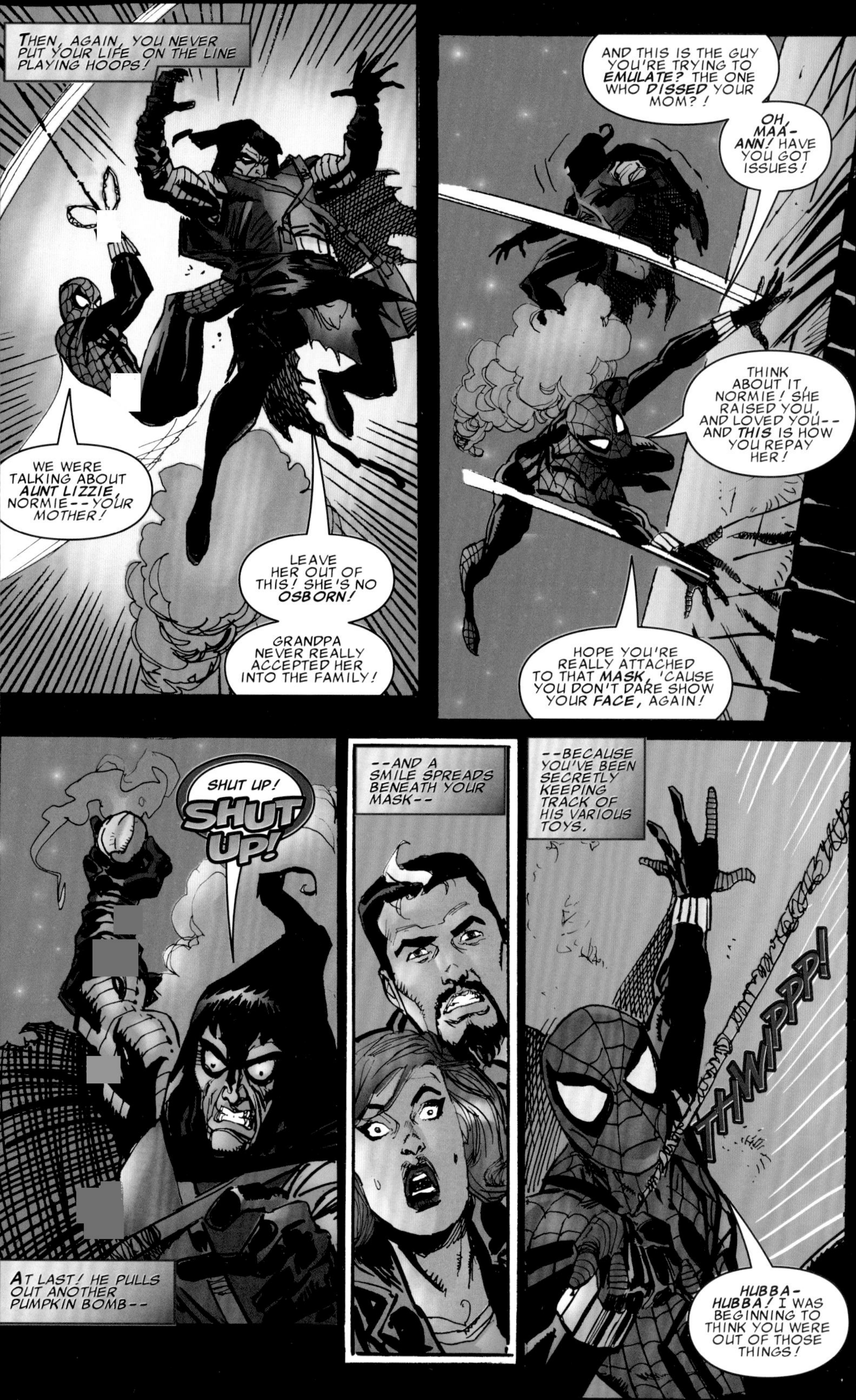
THEN, AGAIN, YOU NEVER PUT YOUR LIFE ON THE LINE PLAYING HOOPS!
WE WERE TALKING ABOUT AUNT LIZZIE, NORMIE--YOUR MOTHER!
LEAVE HER OUT OF THIS! SHE'S NO OSBORN!
GRANDPA NEVER REALLY ACCEPTED HER INTO THE FAMILY!
AND THIS IS THE GUY YOU'RE TRYING TO EMULATE? THE ONE WHO DISSED YOUR MOM?!
OH, MAA-ANN! HAVE YOU GOT ISSUES!
THINK ABOUT IT, NORMIE! SHE RAISED YOU, AND LOVED YOU--AND THIS IS HOW YOU REPAY HER!
HOPE YOU'RE REALLY ATTACHED TO THAT MASK, 'CAUSE YOU DON'T DARE SHOW YOUR FACE, AGAIN!
SHUT UP!
SHUT UP!
AT LAST! HE PULLS OUT ANOTHER PUMPKIN BOMB--
--AND A SMILE SPREADS BENEATH YOUR MASK--
--BECAUSE YOU'VE BEEN SECRETLY KEEPING TRACK OF HIS VARIOUS TOYS.
THWIPPP!
HUBBA-HUBBA! I WAS BEGINNING TO THINK YOU WERE OUT OF THOSE THINGS!

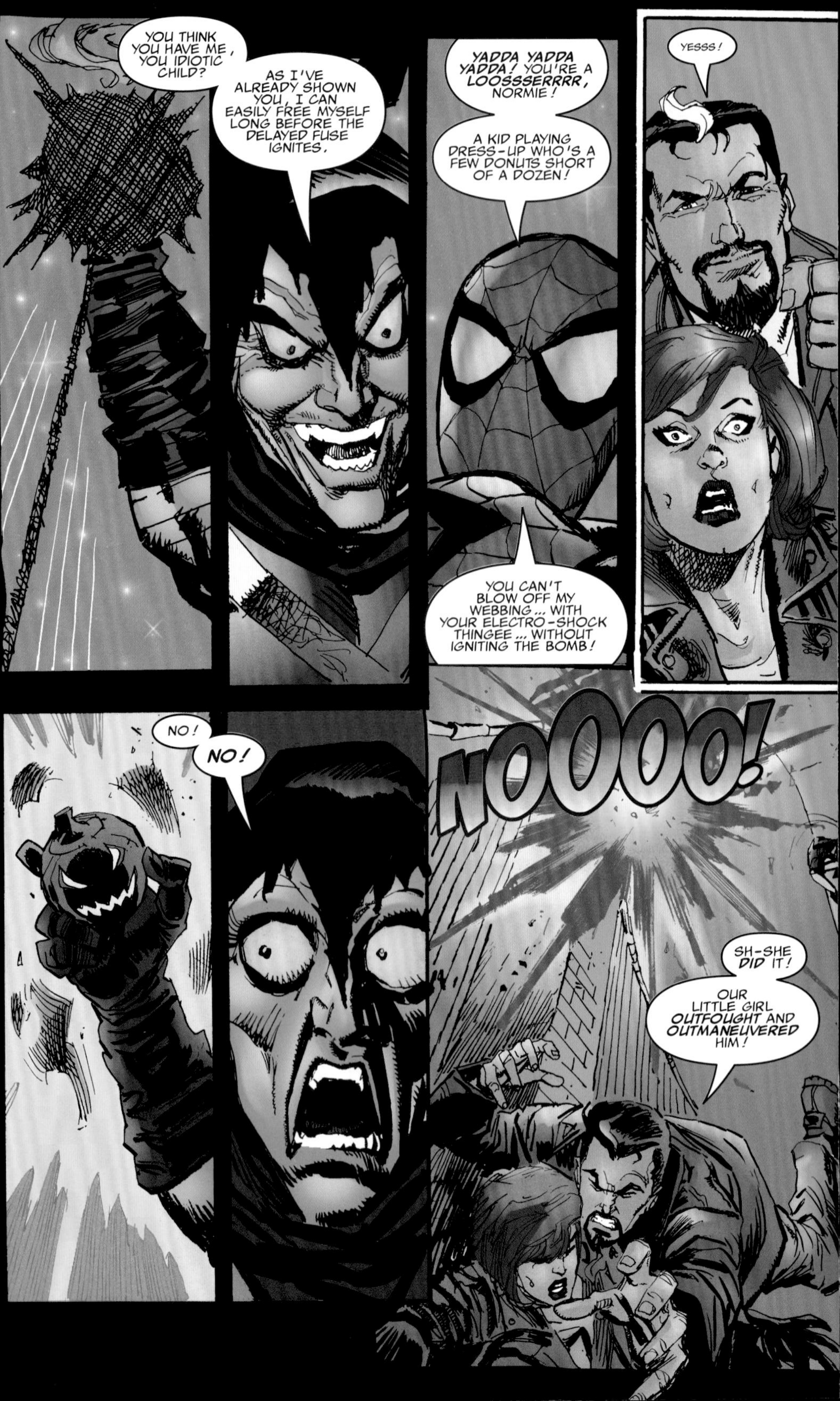
YOU THINK YOU HAVE ME, YOU IDIOTIC CHILD?
AS I'VE ALREADY SHOWN YOU, I CAN EASILY FREE MYSELF LONG BEFORE THE DELAYED FUSE IGNITES.
YADDA YADDA YADDA! YOU'RE A LOOSSSERRRR, NORMIE!
A KID PLAYING DRESS-UP WHO'S A FEW DONUTS SHORT OF A DOZEN!
YOU CAN'T BLOW OFF MY WEBBING... WITH YOUR ELECTRO-SHOCK THINGEE... WITHOUT IGNITING THE BOMB!
YESSS!
NO!
NO!
NOOOOO!
SH-SHE DID IT!
OUR LITTLE GIRL OUTFOUGHT AND OUTMANEUVERED HIM!

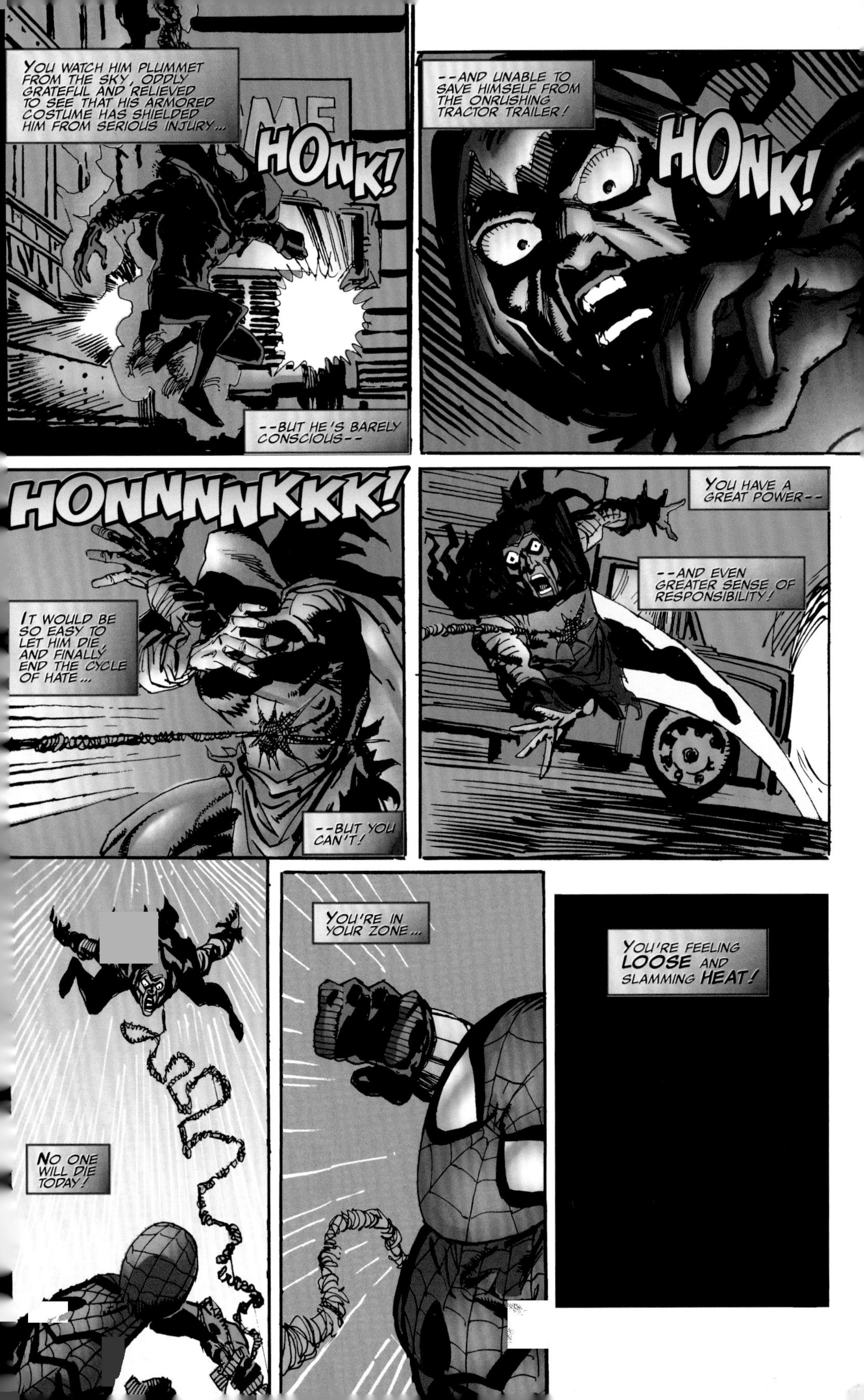
YOU WATCH HIM PLUMMET FROM THE SKY, ODDLY GRATEFUL AND RELIEVED TO SEE THAT HIS ARMORED COSTUME HAS SHIELDED HIM FROM SERIOUS INJURY...
HONK!
--BUT HE'S BARELY CONSCIOUS--
--AND UNABLE TO SAVE HIMSELF FROM THE ONRUSHING TRACTOR TRAILER!
HONK!
HONNNNKKK!
IT WOULD BE SO EASY TO LET HIM DIE, AND FINALLY END THE CYCLE OF HATE...
--BUT YOU CAN'T!
YOU HAVE A GREAT POWER--
--AND EVEN GREATER SENSE OF RESPONSIBILITY!
NO ONE WILL DIE TODAY!
YOU'RE IN YOUR ZONE...
YOU'RE FEELING LOOSE AND SLAMMING HEAT!

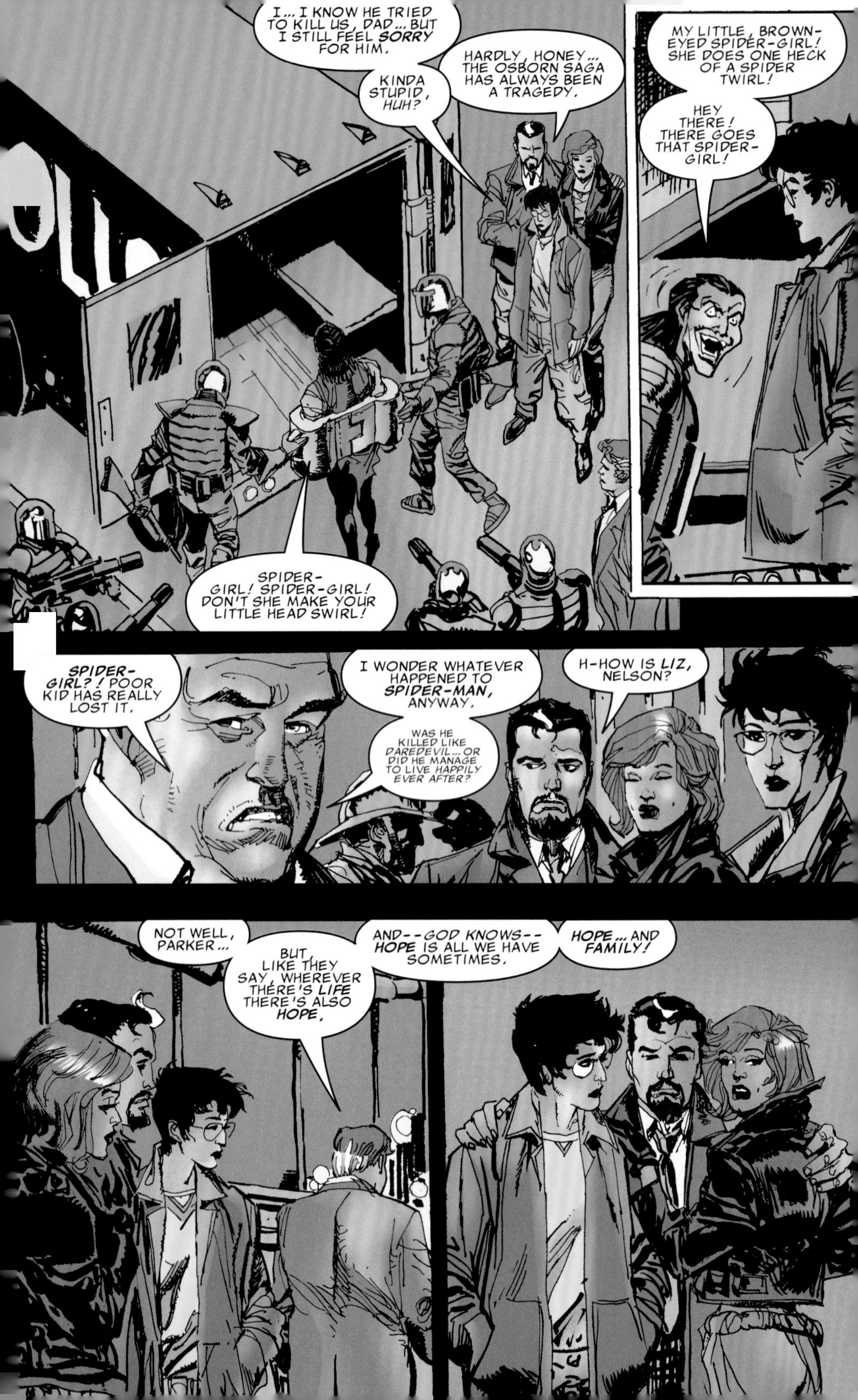
I... I KNOW HE TRIED TO KILL US, DAD... BUT I STILL FEEL SORRY FOR HIM.
KINDA STUPID, HUH?
HARDLY, HONEY... THE OSBORN SAGA HAS ALWAYS BEEN A TRAGEDY.
SPIDER-GIRL! SPIDER-GIRL! DON'T SHE MAKE YOUR LITTLE HEAD SWIRL!
MY LITTLE, BROWN-EYED SPIDER-GIRL! SHE DOES ONE HECK OF A SPIDER TWIRL!
HEY THERE! THERE GOES THAT SPIDER-GIRL!
SPIDER-GIRL?! POOR KID HAS REALLY LOST IT.
I WONDER WHATEVER HAPPENED TO SPIDER-MAN, ANYWAY.
WAS HE KILLED LIKE DAREDEVIL... OR DID HE MANAGE TO LIVE HAPPILY EVER AFTER?
H-HOW IS LIZ, NELSON?
NOT WELL, PARKER...
BUT, LIKE THEY SAY, WHEREVER THERE'S LIFE THERE'S ALSO HOPE.
AND--GOD KNOWS--HOPE IS ALL WE HAVE SOMETIMES.
HOPE... AND FAMILY!

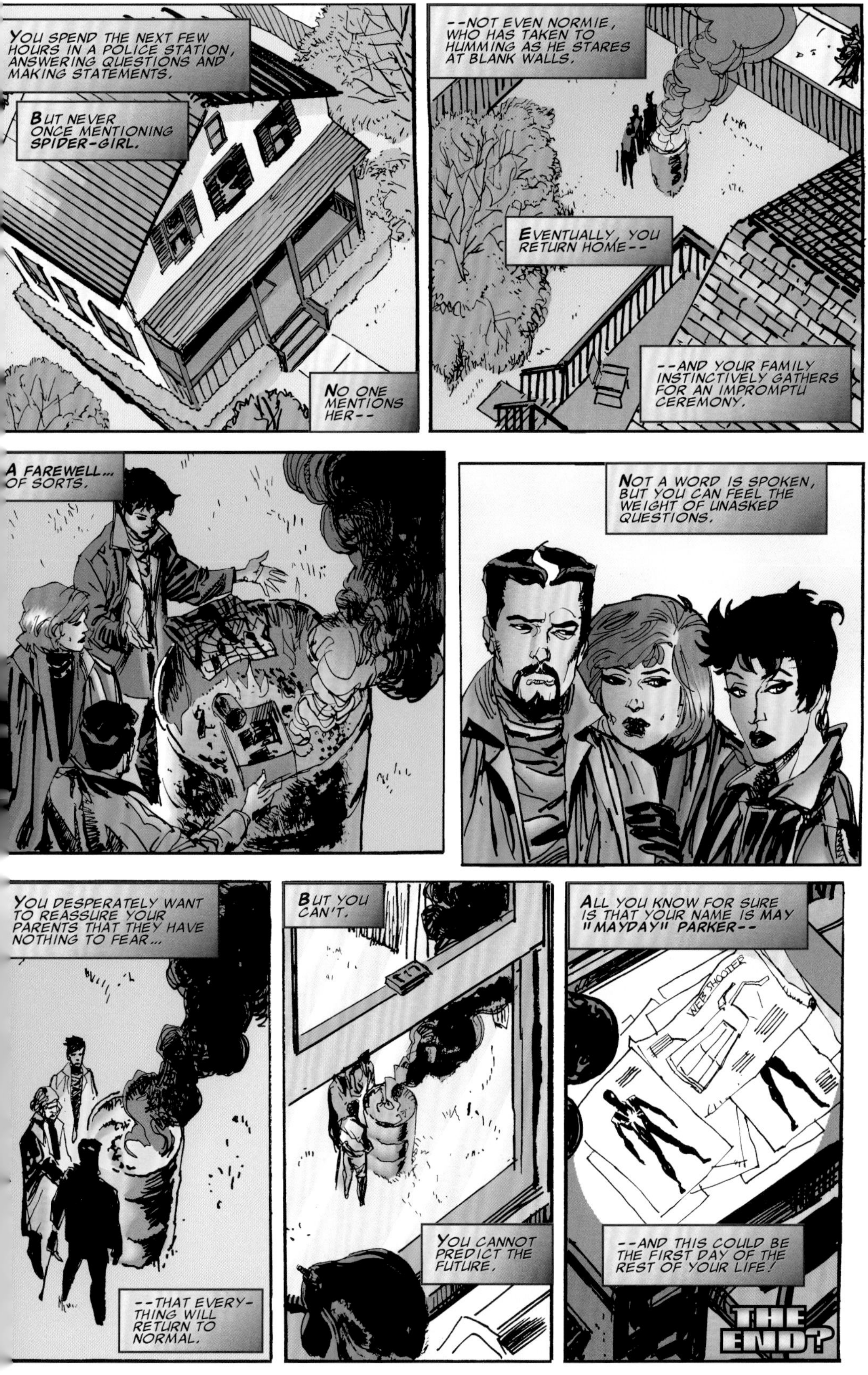
YOU SPEND THE NEXT FEW HOURS IN A POLICE STATION, ANSWERING QUESTIONS AND MAKING STATEMENTS.
BUT NEVER ONCE MENTIONING SPIDER-GIRL.
NO ONE MENTIONS HER--
--NOT EVEN NORMIE, WHO HAS TAKEN TO HUMMING AS HE STARES AT BLANK WALLS.
EVENTUALLY, YOU RETURN HOME--
--AND YOUR FAMILY INSTINCTIVELY GATHERS FOR AN IMPROMPTU CEREMONY.
A FAREWELL... OF SORTS.
NOT A WORD IS SPOKEN, BUT YOU CAN FEEL THE WEIGHT OF UNASKED QUESTIONS.
YOU DESPERATELY WANT TO REASSURE YOUR PARENTS THAT THEY HAVE NOTHING TO FEAR...
--THAT EVERYTHING WILL RETURN TO NORMAL.
BUT YOU CAN'T.
YOU CANNOT PREDICT THE FUTURE.
ALL YOU KNOW FOR SURE IS THAT YOUR NAME IS MAY "MAYDAY" PARKER--
WEB SHOOTER
--AND THIS COULD BE THE FIRST DAY OF THE REST OF YOUR LIFE!
THE END?

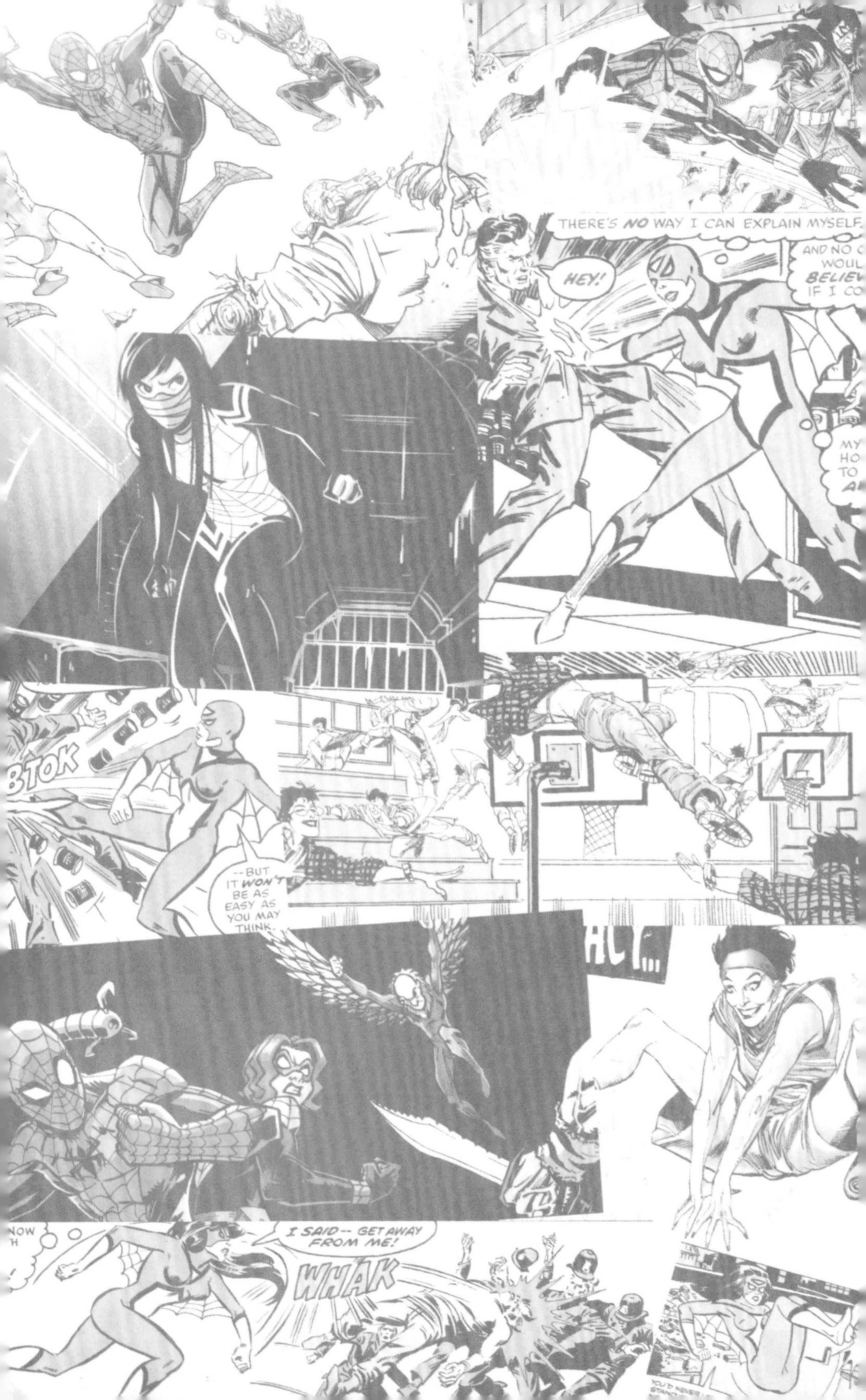
THERE'S NO WAY I CAN EXPLAIN MYSELF,
HEY!
BTOK
--BUT IT WON'T BE AS EASY AS YOU MAY THINK.
I SAID-- GET AWAY FROM ME!
WHAK

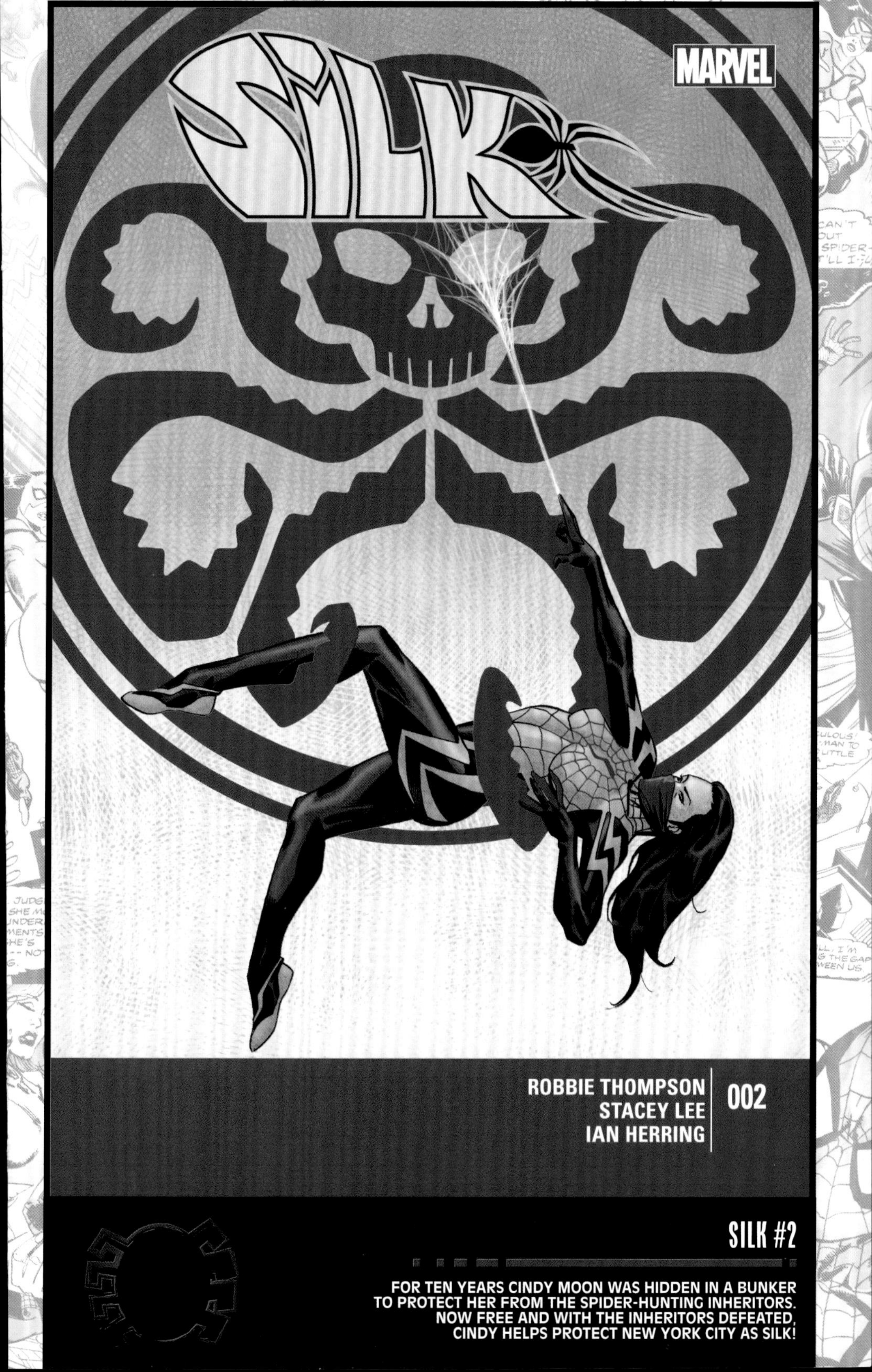
SILK
MARVEL
ROBBIE THOMPSON
STACEY LEE
IAN HERRING
002

SILK #2

FOR TEN YEARS CINDY MOON WAS HIDDEN IN A BUNKER TO PROTECT HER FROM THE SPIDER-HUNTING INHERITORS. NOW FREE AND WITH THE INHERITORS DEFEATED, CINDY HELPS PROTECT NEW YORK CITY AS SILK!

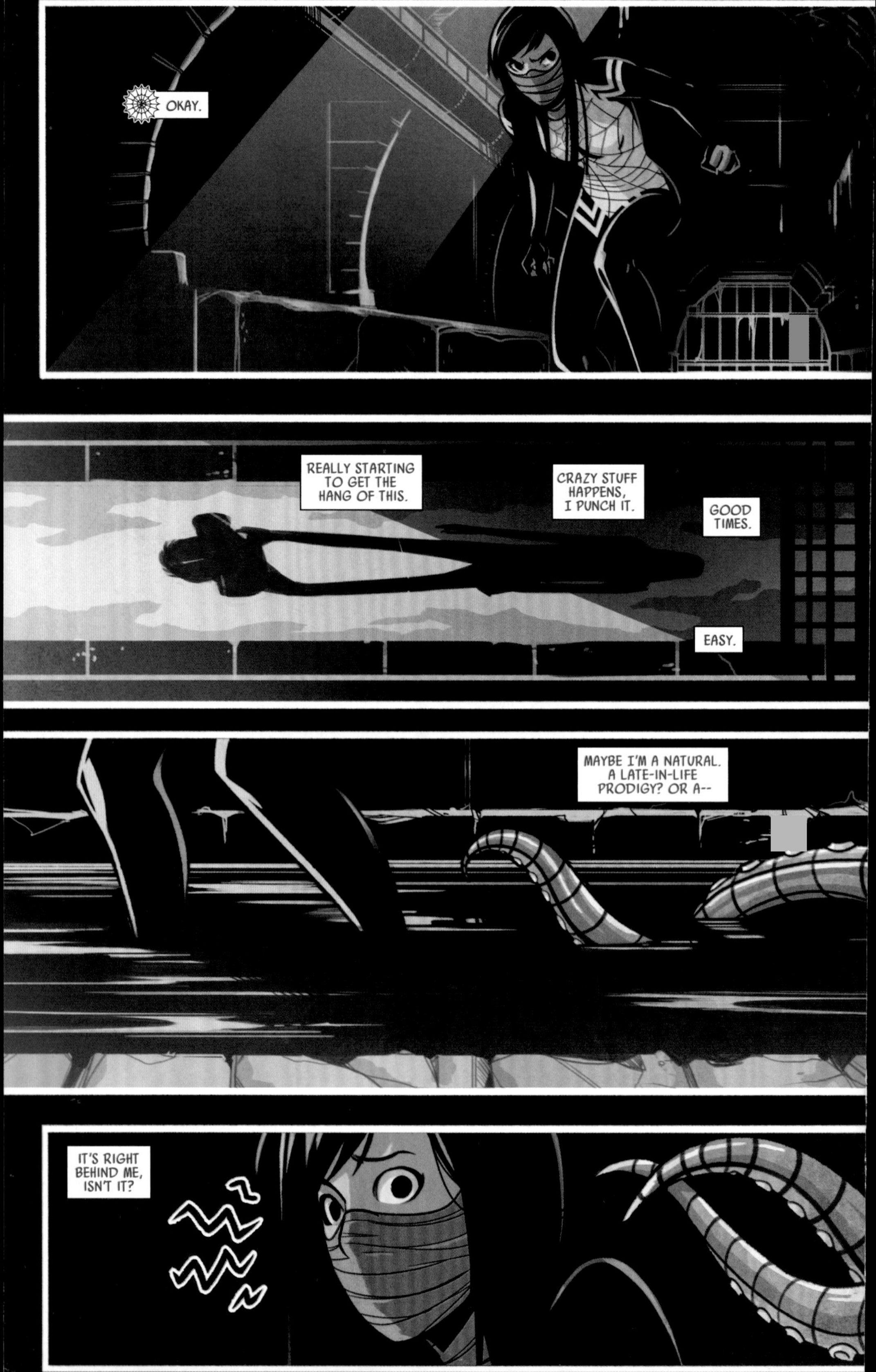
OKAY.
REALLY STARTING TO GET THE HANG OF THIS.
CRAZY STUFF HAPPENS, I PUNCH IT.
GOOD TIMES.
EASY.
MAYBE I'M A NATURAL. A LATE-IN-LIFE PRODIGY? OR A--
IT'S RIGHT BEHIND ME, ISN'T IT?

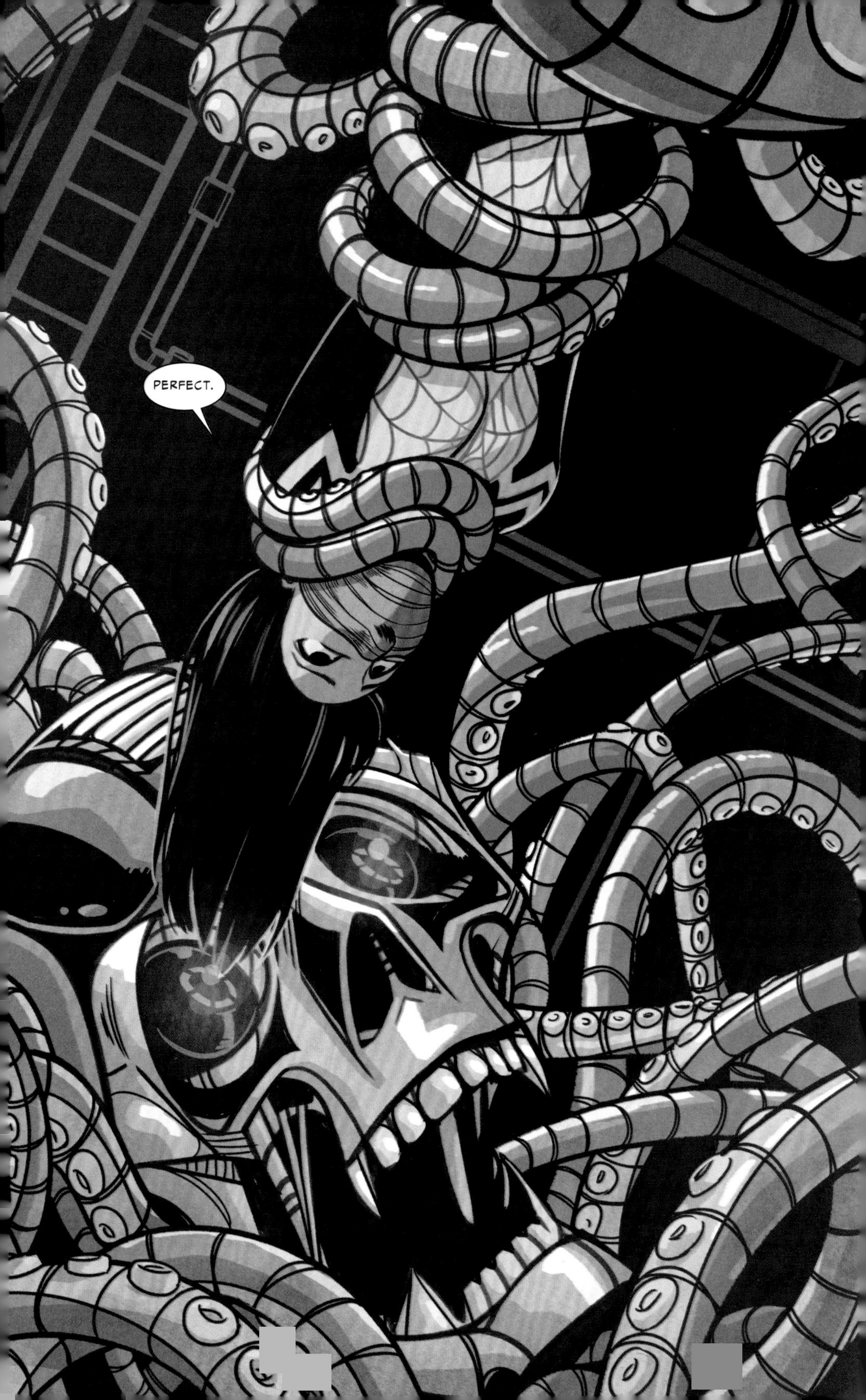
PERFECT.

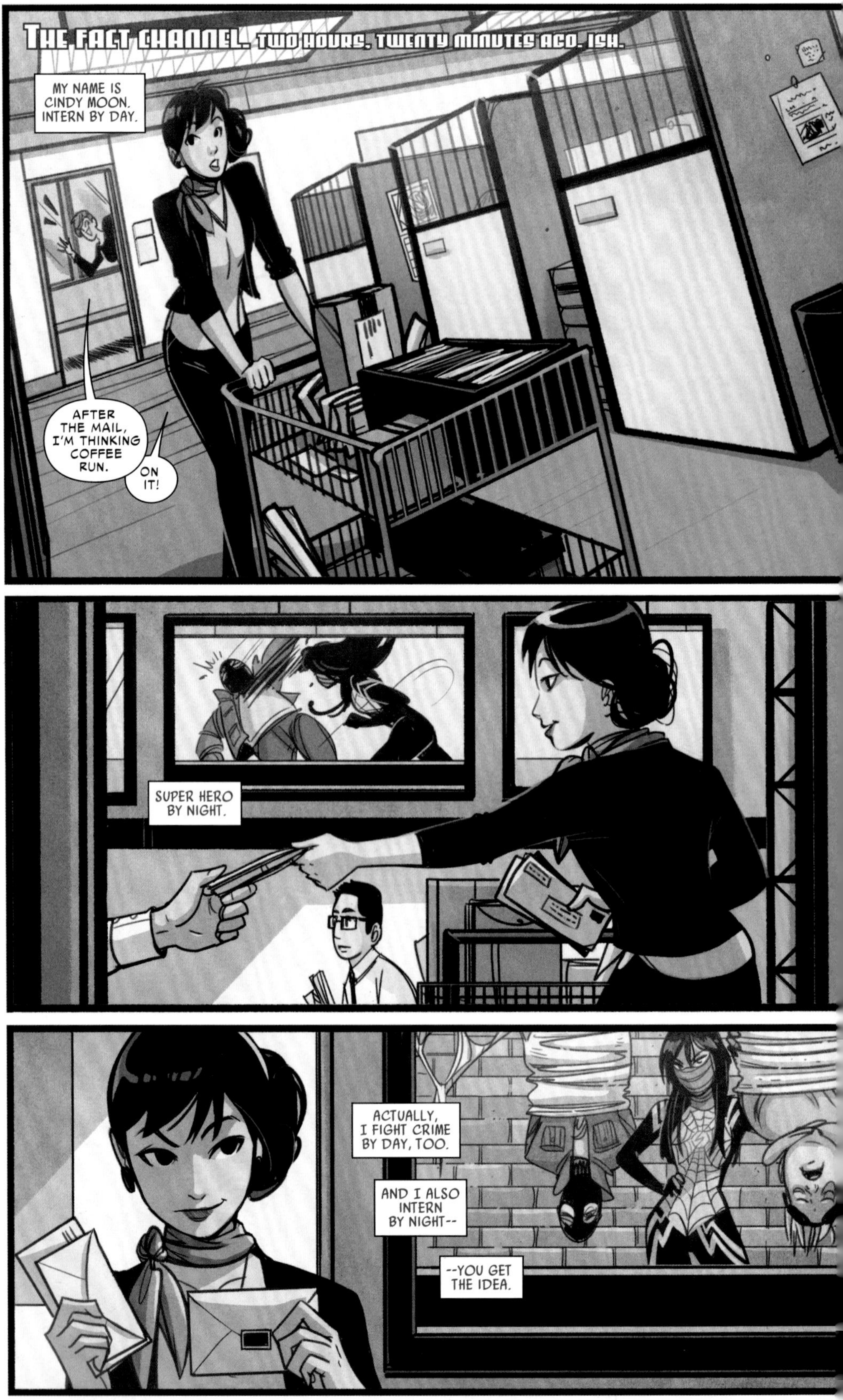
THE FACT CHANNEL. TWO HOURS, TWENTY MINUTES AGO. ISH.
MY NAME IS CINDY MOON. INTERN BY DAY.
AFTER THE MAIL, I'M THINKING COFFEE RUN.
ON IT!
SUPER HERO BY NIGHT.
ACTUALLY, I FIGHT CRIME BY DAY, TOO.
AND I ALSO INTERN BY NIGHT--
--YOU GET THE IDEA.

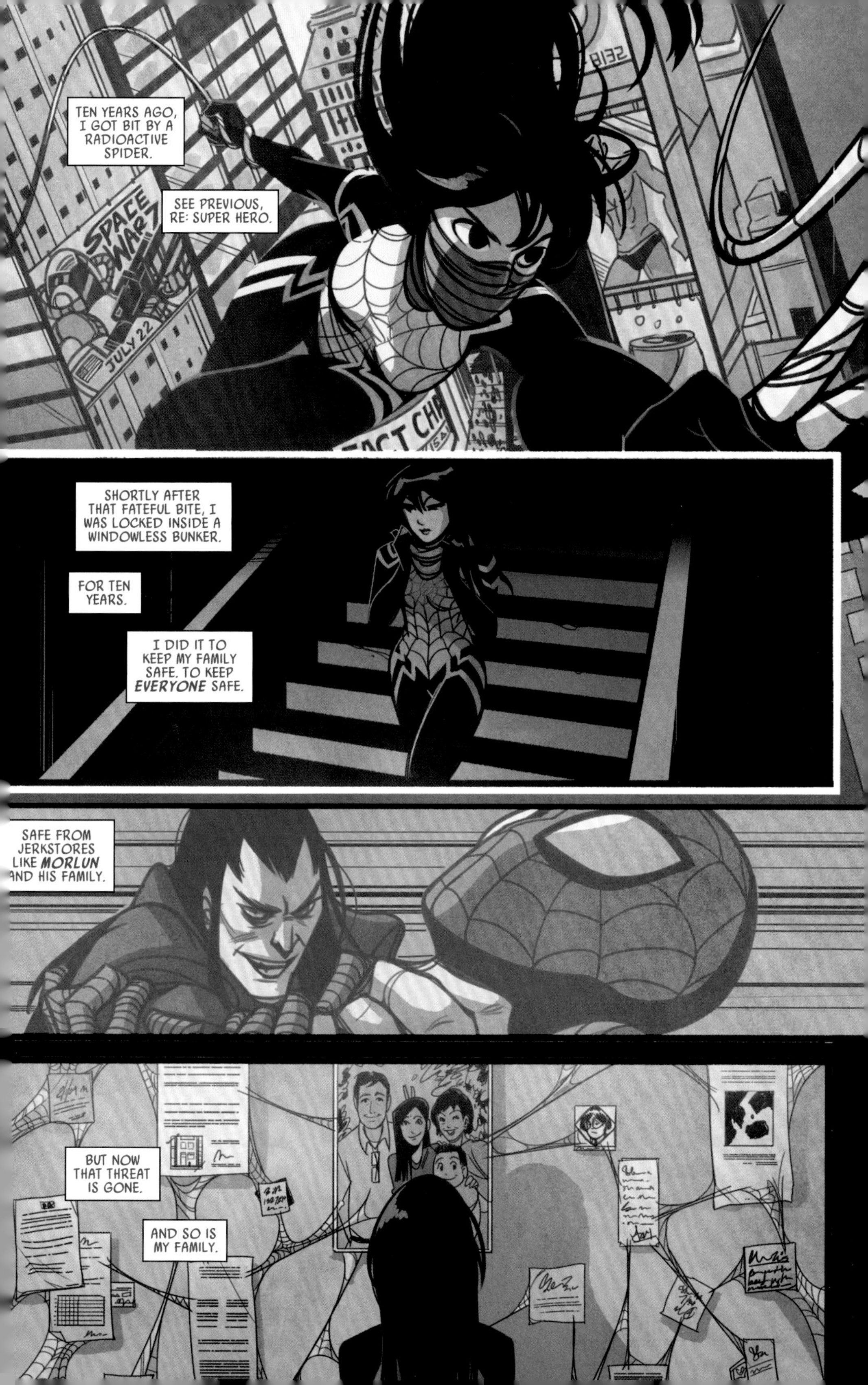
TEN YEARS AGO, I GOT BIT BY A RADIOACTIVE SPIDER.
SEE PREVIOUS, RE: SUPER HERO.
SPACE WAR 7
JULY 22
SHORTLY AFTER THAT FATEFUL BITE, I WAS LOCKED INSIDE A WINDOWLESS BUNKER.
FOR TEN YEARS.
I DID IT TO KEEP MY FAMILY SAFE. TO KEEP EVERYONE SAFE.
SAFE FROM JERKSTORES LIKE MORLUN AND HIS FAMILY.
BUT NOW THAT THREAT IS GONE.
AND SO IS MY FAMILY.

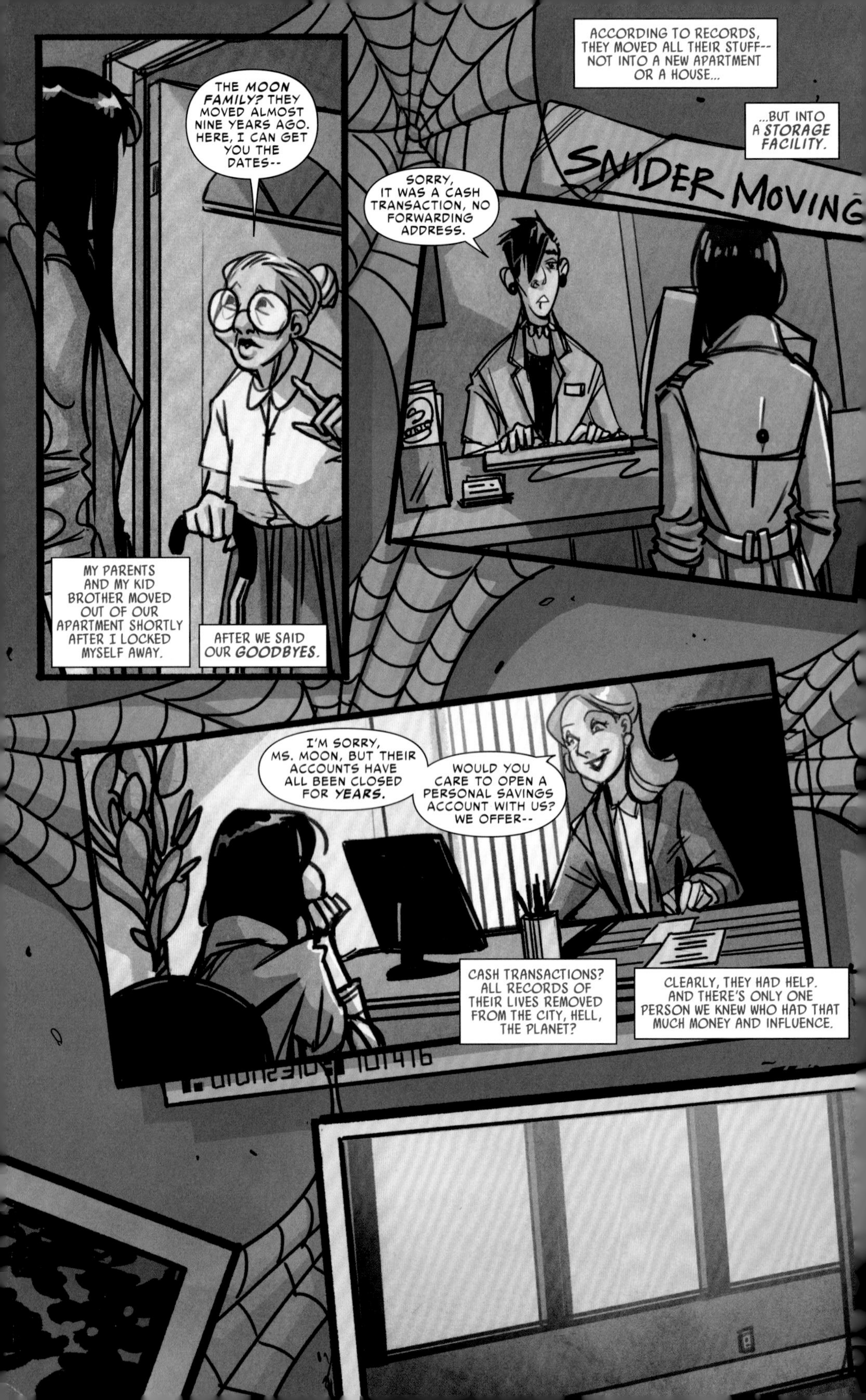

THE MOON FAMILY? THEY MOVED ALMOST NINE YEARS AGO. HERE, I CAN GET YOU THE DATES--
MY PARENTS AND MY KID BROTHER MOVED OUT OF OUR APARTMENT SHORTLY AFTER I LOCKED MYSELF AWAY.
AFTER WE SAID OUR GOODBYES.
ACCORDING TO RECORDS, THEY MOVED ALL THEIR STUFF-- NOT INTO A NEW APARTMENT OR A HOUSE...
...BUT INTO A STORAGE FACILITY.
SNIDER MOVING
SORRY, IT WAS A CASH TRANSACTION, NO FORWARDING ADDRESS.
I'M SORRY, MS. MOON, BUT THEIR ACCOUNTS HAVE ALL BEEN CLOSED FOR YEARS.
WOULD YOU CARE TO OPEN A PERSONAL SAVINGS ACCOUNT WITH US? WE OFFER--
CASH TRANSACTIONS? ALL RECORDS OF THEIR LIVES REMOVED FROM THE CITY, HELL, THE PLANET?
CLEARLY, THEY HAD HELP. AND THERE'S ONLY ONE PERSON WE KNEW WHO HAD THAT MUCH MONEY AND INFLUENCE.

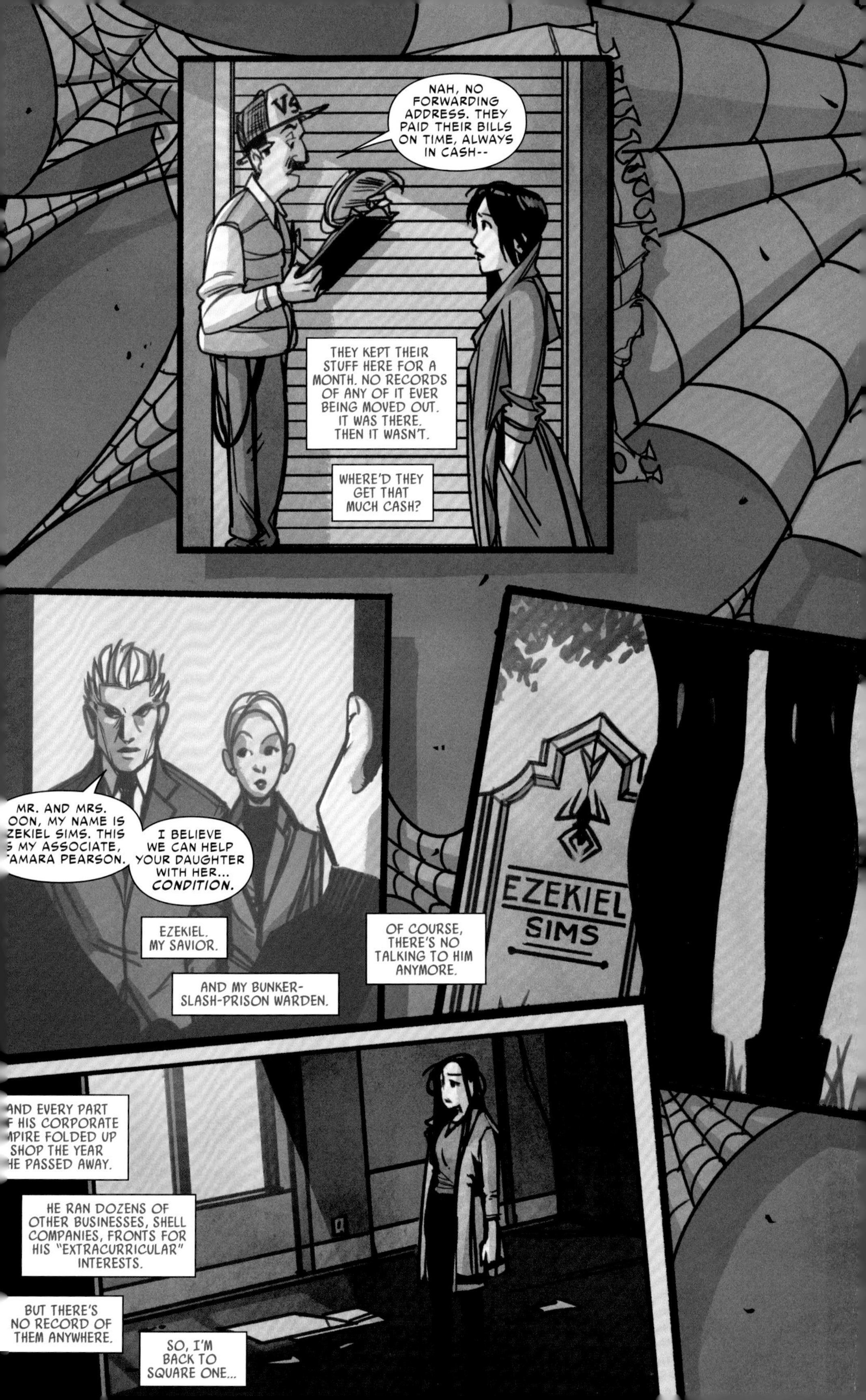
NAH, NO FORWARDING ADDRESS. THEY PAID THEIR BILLS ON TIME, ALWAYS IN CASH--
THEY KEPT THEIR STUFF HERE FOR A MONTH. NO RECORDS OF ANY OF IT EVER BEING MOVED OUT. IT WAS THERE. THEN IT WASN'T.
WHERE'D THEY GET THAT MUCH CASH?
MR. AND MRS. OON, MY NAME IS ZEKIEL SIMS. THIS S MY ASSOCIATE, TAMARA PEARSON.
I BELIEVE WE CAN HELP YOUR DAUGHTER WITH HER... CONDITION.
EZEKIEL. MY SAVIOR.
AND MY BUNKER-SLASH-PRISON WARDEN.
EZEKIEL SIMS
OF COURSE, THERE'S NO TALKING TO HIM ANYMORE.
AND EVERY PART F HIS CORPORATE MPIRE FOLDED UP SHOP THE YEAR HE PASSED AWAY.
HE RAN DOZENS OF OTHER BUSINESSES, SHELL COMPANIES, FRONTS FOR HIS "EXTRACURRICULAR" INTERESTS.
BUT THERE'S NO RECORD OF THEM ANYWHERE.
SO, I'M BACK TO SQUARE ONE...

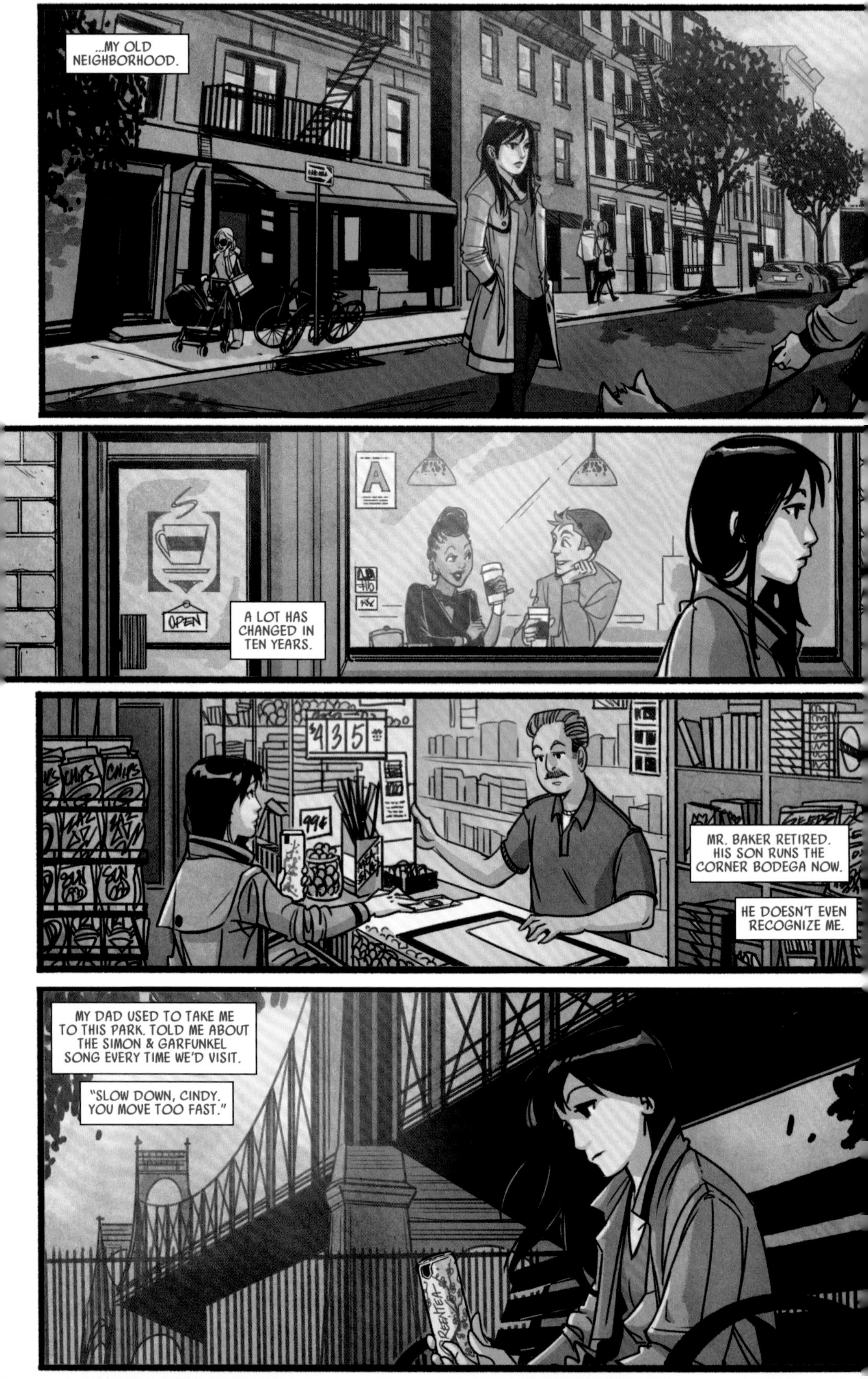
...MY OLD NEIGHBORHOOD.
A LOT HAS CHANGED IN TEN YEARS.
MR. BAKER RETIRED. HIS SON RUNS THE CORNER BODEGA NOW.
HE DOESN'T EVEN RECOGNIZE ME.
MY DAD USED TO TAKE ME TO THIS PARK. TOLD ME ABOUT THE SIMON & GARFUNKEL SONG EVERY TIME WE'D VISIT.
"SLOW DOWN, CINDY. YOU MOVE TOO FAST."

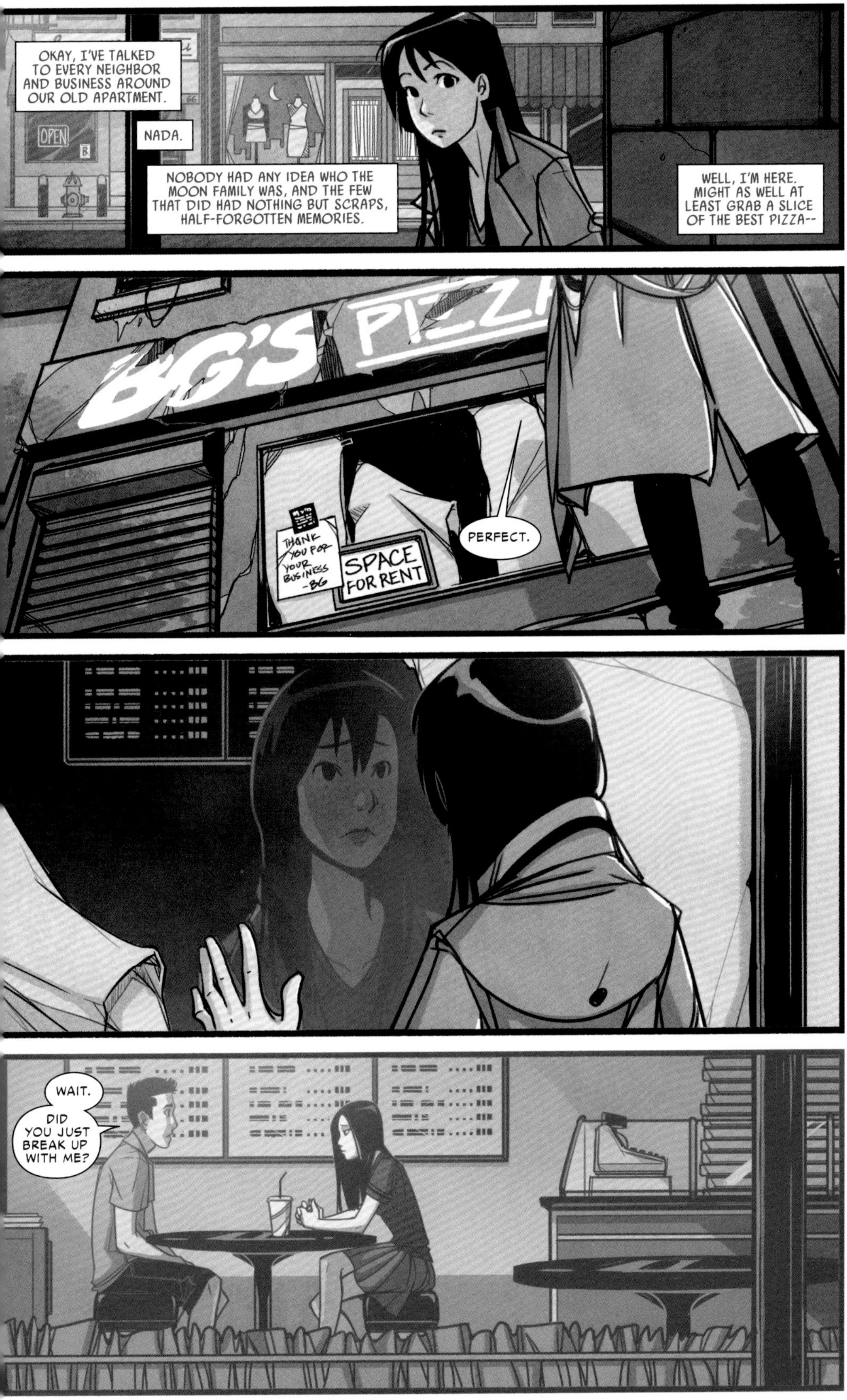
OKAY, I'VE TALKED TO EVERY NEIGHBOR AND BUSINESS AROUND OUR OLD APARTMENT.
NADA.
NOBODY HAD ANY IDEA WHO THE MOON FAMILY WAS, AND THE FEW THAT DID HAD NOTHING BUT SCRAPS, HALF-FORGOTTEN MEMORIES.
WELL, I'M HERE. MIGHT AS WELL AT LEAST GRAB A SLICE OF THE BEST PIZZA--
BG'S PIZZ
THANK YOU FOR YOUR BUSINESS -BG
SPACE FOR RENT
PERFECT.
WAIT.
DID YOU JUST BREAK UP WITH ME?

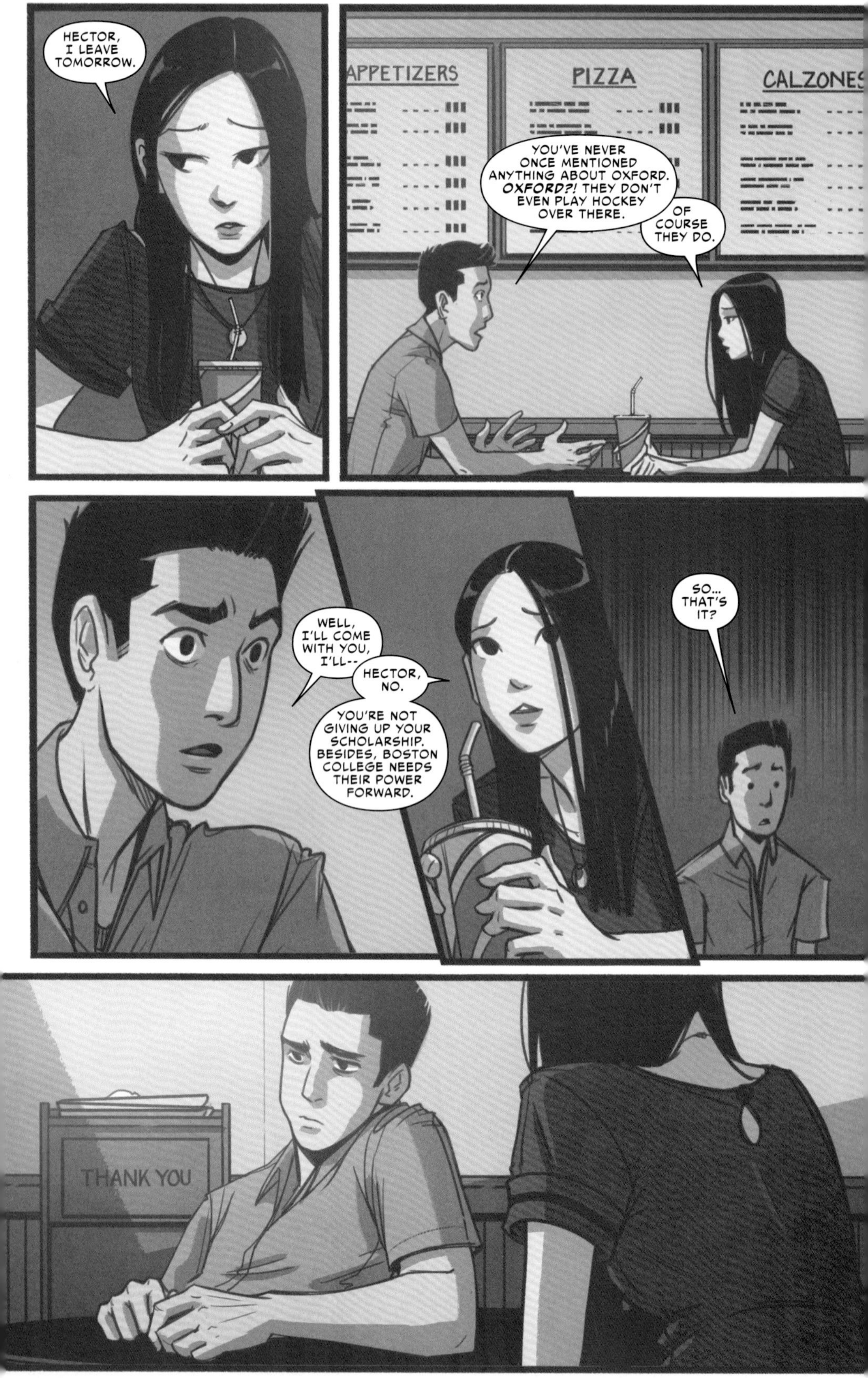
HECTOR, I LEAVE TOMORROW.
APPETIZERS
PIZZA
CALZONES
YOU'VE NEVER ONCE MENTIONED ANYTHING ABOUT OXFORD. *OXFORD?!* THEY DON'T EVEN PLAY HOCKEY OVER THERE.
OF COURSE THEY DO.
WELL, I'LL COME WITH YOU, I'LL--
HECTOR, NO.
YOU'RE NOT GIVING UP YOUR SCHOLARSHIP. BESIDES, BOSTON COLLEGE NEEDS THEIR POWER FORWARD.
SO... THAT'S IT?
THANK YOU

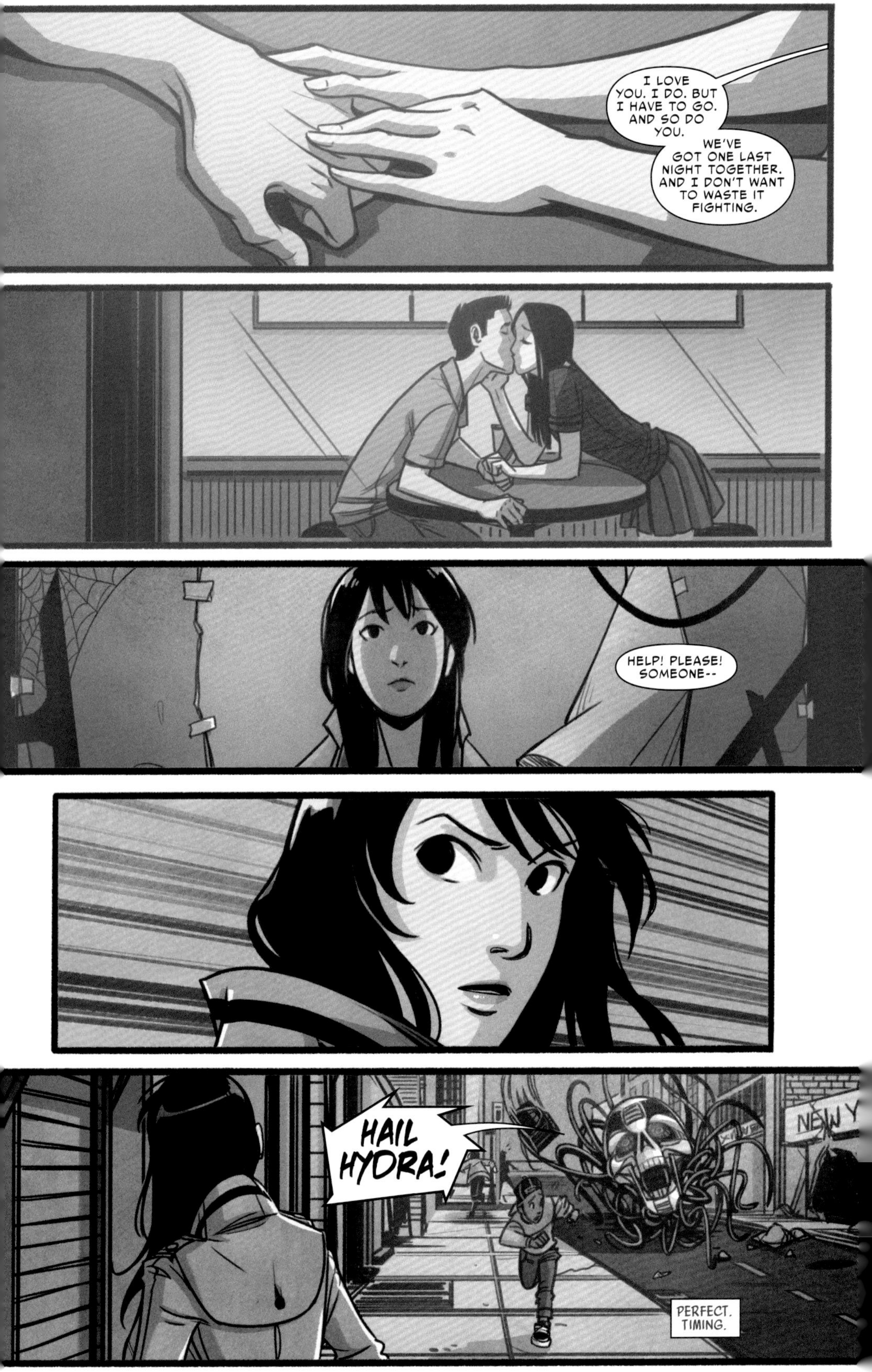
I LOVE YOU. I DO. BUT I HAVE TO GO. AND SO DO YOU.
WE'VE GOT ONE LAST NIGHT TOGETHER. AND I DON'T WANT TO WASTE IT FIGHTING.
HELP! PLEASE! SOMEONE--
HAIL HYDRA!
NEW Y
PERFECT. TIMING.

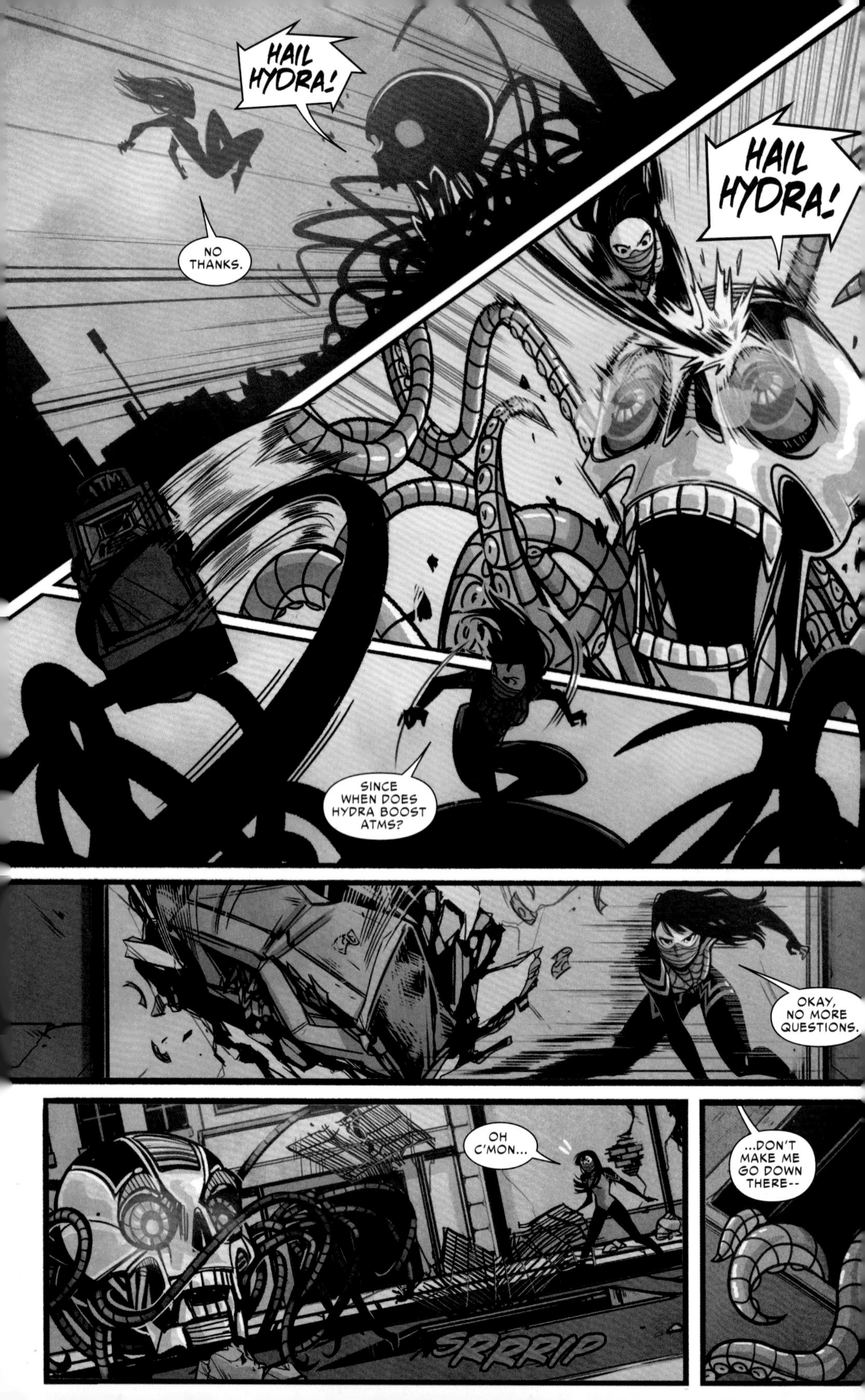
HAIL HYDRA!
NO THANKS.
HAIL HYDRA!
SINCE WHEN DOES HYDRA BOOST ATMS?
ATM
OKAY, NO MORE QUESTIONS.
OH C'MON...
SRRRIP
...DON'T MAKE ME GO DOWN THERE--

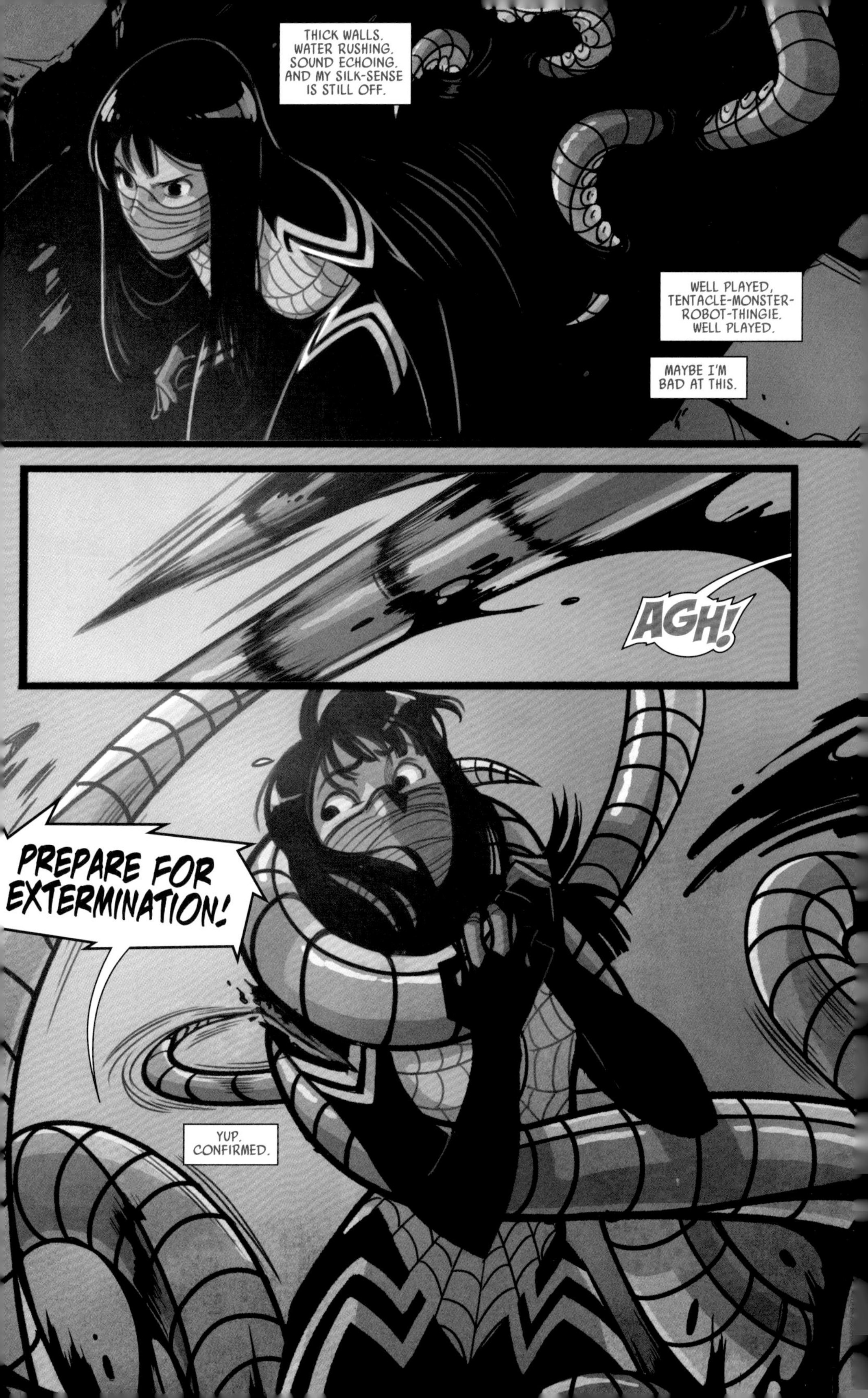
THICK WALLS. WATER RUSHING. SOUND ECHOING. AND MY SILK-SENSE IS STILL OFF.
WELL PLAYED, TENTACLE-MONSTER-ROBOT-THINGIE. WELL PLAYED.
MAYBE I'M BAD AT THIS.
AGH!
PREPARE FOR EXTERMINATION!
YUP. CONFIRMED.

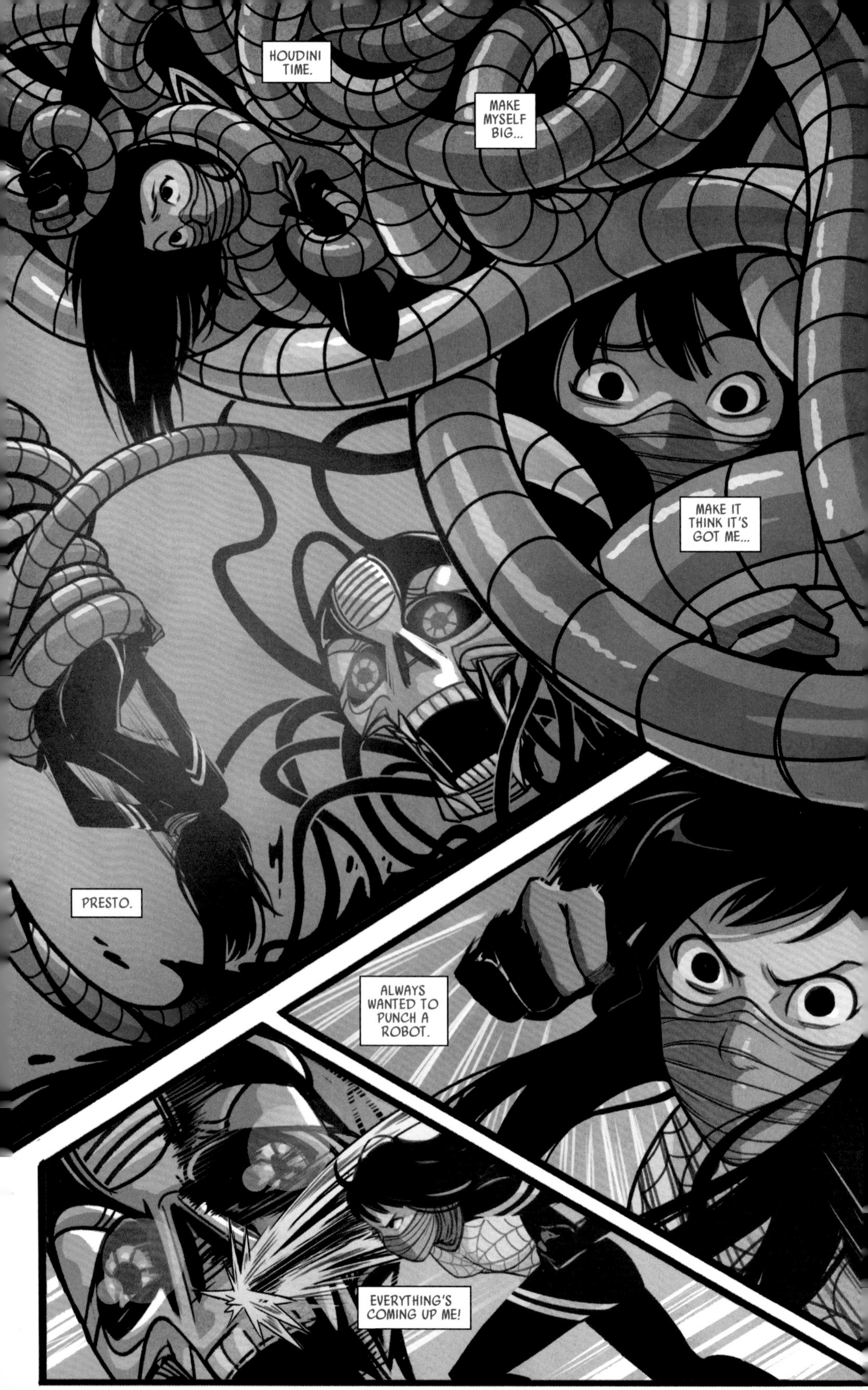
HOUDINI TIME.
MAKE MYSELF BIG...
MAKE IT THINK IT'S GOT ME...
PRESTO.
ALWAYS WANTED TO PUNCH A ROBOT.
EVERYTHING'S COMING UP ME!

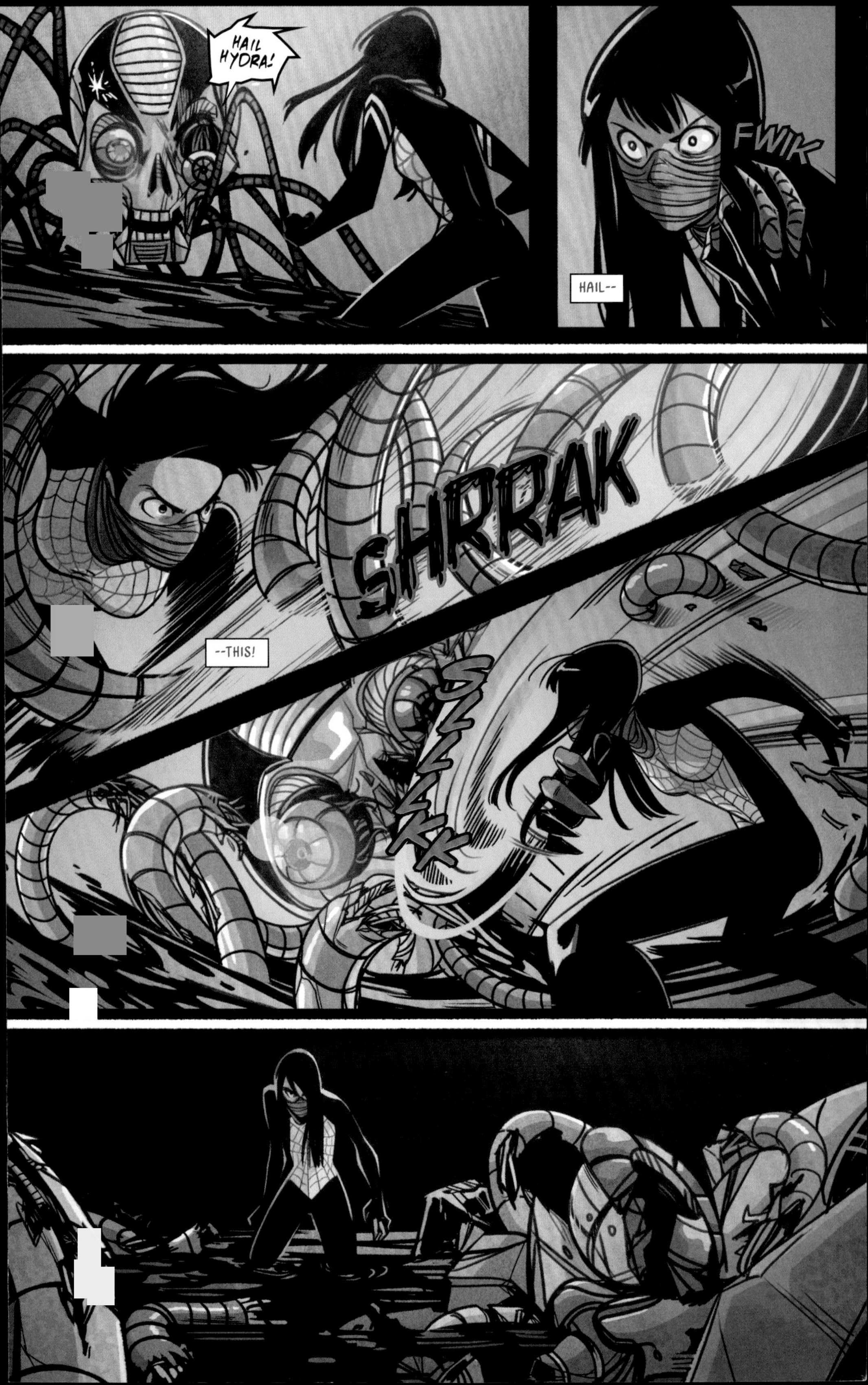
HAIL HYDRA!
HAIL--
FWIK
--THIS!
SHRRAK
SHLLKK

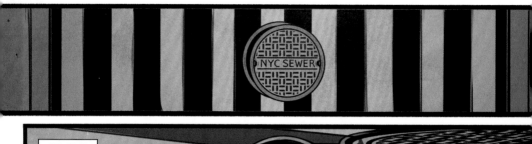

BAD NEWS, I'M COVERED IN...WELL... YEAH.

GOOD NEWS, NOBODY CAN RECOGNIZE MY SILK SUIT--

CINDY?

OH MY GOD. THAT VOICE.

I KNOW THAT VOICE.

CINDY-- I--HI.

HECTOR. UM...DID YOU JUST CLIMB OUT OF A--?

SEWER... YEAH. I'M A NINJA TURTLE.

KIDDING.

MOSTLY.

I WORK FOR FACT CHANNEL. WORKING ON A STORY.

I...I CAN'T BELIEVE YOU'RE BACK.

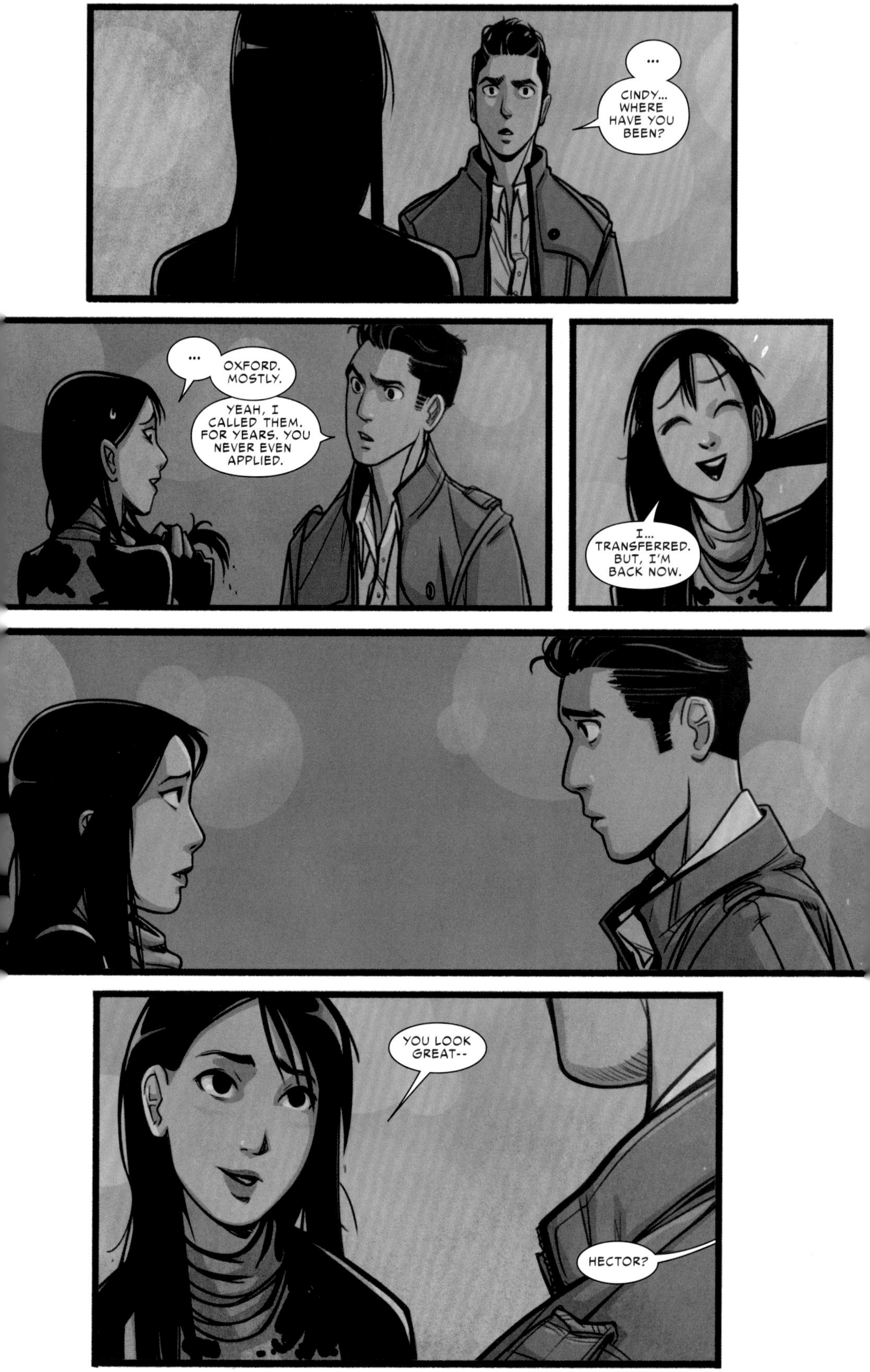
...
CINDY... WHERE HAVE YOU BEEN?
...
OXFORD. MOSTLY.
YEAH, I CALLED THEM. FOR YEARS. YOU NEVER EVEN APPLIED.
I... TRANSFERRED. BUT, I'M BACK NOW.
YOU LOOK GREAT--
HECTOR?

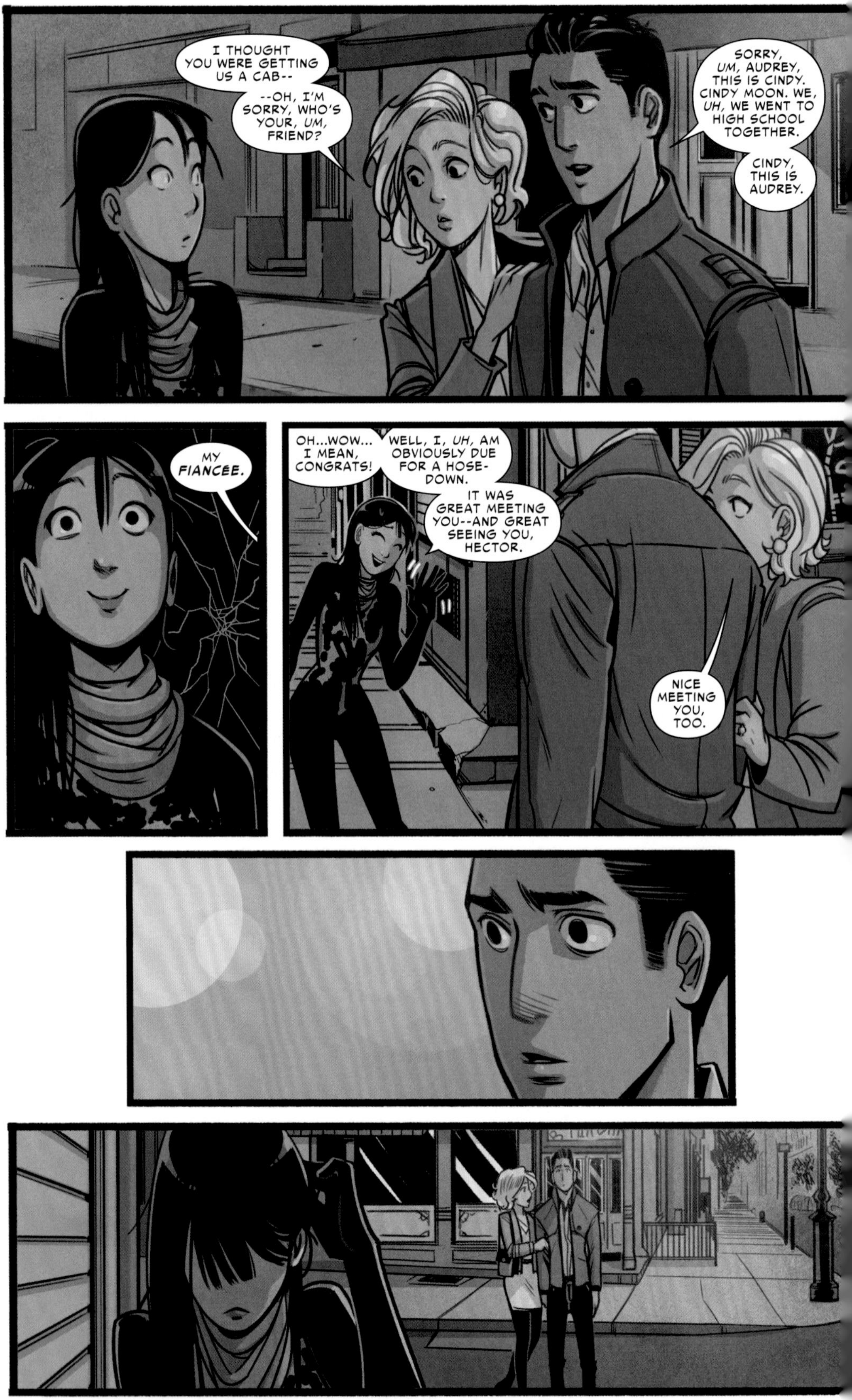
I THOUGHT YOU WERE GETTING US A CAB--
--OH, I'M SORRY, WHO'S YOUR, *UM*, FRIEND?
SORRY, *UM*, AUDREY, THIS IS CINDY. CINDY MOON. WE, *UH*, WE WENT TO HIGH SCHOOL TOGETHER.
CINDY, THIS IS AUDREY.
MY ***FIANCEE.***
OH...WOW... I MEAN, CONGRATS!
WELL, I, *UH*, AM OBVIOUSLY DUE FOR A HOSE-DOWN.
IT WAS GREAT MEETING YOU--AND GREAT SEEING YOU, HECTOR.
NICE MEETING YOU, TOO.

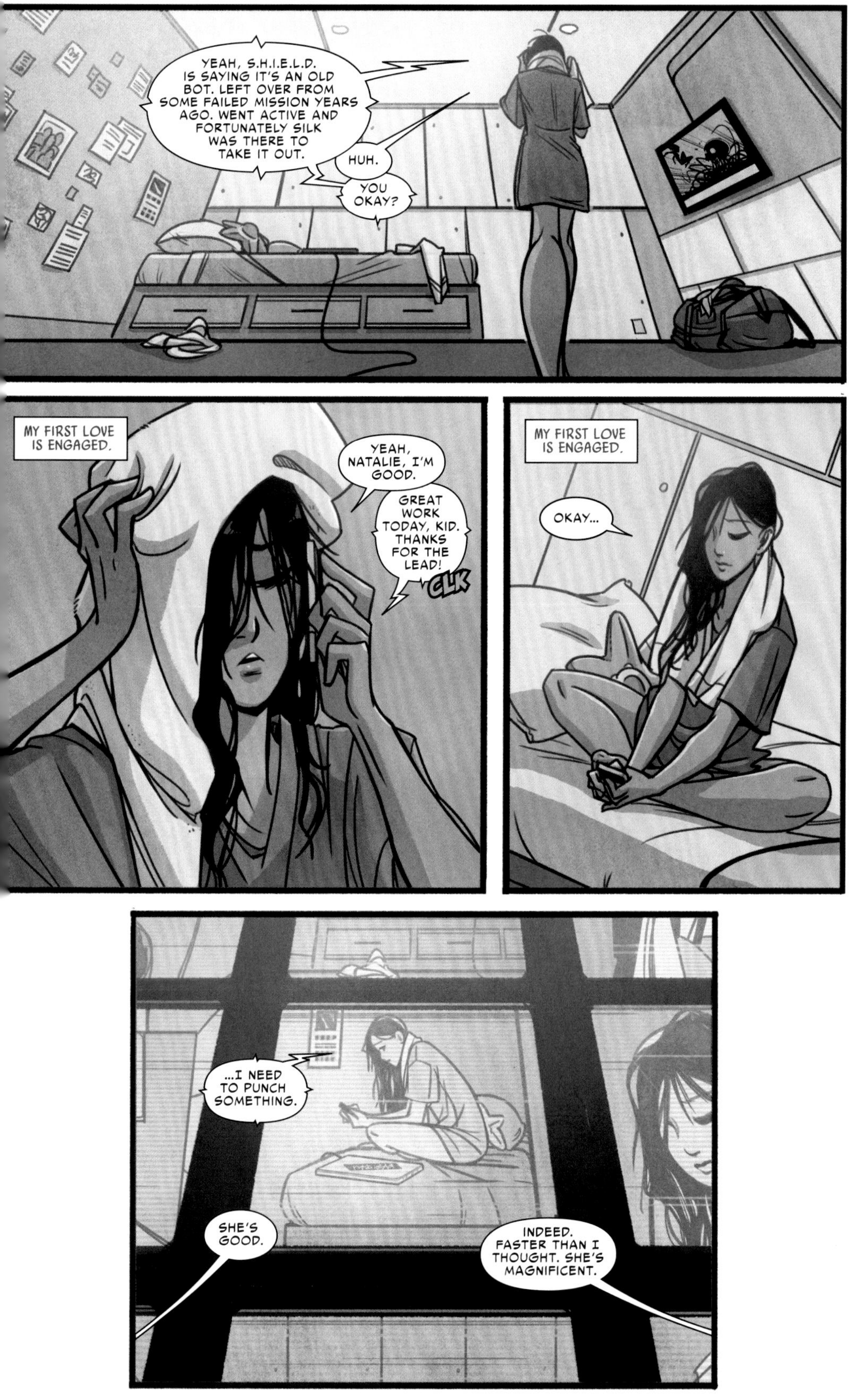
YEAH, S.H.I.E.L.D. IS SAYING IT'S AN OLD BOT. LEFT OVER FROM SOME FAILED MISSION YEARS AGO. WENT ACTIVE AND FORTUNATELY SILK WAS THERE TO TAKE IT OUT.
HUH.
YOU OKAY?
MY FIRST LOVE IS ENGAGED.
YEAH, NATALIE, I'M GOOD.
GREAT WORK TODAY, KID. THANKS FOR THE LEAD!
CLK
MY FIRST LOVE IS ENGAGED.
OKAY...
...I NEED TO PUNCH SOMETHING.
SHE'S GOOD.
INDEED. FASTER THAN I THOUGHT. SHE'S MAGNIFICENT.

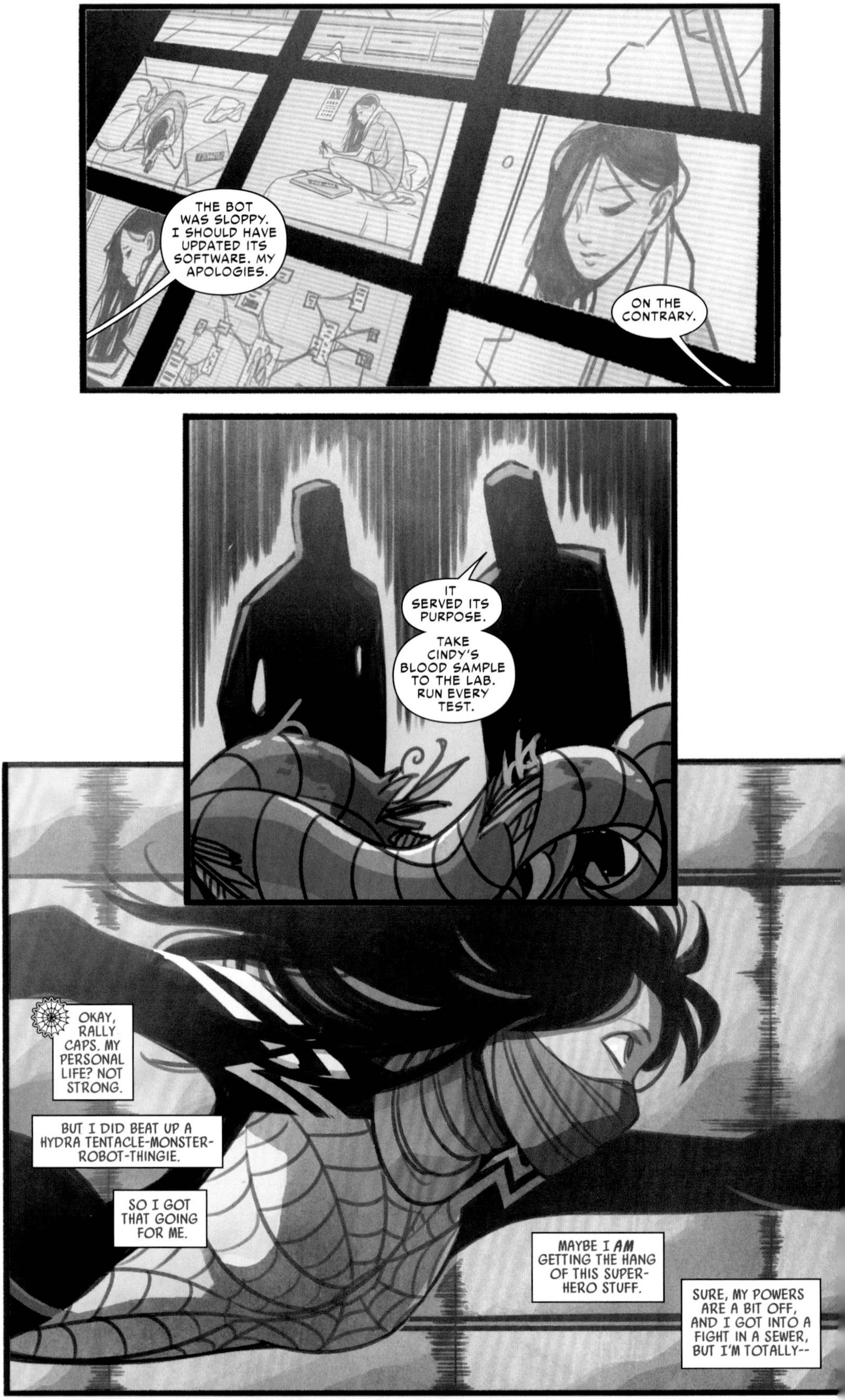
THE BOT WAS SLOPPY. I SHOULD HAVE UPDATED ITS SOFTWARE. MY APOLOGIES.
ON THE CONTRARY.
IT SERVED ITS PURPOSE.
TAKE CINDY'S BLOOD SAMPLE TO THE LAB. RUN EVERY TEST.
OKAY, RALLY CAPS. MY PERSONAL LIFE? NOT STRONG.
BUT I DID BEAT UP A HYDRA TENTACLE-MONSTER-ROBOT-THINGIE.
SO I GOT THAT GOING FOR ME.
MAYBE I AM GETTING THE HANG OF THIS SUPER-HERO STUFF.
SURE, MY POWERS ARE A BIT OFF, AND I GOT INTO A FIGHT IN A SEWER, BUT I'M TOTALLY--

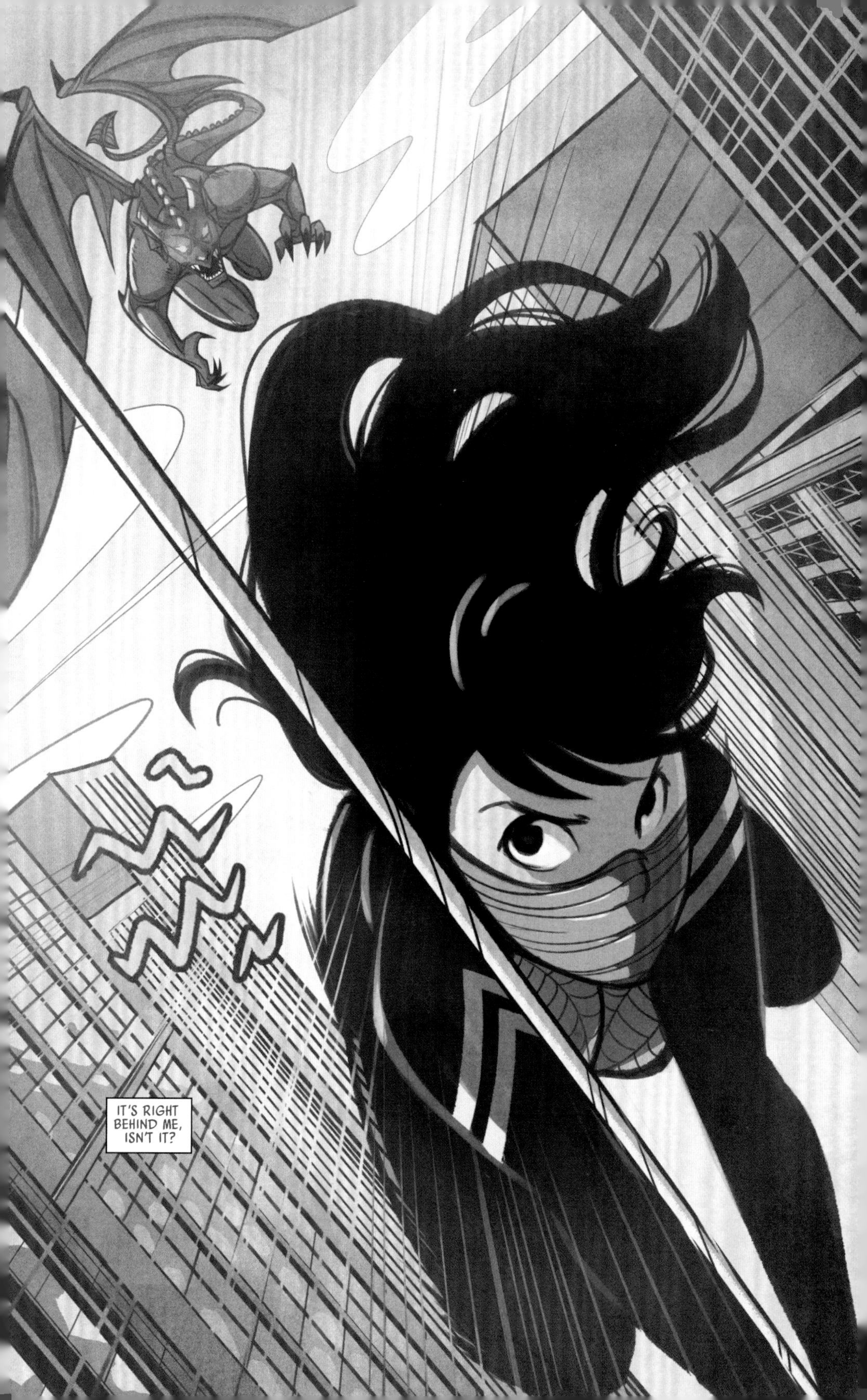
IT'S RIGHT BEHIND ME, ISN'T IT?

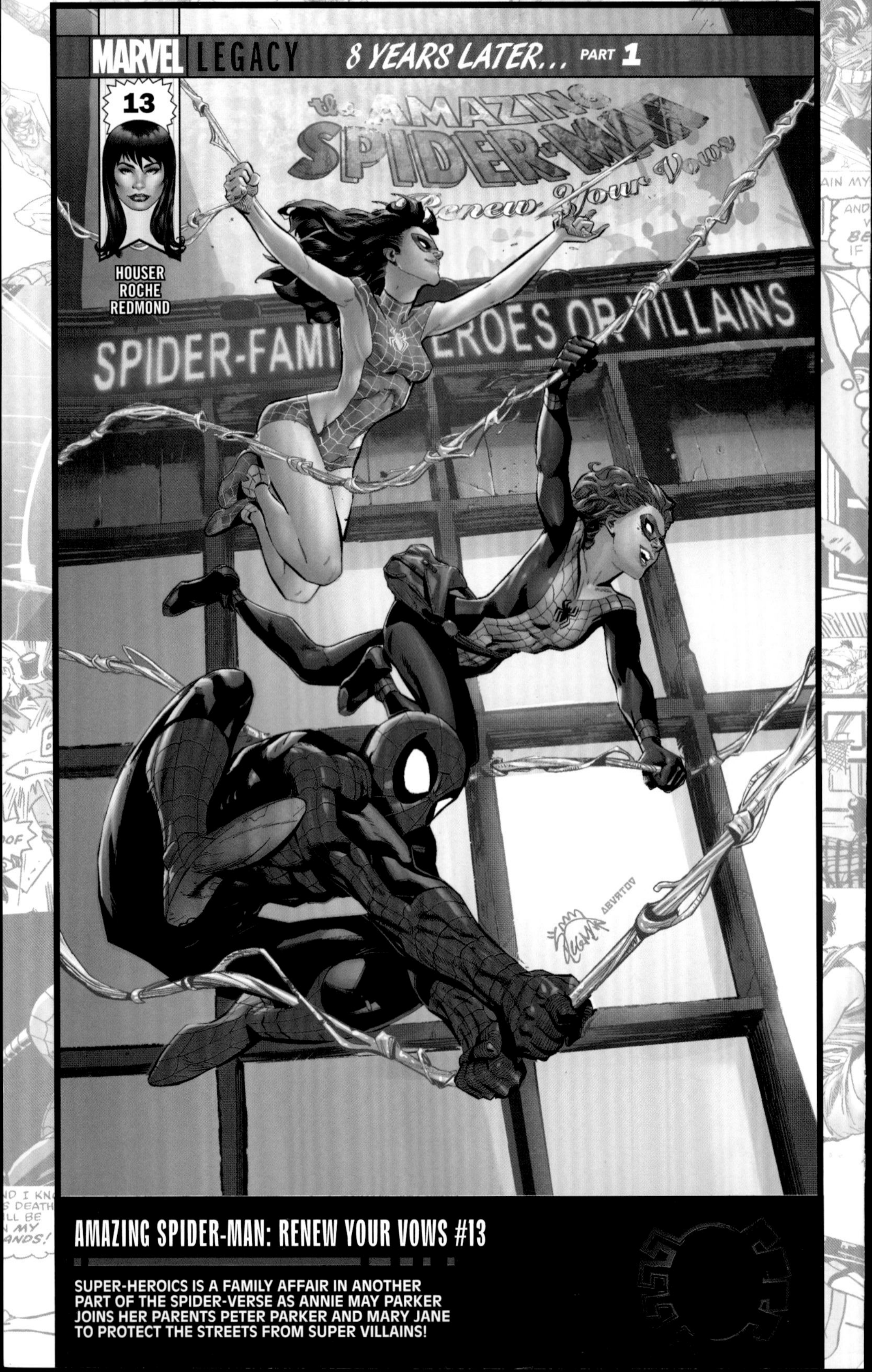
MARVEL LEGACY
8 YEARS LATER... PART 1
13
HOUSER
ROCHE
REDMOND
The AMAZING SPIDER-MAN
Renew Your Vows
SPIDER-FAMI EROES OR VILLAINS

AMAZING SPIDER-MAN: RENEW YOUR VOWS #13

SUPER-HEROICS IS A FAMILY AFFAIR IN ANOTHER PART OF THE SPIDER-VERSE AS ANNIE MAY PARKER JOINS HER PARENTS PETER PARKER AND MARY JANE TO PROTECT THE STREETS FROM SUPER VILLAINS!

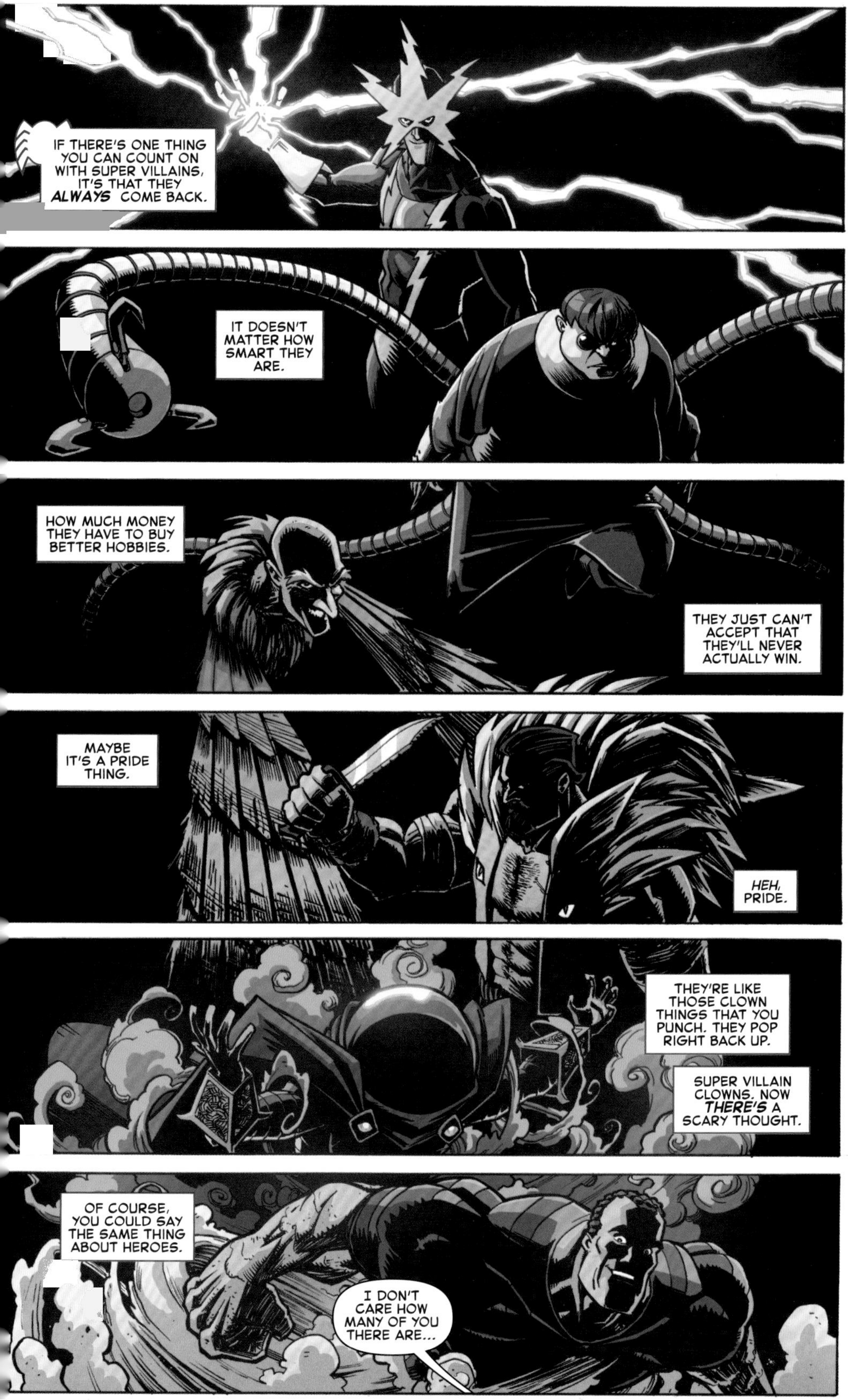
IF THERE'S ONE THING YOU CAN COUNT ON WITH SUPER VILLAINS, IT'S THAT THEY *ALWAYS* COME BACK.
IT DOESN'T MATTER HOW SMART THEY ARE.
HOW MUCH MONEY THEY HAVE TO BUY BETTER HOBBIES.
THEY JUST CAN'T ACCEPT THAT THEY'LL NEVER ACTUALLY WIN.
MAYBE IT'S A PRIDE THING.
HEH, PRIDE.
THEY'RE LIKE THOSE CLOWN THINGS THAT YOU PUNCH. THEY POP RIGHT BACK UP.
SUPER VILLAIN CLOWNS. NOW *THERE'S* A SCARY THOUGHT.
OF COURSE, YOU COULD SAY THE SAME THING ABOUT HEROES.
I DON'T CARE HOW MANY OF YOU THERE ARE...

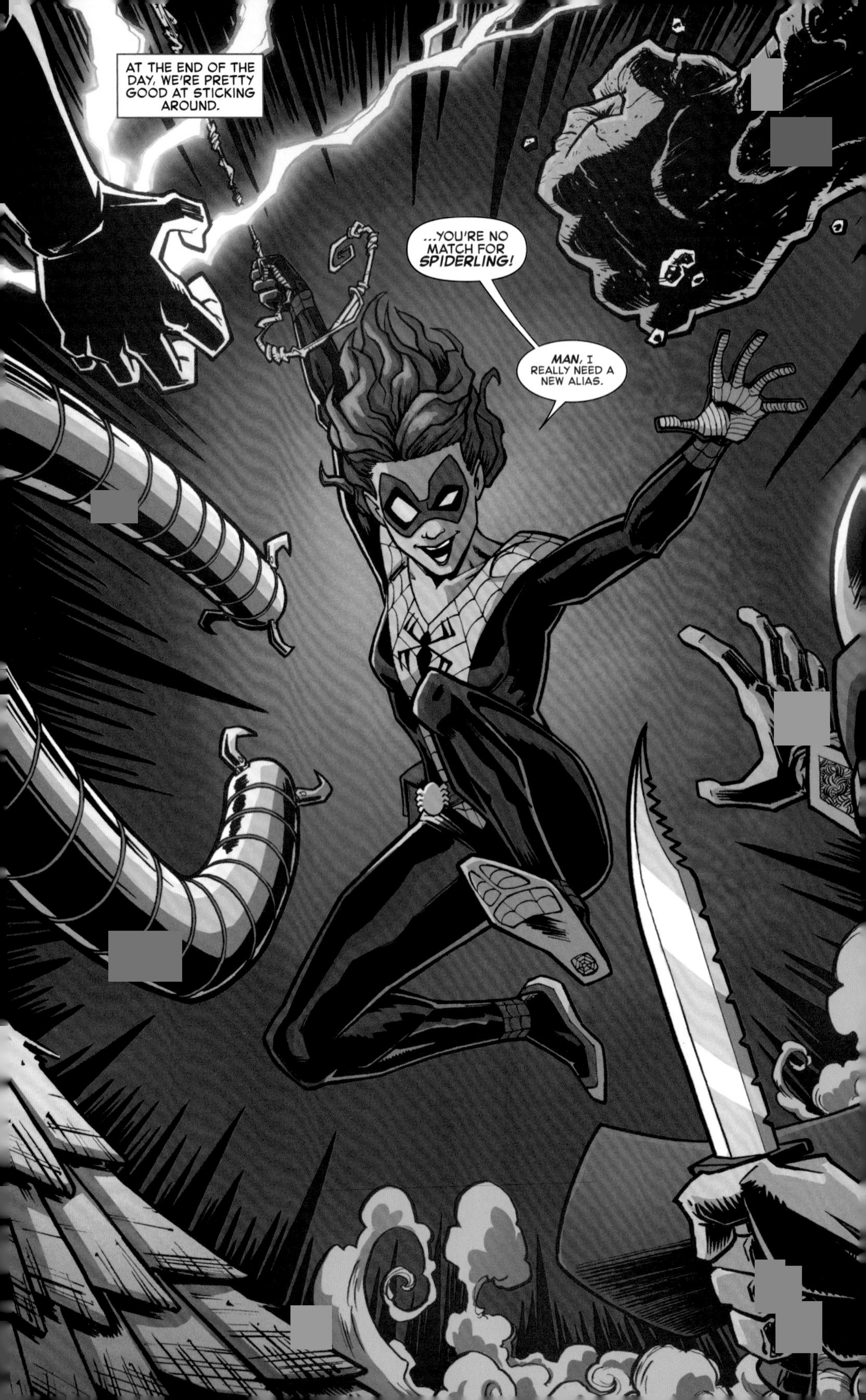
AT THE END OF THE DAY, WE'RE PRETTY GOOD AT STICKING AROUND.
...YOU'RE NO MATCH FOR SPIDERLING!
MAN, I REALLY NEED A NEW ALIAS.

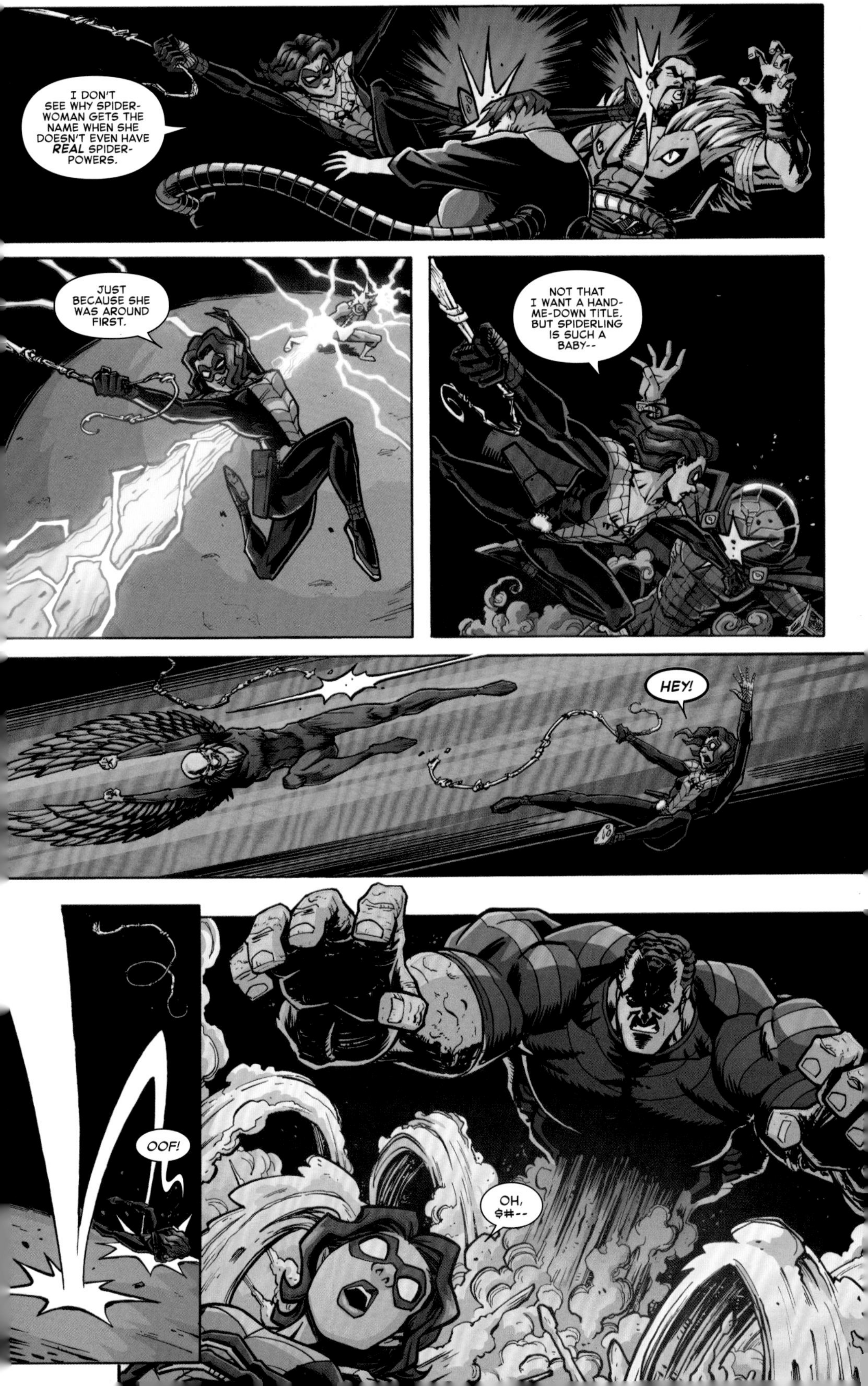
I DON'T SEE WHY SPIDER-WOMAN GETS THE NAME WHEN SHE DOESN'T EVEN HAVE *REAL* SPIDER-POWERS.
JUST BECAUSE SHE WAS AROUND FIRST.
NOT THAT I WANT A HAND-ME-DOWN TITLE. BUT SPIDERLING IS SUCH A BABY--
HEY!
OOF!
OH, $#--

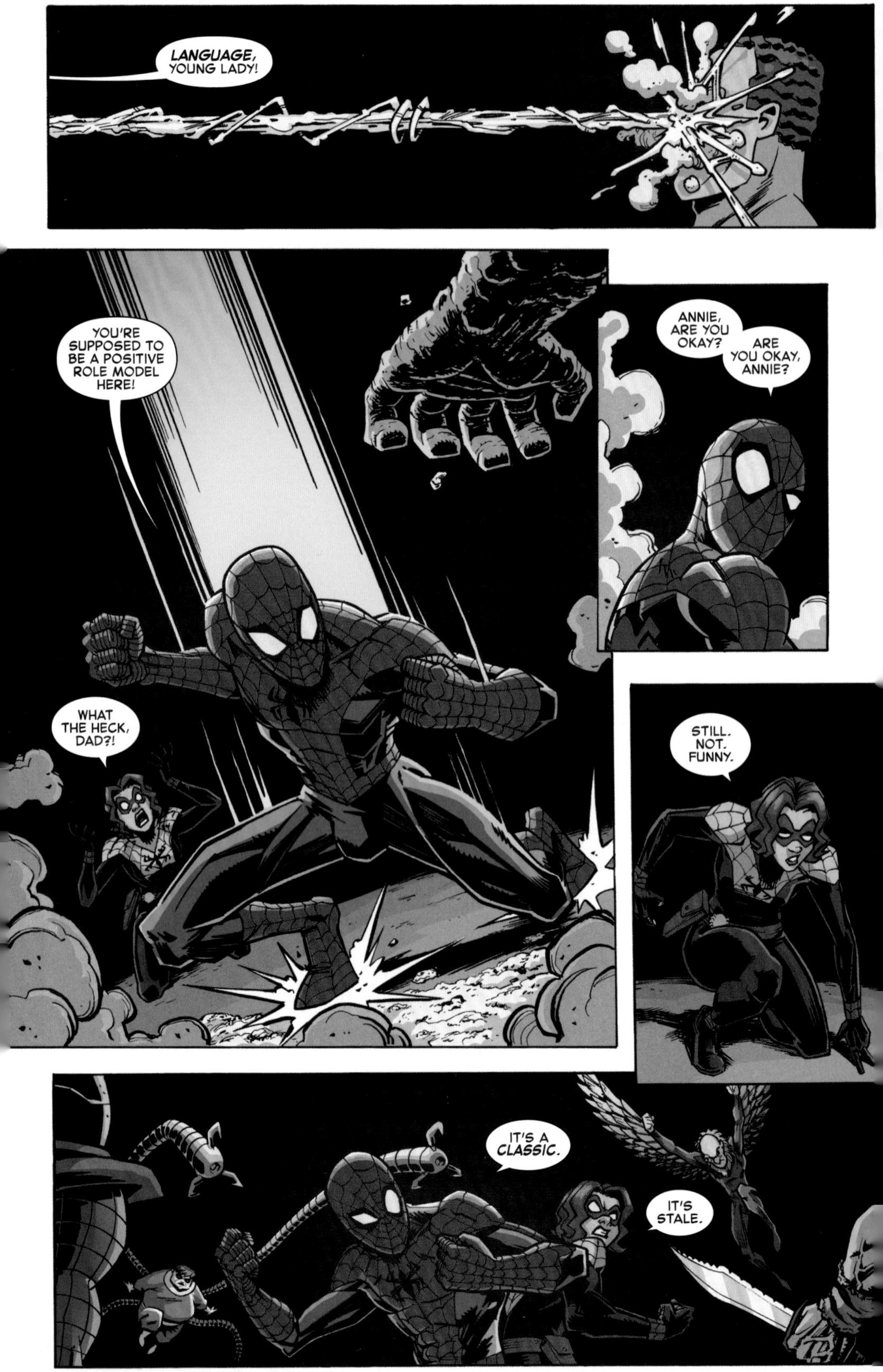
LANGUAGE, YOUNG LADY!
YOU'RE SUPPOSED TO BE A POSITIVE ROLE MODEL HERE!
WHAT THE HECK, DAD?!
ANNIE, ARE YOU OKAY?
ARE YOU OKAY, ANNIE?
STILL. NOT. FUNNY.
IT'S A CLASSIC.
IT'S STALE.

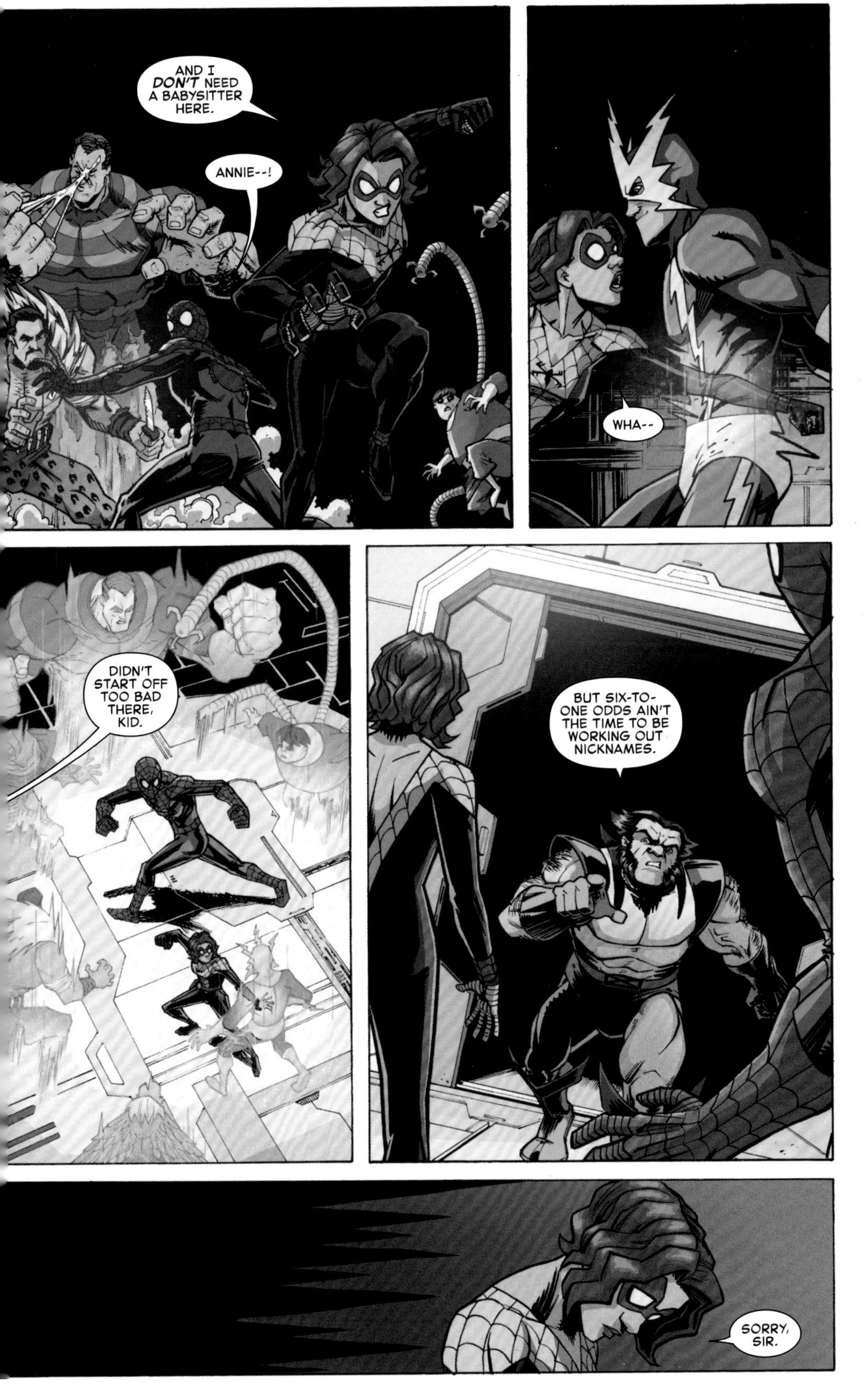
AND I DON'T NEED A BABYSITTER HERE.
ANNIE--!
WHA--
DIDN'T START OFF TOO BAD THERE, KID.
BUT SIX-TO-ONE ODDS AIN'T THE TIME TO BE WORKING OUT NICKNAMES.
SORRY, SIR.

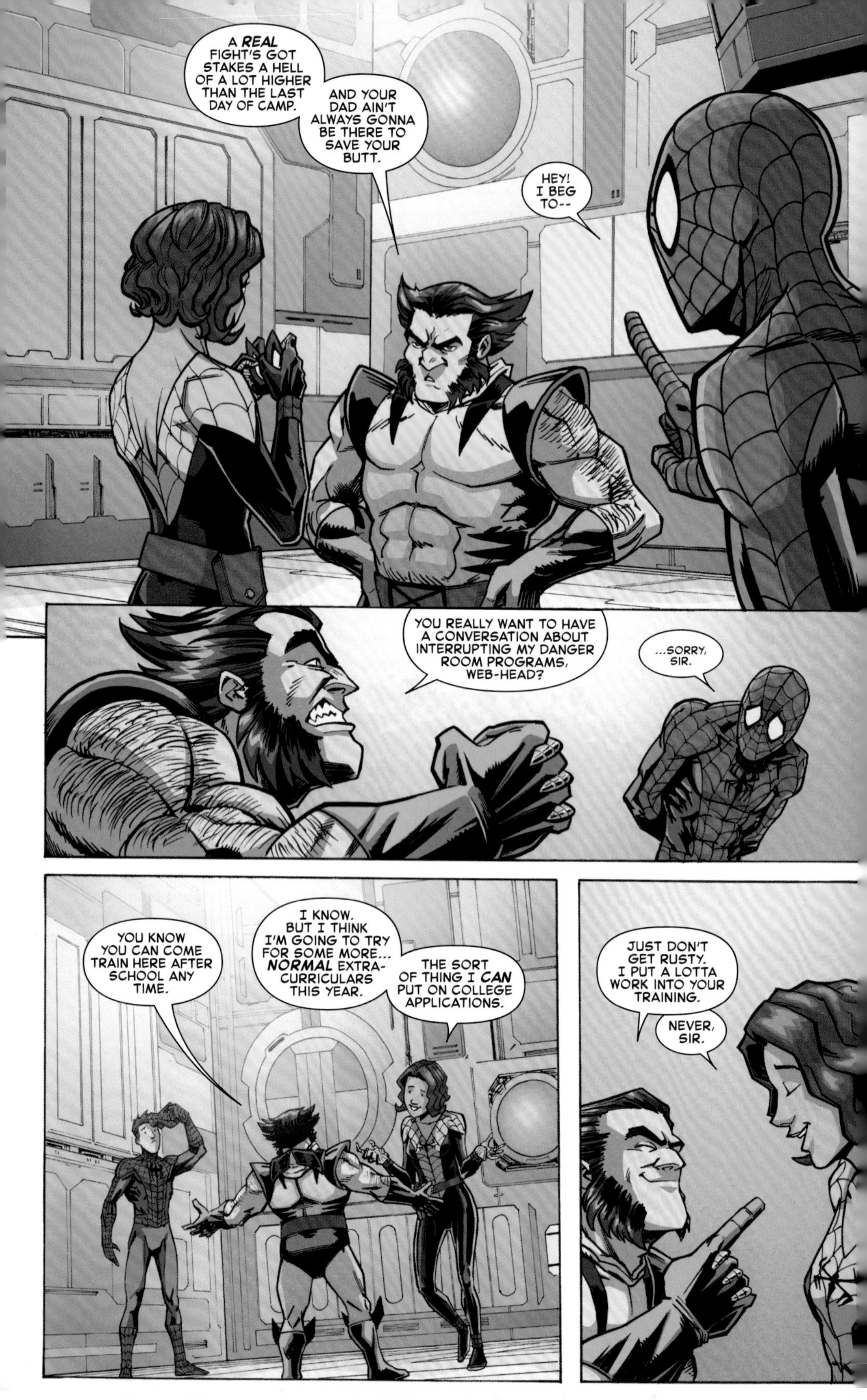

A REAL FIGHT'S GOT STAKES A HELL OF A LOT HIGHER THAN THE LAST DAY OF CAMP.
AND YOUR DAD AIN'T ALWAYS GONNA BE THERE TO SAVE YOUR BUTT.
HEY! I BEG TO--
YOU REALLY WANT TO HAVE A CONVERSATION ABOUT INTERRUPTING MY DANGER ROOM PROGRAMS, WEB-HEAD?
...SORRY, SIR.
YOU KNOW YOU CAN COME TRAIN HERE AFTER SCHOOL ANY TIME.
I KNOW. BUT I THINK I'M GOING TO TRY FOR SOME MORE... NORMAL EXTRA-CURRICULARS THIS YEAR.
THE SORT OF THING I CAN PUT ON COLLEGE APPLICATIONS.
JUST DON'T GET RUSTY. I PUT A LOTTA WORK INTO YOUR TRAINING.
NEVER, SIR.

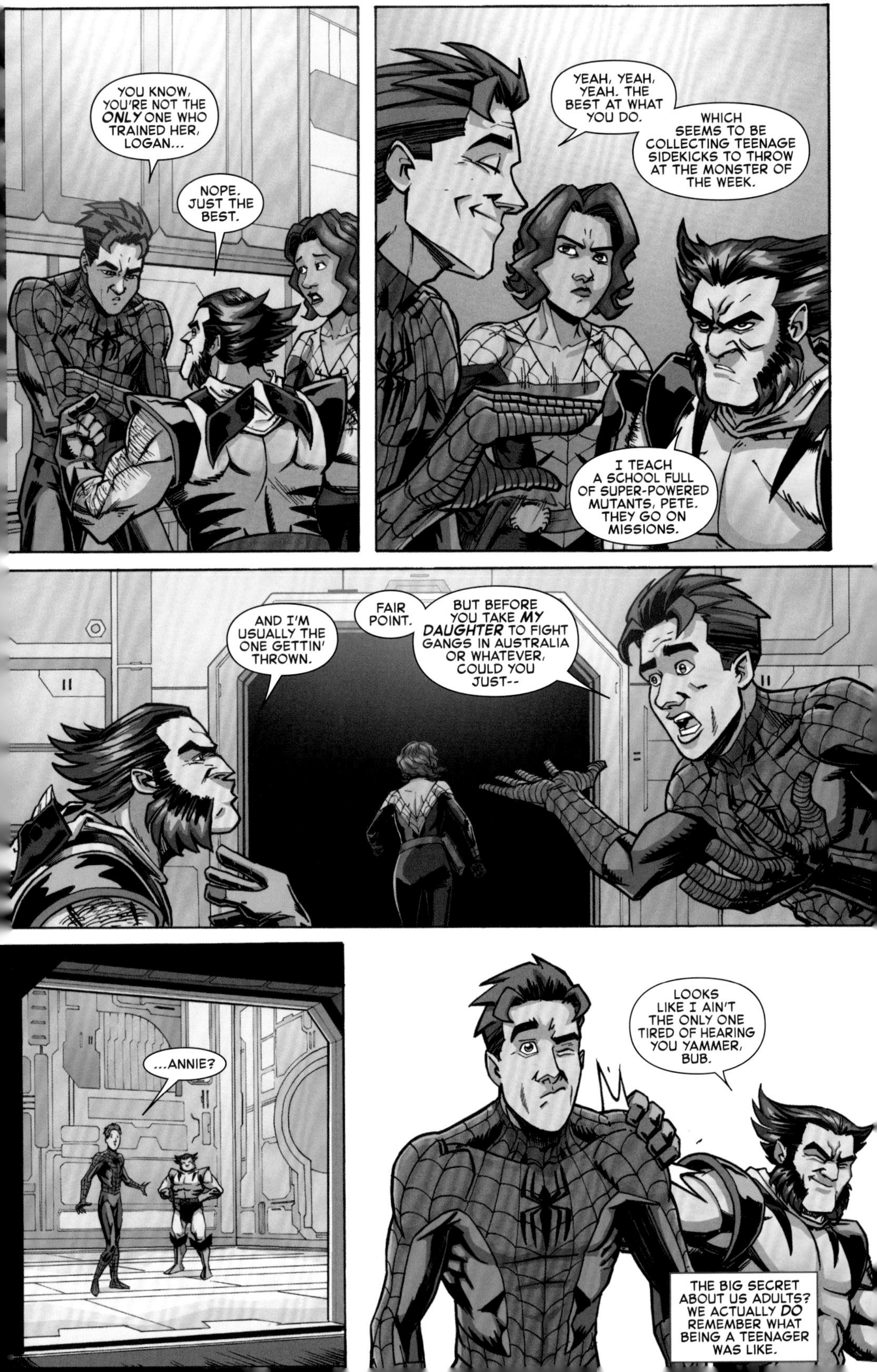

YOU KNOW, YOU'RE NOT THE ONLY ONE WHO TRAINED HER, LOGAN...
NOPE. JUST THE BEST.
YEAH, YEAH, YEAH. THE BEST AT WHAT YOU DO.
WHICH SEEMS TO BE COLLECTING TEENAGE SIDEKICKS TO THROW AT THE MONSTER OF THE WEEK.
I TEACH A SCHOOL FULL OF SUPER-POWERED MUTANTS, PETE. THEY GO ON MISSIONS.
AND I'M USUALLY THE ONE GETTIN' THROWN.
FAIR POINT.
BUT BEFORE YOU TAKE MY DAUGHTER TO FIGHT GANGS IN AUSTRALIA OR WHATEVER, COULD YOU JUST--
...ANNIE?
LOOKS LIKE I AIN'T THE ONLY ONE TIRED OF HEARING YOU YAMMER, BUB.
THE BIG SECRET ABOUT US ADULTS? WE ACTUALLY DO REMEMBER WHAT BEING A TEENAGER WAS LIKE.

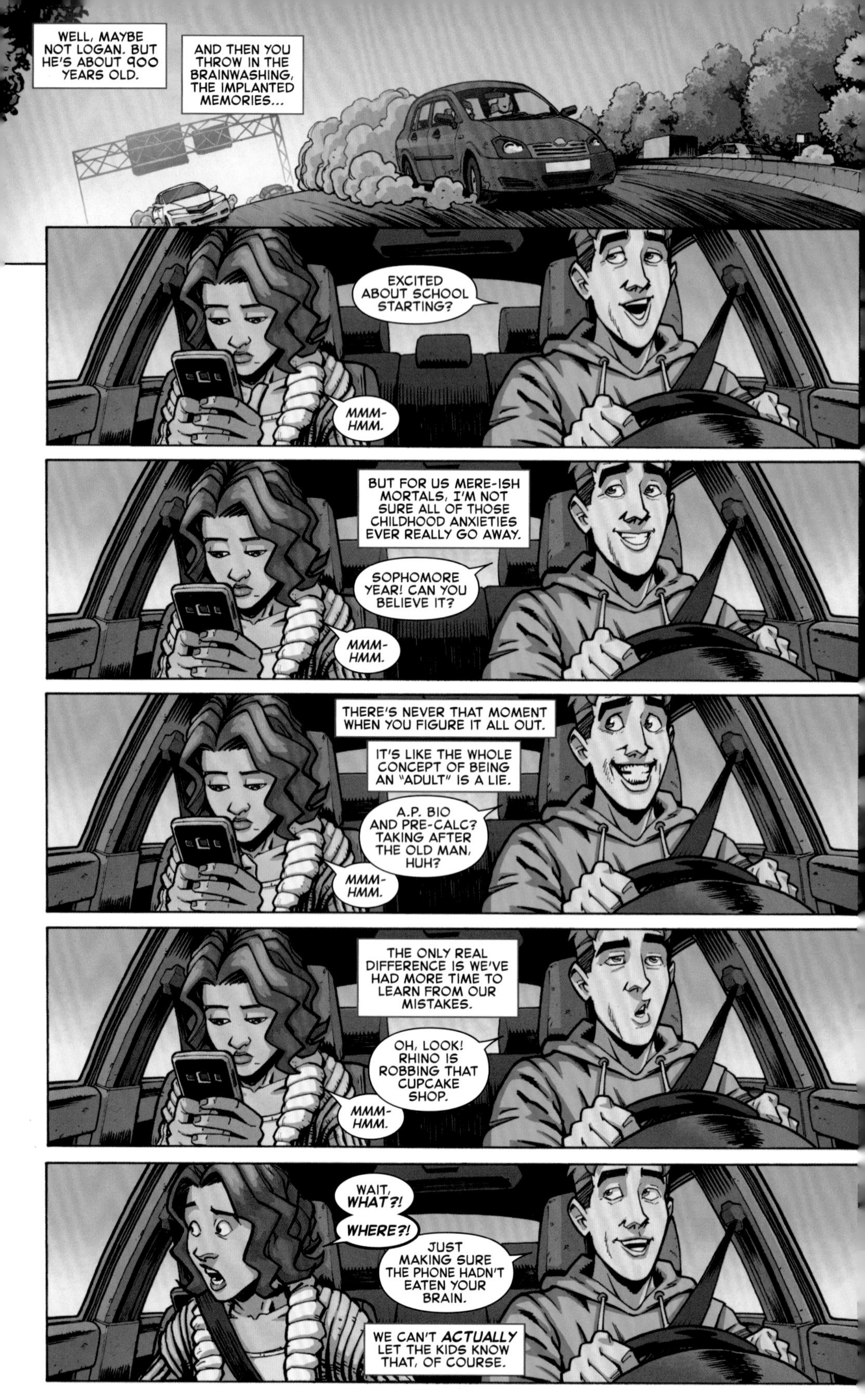
WELL, MAYBE NOT LOGAN. BUT HE'S ABOUT 900 YEARS OLD.
AND THEN YOU THROW IN THE BRAINWASHING, THE IMPLANTED MEMORIES...
EXCITED ABOUT SCHOOL STARTING?
MMM-HMM.
BUT FOR US MERE-ISH MORTALS, I'M NOT SURE ALL OF THOSE CHILDHOOD ANXIETIES EVER REALLY GO AWAY.
SOPHOMORE YEAR! CAN YOU BELIEVE IT?
MMM-HMM.
THERE'S NEVER THAT MOMENT WHEN YOU FIGURE IT ALL OUT.
IT'S LIKE THE WHOLE CONCEPT OF BEING AN "ADULT" IS A LIE.
A.P. BIO AND PRE-CALC? TAKING AFTER THE OLD MAN, HUH?
MMM-HMM.
THE ONLY REAL DIFFERENCE IS WE'VE HAD MORE TIME TO LEARN FROM OUR MISTAKES.
OH, LOOK! RHINO IS ROBBING THAT CUPCAKE SHOP.
MMM-HMM.
WAIT, WHAT?!
WHERE?!
JUST MAKING SURE THE PHONE HADN'T EATEN YOUR BRAIN.
WE CAN'T ACTUALLY LET THE KIDS KNOW THAT, OF COURSE.

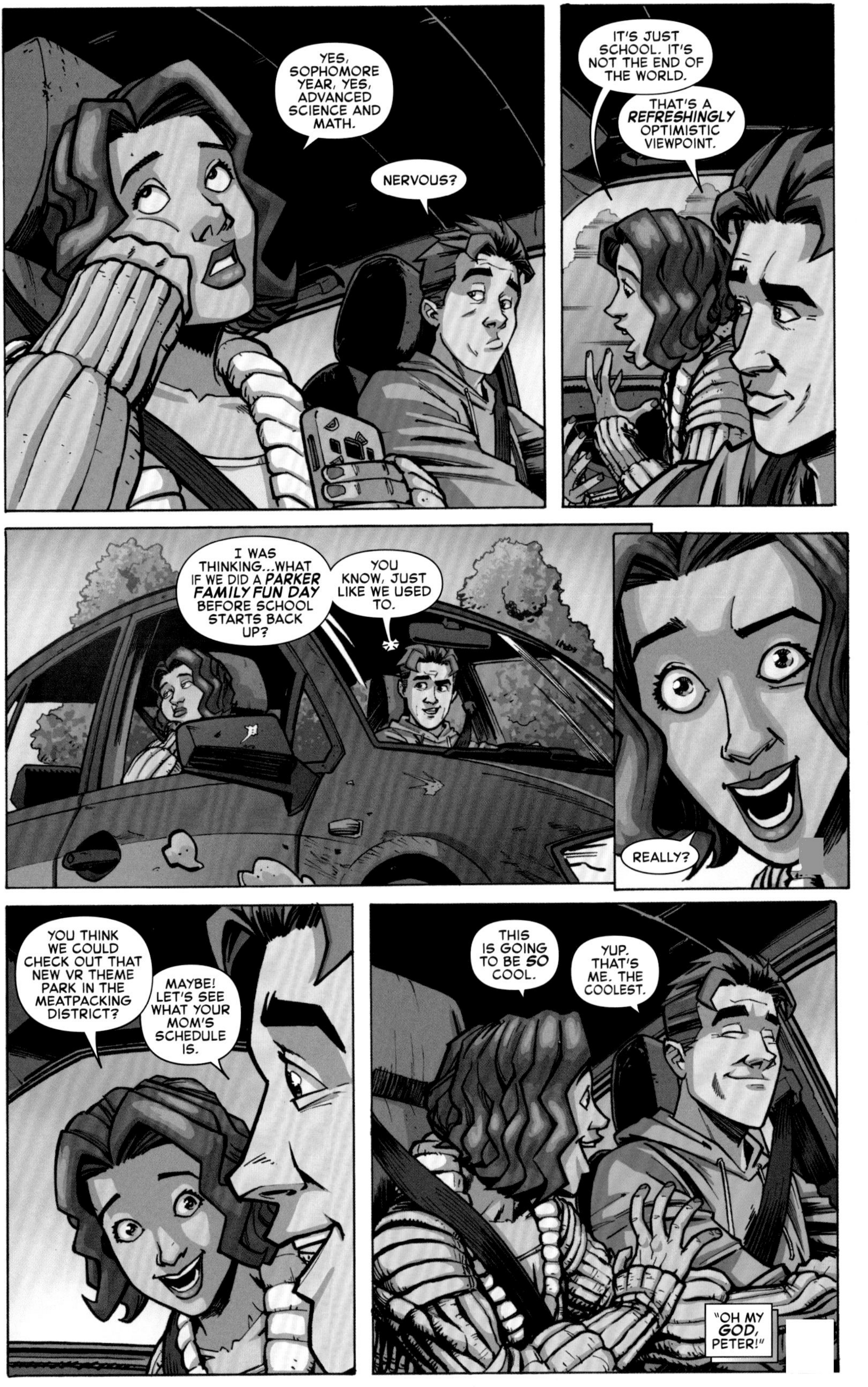
YES, SOPHOMORE YEAR, YES, ADVANCED SCIENCE AND MATH.
NERVOUS?
IT'S JUST SCHOOL. IT'S NOT THE END OF THE WORLD.
THAT'S A REFRESHINGLY OPTIMISTIC VIEWPOINT.
I WAS THINKING...WHAT IF WE DID A PARKER FAMILY FUN DAY BEFORE SCHOOL STARTS BACK UP?
YOU KNOW, JUST LIKE WE USED TO.
REALLY?
YOU THINK WE COULD CHECK OUT THAT NEW VR THEME PARK IN THE MEATPACKING DISTRICT?
MAYBE! LET'S SEE WHAT YOUR MOM'S SCHEDULE IS.
THIS IS GOING TO BE SO COOL.
YUP. THAT'S ME. THE COOLEST.
"OH MY GOD, PETER!"

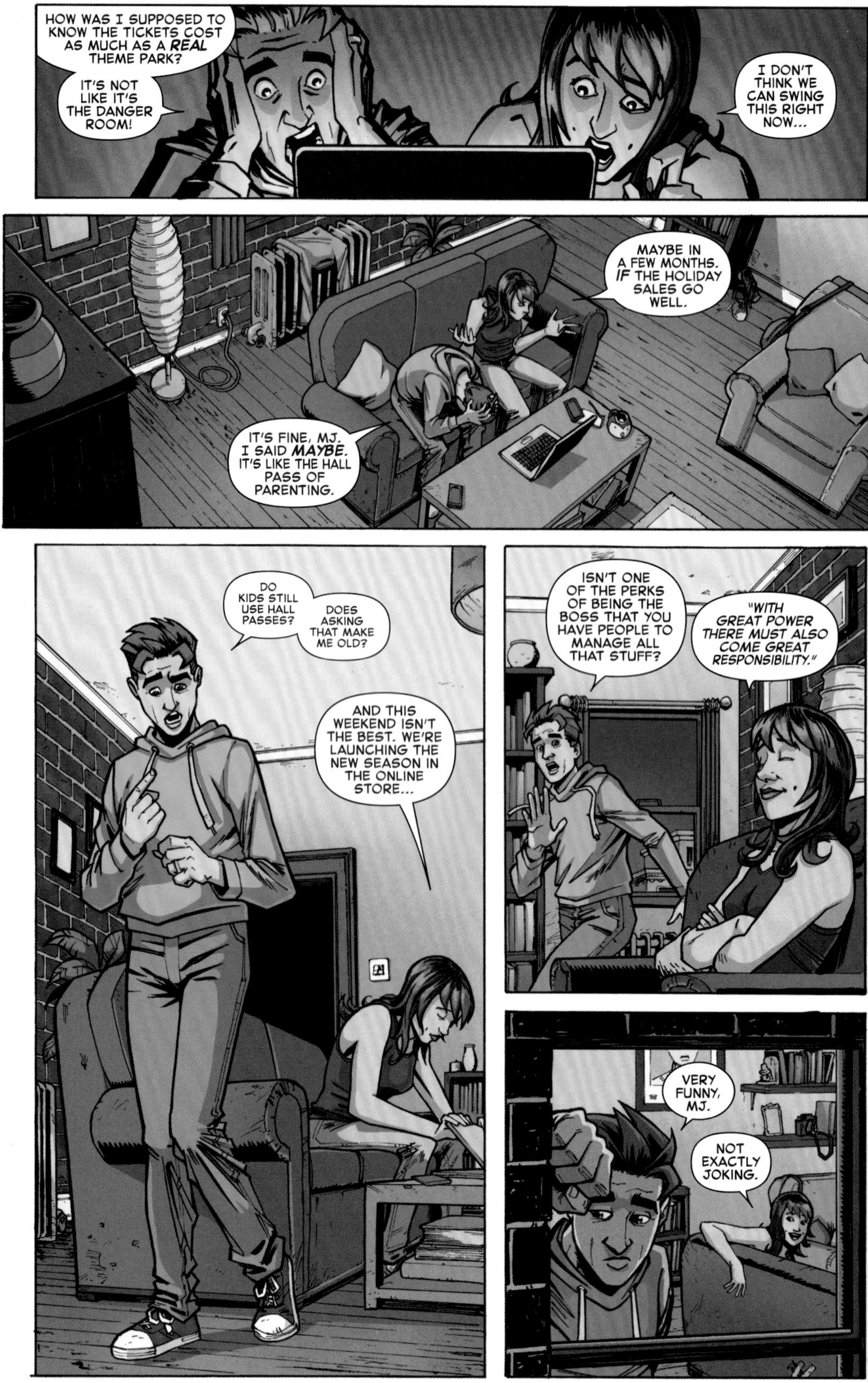
HOW WAS I SUPPOSED TO KNOW THE TICKETS COST AS MUCH AS A *REAL* THEME PARK?
IT'S NOT LIKE IT'S THE DANGER ROOM!
I DON'T THINK WE CAN SWING THIS RIGHT NOW...
MAYBE IN A FEW MONTHS. *IF* THE HOLIDAY SALES GO WELL.
IT'S FINE, MJ. I SAID *MAYBE.* IT'S LIKE THE HALL PASS OF PARENTING.
DO KIDS STILL USE HALL PASSES?
DOES ASKING THAT MAKE ME OLD?
AND THIS WEEKEND ISN'T THE BEST. WE'RE LAUNCHING THE NEW SEASON IN THE ONLINE STORE...
ISN'T ONE OF THE PERKS OF BEING THE BOSS THAT YOU HAVE PEOPLE TO MANAGE ALL THAT STUFF?
"WITH GREAT POWER THERE MUST ALSO COME GREAT RESPONSIBILITY."
VERY FUNNY, MJ.
NOT EXACTLY JOKING.

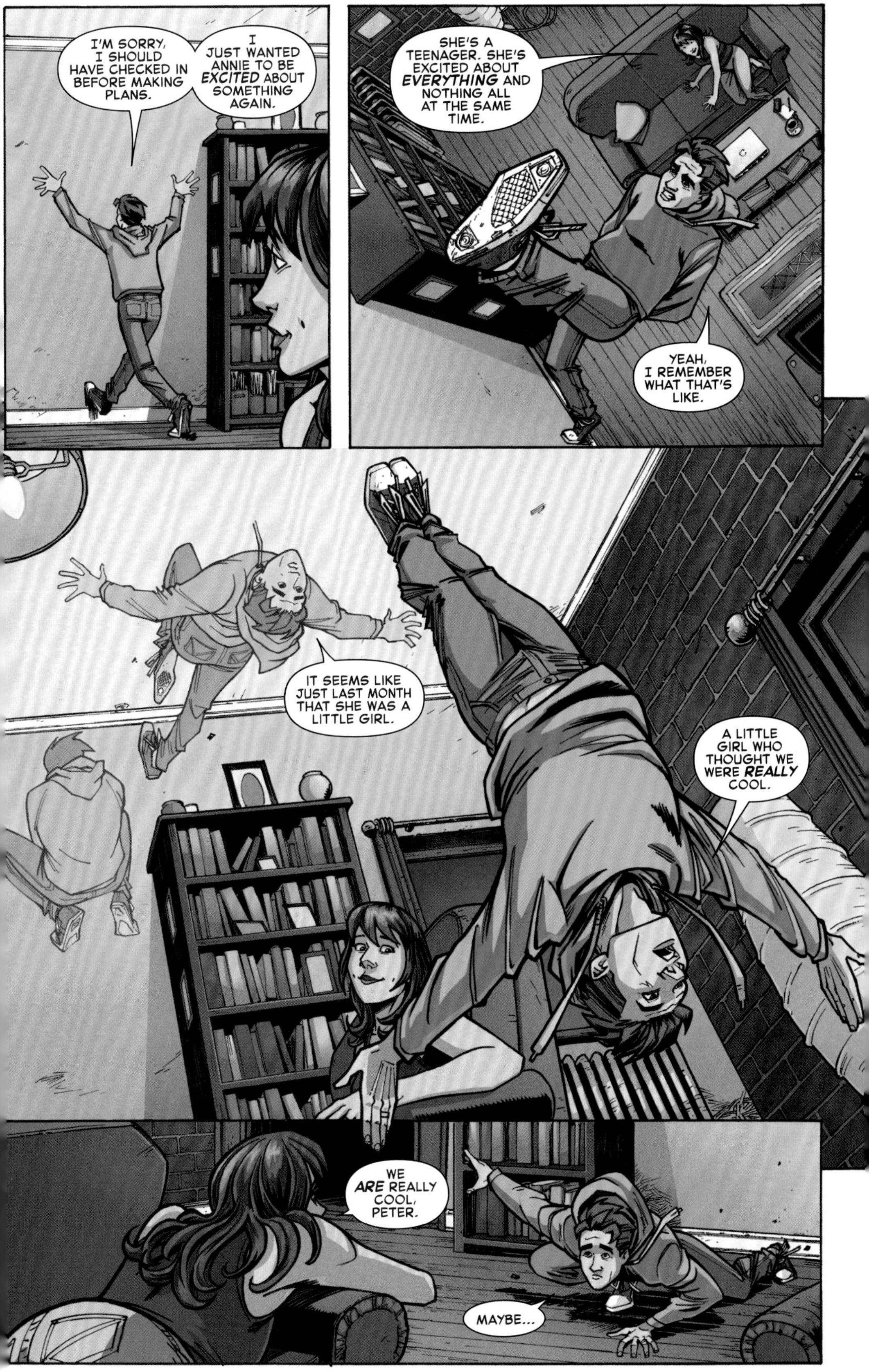
I'M SORRY, I SHOULD HAVE CHECKED IN BEFORE MAKING PLANS.
I JUST WANTED ANNIE TO BE EXCITED ABOUT SOMETHING AGAIN.
SHE'S A TEENAGER. SHE'S EXCITED ABOUT EVERYTHING AND NOTHING ALL AT THE SAME TIME.
YEAH, I REMEMBER WHAT THAT'S LIKE.
IT SEEMS LIKE JUST LAST MONTH THAT SHE WAS A LITTLE GIRL.
A LITTLE GIRL WHO THOUGHT WE WERE REALLY COOL.
WE ARE REALLY COOL, PETER.
MAYBE...

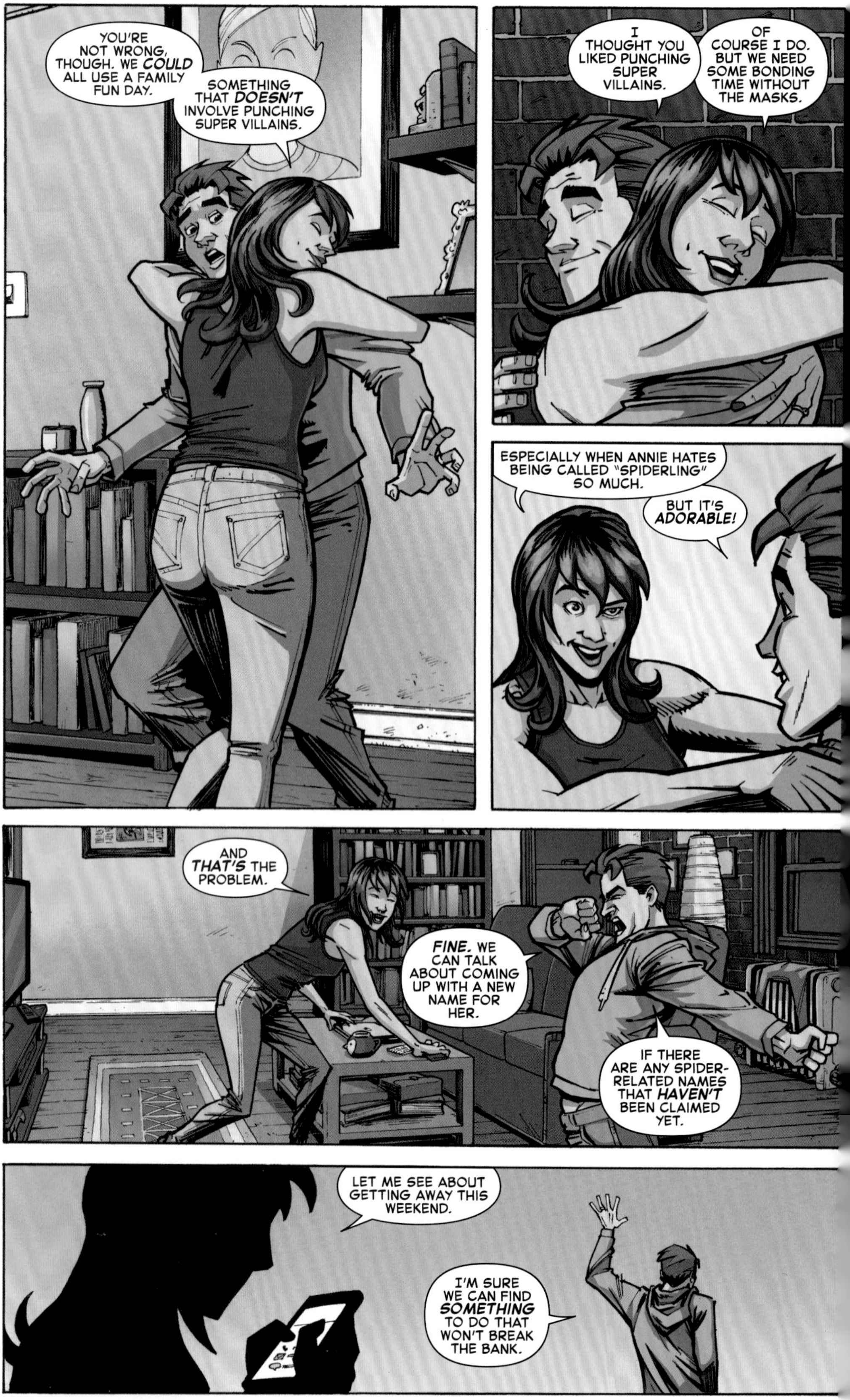
YOU'RE NOT WRONG, THOUGH. WE COULD ALL USE A FAMILY FUN DAY.
SOMETHING THAT DOESN'T INVOLVE PUNCHING SUPER VILLAINS.
I THOUGHT YOU LIKED PUNCHING SUPER VILLAINS.
OF COURSE I DO. BUT WE NEED SOME BONDING TIME WITHOUT THE MASKS.
ESPECIALLY WHEN ANNIE HATES BEING CALLED "SPIDERLING" SO MUCH.
BUT IT'S ADORABLE!
AND THAT'S THE PROBLEM.
FINE. WE CAN TALK ABOUT COMING UP WITH A NEW NAME FOR HER.
IF THERE ARE ANY SPIDER-RELATED NAMES THAT HAVEN'T BEEN CLAIMED YET.
LET ME SEE ABOUT GETTING AWAY THIS WEEKEND.
I'M SURE WE CAN FIND SOMETHING TO DO THAT WON'T BREAK THE BANK.

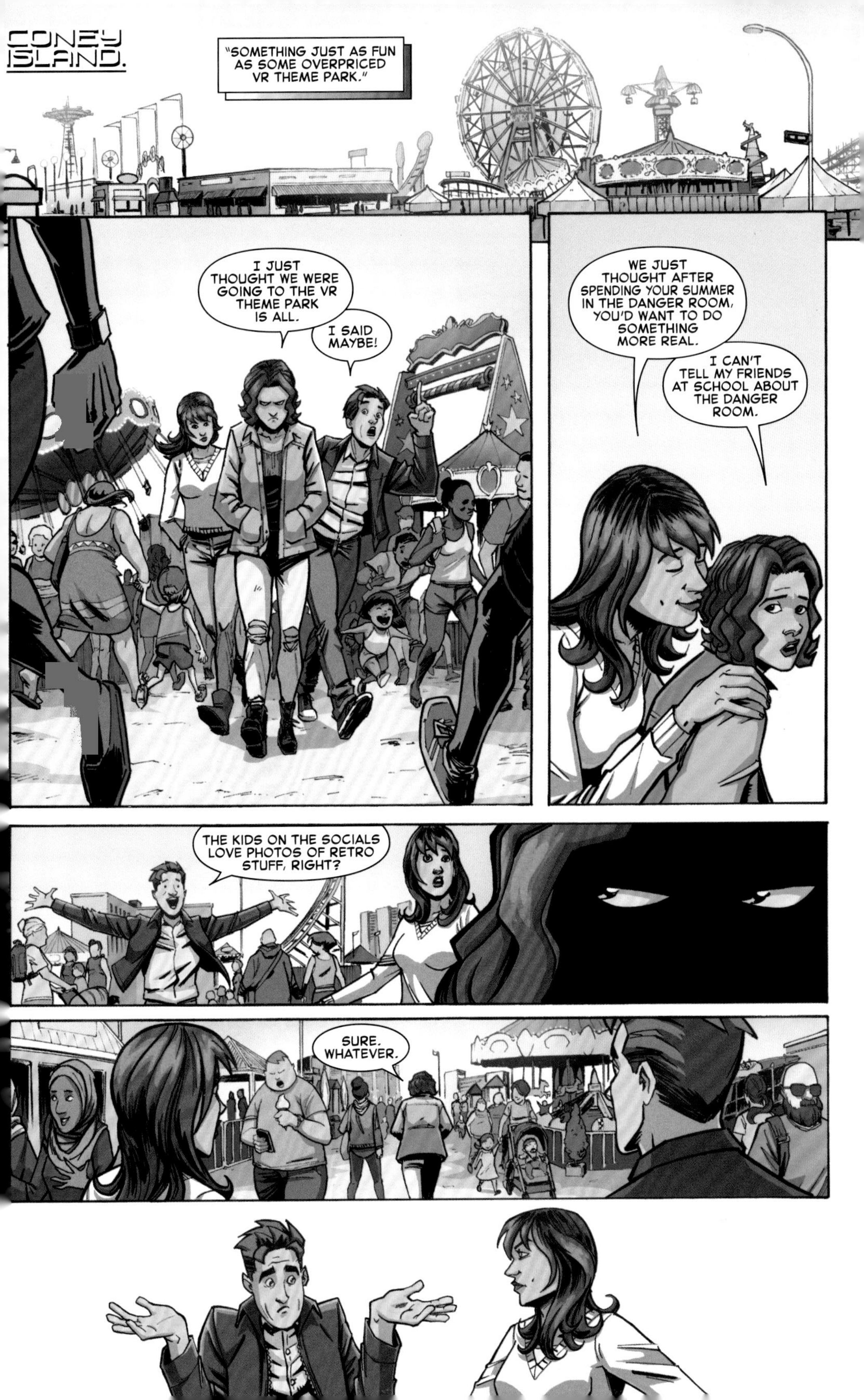
CONEY ISLAND.
"SOMETHING JUST AS FUN AS SOME OVERPRICED VR THEME PARK."
I JUST THOUGHT WE WERE GOING TO THE VR THEME PARK IS ALL.
I SAID MAYBE!
WE JUST THOUGHT AFTER SPENDING YOUR SUMMER IN THE DANGER ROOM, YOU'D WANT TO DO SOMETHING MORE REAL.
I CAN'T TELL MY FRIENDS AT SCHOOL ABOUT THE DANGER ROOM.
THE KIDS ON THE SOCIALS LOVE PHOTOS OF RETRO STUFF, RIGHT?
SURE. WHATEVER.

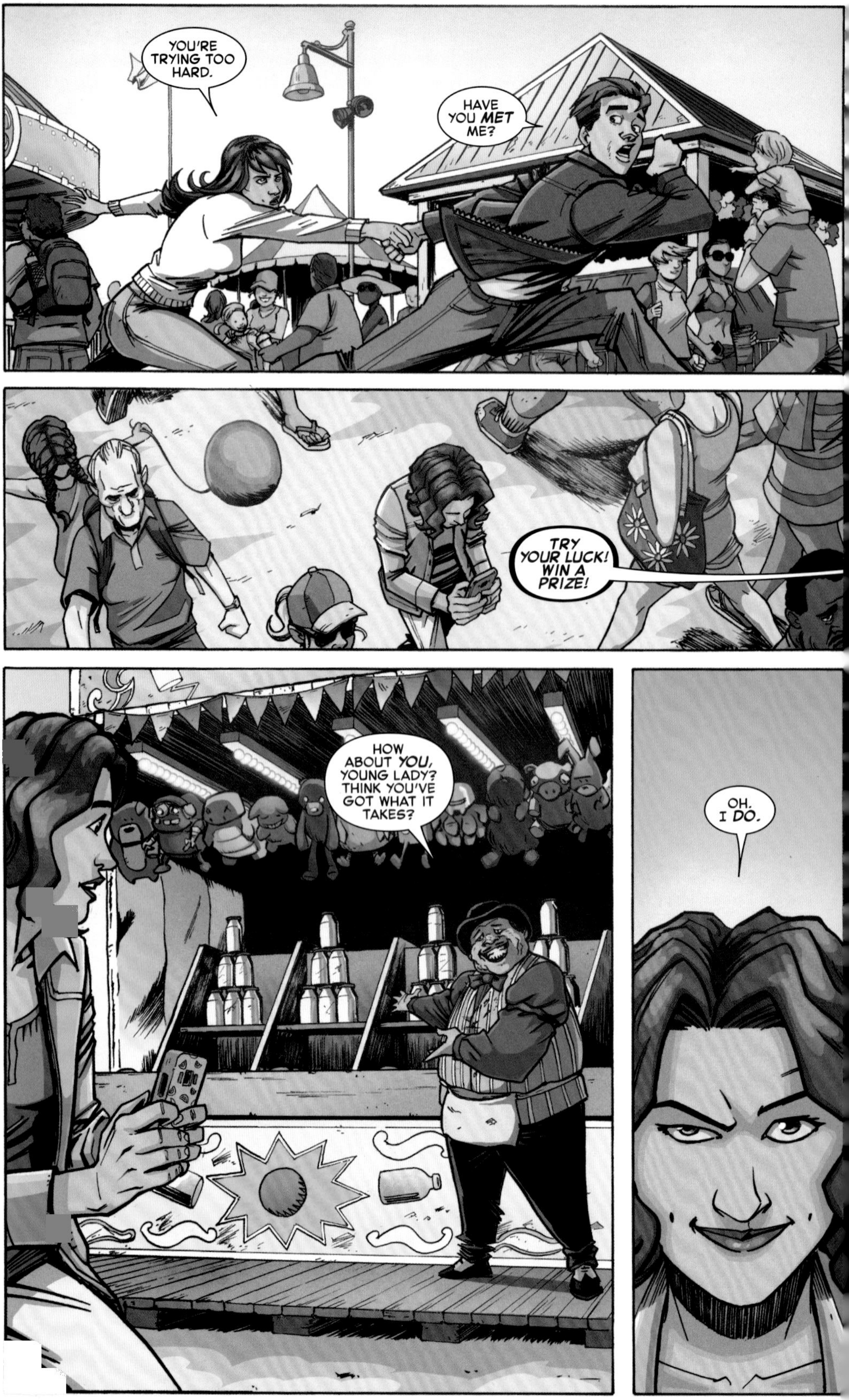
YOU'RE TRYING TOO HARD.
HAVE YOU MET ME?
TRY YOUR LUCK! WIN A PRIZE!
HOW ABOUT YOU, YOUNG LADY? THINK YOU'VE GOT WHAT IT TAKES?
OH. I DO.

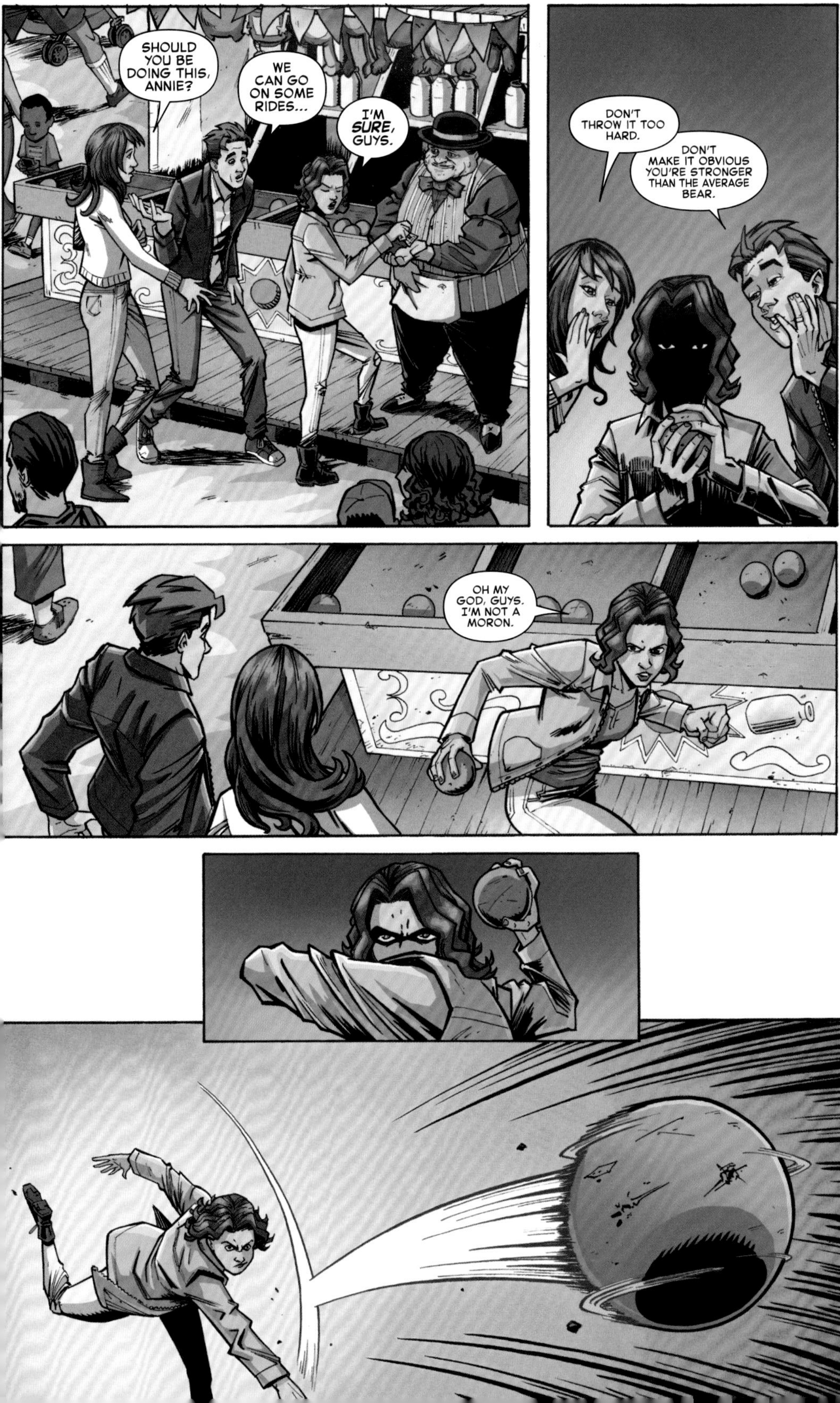
SHOULD YOU BE DOING THIS, ANNIE?
WE CAN GO ON SOME RIDES...
I'M *SURE*, GUYS.
DON'T THROW IT TOO HARD.
DON'T MAKE IT OBVIOUS YOU'RE STRONGER THAN THE AVERAGE BEAR.
OH MY GOD, GUYS. I'M NOT A MORON.

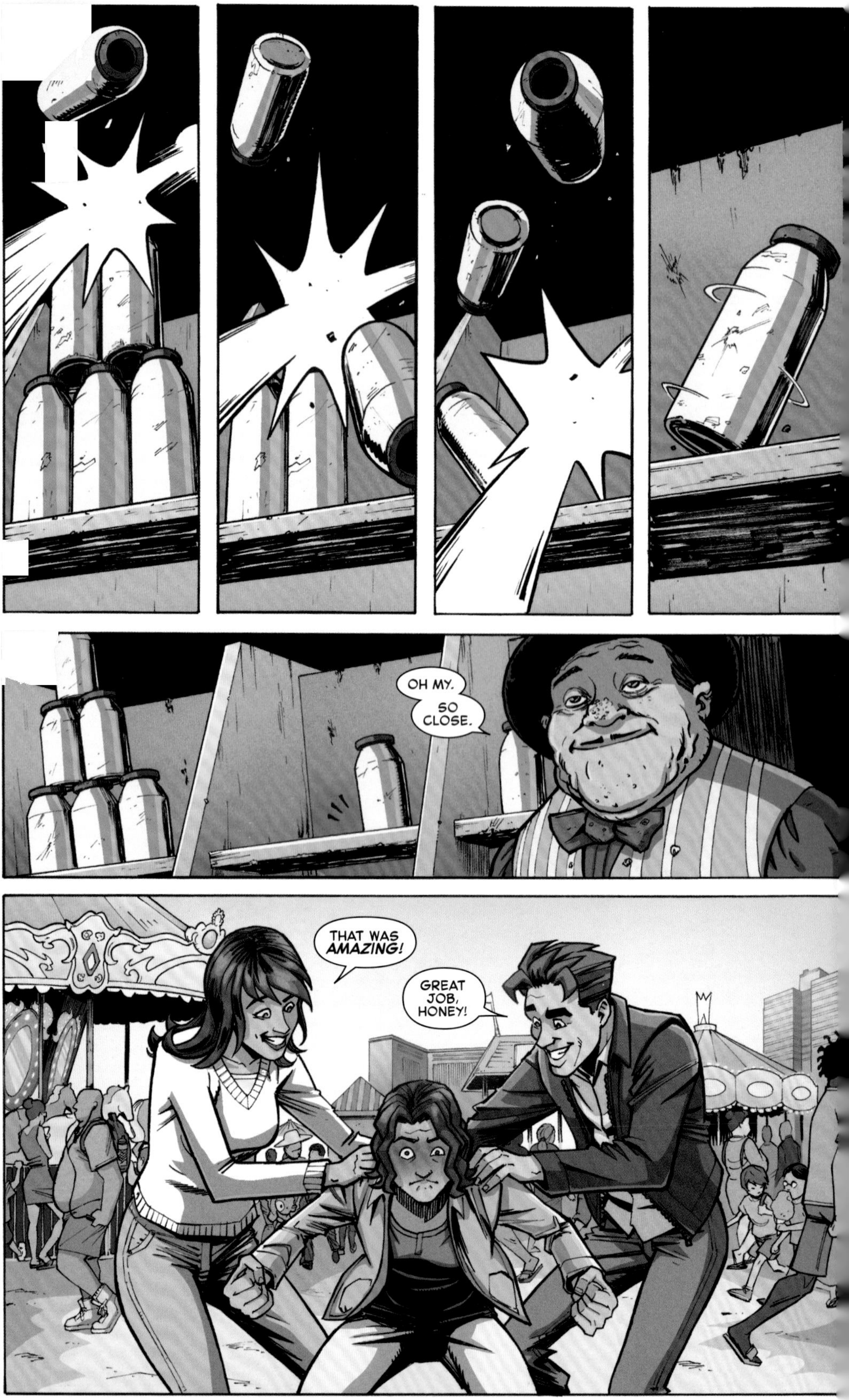
OH MY.
SO CLOSE.
THAT WAS *AMAZING!*
GREAT JOB, HONEY!

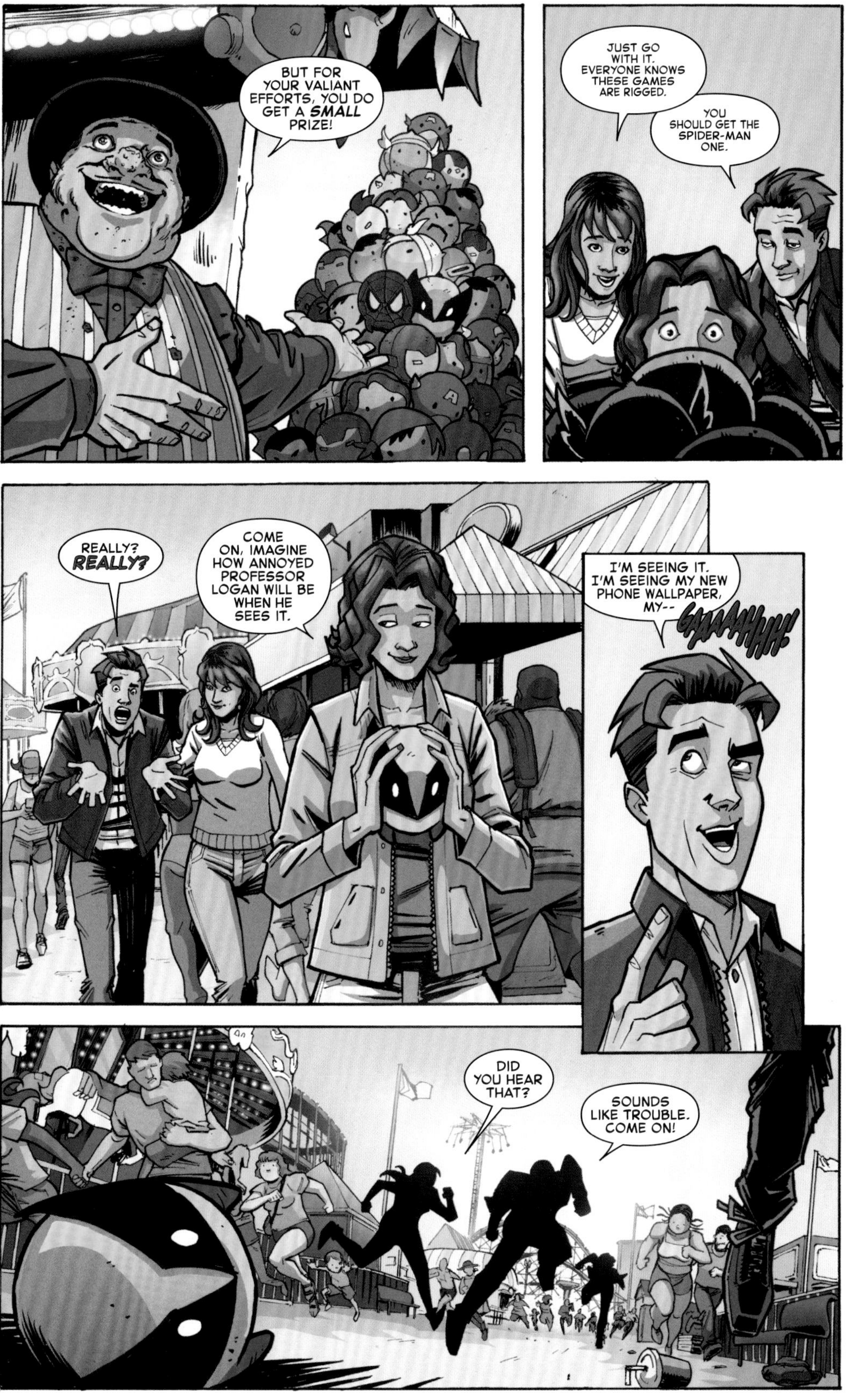

BUT FOR YOUR VALIANT EFFORTS, YOU DO GET A *SMALL* PRIZE!
JUST GO WITH IT. EVERYONE KNOWS THESE GAMES ARE RIGGED.
YOU SHOULD GET THE SPIDER-MAN ONE.
REALLY? *REALLY?*
COME ON, IMAGINE HOW ANNOYED PROFESSOR LOGAN WILL BE WHEN HE SEES IT.
I'M SEEING IT. I'M SEEING MY NEW PHONE WALLPAPER, MY--
GAAAAAHHH!
DID YOU HEAR THAT?
SOUNDS LIKE TROUBLE. COME ON!

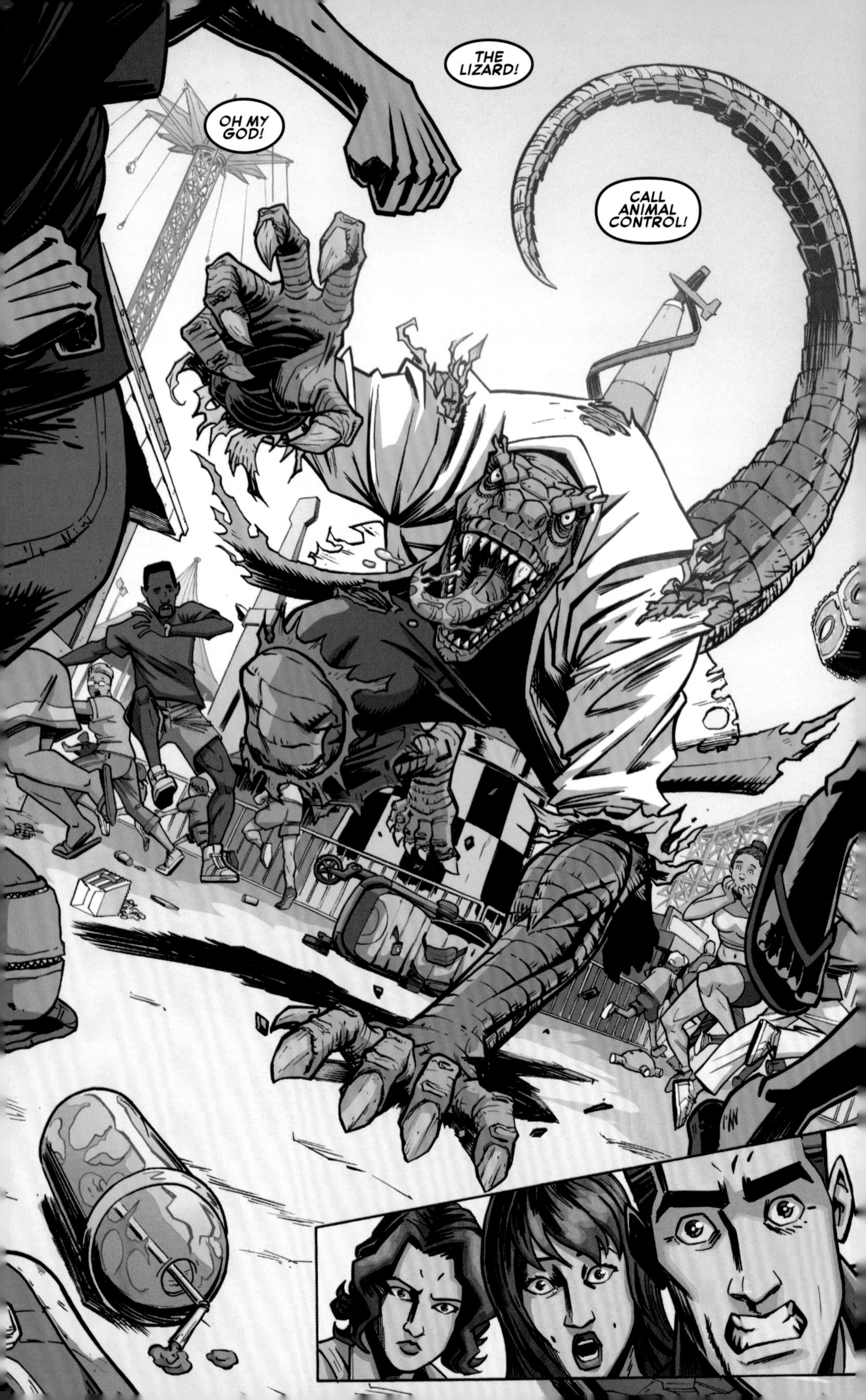
THE LIZARD!
OH MY GOD!
CALL ANIMAL CONTROL!

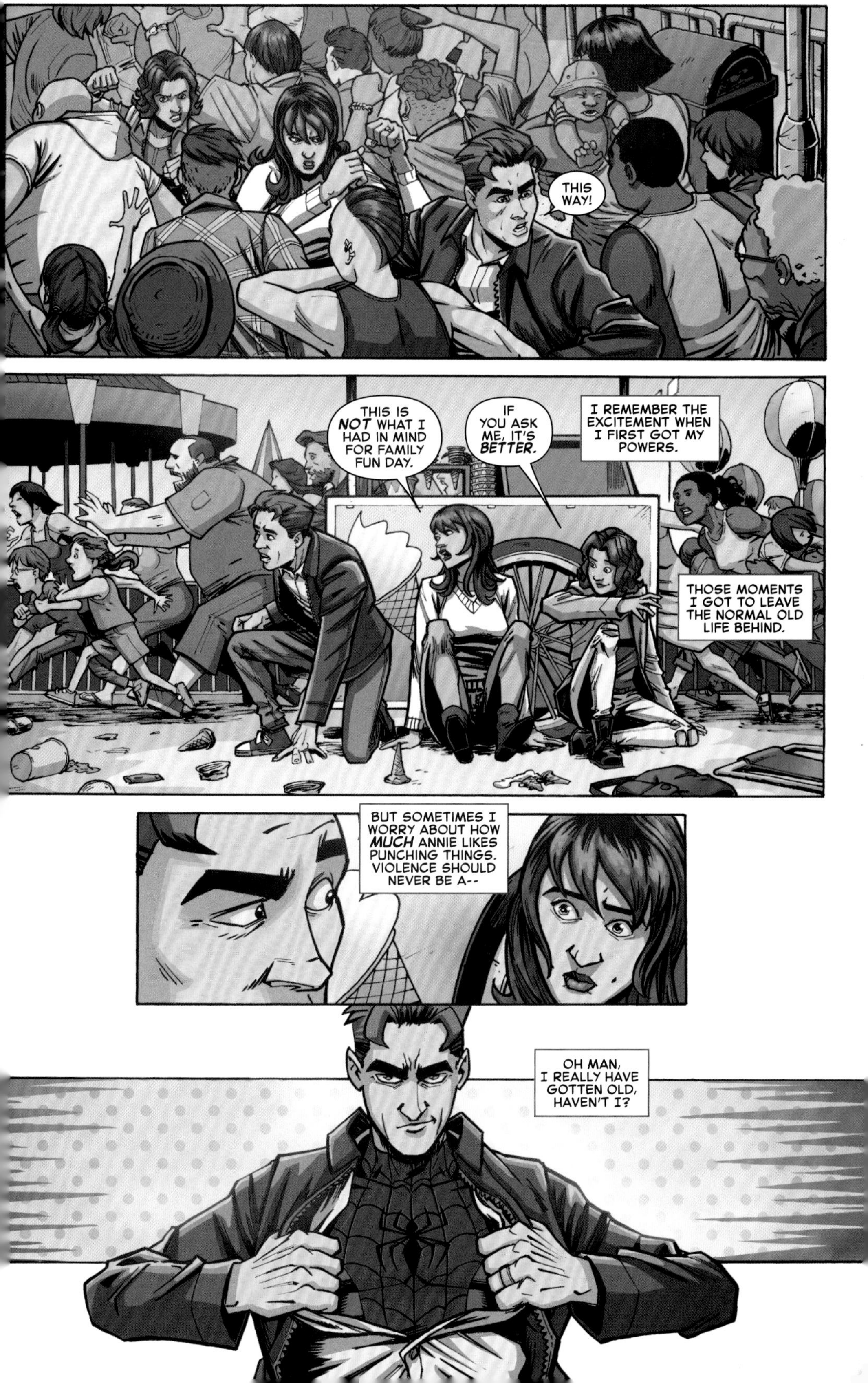
THIS WAY!
THIS IS NOT WHAT I HAD IN MIND FOR FAMILY FUN DAY.
IF YOU ASK ME, IT'S BETTER.
I REMEMBER THE EXCITEMENT WHEN I FIRST GOT MY POWERS.
THOSE MOMENTS I GOT TO LEAVE THE NORMAL OLD LIFE BEHIND.
BUT SOMETIMES I WORRY ABOUT HOW MUCH ANNIE LIKES PUNCHING THINGS. VIOLENCE SHOULD NEVER BE A--
OH MAN, I REALLY HAVE GOTTEN OLD, HAVEN'T I?

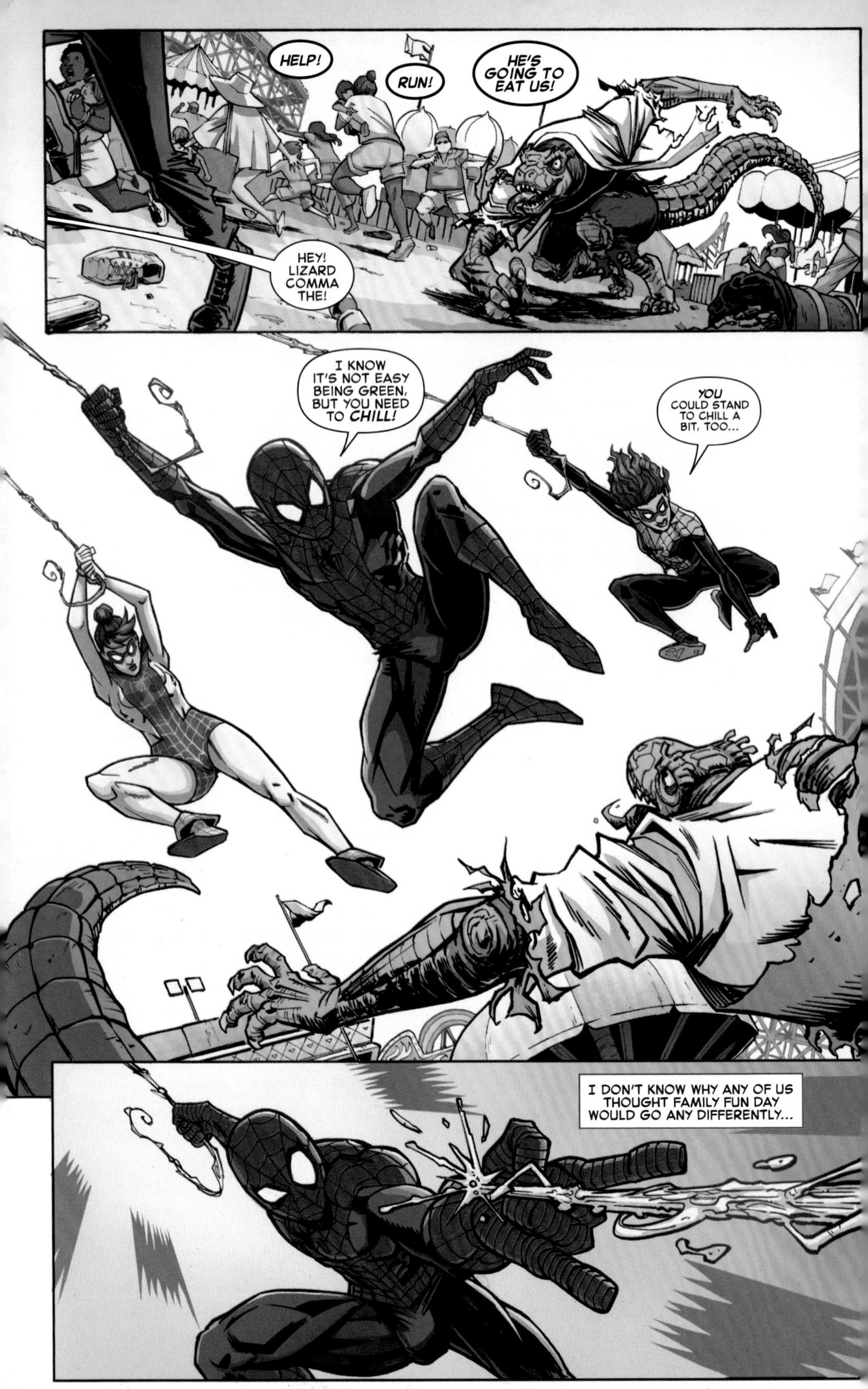
HELP!
RUN!
HE'S GOING TO EAT US!
HEY! LIZARD COMMA THE!
I KNOW IT'S NOT EASY BEING GREEN, BUT YOU NEED TO CHILL!
YOU COULD STAND TO CHILL A BIT, TOO...
I DON'T KNOW WHY ANY OF US THOUGHT FAMILY FUN DAY WOULD GO ANY DIFFERENTLY...

SILK #1 VARIANT

BY W. SCOTT FORBES

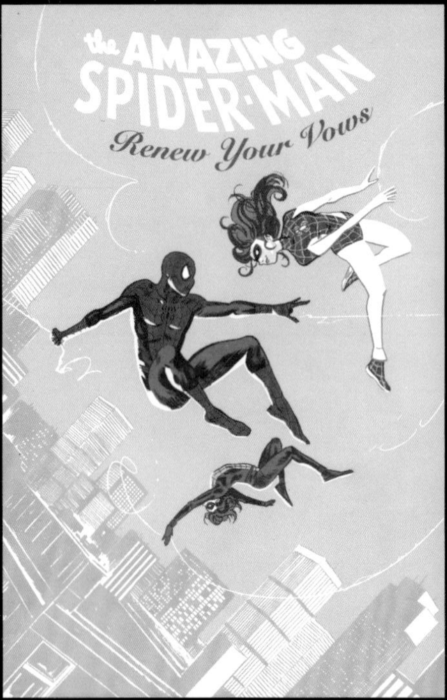
the AMAZING
SPIDER-MAN
Renew Your Vows

AMAZING SPIDER-MAN:
RENEW YOUR VOWS #13 **VARIANT**
BY MICHAEL WALSH

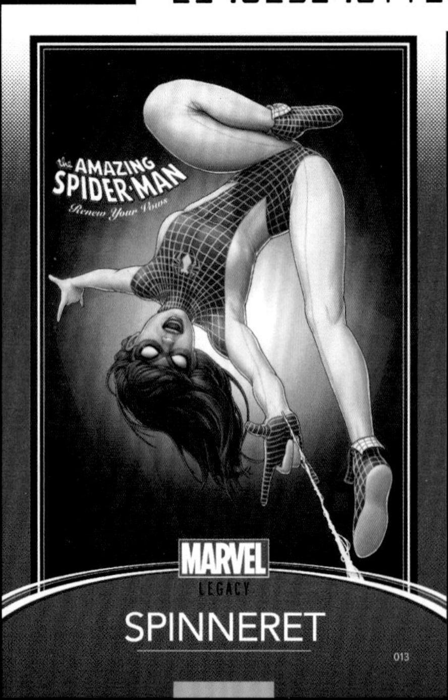
the AMAZING
SPIDER-MAN
Renew Your Vows
MARVEL
LEGACY
SPINNERET
013

AMAZING SPIDER-MAN:
RENEW YOUR VOWS #13 **TRADING CARD VARIANT**
BY JOHN TYLER CHRISTOPHER

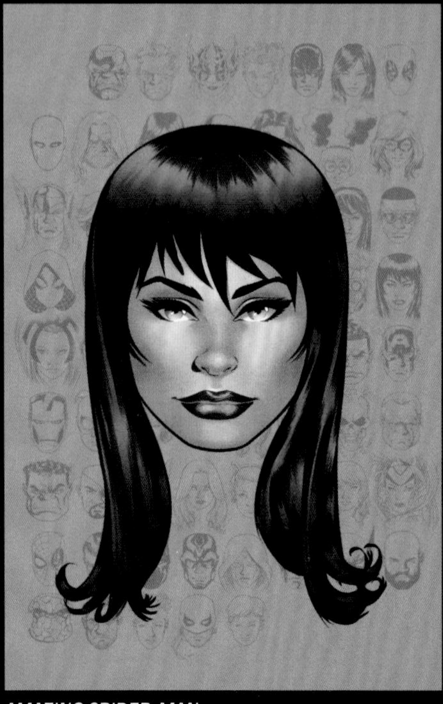

AMAZING SPIDER-MAN:
RENEW YOUR VOWS #13 **HEADSHOT VARIANT**
BY MIKE McKONE & RACHELLE ROSENBERG

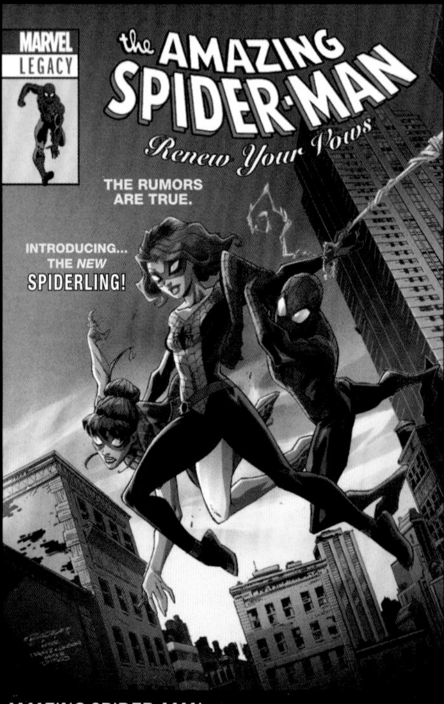
MARVEL
LEGACY
the AMAZING
SPIDER-MAN
Renew Your Vows
THE RUMORS ARE TRUE.
INTRODUCING... THE NEW SPIDERLING!

AMAZING SPIDER-MAN:
RENEW YOUR VOWS #13 **HOMAGE VARIANT**
BY KHARY RANDOLPH & EMILIO LOPEZ